The Girl with the Red Ribbon

LINDA FINLAY

PENGUIN BOOKS

PENGUIN BOOKS

UK | USA | Canada | Ireland | Australia
India | New Zealand | South Africa

Penguin Books is part of the Penguin Random House group of companies
whose addresses can be found at global.penguinrandomhouse.com.

First published 2015
001

Copyright © Linda Finlay, 2015

The moral right of the author has been asserted

Set in 12.5/14.75 pt Garamond MT Std
Typeset by Jouve (UK), Milton Keynes
Printed in Great Britain by Clays Ltd, St Ives plc

A CIP catalogue record for this book is available from the British Library

ISBN: 978-1-405-91897-8

www.greenpenguin.co.uk

To Pern for his continued support
and encouragement

Chapter 1

Brigid, beloved Brigid, pray listen, I beseech thee.
On this sweet night of Imbolc, set the freeze of winter free,
Fan your flames, warm the tilth, release energy that wilth
Bring these new seeds to birth.

Raising her arms to the heavens, Rowan chanted the ancient rhyme as she danced around the circle cast on the ground before her. The mirror glinting among the frosted blades of grass reflected her lithe form as she leaped high into the air, her movements becoming more frenzied as she gathered the energy of the night. Her riot of copper curls tumbled over her shoulders, fanning out around her slender waist as she dipped and swayed in the darkness of true midnight.

As if on cue, the full moon climbed from behind a curtain of cloud, silvering the girl's white nightgown, contrasting vividly with the slash of red around her wrist. Falling to her knees, Rowan reached out with her right hand and scooped up seeds she'd saved from the last year's harvest. Carefully cupping her left hand over them, she completed the rhyme.

Brigid, beloved Brigid,
Bless all that lives
Between my right hand and my left.
So mote it be.

Taking a deep breath for each seed, she thrust them into the holes she'd made in the frozen soil. Finally, to complete the magic charm, she leaned forward and kissed the earth three times.

From his bedroom window Edward watched proudly as his daughter performed the primordial ritual just as her mother had taught her. She looked so like his beloved Hazel before she'd been cruelly taken that the breath caught in his throat. Lost in thought, he didn't hear his new wife creep up behind him and he jumped when she placed her arm through his.

'It's cold, Edward. Come back to bed,' she murmured enticingly. Then, catching sight of Rowan dancing on the earth below, she stiffened. 'That girl will catch her death if she's not careful, cavorting around half naked like that. Why, it's enough to spook the spirits,' she muttered, striving to keep the venom out of her voice.

'Don't fret, my dear. You'll soon get used to our country ways,' Edward said, patting her hand before turning away from the window and sinking down onto the mattress. 'Come on then, my dear, time for roost.' But Fanny pursed her lips and stayed where she was.

As always after carrying out her nocturnal rituals, Rowan felt both exhausted and energized as she made her way back to the thatched farmhouse, built beneath a rocky outcrop on the Devonshire slopes for protection against the elements. Trees surrounded the fields like sentinels, dark and eerie against the soft light of the moon, and a fox padded towards her, amber eyes gleaming as it nodded a greeting in passing. She smiled back, safe in the knowledge that all the chickens were secured in their coops. When the white spectre of a barn owl glided from its roost she stopped to watch, marvelling at the magnificent sight as it swept silently by so close she could feel the stir of air beneath its wings. How she loved being at one with nature and she revelled in the stillness and quietude of the night.

It was some time before she noticed the silhouette of her stepmother watching her from behind the curtain. Even from this distance Rowan could feel waves of hostility emanating from the woman towards her on the midnight air, and her good mood evaporated like dew in the rays of the sun. Remembering the warmth of her own mother's love, Rowan instinctively rubbed the red ribbon on her wrist and clutched the precious mirror tighter to her chest. She'd known her father's remarriage would bring changes, and now realized with a shudder they weren't going to bode well for her.

With a shudder, she hurried indoors and stood in front of the fire, but the heat from the glowing embers failed to penetrate her chilled insides. Knowing she had to be up early in the morning, she made sure the fire was safe for the night and then tiptoed up the stairs. Despite her misgivings, she fell into a dreamless sleep.

Woken by the cock's first crow, Rowan groaned. She was tempted to pull the covers over her head and go back to sleep, but the lowing of cattle in the shippon below penetrated her befuddled thoughts. Aware that her father and Sab would be hungry, she forced herself out of her cosy bed. She rinsed her face and hands, shuddering as the icy water tingled her skin. Dressing quickly, she was about to go downstairs, when some instinct stopped her.

Going over to the bed, she removed her precious mirror from under her pillow and, without really understanding why, carefully wrapped it in an old flour sack and thrust it beneath the mattress.

In the kitchen Rowan stoked the fire into a blaze, lifted the pot over to heat and set about preparing breakfast. The aroma of simmering oats was wafting temptingly from the pot when her father came indoors, rubbing his hands together.

'Morning, Rowan, my dear, and a mighty raw start to February it be too,' he said, tossing his woollen cap onto the bacon settle before going over to the hearth and holding his hands up to warm.

'Morning, Father,' she answered, ladling a generous portion of porridge into his bowl and setting it down on the long scrubbed table.

Moments later the door clattered open again and Sab came in, sniffing the air appreciatively as he tossed an armful of faggots down beside the hearth.

'Thought you'd need these for your bread making later,' he said. 'Ah, that smells good.'

Rowan smiled and shook her head at the freckle-faced youth with hair like cropped corn, who'd been raised alongside her like a brother.

'Oh, Sab, you say that every morning, even though we always have the same thing, apart from on the Sabbath, of course,' she said.

'Yes, well, happen I can remember a time when I was hungry,' he said, his cheeks flushing as he held his hand out eagerly for the dish Rowan was filling for him. She watched as he settled himself beside her father. Poor Sab, she thought. Memories of the miserable start he'd had in life obviously still haunted him all these years later. Her parents had told her how they'd rescued him from the foundling hospital when he was four and a half years old. Their hearts had gone out to the half-starved, miserable waif who'd seemed afraid of his own shadow, and they'd brought him home to Orchard Farm where they'd raised him as their own. Now, all these years later, she and Sab were as close as any siblings could ever be.

'No Fanny yet?' her father asked, interrupting her thoughts.

Rowan shook her head.

'Why, it's only just past milking,' Sab quipped, winking at Rowan. 'And I'm surprised you're up this early after all that prancing around last night, young lady.' He wagged his finger at her.

'You know how important it is we observe the natural rhythms of nature and pay our respects if we want to reap a bountiful harvest,' she replied, her emerald eyes glistening with sincerity.

'Ah, but it's the moon's phases affecting the rising of the water in the ground that really makes the difference to our crops,' Sab countered.

'Now, you two, I've told you before, there's wisdom in both practices, and everything we can do to ensure a good harvest is to be encouraged,' said Edward, stroking his wiry beard thoughtfully, 'although Fanny was quite concerned in case you caught a chill last night.' Rowan stared at him in surprise, but before she could say anything, he'd risen to his feet. 'I'd best go up and check she's all right. She was saying yesterday that this move down to

Devonshire has taken it out of her,' he said as he mounted the stairs.

Sab raised his eyebrows at Rowan. 'Uncle Ted's been seeing to the animals since before daybreak yet that woman lies in her bed like Lady Muck. 'Tis not right, Rowan,' he muttered, shaking his head.

'I know, Sab, but Father's that smitten, she can do no wrong in his eyes. Still, I must get on. The bread oven won't light itself, nor will the flour magically turn into loaves, more's the pity,' she said, scraping her bowl then putting it on the side.

'And with the moon starting its third quarter it's time for fertilizing, so I've to empty the privy ready for spreading its wonderfully ripe contents over the top field as soon as this frost starts to melt,' Sab said, wrinkling his nose.

'You get all the good jobs,' Rowan teased.

'Talking of which, you have so much to do, I hope Fanny's going to help you with the chores around here.'

Thinking of her stepmother's pristine appearance, Rowan thought that was highly unlikely, but before she could say anything Edward came back into the room.

'I know you're busy, dear, but Fanny wondered if you could take her up a slice of fresh bread. She'd also like some warm water for washing,' he said, looking sheepishly at Rowan.

'But I left a jug of water on the washstand last night, Father,' Rowan said. 'And as for fresh bread, I've yet to start on the baking.' Then, seeing her father was looking uncomfortable, she forced a smile. 'Still, I'm sure I can find her something.'

'Perhaps she'd like a nice thick layer of bramble jelly on

it, too,' Sab said sarcastically, but Edward had missed the tone and his eyes lit up.

'Yes, that would be grand. And if you could heat up some water for her ablutions, Rowan . . .? Apparently her soap doesn't lather in cold. We must remember everything's new to her here and try to make her feel at home,' he said, tugging his woollen cap right down over his ears so that his soft brown curls sprang around his shoulders.

'Ready, my boy?' he asked Sab. 'After we've seen to the privy and muck spreading, we'll be hedging up in Five Acre Field, Rowan. Tell Fanny I'll see her for supper,' he called over his shoulder as he disappeared outside.

Sab raised his eyebrows again at Rowan, then followed after him, whistling for the dogs as he went. She heard their joyful barking as they bounded to meet him and she couldn't help looking over to the fireside. The kitchen seemed soulless without the dogs' companionable presence, and Rowan could still barely believe Fanny had banned them from the house, or that her father had gone along with it, even if they had growled every time they saw her.

As the door clattered shut behind them, Rowan looked at the pile of dishes that needed cleaning before she could begin making the bread. Sighing, she picked up the pot and went outside to the well house. Really she had enough to do already without pandering to her stepmother's whims, she thought. Then she chided herself for being mean. Her father was right about making Fanny feel at home. Not that she could ever take her mother's place, of course, but Rowan could at least try to make the woman welcome. The slosh of cold water over her bare feet stung like needles, bringing her thoughts sharply back to the task in hand.

Back indoors, she set the pot over the fire, then stacked the bread oven with the faggots, before setting light to them. At least it would be heating up whilst she got on with her chores. In the scullery she cleared away their dishes, then got out the big mixing bowl and took it through to the kitchen. Once she'd gathered her ingredients, she set about her task. As usual, the rhythmic kneading of the dough soothed her spirits and she found herself wondering how her life was going to be affected now that Fanny had moved into the farmhouse. Although the family had been devastated when her mother had died, the years had turned grief into acceptance and gradually they'd sorted themselves into their daily routine.

However, Rowan did miss the female things she and her mother had done together. They'd always been close, sharing an affinity with nature. Her mother had trained her to recognize which plants and herbs could be used for cooking and healing, and she'd taught Rowan the importance of celebrating the change of the seasons.

'I'm that hungry my stomach thinks my throat's been cut,' Fanny's querulous voice cut across Rowan's thoughts, making her jump guiltily. She'd been so absorbed in her task she'd quite forgotten to take her stepmother any breakfast. It was strange, though, Rowan thought, frowning, she didn't recall her voice being shrill like that before now.

'Just coming, Fanny,' she called back. Hurrying out to the dairy, she picked up the dish of butter, hoping that if she spread it thickly over the heel of two-day-old bread, her stepmother wouldn't notice its hardness. Then, having poured a jug of small beer, she made her way upstairs.

Her stepmother was sitting up in bed, a lacy shawl draped elegantly around her shoulders, fair hair still hidden beneath her nightcap. Rowan smiled and set down the tray before her.

'It's a beautiful morning with the frost sparkling like diamonds,' she said brightly.

'And what would you know about diamonds?' Fanny asked, sharp grey eyes studying her curiously.

'Well, I've never actually seen any real ones, of course, but Mother Nature scatters the grass with hers, doesn't she?' Rowan answered.

'Indeed? Which reminds me, what on earth were you doing dancing outside in the dark last night? And, heaven forbid, in your nightgown too. Muttering away to yourself, you were. Are you mad or something?' Fanny asked.

Rowan laughed.

'I don't happen to think that's funny, young lady,' her stepmother admonished, pursing her lips.

'No, of course not, it was just the way you said what on earth I was doing. Last night was Imbolc, you see.' Then seeing Fanny's puzzled look, she added. 'It marks the retreat of winter and the approach of spring. Before we can sow the crops we need to ask for the earth to warm, and you asked what on earth I was doing,' Rowan said, grinning.

'Oh, for heaven's sake, I've never heard such nonsense,' Fanny retorted. 'And talking of warmth, it's perishing in here. Doesn't this fire ever get lit?'

Rowan stared at the empty grate, her stomach churning

as she remembered the last time a fire had blazed there. It had been seven years ago, when her mother's life had been ebbing away. She could remember sitting by the side of this very bed, stroking her tawny hair and holding her birdlike hand. Her mother's usually olive skin had been quite white, her touch light as, with trembling hands, she'd removed the ribbon from around her wrist and handed it to Rowan. Then, in a voice soft as a summer breeze, she'd clutched Rowan's hand and whispered the words she would treasure forever. *I was blessed with the greatest of fortunes the day you were born, my darling daughter. This red ribbon symbolizes the circle of life. Wear it as I have and know I'll be with you always.* Those were the last words her mother had ever uttered. As the memory faded back into the mists of time, Rowan felt a lump rise in her throat and her hand went to her wrist, where the ribbon had tightened its grip.

Chapter 2

As memories of that terrible day replayed themselves in her head, Rowan felt as though her heart was being pierced with a shard of broken glass. Hot tears pricked the back of her eyelids and, determined not to lose control in front of her stepmother, she muttered an excuse and fled back to the kitchen.

Slumping down on the bacon settle, she struggled to bring her emotions under control. Even after all this time, she missed her mother so much it physically hurt, she thought, absently stroking the red ribbon, which seemed to have eased its grip and felt comfortable once more. They'd been such a happy family. Her father had called his wife and daughter his two blossoms, and whilst her mother's real name had been Hazel, he'd always referred to her as Catkin because of the graceful way she moved. Unlike Fanny, she'd been softly spoken. It might have been years since her passing, but the recollection of her tiny form lying in the bed beside the fire was once again vividly brought to mind.

A wet nose snuffled her arm and looking up, Rowan saw Magic gazing at her with those all-knowing, all-seeing eyes. Smiling through her tears, she stroked the cat's velvety ears, drawing comfort from the warmth of the soft black fur. As the gentle purring soothed her spirits, another memory surfaced. That of her mother saying self-pity was only for fools.

'Right, this won't do at all,' Rowan announced, startling Magic, who, with a baleful glare, jumped from her lap. Wiping her eyes, Rowan got to her feet. Then seeing the dough still waiting on the table she shook her head. Really, she was so behind with the chores this morning, she thought. Knowing how important a strict routine was to the good running of the farm, she vigorously swept the ashes from the oven before sliding the loaves inside. She was just sealing the edges of the door with flour paste when Fanny appeared, the heavy aroma of rose drifting in her wake.

'Oh, you smell of roses, Fanny,' Rowan exclaimed.

'Since no warm water was forthcoming, I gave up waiting and used some of the precious rose scent I brought with me from London,' her stepmother announced in a martyred voice.

'Sorry, Fanny, I'll make sure you have some tomorrow morning,' Rowan assured her, comparing the cloying smell with the gentle fragrance her mother had worn. How they'd enjoyed collecting the fresh petals from the bushes and putting them in jars. Her mother would cover them in clear water from the stream and, after giving them a vigorous shake, they'd leave them in the well house to steep. 'I didn't know you lived in London,' she said.

'Yes, well, I'm here now and so far all I've seen is the parlour and my bedchamber. I'd like you to show me around the rest of the farmhouse,' she instructed, her eyes darting around the room. Rowan sighed again. She really had so much to do.

'Right, this is the kitchen, of course. Then there's the scullery, the dairy and the well house,' Rowan, said hurrying to the door.

'You can't go outside like that. Where are your boots, girl?' her stepmother asked, frowning down at Rowan's bare feet.

'I only ever wear them when I go to the market or up to the fields,' Rowan explained.

'For heaven's sakes! Why don't you wear them all the time like normal people?'

'I like to feel the earth beneath my feet. It makes me feel grounded. Mother always said . . .'

'Yes, well, come along then,' Fanny said, cutting her short. Rowan looked down at her stepmother's dainty shoes and thought they seemed even less suitable for tramping around in the dirty yard than bare feet, but deemed it better not to say so.

The wind was whistling through the passageway as they made their way outside, and Fanny shivered, pulling her shawl tighter around her. Rowan headed towards the scullery, little realizing her stepmother had gone the other way, until she heard her scream.

'What's the matter, Fanny?' she asked, hurrying back.

'There's a beast,' Fanny squeaked, pointing to the head that was peering through the open shippon door.

Rowan smiled at the docile cow that was eyeing them curiously, but before she could say anything, it turned, lifted its tail and deposited a steaming pat right in front of her stepmother.

Fanny's eyes widened in horror as she snatched a lacy hanky from her pocket and held it to her nose. 'That's quite the most disgusting thing I have ever seen,' she exclaimed. Then, as the sounds of munching and mooing emanated from the stalls behind, her hand went to her heart.

'What on earth's going on in there?'

'That's where the livestock are housed over winter.'

'You mean those animals actually live inside the house?' Fanny exclaimed, wrinkling her nose.

Rowan laughed. 'Oh, you are funny. Of course, we share the accommodation with the livestock. They are literally that, after all: our livelihood,' she elaborated, having been schooled on the importance of animal welfare since she was a young child. Seeing the perplexed look on her stepmother's face, she shook her head. 'Come on, I'll show you the dairy and well house.'

Rowan led her stepmother round to the back of the farmhouse, explaining what everything was used for. She then pointed out the linhay and stables off the cobbled farmyard to the front, but could see the woman was more concerned with keeping her fine skirts out of the dirt than hearing about the farm.

'You mean that was it?' Fanny exclaimed as they made their way back into the warmth of the kitchen. She glared down at the muck on her shoes and kicked them off in disgust. Then as Rowan took a handful of straw and wiped her feet, she wrinkled her nose. 'I shall have to speak with Edward about moving those wild beasts out. Really, I can't have animals living in my house. Whatever will my friends think when they visit, and where will I entertain them?'

'But that's what the parlour's for,' Rowan said. Then as

the aroma of cooked bread wafted towards her, she hurried to the oven, peeled away the dough sealing the door and carefully lifted out the loaves. As she turned them out on the table to cool Fanny watched, frowning.

'Why are you doing that?'

'Because I always bake every second day –'

'No, I mean, why are you doing the cooking? Who keeps house here?'

'I do,' Rowan began, then seeing the woman's set face she added, 'although, of course, I expect you'll want to now.'

'Me? I hardly think so,' Fanny exclaimed. 'No, I'm certain Edward said you had hired help.'

'Well, it's quite a small place really, and we do most things ourselves. Of course, we do have some help on the farm itself, especially at harvest. Sally comes in to see to the dairy when there's hard cheese to be made, and Mrs Stokes does most of the laundry. Which reminds me, when you empty your chamber pot there's a jar by the copper where we store the urine for ammonia . . .'

'Empty my chamber pot! Store the urine! My dear child, I hardly think I shall be concerning myself with such trifles,' Fanny said shrilly, putting her nose high in the air as if it was fresher up there.

'But then, how . . .' Rowan began, but her stepmother cut her short.

'I've had quite enough of this disgusting conversation. You might live with animals but there's no reason to act like them. Please tell Edward I wish to see him immediately.'

'Father will be up in Five Acre Field by now. He said he'd see you at supper time,' Rowan replied.

'Supper time! And what am I meant to do until then?' the woman demanded, looking around the room with distaste.

Rowan thought of everything that needed to be done before their evening meal could be put on the table. 'Well, there always seems to be more work to do than time to do it in. The men have been up in the field since breakfast and will be getting hungry so why don't we start preparing their noon pieces?' she suggested, but Fanny was already heading towards the parlour.

Rowan breathed a sigh of relief. Perhaps she could get on now, otherwise her father and Sab would be wondering where she'd got to. Quickly she cut into a cooling loaf, then spread it liberally with soft cheese flavoured with chives, which she'd picked from her garden. She was just adding pickled gherkins and a flagon of small beer to her basket when Fanny reappeared.

'It's so cold in there, I shall catch my death. Why hasn't the fire been lit?' she asked, looking at Rowan with the pebble-like eyes the girl was beginning to find unnerving. They reminded her of the ones on the beach at Salterton, cold, flat and grey.

'We only light the fire in the parlour on high days and holidays, Fanny,' she explained.

Her stepmother pursed her lips in a gesture Rowan was coming to recognize. 'Edward had a nice fire blazing in there when he brought me back after our wedding,' she said, shivering and glaring at Rowan as if it were her fault.

'We usually gather around the fire in here at the end of the working day,' Rowan pointed out, emphasizing the word 'working', but Fanny was eyeing the food spread out on the table.

'What's that?' she asked, picking up the dish of cheese and sniffing it.

'It's just some soft cheese I made yesterday.'

'Well, I've never seen cheese like that. You say you made it?'

'Yes, it's from a receipt in Mother's book. She used to write down all the food my father really liked in it. She said, feed a man his favourite foods and he'll love you for ever,' Rowan continued.

A spark of interest flashed in Fanny's eyes. 'Is that a fact? Perhaps you'd care to show me this famous book some time,' she said, smiling at Rowan for the first time that morning.

Surprised at the change in the woman's demeanour and relieved something had pleased her stepmother, Rowan replied, 'Of course.'

'For now, though, I'll sample some of your bread and cheese,' Fanny said magnanimously. 'It actually looks quite appetizing.'

'You help yourself whilst I take the men their noon pieces,' Rowan said, bending to put on her boots, grabbing her shawl and placing the basket over her arm.

Thankful to be outside, she noticed the wind had dropped and a watery sun was making a brave attempt to warm the frozen ground. Feeling her mood lighten, Rowan made her way along the track towards Five Acre Field. As she passed the privy she couldn't help grinning at Fanny's reaction to the word 'urine'. Did they not use chamber pots in London, she wondered. Chickens strutted and flapped around her feet, hopeful of extra feed, and she could hear the sheep bleating from the hills high above. Her father would be bringing them down soon to check how many ewes were in lamb, she thought. Then her attention was caught by a clump of snowdrops and she couldn't resist bending to stroke their creamy petals. The first harbingers of spring, her mother had always said.

'Hey, Rowan,' she heard Sab call. Looking up, she smiled as she saw him hurrying towards her.

'Sorry, I'm late with your piece, Sab. Fanny wanted a grand tour of the farmhouse,' she said.

'And did it meet with madam's approval?' he enquired, and although his voice was light, his eyes showed concern.

'No, I don't think it did, Sab, especially the animals in the shippon. She wanted me to go and get Father.'

'Well, he's had to go to Sudbury. He went on Blackthorn. Said he'd get a bite there. Thought I'd come and see if you were all right,' he grinned, peering eagerly into the basket.

'Fresh bread, chive cheese and gherkins,' Rowan laughed.

'Have you eaten?' Sab asked. She shook her head. 'Come on then,' he said, taking her arm and leading her back towards the barn; feral cats scattering in their wake. 'You can have Uncle Ted's share and tell me more about what's been going on.'

Rowan glanced back towards the farmhouse but she'd had enough of Fanny for one morning.

Settled on bales of straw, they tucked into the food as

if they'd not eaten for weeks. Then, as they shared the bottle of small beer, Rowan told Sab about her morning. 'You should have seen her face when Daisy dumped one in front of her; it was a right steamer, too,' she said, giggling. 'Then she insisted the animals would have to be moved out of the shippon so that she would have the whole farmhouse for entertaining her friends.'

Sab shook his head in disbelief. 'That one's going to be trouble and no mistake. Can't think what Uncle Ted was doing bringing someone like that here,' he grimaced, turning up his nose.

'Apparently, she comes from London,' Rowan explained. 'Father thinks she's wonderful and he did say we were to make her welcome. Perhaps I'd better cook something special for dinner.'

'What did you have in mind?' Sab asked, licking his lips.

'I was looking through Mother's cookbook the other day and found a receipt for chicken and ham pie. I know it's a bit extravagant, but we've got some of the chicken left from the roast and there was gammon in the settle, which I've put to soak. Not that I've attempted pie crust before, but I could at least try something different in her honour, couldn't I?' she asked.

'You're a kind girl, Rowan, and pie – well, that would be a feast for a king.' He rubbed his stomach appreciatively. 'And if there were baked potatoes, too ...' he added, looking hopeful.

'I think we might still have a few potatoes in the sack,' she replied, frowning as she remembered how quickly their winter crop store was dwindling. 'Well, I'd better get back and start preparing it all. I've a feeling it's going to take some time but at least I'll have made the effort for Father. It'll mean relighting the bread oven, though,' she said, gathering up the remains of their impromptu picnic.

'And I'd better get back to the hedging before Uncle Ted reappears. Do you want me to tell him what's in store for dinner?' he asked.

'No,' Rowan said. 'Let's keep it as a surprise. I think we still have some cider left, so perhaps you could bring in a flagon when you come? We'll make it a welcome party for Fanny.'

'I just hope she appreciates all the trouble you're going to. You'll be needing more faggots for the fire so I'll bring some in with me as well,' Sab offered, smiling.

As they went their separate way, neither of them noticed Fanny watching from her bedroom window.

Chapter 3

Back at the farmhouse, Rowan found the kitchen empty, apart from the remains of Fanny's meal strewn across the table. As she kicked off her boots she saw, to her dismay, that her stepmother had cut the tops off the remaining loaves and eaten those, leaving behind the charred bottoms. All her hard work had been wasted, she thought, anger rising in her chest. She had a good mind to go and have it out with the woman. Then she remembered she'd promised her father she'd try to make her stepmother feel welcome. Swallowing down her disappointment and deciding she would soak the remaining crusts in warm milk sprinkled with salt and turn them into brewis for their breakfast, she carried the remaining crusts through to the pantry.

Taking down the receipt book from the dresser, she settled herself on the floor beside the fire and turned to the relevant page. As always, the sight of her mother's beautiful flowing writing brought a lump to her throat, and the fact that the receipt for the chicken pie was the last entry made it more poignant. Stroking the ribbon around her wrist, she forced herself to concentrate on the instructions. Although the list of instructions was long, each stage seemed straightforward so Rowan was feeling confident as she stacked the bread oven with the remaining faggots. Then, having set fire to them, she lined up all the ingredients along the table.

The preparations took Rowan the rest of the afternoon, but to her immense satisfaction she managed to form the pie crust, fill it with the meats and pour in stock without it leaking. Finally, sealing it with its pastry lid, she stood back and admired what, to her, looked like a very passable effort indeed. With the shadows lengthening, she lit the candles and put another log on the fire. Then, after raking out the ashes from the oven for the second time that day, she placed her pie carefully inside, adding a few potatoes to bake at the same time. Magic tangled herself around her feet and, laughing at her antics, Rowan settled herself on the floor beside the fire, stroking her soft black fur.

After a while, her eyes grew heavy. Shaking herself, she jumped to her feet and began clearing away. Soon the aroma of cooking pie filled the kitchen, and she felt excitement stirring. Wait until her father saw what she'd made from her mother's book. Carefully she spread the bright cotton cloth they kept for special occasions over the table and set out the utensils they'd need.

'Something smells good,' Fanny said, gliding down the stairs. Pity she couldn't say the same, Rowan thought as the pervading scent of rose threatened to overpower the appetizing aroma of her cooking. She noticed her stepmother had changed into yet another fancy dress. How many did the woman have, she wondered, looking down at her own homespun gown. Although she'd dyed it green with leaves from the elder, and had been pleased with the result, beside Fanny's brightly sprigged material it looked quite drab. Her stepmother had styled her hair, too, clipping it back with an ornate clasp. Hastily, Rowan smoothed back her own mane of copper curls, reminding herself to take off her apron once she'd served the meal.

'Well, aren't you going to tell me what's cooking?' Fanny asked, looking enquiringly at Rowan.

'It's chicken and bacon pie,' she said proudly. 'It's from a receipt in Mother's book. I've never made a pie before so I hope it tastes as nice as it smells.'

'Did your mother make it often?' Fanny enquired.

'Yes, it was one of her favourite dishes. She always cooked it on special occasions,' she whispered, blinking back the tears so that she failed to notice the interest sparking in Fanny's eyes.

'My goodness, something smells inviting in here,' her father said, striding into the room and throwing his cap onto the settle. 'And what a delightful sight to welcome a man home,' he exclaimed, smiling at his new wife.

'Edward, my dear,' Fanny simpered in a soft voice, as she went over and kissed his cheek. Although he flushed and turned away, Rowan could tell he was pleased. Then the door swung open again and Sab clattered in, a flagon under one arm and a bundle of faggots under the other. He sniffed the air appreciatively.

'I heard there's a bit of a celebration going on, so I brought this in.' He proudly held up the cider and winked at Rowan.

'How clever of you to know that, Sab,' Fanny gushed, beaming at him as he carefully set the flagon on the table before tossing the faggots beside the hearth.

Surprised at the change in the woman's manner, but

putting it down to her afternoon rest, Rowan proudly set the pie on the table.

'Right, Sab, my boy, if you'd like to pour the drinks, I shall dish our dinner,' Fanny announced nudging Rowan out of the way and picking up the serving spoons. Rowan stared at her in surprise, but her stepmother was making such a performance of placing a generous portion of the pie in front of her new husband, she didn't notice.

'Now come along, Edward. Tell me what you think of your new wife's pie crust,' she said coyly.

'But, Fanny . . .' Rowan began.

'Do help yourselves to some pie, my dears, I've made plenty,' Fanny said, cutting Rowan short and regally making a sweeping gesture towards the food. Really, it was as if she were speaking to servants, Rowan thought.

'Why this looks absolutely delightful, my dear,' Edward murmured, oblivious to what was going on around him as he raised the crust to his mouth.

'But, Father . . .'

'Now Rowan, let your father enjoy his meal,' Fanny interrupted quickly. 'He must be famished after working out in the fields all day,' she purred, leaning across and patting his hand tenderly.

'Hmm, delicious, Fanny,' her father enthused. 'If you are going to cook dinners like this every night, I shall be a very happy man indeed.'

Rowan stared at Fanny, waiting for her to correct him, but her stepmother just smiled sweetly. 'Why, Edward, my dear, this is just a little pie I knocked up this afternoon.'

Sab, who was taking a swig of his cider, almost choked on his drink.

'Are you all right, Sab, dear?' Fanny asked solicitously.

'No, Fanny, I'm not. Something I just heard stuck in my throat and made the cider go down the wrong way,' he grunted, his clear eyes challenging.

'Oh?' Fanny said sweetly, her face a picture of innocence, but Rowan saw those pebble eyes hardening.

Oblivious, Sab continued, 'Yes, you see I understood it was Rowan who . . .'

But Fanny shrugged dismissively. 'Do eat your meal, Sab. I hate to see good food wasted,' she ordered, then promptly turned back to Edward and began regaling him with a story about eating out in London. Rowan raised her eyebrows, thinking about the remains of bread she'd left strewn over the table earlier.

Sab's mouth tightened, a sure sign he wasn't going to let the matter drop, but Rowan could see how her father was lapping up her stepmother's attention and shook her head. As she passed Sab his meal, she whispered, 'Don't forget about the crust, will you?'

'I'm no fool, and I don't like seeing you being taken for one either. It must have taken you ages to put this together,' he said, taking a mouthful of meat and sighing. 'This is right tasty. I don't see why she should get away with taking the credit for it, though.'

Rowan looked down the table.

'Come along, Edward, I insist you have another portion of my pie,' Fanny was saying, heaping another helping onto his plate. Then she saw Rowan watching and shot her a triumphant look. Why, she's gloating, Rowan thought. As her hand went instinctively to the red ribbon around her wrist, she found herself remembering one of her mother's favourite sayings.

'Don't worry, Sab, what goes around comes around,' Rowan replied, turning back to him and winking.

'That was a fine meal, Fanny, my dear,' Edward said, downing the rest of his drink. 'You must be quite worn out after all that work.'

'I must admit I am rather fatigued,' Fanny agreed, smiling at him apologetically as she made a half-hearted effort to collect their plates together.

Edward put a restraining hand on her arm. 'After making us a lovely meal like that, I'm sure Rowan will be only too happy to clear away, won't you?' he asked, turning towards her. Not trusting herself to speak, she nodded. 'We'll take ourselves up and have an early night, shall we, Fanny, my dear?' he said, smiling at her.

'Oh, Edward, you are so kind and thoughtful,' she simpered.

'Well, we can't have you wearing yourself out, Fanny, now can we?'

'Good night, Rowan. Good night, Sab. You'll see the livestock's settled?' Edward called over his shoulder as he led his new wife up the stairs.

'I want to do my best by you, Edward, but I can't deny that it's hard work cooking for you all. Now, my friend was telling me about these new open ranges you can get. Apparently, they really make a woman's life much easier.'

As their voices faded away, Rowan turned to Sab. 'Father can't afford things like that.'

'That's as may be, but I somehow think she'll get her own way,' he said, shaking his head. 'That one's perfected the art of looking like an innocent child when underneath she's cunning as a serpent. Her eyes give her away, though. Bet she's already got her plans worked out for this place. Uncle Edward won't stand a chance.'

Remembering the earlier conversation with her step-mother by the shippon, Rowan couldn't help thinking he was right.

'Well, I'm too tired to clear this lot away tonight so I'm off to the privy while I can still get in there,' she said, grinning mischievously.

'I'll guide you and then see to the animals,' replied Sab, lighting the lantern. He opened the door and the dogs seemed to appear at his side from nowhere. 'Can't believe the old dragon's banned them from the kitchen, poor things. They enjoy a laze by the fire after a day's work, just as we do,' he said, bending and fussing them.

It was a crisp night with the full moon shining, the countryside peaceful. Sab looked up at the sky and shook his head.

'Uncle Edward will need to come back down to earth soon if we're to sow the first of the crops when the water table next rises.'

'Perhaps the novelty of early nights will have worn off by then,' Rowan said.

'I certainly hope so. It's him who insisted on this lunar lark in the first place,' Sab reminded her.

'Father says it's scientific and it always seems to work, along with a little help from my rituals, of course. We certainly had a better crop than our neighbours last year, didn't we? Well, I can manage now, thanks, Sab,' she said, as they reached the privy.

'Night, Rowan, and thanks again for a truly delicious meal. I'm just sorry Uncle Edward didn't realize you made it.'

'Don't worry, Sab. I've a feeling that come tomorrow Fanny will be wishing she'd told him I had,' and, laughing, she dived inside the wooden hut.

After washing her hands in the crystal waters of the stream, Rowan slowly made her way back to the farmhouse, the quietude of the night restoring her equilibrium. She could hear Sab's gentle voice coming from the shippon as he settled the animals for the night. It was as if they were his children, she thought smiling. He'd been at one with the animals ever since he'd arrived, insisting on sleeping in the hayloft above them, even though her parents had offered him the small room next to her own.

Candle in hand, she crept up the stairs but the sounds of muffled laughter and creaking of the bed coming from her father's room wiped the smile from her face. She knew what they were doing, of course. Mrs Stokes had taught her about such things the day she'd found Rowan shivering with fright having seen her first blood nearly two years back. The kindly woman had made her a hot drink and explained to Rowan how her body was developing and preparing itself for motherhood. She'd gone on to outline what happened between a man and a woman, likening it to sheep at tupping, but Rowan had grimaced, not wanting to dwell on such details.

Now, hearing Fanny giggle, she hurried into her own room, shutting the door firmly behind her. But as she placed her candle on the chest, the overwhelming scent of rose hit her. Fanny had been in her room! A quick inspection revealed her things had been disturbed. Nothing had been taken as far as she could see, but it was obvious her possessions had been searched and she had a terrible sense of her privacy having been invaded.

Then a thought struck her and, hurrying over to the bed, she felt beneath the mattress. As her hand closed over her precious mirror, she breathed a sigh of relief. Carefully, she drew it from its covering and sat there tracing the trumpet scroll design decorating the grip that held the handle to the mirror. She remembered how excited her mother had been the day she'd found it. She'd been digging over their vegetable plot when her spade had hit a hard object. Fascinated, Rowan had watched her carefully wipe away the earth to reveal the find. Her father had deduced from the layer of rich clay in which it had been encrusted that it must have lain there undisturbed for hundreds, maybe even thousands of years. It had become her mother's most treasured possession and she'd used it often. After she'd died Rowan's father had given it to her. Smiling at the memory, she turned the mirror so that, with the handle at the top, it looked like the face of a cat grinning back at her, and she sighed at the recollections of happier times.

Then she caught another whiff of rose and anger whirled up inside her like a snake uncoiling. Privacy had always been an important part of their lives. Her mother had taught her that. Privacy of thought, privacy of deed, privacy of space, and now her stepmother had invaded all three. Rowan could not and would not allow that to happen again. Instinctively her hand went to her wrist and as her fingers stroked the soft red ribbon they were charged with energy. She knew then what she had to do and the mirror would be her ally.

Quickly snuffing out the candle, she went over to the window and laid her claim, acknowledging the full moon as mistress of truth and illusion. Then, relighting her candle, she cleansed her space with water and salt and carefully cast her circle. After lighting more candles and placing them to the north, south, east and west, she sat cross-legged in the centre of them. Pointing in the direction of sunrise, she drew energy upward from her feet and made her declaration. Snuffing out all but one of the candles, she held the mirror in front of the flame and concentrated on the rhyme. Visualizing the bad energy being returned to its sender, she intoned the final words aloud.

> *Confusion to the enemy,*
> *As I have spoken,*
> *So mote it be.*

Placing the mirror on the door for it to continue its work, she snuffed out the candle and climbed into bed.

Lying in the moonlight, she thought back over her day. And what a day it had been. Did Fanny really think her father would move the animals to make more space in the farmhouse for her to entertain her friends? Was he really going to buy her a range? If so, then where would he get the money? Rowan knew to the last farthing how much the farm had in its kitty. Since her mother had died she'd kept the accounts, going through them with her father at the end of each month. Although, thinking about it, she realized since he'd met Fanny he hadn't had time to do that. She must ensure they went through the figures very soon. Her final thought before she went to sleep was that it was a shame her father hadn't listened when she'd tried to explain about the pie.

Finally she drifted off to sleep, only to be woken some time later by the sounds of groaning coming from the next room, followed by the chink of the chamber pot and then footsteps running outside to the privy. Oh, well, there was nothing she could do, she thought, turning over and going back to sleep.

Chapter 4

The first thing Rowan noticed when she entered the kitchen the next morning was that the remains of the previous night's meal had been cleared away. Good old Sab. He knew showing Fanny around the farmhouse and making the pie had put her behind with her chores, and had obviously wanted to help. Today, she decided, she would prepare a simple broth for their evening meal and leave it simmering over the fire, whilst she caught up. First, though, she needed to get some water on to heat for breakfast. How much more time she'd have if they didn't have to eat, she thought, lifting the empty pot from its arm beside the fire and making her way outside to the well house. Her mother had always seemed to take cooking in her stride but Rowan would much rather be mixing ingredients for her potions and salves than for stews.

As soon as she opened the door to the passage, she could hear insistent lowing coming from the shippon. Peering round the open door, she saw Sab milking Daisy, whilst the other cows restlessly pulled at their tethers.

'Need a hand?' she called, setting down her pot.

Sab looked up and nodded gratefully. 'That would be grand, Rowan. We're running late this morning and these beasts are impatient to let down their milk.'

Placing a pail beneath the cow in the next stall, Rowan perched on a stool.

'Come along, Dolly, give unto me your richest, creamiest milk,' she crooned encouragingly, leaning against the animal's warm flanks and breathing in her hot grassy breath. 'No Father this morning?' she asked.

'He came down first thing, but was doubled over with stomach gripes before he'd even finished milking the first one.'

'Poor Father; still, it'll soon pass,' she said philosophically.

'Bet her majesty's making a fine tap and tune, though. I can see she's going to lead Uncle a right jig,' Sab commented, pulling vigorously on the cow's udders so that she kicked out in protest.

'Steady on, Sab. That's not like you,' Rowan admonished.

'Yes, sorry, Daisy old thing,' he apologized, patting the animal's rump. 'I was musing last night. If Fanny's from London, then happen her fancy friends are too. Are they really going to come all this way to visit? Doesn't make sense to me.'

But Rowan had no answer and they carried on milking in silence, both lost in their own thoughts.

'Quite like old times, this,' she commented after a while. The rhythmic pulling and soft rush of sweet, warm liquid filling the pail soothed her senses, reminding her how they'd used to milk the cows together, before the domestic duties of the farmhouse had claimed her time. 'Thanks for clearing up the kitchen, Sab. I hate starting the day with a dirty table.'

'I just stacked everything in the scullery. After that fine meal, it was the least I could do. I'll help you wash the dishes later,' he said, moving his stool over to milk the next fidgeting animal.

'All right in here, you two?' Rowan's father called from the doorway. 'I'm afraid my visit to the privy took longer than I thought, and then Fanny needed me urgently,' he explained, looking sheepish.

'Are you feeling better now?' Rowan asked, taking in his pale face and dishevelled appearance.

Her father nodded. 'Better than I was earlier, that's for sure,' he said, grinning ruefully.

'Don't worry, Father. Sab and I have almost finished here,' Rowan said, indicating the pails foaming with their creamy contents.

'You two haven't suffered any ill effects then?' he asked.

Rowan and Sab exchanged knowing looks before shaking their heads.

'Well, I'm pleased, of course, but it does seem strange when we all ate the same meal,' he muttered, stroking his beard thoughtfully.

Rowan opened her mouth, but before she could say anything to her father, the querulous voice of Fanny had him scuttling back inside.

'Poor Uncle Ted,' Sab said.

'Yes, it's a shame he's been ailing,' Rowan answered.

'That wasn't what I meant. If that's married life, then I'm staying well clear,' he said with feeling. 'Look, thanks for helping, Rowan, but I can manage now. I'll drive this lot out into the yard then swill down the shippon. That'll leave you free to get on with breakfast. I'm starving,' he declared, his usual cheeky grin replacing his sombre look.

'You and your stomach,' Rowan said, laughing. As she reached down to retrieve the pot, she saw her feet were covered in muck and straw. Remembering Fanny's disparaging look the previous day, she thought she'd better rinse them before going back indoors. Hurrying over to the brook, she hitched up her skirts and waded in, gasping as the icy waters took her breath away. Then she noticed the sun peaking up from behind the treetops on the upper pastures. Even as she watched, the rosy glow spread ever wider and she felt excitement bubbling up inside her. Spring was just around the corner, bringing with it new growth and longer hours of daylight. She couldn't wait to be out harvesting herbs for healing and flower heads for her dyes and potions. Remembering Fanny's brightly coloured dresses, she had a sudden yen to experiment with the bright blue juice of cornflowers. She would show her stepmother that living in the country didn't mean being drab.

Before then, she would need to sow her vegetables. Growing food for the kitchen was one of her most important tasks, and she began working out the moon's phases and the best time for planting. It was some moments before she spotted the empty pot by the side of the bank. Gosh, here she was dreaming away the time when there was work to be done. Climbing out of the waters and drying her feet on the grass, she hurried to the well house.

Having set the water to heat, she let out the chickens and began collecting their eggs, humming happily as she revelled in the familiarity of her routine. However, when she returned to the farmhouse to make their breakfast, her happy mood quickly turned to one of dismay for the pot of water was all but empty. As she stood there shaking her head in disbelief, her father hurried down the stairs.

'Sorry, Rowan, Fanny was complaining she needed a wash so I took her up some hot water,' he explained. 'She intends going back to bed for a lie-down after her disturbed night and says not to worry about taking her any breakfast up until later.'

Take her up breakfast again? Rowan bit down the angry words that sprang to her lips.

Her father noticed her frowning and he shrugged. 'Guess I'd better go and see how Sab's getting on,' he said ruefully.

Rowan opened her mouth to say something, then, seeing how pale he still looked, her mood softened.

'You can't go outside without something to line your stomach, Father. You sit down and I'll fry you an egg with a rasher.'

Edward grimaced. 'Thanks Rowan, but I don't think I could face it.'

'Well, at least have some bread and milk. I made some brewis yesterday; that'll settle you. Haven't you always told us we can't work effectively on an empty stomach?' she asked, repeating his well-worn mantra.

'A man knows when he's beaten,' he said, grinning as he seated himself at the now tidy table. Rowan hurried to the pantry and was just pouring their milk, still warm from the cows, into mugs, when the door clattered open. Sab, true to form, stood there, his face splitting into a wide grin when he saw the food set out on the table.

'Good timing, eh?' he quipped, settling himself alongside her father.

They ate in companionable silence, no one seeming to mind they only had the brewis. As Rowan sat there, listening to the crackle of logs on the fire and the now contented lowing of the cattle in the shippon on the other side of the passage, she began to relax. Then she glanced over to the fireplace where the dogs had always sprawled on the hearth, and felt a pang. When she turned to her father, intending to ask if they could be allowed in again, she saw he was frowning.

'Is something wrong, Father? You're not feeling ill again, are you?'

He shook his head. 'I've upset Fanny,' he burst out. 'I was saying earlier how strange it was that you two haven't felt any ill effects after our meal last night when we all ate the same thing, and she flew into a rage. Reckoned you must have added something to it,' Edward said.

'What?' Rowan exclaimed.

'Just to the part you and she ate? How stupid is that?' Sab spluttered. 'Rowan didn't even know Fanny was going to dish up the pie, which she made, by the way.'

Edward stared at Rowan. 'Is that right, Rowan? You mean it wasn't Fanny's cooking at all?' he asked.

Taken aback, Rowan said quickly, 'Look, Father, it was the pie crust that upset you both. It's only used to contain the meat while it cooks, remember?' She watched as understanding dawned. 'Neither Sab nor I ate it. I did try to warn you, but you were busy listening to Fanny,' she said gently.

Her father looked shame-faced. 'Well, I've gone and put my hoof in it good and proper,' he said, stroking his wiry beard.

'Why, Father?' Rowan asked.

'When I told her you wouldn't have done anything like

37

that, she got right cross and accused me of taking your side against her. Now she's refusing to do anything until I promise to buy her one of those newfangled open ranges. Where am I going to get money for something like that?' he groaned.

'I don't mean to be funny, Uncle, but can Fanny actually cook?' Sab asked.

Edward frowned. 'Of course; she told me she used to host supper parties in London,' he said.

'Ah, but did she do the cooking for them?' Sab persisted.

The furrows on Edward's brow deepened.

'What did Fanny actually do in London, Father? You never did say,' Rowan asked.

'Well, I'm not rightly sure,' he said, scratching his head. 'We spent more time discussing life at Orchard Farm. She was so interested and wanted to know everything about it. I do remember her telling me she was used to dealing with children and that running the farmhouse here would be a simple affair.'

Sab raised his eyebrows at Rowan.

'Anyway, talking of Fanny reminds me, I have to go to Honiton this morning. It seems there are some things she needs to help her settle in, so as it's quiet at the moment, I'll head off,' Edward said, getting to his feet and snatching up his cap.

Remembering her thoughts of the previous night, Rowan frowned.

'You're not going out to buy a range, are you, Father? Only we need to go through the farm accounts.'

'Stop worrying, Rowan. I'm not one for spending

money we don't have, you know that,' assured her father, patting her shoulder. 'You carry on with the hedging whilst I'm gone, Sab, and I'll be back some time after noon.'

As the door clattered shut behind him, Rowan and Sab stared at each other.

'Twice in two days Uncle Edward's left the farm during working time,' Sab said, shaking his head. 'It's not like him at all. I'd like to know what it is she needs so urgently.'

'Shouldn't you be about your work?' The sharp voice made them jump. Fanny was standing in the doorway, hands on hips, an unfathomable look on her face. 'I don't think a servant should take advantage just because his master isn't here,' she snarled, her pebble eyes boring into Sab.

'Sab is no servant, Fanny,' Rowan retorted, jumping to her feet. 'He's part of our family.'

'It – it's all right, Rowan. I – I'm off to finish the hedging, anyway,' Sab said, his cheeks glowing red as the fire. Rowan looked at him in dismay.

'Fanny . . .' she began, but her stepmother cut across her.

'Before you go, Sab, you can empty my chamber pot. It's full to overflowing,' Fanny declared, wrinkling her nose.

Rowan stared at her aghast. 'We all see to our own here, Fanny,' she said. 'Besides, Sab has enough to do around the farm, especially with Father having to go out shopping for you.' Although Rowan felt her legs trembling, she wasn't about to let Fanny order Sab around like that.

Her stepmother shot her a look of pure loathing. 'Now, you two, let's get one thing straight. I am now the lady of Orchard Farm,' she stated, giving them each a hard stare. 'Sab, you will do as I say, right this minute,' she ordered. Sab opened his mouth, closed it again quickly and hurried up the stairs. When he returned moments later with the pot held at arm's length, Fanny was waiting.

'When you've emptied that, you can leave it on the doorstep, cleaned mind and then be about your business.'

Rowan saw Sab clench his jaw, but he said nothing and disappeared outside.

'Well now, Rowan, let us go and sit by the fire. I think you and I need to have a little chat,' Fanny said smiling graciously, but Rowan noticed the smile didn't reach her eyes.

'Perhaps we could have a chat later, Fanny. I really don't have time . . .'

'When I say we need to talk, I mean now,' her step-mother said, standing up so that she towered over Rowan's diminutive form. 'There are certain things we have to get straight.'

Knowing she was beaten, Rowan slumped down on the floor beside the fire, idly toying with the ribbon on her wrist. But as Fanny crossed the room, Magic jumped down from the bacon settle, arched her back and spat at her.

'That creature will have to go,' she declared, aiming her foot in the cat's direction.

'Magic's never done that before, Fanny,' Rowan said, watching Magic shoot up the stairs. However, her step-mother had perched herself on the edge of the chair and was making a show of arranging the skirts of her dress. Yet another one, Rowan noted. She saw Fanny frowning down at her bare feet and quickly tucked them beneath her skirt.

'Right, young lady, just what do you think you were doing trying to poison me last night?'

'Poison you?' Rowan spluttered. 'I never did any such thing and if you hadn't been so busy making a performance of dishing the pie that you professed to have made, you'd have heard me warn you about the crust.'

'Ah, so you admit there was something wrong with it?' her stepmother said triumphantly.

'There was absolutely nothing wrong at all. The crust is only used as a container for baking the meat in, as any cook knows,' Rowan said, watching Fanny's reaction closely. Sure enough, the woman's cheeks began to redden.

'Yes, well, where I come from we have dishes for that,' she said quickly. Then her voice changed, becoming sweet as honey. 'Anyway, let's forget that for now. The real reason I want us to have this little chat, Rowan, is because I feel, as your stepmother, it is my duty to take on the role of lady of the house. I was saying to Edward that you are too young to have so much responsibility. The way you have looked after your father and the farmhouse is admirable, of course. However, you should be out having fun,' she said, leaning forward and patted Rowan's arm. Immediately the ribbon around her wrist tightened.

'Does that mean you will be taking over all the house-keeping and cooking duties?' she asked, smiling innocently up at Fanny.

'I shall assist, of course,' her stepmother said quickly. 'However, as I explained to your father, I can't possibly venture outside in all that dirt. My nicest shoes are already ruined, and as for that awful smell from the animals . . .' She shuddered so theatrically that Rowan had to bite her tongue to stop herself from laughing out loud. As far as she was concerned, the smell from the farmyard was like new-mown hay compared to the all-pervading reek of artificial rose that wafted in her stepmother's wake.

'Now in order for me to oversee things, Rowan, you need to tell me more about the daily duties of the hired hands.'

Rowan stared at her stepmother. 'But, I've already explained, Fanny. We don't have help every day. As a family, we pitch in with the chores around the farm. And then at harvest time, we all lend a hand on each other's land.'

Fanny shuddered. 'I mean in the house, Rowan. You truly don't expect me to believe one person sees to everything around here.'

Rowan nodded. 'Mostly, I do.'

'Then that will have to change. I shall discuss finances with Edward this evening and make the necessary arrangements.'

As Fanny sat back in her chair with a self-satisfied air, Rowan couldn't help it. She burst out laughing.

'Oh, Fanny, you make it sound as if this is some grand manor, not a modest farmhouse,' she gasped, tears of mirth running down her cheeks.

'Don't think you can deceive me, Rowan. When Edward proposed, he assured me Orchard Farm was a lucrative business, and that I would be lady of it. Now I'm sure you don't wish to upset your father, so from now on you will do as I say. Do I make myself clear?' Fanny barked, shooting each word out like shot from a musket. 'Things are going to be very different around here and, for a start, you can stop wearing that filthy ribbon round your wrist.'

'Never,' Rowan cried, and before her stepmother could say another word, she fled to the sanctuary of her room.

Chapter 5

Rowan slammed the door behind her then cautiously sniffed the air. To her relief there was no smell of rose in her room. Blessings, wondrous mirror, she intoned mentally, tracing the outline of the trumpet scrolls on its handle and thinking that her need to have a safe haven from the horrible Fanny was even greater now. Throwing herself onto the bed, she stared up at the ceiling. How dare that woman tell her what she could and couldn't wear she thought, her fingers automatically going to the red ribbon. Who the devil did she think she was? And where did those delusions of grandeur come from? Surely her father, ever a truthful man, would never have exaggerated how prosperous their farm was? Although they got by quite well, there was never much left over at the end of the year and certainly not for fancy goods. Lady of the farm indeed! Well, if Fanny wanted to be in charge then she could and that included seeing to today's meals.

Jumping up, she threw her shawl around her shoulders and crept downstairs. In the kitchen she stepped into her boots, snatched the last of the bread from the table then quietly lifted the latch and fled out of the door. Ignoring the chickens that flapped around her feet, she hurried off in search of Sab.

The air was brisk, but with anger fuelling her steps, Rowan reached Five Acre field before she'd even noticed.

Leaning against the five-bar gate, her breath rising in steamy clouds, she looked around but could see no sign of Sab. Inroads had been made into the repair of the hedges but there was still much left to do. It wasn't like him to leave a job half finished, and she fervently hoped Fanny hadn't upset him too much.

Feeling an overwhelming need to be near her mother, Rowan picked her way up the steep track until she came to the copse and her mother's final resting place beneath the hazel. A profusion of snowdrops were blooming on her grave and Rowan couldn't help smiling through her tears. Never one for show, her mother had insisted they shouldn't waste money on a fancy cairn, but were to leave it to nature to mark where she lay. 'When the blossoms show, remember me,' she'd said that final day, her voice coming in ragged, raspy breaths.

'Oh, I do, Mother,' Rowan cried now as, heedless of the damp ground, she threw herself down beside the flowers. 'How I wish you were still here,' she whispered, burying her head in the soft creamy petals. And then all the pent-up anger burst out of her. 'This woman Father's married is horrible, really nasty. I made a pie and she claimed it was hers. She even insisted Father ate it all, including the crust. They had bad stomachs this morning. Come to think of it, though, Fanny seems to have recovered very quickly. She must have a system of steel. Just like her smile, which never reaches her eyes. She wants to change things around the house. But don't worry, I won't let her, Mother. I shall make sure everything stays just as you left it . . .'

Finally her ranting came to a halt, leaving her drained

and spent. As she sat in the ensuing silence, staring down at the bell-shaped flowers, the ribbon around her wrist tightened and she knew her mother was trying to tell her something. But what?

Suddenly, seemingly from nowhere, a breeze blew up. It gathered in strength, swirling Rowan's copper curls around her face and lifting her skirts. She shivered, pulling her shawl tighter round her.

'Goodbye, Mother,' she whispered, jumping to her feet. As if in answer, the wind gusted around her, rippling the snowdrops into what looked, just for a second, like the shape of a heart. She gasped, but then another gust swirled, returning the flowers to their upright state.

Her mother had been listening! With warmth flooding her insides, Rowan flew back down the hill as if she'd grown wings. Passing the mighty oak, its branches creaking and cracking in the increasingly strong wind, she saw rich green moss growing to the north of its trunk. Knowing it would make a wonderful rich dye, she hesitated, but the wind gusted powerfully again and she knew it would be foolish to stop. Resolving to return when the storm had passed, she continued on past the saplings, which were swaying and bending to the will of the wind.

Then, as she regained the path, as quickly as the wind had blown up, it dropped, returning to a gentle breeze. Not wanting to confront Fanny any sooner than she had to, Rowan slowed her steps. Maybe she could hide away in the dairy and busy herself preparing for butter making the next day? As she stood there deliberating, she heard the sound of a cart and horse making its way towards the farmhouse. It must be her Uncle Silas and Auntie Sal, and, spirits lifting, she tore down the hillside.

By the time she reached the farmhouse, even the gentle breeze had died. To her surprise, she saw her aunt and uncle were standing on the step with Fanny, arms folded, presiding in the doorway.

'Auntie Sal, Uncle Silas,' Rowan called. 'Why are you standing out here? Come on in and have a warm. I've been to see Mother and there was a fine old wind blowing ...' She stopped as she saw their serious faces. 'Is something wrong?'

'We came to visit, Rowan, but it seems we've chosen the wrong time,' her uncle said, and although he spoke in his usual gentle West Country burr, Rowan saw the glint in his eyes.

'Don't be silly, there can never be a wrong time for coming to see us, can there?' she questioned, turning to Fanny, who was pursing her lips.

'Now don't you go worrying, dearie. We can call another time,' her aunt said, smiling awkwardly as she held out a basket covered with a muslin cloth. 'I was baking earlier and thought you might find these useful. You know how I always make too much.'

Rowan grinned wryly, knowing her aunt, a thrifty housewife, would never cook more than she intended.

'But you must come in. Father will be returning soon and he'll be sorry if he doesn't see you,' Rowan insisted.

'Well, if you're sure ...' her aunt said doubtfully, but followed her in anyway.

'I am. If we can't offer our family refreshment when they come to visit, then it's a sorry day for the Clodes,'

Rowan said, and although she didn't look in Fanny's direction, she could feel the woman's hatred emanating her way. Pushing past her stepmother, she caught a waft of overpowering scent, and noticed her aunt wrinkling her nose.

Belatedly remembering her manners, Fanny turned towards Silas and Sal and forced her lips into a smile.

'Now that Rowan has returned, of course you must come in,' she said graciously.

In the kitchen Rowan shivered and, going over to the fire, she saw that it had burned right down. Riddling the embers and adding more wood, she noticed with dismay that yet again the pot was empty.

'I'll just go out to the well,' she said, lifting the pot and fighting down the urge to comment on her stepmother's lack of housekeeping skills. 'You'll be wanting a hot drink after riding through that storm.'

Her aunt and uncle stared at her in surprise.

'We never passed no storm,' her aunt said, shaking her head as she picked up her basket. 'I'll come with you and unpack these,' she added, frowning at Fanny, who was now sitting in front of the fire, holding her hands in front of the kindled flames.

'Whilst they do that, you can come and sit by me, Silas,' Fanny gushed, smiling and patting the seat beside her. 'You'll have to forgive me if I seemed inhospitable earlier, but in London we never let anyone we don't know over the threshold. One can't be too careful,' she added.

'Well, if we'd been invited to the wedding, she would have known who we were,' Aunt Sal muttered as she followed Rowan through the cross passage.

'I know, Auntie. Even Sab and I weren't invited,' Rowan said. 'It wasn't like Father not to include us all, but he says everything happened so quickly.'

'Hmm,' her aunt growled, and Rowan could remember her mother saying Aunt Sal had a way of expressing everything she meant without using words. Now she understood. 'Is everything all right here, Rowan?' she asked. Her voice was so soft and caring, Rowan wanted to tell her everything was far from all right, but knew that would be disloyal to her father. Smiling brightly, she nodded. Her aunt wasn't fooled, though. 'Just remember you can tell me anything, dearie. Your mother was the sister I never had, God rest her soul, and she'd never forgive me if I didn't look out for you.'

'Oh, Auntie, you've looked after us so well since Mother died, and still are, by the look of things,' she said, nodding down at the basket her aunt was still holding.

'Dearie me, here's me forgetting my manners. Now, I've brought some bread, butter, cream and cheese. There's cold meat and pease pudding, some of my Devon splitties, oh, and an apple pudding, too. I know how your father's partial to that,' she said, unpacking everything and placing them on the shelf in the pantry. 'Of course, if you think I'll be impinging on Fanny's housekeeping, then you must tell me, dearie. It doesn't do to interfere with another woman's cooking,' she murmured, suddenly looking unsure.

Rowan burst out laughing. 'There's no chance of that, Auntie,' she said. Then seeing her aunt's look of surprise, she quickly told her about the pie crust. 'So you see, Auntie, Sab and I don't think she can even cook,' she finished up.

Her aunt stared at Rowan as if she'd taken leave of her senses. 'That can't be true, Rowan. Why, if there's one thing we all know about your father it's his fondness for his stomach. You've been looking after him for many years now, and a right good job you've done of it. Perhaps Fanny's just afraid of stepping on your toes, so to speak.'

Rowan shrugged. 'I don't think so, Auntie.'

'Well, we'd best be getting back inside, dearie. Your uncle will be wanting to leave before it gets too late. This cold, wet winter's made his joints play up something rotten.'

Rowan turned and picked up a bottle from the shelf.

'Take this sage oil, Auntie, and get him to rub it on his joints every morning and night. I'm sure it will help.'

'Why, thank you, dearie. You really are a clever girl with all your lotions and potions. If this works as well as that elder salve you made for his sore foot, he'll be better in no time.'

As they went back indoors, her uncle jumped to his feet, looking relieved to see them. Taking the pot from Rowan, he carefully placed it over the now blazing fire.

'I'll prepare some of your tasty splitties whilst the water's heating, Auntie,' Rowan said. Then, she turned to her stepmother. 'That is, unless you've already baked today, Fanny. I'd hate to interfere with your housekeeping,' she added innocently, keeping her face deadpan.

Her stepmother looked startled but, as ever, quickly recovered her composure.

'Of course we must have your splitties, Sal. I may call you Sal?' she asked, her voice rising in that false way Rowan had come to recognize. 'It's most kind of you to bring them.' Although her aunt smiled politely, Rowan noticed she was giving her stepmother one of her long level looks. She smiled inwardly. Aunt Sal was a shrewd woman and Fanny would be hard pressed to fool her.

By the time she'd spread the little sponges with cream and jam and arranged them on a platter, her father had returned. His enthusiastic welcome put paid to any doubt Rowan's aunt and uncle had about staying for refreshments and they all gathered around the scrubbed table catching up on their news.

'Do tell us about your life in London,' said Aunt Sal, turning to Fanny. 'What did you do there?'

There was a moment's silence and Rowan watched as her stepmother painted on her bright smile, the one that didn't reach her eyes.

'It's kind of you to ask, Sal. However, as I am now living here in beautiful Devonshire, I'm much more interested in finding out about you all.'

To give her aunt her due, she answered all of Fanny's questions but Rowan could see she was biding her time. Sure enough, when there was a lull in the conversation, her aunt turned towards Fanny, smiling brightly.

'Now that really is enough about us, except to say that we are really proud of the way Rowan has coped these past years. It will be good for her to have the company of another female. There's always so much that needs to be done in a farmhouse.'

Fanny looked around the room and frowned. 'Well, of course, there are a lot of changes to be made. We've already spoken about getting a range, haven't we, Edward?' she said, smiling at her husband. 'And then, of course, there will be other additions,' she said, pausing and lifting her cup to her lips.

'Perhaps the patter of tiny feet will be heard again at Orchard Farm in the not-too-distant future, then,' Aunt Sal suggested, winking at her brother.

Fanny burst into a fit of coughing, spraying her tea in an unladylike manner whilst Edward sat there beaming. Clearly her father liked that idea, Rowan thought. She'd never given any thought to the fact that she might one day have a stepsibling. Her mother, being so petite, had suffered badly when she'd been born and had been told there could be no more children. It had come as a great disappointment to her parents, for they'd hoped to have a large family. In time, of course, they'd come to terms with the fact and adopted Sab. Sab, where was he? It wasn't like him to miss out on a meal. But Fanny, having recovered her composure, was already preparing to show her guests out.

'It's so kind of you to have paid us a visit but we mustn't keep you,' she said with her superficial smile.

Politely, Rowan's aunt and uncle got to their feet.

'Before you go, Auntie, I've finished those socks you asked for,' Rowan said, jumping up and going over to the dresser.

'Why, thank you, Rowan. As ever, they're beautifully knitted. Now what do I owe you?' Sal asked, putting them down and rooting around in her basket.

'Nothing, Auntie, I enjoyed making them,' Rowan said, thinking of all the things her aunt had done for her over the years.

'Now, Rowan, it must have taken you ages, for we all

know your uncle has big feet,' Sal laughed, nudging her husband. 'Then there's the wool.'

'Which you spun,' Rowan replied.

'And you dyed,' her aunt countered, laughing. 'So, I insist. Oh, and then there's the sage oil, too.'

Rowan shook her head. 'No, that's a present for Uncle Silas. I've been working on a new formula, so do let me know if it works.'

'I will that, Rowan, my dear. I've no doubt it will do the trick. Your magic potions always do,' her uncle said, smiling. Despite her protests, Auntie Sal insisted on pressing some coins into Rowan's hand. Fanny looked on, her sharp eyes taking in the exchange.

''Treat yourself to a little something, dearie; you deserve it,' her aunt said quietly, enveloping Rowan in her motherly arms. As the girl breathed in the sweet smell of her country freshness, she couldn't help wishing her new stepmother was more like her aunt.

''Bye then, our Rowan,' her uncle said. Then, leaning forward, he whispered, 'That one's like a fox with her cunning ways. She's got your father eating out of her hand, and I'm thinking it'll be better for you if you go along with her changes. You know where we are if you should need us.' And with a rueful grin he followed his wife out of the door.

Rowan watched as her aunt and uncle trundled away, wishing with all her heart she was going with them. Her uncle, ever wise, was right about Fanny, but Rowan couldn't just stand by and let her change everything, could she?

Chapter 6

Rowan stood on the step waving until her aunt and uncle were swallowed up by the twilight. For the first time in ages, she felt really alone, almost abandoned. Shaking herself for being so fanciful, she hurried across the yard and began shooing the chickens back into their coops. She was just shutting them in for the night when she heard a whinny and saw Bramble peering over the stable door. Sab was back. He looked up and nodded as she entered the shippon, and then returned to milking Daisy without saying anything. Shooting him a grin, she pulled up a stool alongside Buttercup, and began rhythmically pulling on the cow's udders. The smell of hay and the steady munching of the cattle were comforting and she felt herself relaxing as they worked together in the flickering light of the candle lantern.

'Quite like old times again,' she said, after a few moments. 'You missed a lovely tea earlier, Sab. Auntie Sal brought us some of her splitties.' He shrugged, looking despondent. 'Don't worry, I've saved one for you,' she added. He gave a quick grin of acknowledgement, but still didn't say anything.

Rowan continued with her milking, giving him time to collect himself before telling her what was on his mind. Finally, though, impatience got the better of her.

'I went up to Five Acre Field this morning but couldn't

see any sign of you,' she said, staring at him through the animal's legs.

'Took the wagon down to Saltcombe and collected a load of seaweed for the vegetable garden,' he grunted.

'Oh, Sab, why didn't you come and get me?' she cried in disappointment. 'You know how I love to go to the beach. We're nearly out of chalk and I could have collected some.'

'Sorry, Rowan. I'd had it up to here with that woman and her orders,' he said, raising his hand above his forehead. 'Had to get away before I exploded. At least the dogs got a good run.'

'Lucky them,' she said with feeling. 'I knew Fanny ordering you to empty her chamber pot was too much. Did you put the urine in the collecting pot?'

'No I did not!' he exclaimed. 'It was the most revolting mess . . . Well, you don't want to know. But that wasn't all. She wanted me to light the fire in the parlour and then change the furniture around. When I'd finished that, she insisted I move their bed so it faces the window, even though I pointed out the draught from the loose sash would blow over her head at night. She got right on her top note, insisting she had to see the view. I ask you, have you ever heard anything like it?'

Rowan shook her head and moved her stool over to the next impatient cow. Then a thought struck her.

'You must have got caught in that storm then,' she said.

'What storm? I didn't drive through any storm,' he said.

'That's strange. It must have been very local then, because Aunt Sal and Uncle Silas didn't catch it either. I was up the top visiting Mother and it blew up out of nowhere,' she explained, thinking back. Lost in their own worlds, they continued milking.

'Well, that's me finished,' Sab announced some time later, carefully setting his full pails outside the shippon door and returning to collect hers. 'Thanks for helping, Rowan. Don't know what's happened to Uncle Ted. Or perhaps I do,' he said, looking at her meaningfully. 'I'll carry these over to the dairy. I dare say you'll be wanting to see about our meal,' he added hopefully, his usual cheeky grin returning.

Rowan wiped the beads of perspiration from her forehead and got to her feet.

'No, I won't, Sab. Fanny's made it clear she is lady of the farm now, so as far as I'm concerned that includes preparing our meals,' Rowan stated.

'Heaven help us then,' Sab groaned. 'My stomach's already rumbling and grumbling like blasts from the quarry.' As he stood there looking crestfallen, Rowan's heart went out to him. A full stomach and Sab went together.

'I'll go and see if there's any sign of supper,' she said, patting his arm. Quickly wiping the muck from her feet on the straw, she made her way through to the kitchen.

Inside, her father and stepmother were sitting side by side on the bacon settle with Fanny admiring a pair of house shoes she'd just unwrapped.

'Edward, these are truly delightful. How clever of you to have chosen them,' she gushed, holding them up for Rowan to admire.

Gritting her teeth, Rowan forced a smile. They must have cost her father a pretty packet.

'Well, you made such a fuss about ruining your others, my dear, I thought I'd better do something about it. Now, come on, open your other parcel,' he said excitedly.

Fanny didn't need telling twice and tore open the paper, anticipation lighting her face. Then her expression changed and she held up the contents enquiringly.

'What on earth are these ugly things?' she exclaimed, wrinkling her nose.

'They are pattens, my dear. You place them over your shoes to protect them from the mud and dirt. They're ideal for walking through the farmyard, and you did say you couldn't go outside again until you had something serviceable to wear.'

Rowan grinned as she watched her stepmother hastily rewrap them.

'I should imagine you'd have more use for these – these patten things, Rowan,' Fanny scowled, thrusting the parcel into her hands. Then seeing the crestfallen look on her husband's face, she smiled and patted his arm. 'It's for the best, Edward. You know how worried I've been about her going barefoot in this weather. You really are a kind and clever man to have thought of both of us, isn't he, Rowan, dear?'

'But I never wear anything on my feet unless I go up to the fields. Never have and never will,' Rowan insisted. 'Mother never did either. As I've said before, we like to feel connected to the earth and . . .'

'Yes, quite,' her stepmother said, cutting her short. 'Now, Edward, I'm sure you must be hungry.' Rowan watched open-mouthed as Fanny deftly deflected the subject by leaning forward and kissing her father's cheek. He flushed, but smiled adoringly at his new wife.

'You are already becoming quite the farmer's wife, my dear,' he said. 'I'll go outside and have a rinse before we eat.'

As soon as the door had closed behind him, Fanny turned to Rowan. 'Well, what's for our meal then?' she barked.

Remembering their earlier conversation, Rowan stared at her stepmother in surprise. 'I'd have thought as lady of the farm you'd know,' she quipped. Then she saw the pebble eyes harden and wished she'd kept quiet.

'I'm sure your father would hate to think you were being unhelpful to his new wife,' Fanny said in a tight voice. As Rowan opened her mouth to protest, Fanny moved closer, towering over her slight form. 'Either you co-operate, missy, or there'll be trouble. If it comes to having to make a choice between us, you can be sure your father will choose me. A man has other needs besides a full stomach, and you can rest assured I satisfy those extremely well.'

Hearing the venom in Fanny's voice, Rowan swallowed hard. What did she mean, 'choice'? Why would her father have to choose between them?

At that moment he came bounding back into the room like an eager puppy and Fanny hurried over to him, kissing his cheek. As he beamed at her in delight, she gave Rowan a triumphant smirk over his shoulder. Not able to stand it a moment longer, Rowan went out to the pantry and leaned her forehead against the stone shelf, willing herself to calm down. Surely Fanny would never really make her father choose between them? No, that could never happen. They'd always been close, especially since her mother had died. Yet something was nagging at the back of her mind. Of course, the storm. Nobody else had experienced it, so could it have been a warning from her mother? How she wished Sab would appear so she could discuss it with him. Blinking back tears, she caught sight of the fresh bread and cold meat her auntie had brought with her and snatched them up.

Back in the kitchen, her stepmother was still fawning over her father and it took all of Rowan's willpower not to slam the food down on the table. Luckily Sab clattered through the door before she had time to say something she'd regret.

'That looks good,' he said, his face lighting up at the sight of food as usual. 'I'm that starving I could eat a whole pig to meself.'

'Sorry, we're clean out of pigs, Sab,' Rowan teased, smiling, her mood lifting at his characteristic banter. 'Aunt Sal did bring us some cold beef and a loaf of her freshly baked bread, though,' she added, carefully emphasizing the words 'Aunt Sal'. Fanny, however, chose to ignore her, busying herself slicing the meat then passing a piled platter to Edward.

'There you are, my dear. I do hope you find the beef cooked to your liking.'

'It looks perfect, Fanny dear. If you carry on feeding me like this, I shall have to loosen my belt before much longer,' he said, giving her a grin.

Rowan stared at him in amazement, the knife piercing a hole in the bread she was buttering. Sensing her tension, Sab quickly intervened.

'It's been a really busy day, Uncle. First I had to . . .' he began.

'Don't worry Edward with trivialities, please, Sab,' Fanny interrupted. 'Let him enjoy his meal. He's had a busy day, too, and needs to relax.' She was looking at Sab so pointedly he turned as red as the flames licking the grate. Miserably he stared down at his empty plate. Rowan passed him meat and bread, but barely got a nod in response.

Only the logs crackling in the grate and the clatter of cutlery against their platters broke the silence as they ate. As soon as they'd finished, though, Fanny turned to Edward.

'A little bird tells me you're partial to something sweet, my dear,' she said, smiling across at him. Getting to her feet, she returned moments later and with a flourish placed the pudding on the table before him. As her father's eyes lit up, Rowan could hardly contain her anger. Surely her stepmother wasn't going to pass this off as her own as well?

'Oh, Fanny, my dear, apple pudding, my absolute favourite,' Edward exclaimed, only to watch in astonishment as she carefully cut away the sponge and spooned out some of the fruit.

'See, Edward, my dear, already I've learned how you do things here in Devonshire,' she gushed, triumphantly placing the dish of apple before him.

Edward's face fell as he looked from the apple to the soft, feathery sponge left behind on the plate. Rowan saw him swallow and then smile bravely as he picked up his spoon. 'Well done, Fanny, my dear,' he uttered faintly.

Sab looked across at Rowan and raised his eyebrows, and she didn't know whether to laugh or cry.

'Don't worry, I'll rescue the pudding later,' he whispered, grinning.

Sure enough, as soon as they'd finished eating, he jumped to his feet, gathered their empty dishes and took them, along with the sponge, to the scullery. As he went out of the door, Magic shot past him, sniffing the air hopefully. Then she spied Fanny and skidded to a halt. Arching her back, she began hissing and spitting at her.

Fanny's eyes narrowed and she raised her hand, but before she could do anything, Sab returned. Glaring at Fanny, he snatched up the cat and took her outside, and Rowan could hear him crooning as he gave her a dish of milk.

'And what have you been up to today, my dear?' Edward asked in the intervening silence.

Recovering her composure, Fanny smiled and turned to Rowan.

'First thing this morning, Rowan and I had a lovely woman-to-woman chat, didn't we, my dear?' she said, her voice rising in that sickly sweet way Rowan had come to recognize.

First thing? It had been halfway through the day before the woman had even surfaced. She opened her mouth to say as much but saw her father beaming at them in delight and held her tongue.

'I explained that now I'm here, she needn't worry about the running of the farmhouse, for, of course, that will be my responsibility,' Fanny continued. Leaning across, she patted Rowan's hand and gave her one of those nauseating smiles which never reached her eyes. Quickly, Rowan snatched her hand away.

'Good, good,' her father said, blissfully unaware of the undercurrent going on around him.

'Now,' Fanny went on, reaching for her writing paper, 'although Rowan has done her best around here, changes need to be made to bring things up to an acceptable standard.'

Rowan gasped in protest and Edward blinked in surprise.

'Changes?'

'Yes, Edward, changes, and we will start with you. You are a handsome devil, my dear, but sporting bristles is a common look. Now, it appears our prince has taken to wearing sideburns, and you may too, although the rest of your face is to be clean-shaven.'

Frowning, Edward stroked his beard. 'But I like my beard, and shaving takes precious time out of the day.'

'Don't be difficult, Edward, my dear. A new wife, a new start, isn't that what they say?' Fanny smiled as she patted his hand.

'Rowan, you are to wear boots or those patten things your father has kindly bought for you. And, with immediate effect, you will stop wearing that ridiculous rag round your wrist.'

Instinctively, Rowan's hand covered her ribbon. 'Never,' she cried, jumping to her feet.

'Sit down, please, Rowan,' her stepmother ordered. 'You have been without a woman's guidance for too long and it is my duty as your stepmother to see that you grow up in a ladylike manner and not roam the farm like some hoyden.'

'I s-say, th-there's no n-need for that,' Sab stuttered,

coming back into the room. Fanny held up her hand to silence him.

'Ah Sab, that brings me to you. If you don't mind me saying, Edward, you give this lad far too much freedom. From what I've seen, he comes and goes as he pleases. I require a path to be built from the farmhouse to the privy and you can make a start on it tomorrow.'

'B-But we n-need to finish f-fertilizing the soil for the v-v-vegetables. We're already g-getting b-behind and the m-moisture . . .'

Again Fanny held up her hand. 'If you wish to speak, then please do so properly.'

Sab shook his head. 'Uncle T-Ted, you know the m-moon'll be on the w-wane soon. We must get this done if we're to p-plant . . .'

'For heaven's sake, boy, whatever's the matter with you?' Fanny cut in. 'All this talk about the moon is sheer lunacy. It's a farm you're running here.'

'Yes, my dear, it is,' Edward said, having finally found his voice. 'But by working with the lunar phases we can ensure maximum results. As Sab was trying to explain, fertilizing when the water table's falling means the nutrients get taken deeper into the soil and . . .' As Fanny held up her hand again, Edward came to a halt.

'Edward, my dear, all this is not my concern. You are the farmer around here and it's your job to make the money, preferably lots of it,' she urged, giving a brittle laugh. 'I shall assist by ensuring your farmhouse runs smoothly, your children behave, and speak in such a manner they become a credit to you,' she said, staring pointedly at Sab.

'Ex-Excuse me, Uncle T-Ted,' Sab started, ignoring Fanny. 'I kn-know what n-needs to be d-done and I'm g-going to see to it right n-now.' Without waiting for an answer, he shot out of the door.

'Whatever is wrong with that boy? You need to have stern words with him, Edward,' Fanny blustered.

Rowan got to her feet. 'It's you, Fanny. You've upset him. He's hasn't stammered like that for years. I'm going to help him,' she said to her father.

'All in good time, Rowan. If that's the way the boy gets attention it's a pretty poor show and needs to be sorted out. Now, I'd appreciate it if you would give me the courtesy of letting me finish what I was saying,' Fanny growled. 'When I went into your room yesterday, I was dismayed to find it littered with half-used candles. Now, one at a time, I can understand, but that many together pose a fire risk and I must . . .'

'How dare you go into my room,' Rowan burst out. 'We respect people's privacy around here. I knew by that terrible smell you'd been in there.'

'Now, Rowan, that's no way to speak to your stepmother,' Edward admonished. 'However, I must agree that we have always respected each other's privacy, Fanny. Not that you were to understand that,' Edward added quickly, when he saw Fanny's lips purse.

'It is for the girl's own good, Edward. However, when I went to go in there this morning to check on things, the door wouldn't budge, no matter how hard I pushed it. You'll need to take a look at it.'

'Blessings and thank you, oh mirror,' Rowan muttered under her breath.

'Now, my child, I will not have you . . .' Fanny began, but Rowan had had enough.

'I am not a child and certainly not yours,' she retorted. 'I'm going outside to help Sab. Please note I am putting on my boots, but only because I shall be working on the vegetable plot,' she tossed over her shoulder as she fled from the room.

Chapter 7

Rowan found Sab by the kitchen garden, furiously forking the seaweed down from the cart.

'I'll dig it in and pretend it's her,' Rowan raged, stressing the word 'her'. Working together, anger fuelling their energy, they tackled the pile with a vengeance. The bright moon was shining from a clear sky, making it easier for them to see what they were doing.

'Who does that woman think she is, coming here and throwing her weight around?' Rowan asked, some moments later. 'I am not going to listen to a word she says.'

'I know how you feel, Rowan,' Sab agreed, his stutter completely gone now he'd calmed down. 'But I've been thinking. Uncle Ted's really smitten with this Fanny and in his eyes she can do no wrong, so it might be easier to go along with what she suggests for the moment. I've just got this feeling it'll be us who come off worse if we don't.'

Rowan considered this in silence. The more she deliberated, the harder she dug. Hadn't her uncle said virtually the same thing earlier? A movement caught her eye and she saw an owl take flight from its perch through a hole in the barn. It hovered over the adjacent field and then swooped. As the pitiful squeaks of its prey broke the silence of the night, Rowan and Sab watched the bird, dinner in its talons, fly off towards the big oak. Fanny was just like that, she thought. A hunter, only it was Rowan she had set her sights on. She shivered. Thick clouds were now gathering, and she didn't know whether it was those or the dawning comprehension about Fanny that had cooled her blood. She resumed her shovelling with renewed vigour, but moments later, Sab stopped what he was doing and turned to her.

'Remember what your mother used to say about the oak standing proud against the wind only to break in the end, while the sapling that sways along with the storm weathers it?' he asked, his breath rising like mist in the plummeting temperature. 'Happen we should be like the saplings here.'

Of course, the storm! That's what her mother had been trying to tell her.

'I think you're right, Sab,' she agreed eventually. 'It's not going to be easy, though, is it?'

'No, but I guess for Uncle's sake we'll have to try to go along with what Fanny suggests,' he sighed, returning to his work.

Well, she might go along with some of Fanny's suggestions but that woman was never going to enter her room again. Her mirror would see to that, she thought, digging furiously.

It was another hour before the job was finished. Stretching to ease her back, Rowan saw the clouds had completely covered the moon. She sniffed the air. Snow was on the way. Sab had noticed too.

'Come along, Rowan, I reckon we can call it a night now. Thanks for helping. I'd never have got this lot dug in on my own before the weather breaks. If it hadn't been done tonight we'd have missed the opportunity of the nutrients being taken down into the soil with the falling water table. This ground will be white and frozen come morning,' he said.

'It's unlike Father to leave it all to you, Sab. I'm going to speak to him. It's all right saying he's besotted with that besom, but that doesn't mean he can neglect things around here.'

'Sleep on it, Rowan,' he advised, looking serious. 'Come on, let's go inside. We'd better take some wood with us if we want a hot breakfast and tea in the morning,' he added, grinning, and Rowan was pleased to see he was back to his usual cheeky self.

'Oh, you and your stomach, Sab,' she teased as they made their way over to the faggot rick by the light of his candle lantern.

They were just stacking the wood beside the grate when Fanny, candle in hand, emerged from the parlour.

'About time,' she snapped. 'The fire has burned low in the other room so you'd better take some of that in there, Sab,' she ordered, nodding to the wood he was carrying. Silently, he continued what he was doing. Fanny pursed her lips, but before she could say anything, Rowan, mindful of her earlier promise to be helpful, explained.

'We reckon we're in for some late snow, Fanny, so we need to conserve our stocks. I did tell you, we only light the fire in the parlour for special occasions. I'm surprised Father allowed it,' she added.

'Your father wishes me to be happy here, young lady, which is more than can be said for you,' she snapped. Going over to the window, she pulled back the curtain

68

and peered into the darkness, her reflection making a sinister picture in the light of the flickering candle. 'Snow indeed! It's all cloudy out there,' she scoffed.

Sab snorted. 'I'm going to check on the stock and then turn in. Good night,' he said, snatching up his lantern and hurrying out.

'Night, Sab,' Rowan called. 'Where's Father?' she asked, turning to Fanny.

'Sprucing himself up, if he's got any sense,' the woman answered briskly. Rowan waited but her stepmother didn't elaborate.

'It's been a long day, so I'll take myself up to bed,' she said, not wishing to be alone with her stepmother, who seemed even more belligerent than usual.

Rowan opened her eyes the next morning to find a pearlescent brightness flooding the room. Worried she'd slept in, she sat bolt upright but could hear no sound coming from outside. In fact, everything was ominously silent. The silence of snow, she thought, jumping out of bed. Sure enough, the yard below and the fields beyond were glistening with stark whiteness. Not much could be done outside today after her father and Sab had seen to the stock.

Recalling her discussion with Fanny yesterday, she decided she'd leave the cooking to her. She would use the time to catch up on her mending, which had been sadly neglected recently. Then she'd start knitting some new pop-over mittens for Sab, for she'd noticed last night that his were more hole than wool, and quite beyond darning. Feeling brighter than she had for some time, she dressed and made her way downstairs.

Her father was sitting at the scrubbed table, dejectedly rubbing his chin.

'Morning, Father. Is something wrong?' Rowan asked, frowning as she took in his reddened, blotchy skin. 'Whatever's happened to your face?'

'Had to shave off my beard and shape these,' he answered, tugging at the wiry tufts of hair that now sprang around his ears like tussocks.

'That skin looks really raw. I'll get you some of my lavender salve,' she offered, hurrying over to the dresser. She'd just finished rubbing some into the areas around his newly clipped moustache when Sab appeared in the doorway. He shook the snowflakes from his jacket and then rubbed his hands together.

'It's a cold un and still snowing. Good job we got that weed dug in last night,' he said, looking pointedly at Edward.

'Sorry I didn't help. Hurry up and come in, boy. You're letting all the heat out,' Edward snapped.

'Blimey, what's happened to you, Uncle Ted?'

'I had to spruce myself up,' Edward muttered, looking wretched as he gingerly touched his chin. 'That feels better already, Rowan. The pot's heating for our breakfast.'

'Good, I'm starving,' Sab said. 'I've seen to the livestock and old Davey called by with a couple of rabbits he'd snared. I've put them in the scullery. He reckoned this snow will continue for some time so he's taken the dogs to drive the sheep down the hill while the track's still passable.' Sab took a seat beside Edward. 'Did someone mention breakfast?'

Rowan shook her head, laughing as she went over to

the fire and gave the pot of oats a good stir. 'Good, nearly ready,' she said, and minutes later they were eating their thick, creamy porridge. 'Honestly, Father, there's double the amount of milk I normally use in here,' she teased. 'But it is delicious,' she added quickly, seeing his crestfallen look. She guessed his pride was hurting as much as his face.

'What are you going to do today then, Rowan?' her father asked.

'I intend making the most of this cold weather by catching up on all the jobs that have been neglected lately,' she said. 'I shall enjoy the luxury of sitting by the fire and doing some mending. Your shirt sleeves need darning as well as your socks, Father.'

'I'll skin and draw those rabbits. They'll make a tasty stew.' Sab looked at Rowan hopefully.

'Well, you'll have to ask Fanny about that, Sab,' said Rowan. Edward stared at her in surprise. 'It wouldn't do to interfere with the lady of the farm's housekeeping, Father,' she continued, quoting her aunt's words.

'When did you get so wise, daughter?' he asked, grinning at her.

'Or you could say so foolish,' Sab groaned. 'I'd hate to see good meat ruined.'

'Now, Sab, it's only fair to give Fanny a chance,' Rowan said, tongue in cheek. Then felt guilty when her father brightened.

'It's good that you two are getting on. I told Fanny you were a sensible girl and everything would soon shake down. Although perhaps she could do with some guidance when it comes to dishing up sponge puddings,' he said, grimacing at the memory. 'Well, I'm off to prepare the pens in the barn for those sheep.'

Watching as he shrugged into his heavy coat and tugged his woollen cap over his curls, Rowan couldn't help thinking he looked strangely out of balance without his beard. That wispy moustache and burly sideburns didn't look right on him and although she had seen only one picture of Prince Albert, she didn't think her father resembled him in any way. Sab raised his eyebrows, catching her train of thought as usual.

'Come along, lad,' Edward said. 'Oh, by the way, Rowan, I took a look at your door last evening and it opened easily enough.' She smiled at her father, thinking that it would have done for him, thanks to her trusty mirror.

She cleared away their dishes. Then, peering out of the window and seeing the large white flakes still falling from a leaden sky, she decided to leave venturing out to the well until later. Tossing more wood onto the fire, she settled beside the blaze with her mending on her lap. Magic padded over and settled her weight on Rowan's feet.

'That's wonderful,' Rowan sighed to the purring animal, her skin warming beneath the animal's soft fur. As her fingers nimbly sewed and darned, she relaxed, enjoying the opportunity of being indoors on such a bitter day. The crackle of logs made the room feel cosy and she couldn't help reminiscing how, on snowy days like this, she'd sat beside her mother while she taught her to sew to her own exacting standard. Putting her mending down, she stroked the red ribbon, not for the first time wishing things could have stayed the same.

As footsteps sounded on the stairs, Magic leaped to her

feet, fur standing on end so that Rowan was reminded of her father's dishevelled appearance earlier.

'Hush, Magic,' she murmured, bending to stroke the agitated animal. But as Fanny entered the room she hissed and bolted beneath the table.

'Good morning, Rowan, my dear,' Fanny gushed in her false fashion. 'What are you doing?' she asked coming over and looking quizzically at neatly folded garments.

'Just catching up on some mending, while it's snowing.'

'Goodness, why don't you just get new clothes?' Fanny asked. Without waiting for an answer, she peered into the pot and then pouted. 'There's no hot water for tea! I haven't had a thing to eat this morning either,' she exclaimed.

'I expect Sab will bring some water in with him when he comes. Of course, if you don't want to wait, you could always go out to the well yourself,' Rowan pointed out. 'It's a pity you weren't up when we had breakfast. The porridge was extra creamy this morning,' she couldn't resist adding. Her stepmother gave her a martyred look.

'I'm not going out in this awful weather,' she said, shivering dramatically even though she was standing right in front of the fire. 'Sab will need to empty my chamber pot soon, though.'

Not trusting herself to speak, Rowan continued stitching furiously. Oblivious to the atmosphere, Fanny perched elegantly on the chair beside her, drawing the folds of yet another dress Rowan hadn't seen before around her ankles.

'Are the men outside?' she asked. Rowan nodded, trying not to wrinkle her nose as the all-pervading scent

73

of roses wafted her way. 'Good. We can use the opportunity to have a chat,' her stepmother said. Had she forgotten their words of the previous day already, Rowan wondered.

As her stepmother prattled on about inconsequential matters, Rowan found herself becoming increasingly uncomfortable. When she'd pricked her finger for the third time, she admitted defeat and put her sewing to one side.

'That's better, dear,' her stepmother said. 'Now we can really get to know one another. Why don't you tell me more about life around here? You must find it very quiet. What do you do for fun?'

'Well, the fair visits sometimes, and we ride into Sudbury on market day. If we sell all our wares we treat ourselves to a pie to eat on the way home. If it continues snowing, we won't be able to go this week.'

'Why ever not?' asked her stepmother. 'I was looking forward to getting away from here for a day.'

'The cart will never make it down the steep path to the village,' Rowan said, frowning at such an obvious question. 'You mean you were intending to come with us?'

'Of course I was. I need to get to know people. How often do you usually leave the farm?' Fanny persisted.

'Once a week, I suppose. There's always so much to do here. Why?' She watched her stepmother's lips tighten but then, in an instant, she was giving Rowan that sickly sweet smile again.

'Well, a pretty young girl like you must have a beau. Are you courting anyone? You'll be wanting to marry and have a home of your own before much longer, I dare say.'

'There's plenty of time for that. I'm only fifteen, Fanny,' she said, shocked at such a thought.

'But I am married and I am only a few years older than you,' Fanny said.

Rowan looked at her in surprise. She'd never given any thought to the woman's age. Now she could see she was years younger than her father.

'You must leave me to run things around here. You go out and enjoy yourself whenever you want,' her step-mother said magnanimously.

'Thank you, but at the moment I'm happy staying indoors, especially in this weather,' she quipped. Then sensing she wasn't giving the woman the answers she wanted, she added, 'Of course I'll be happy to leave the cooking and housekeeping to you. You must have more experience than I do.'

Fanny smiled, acknowledging the perceived compliment. 'Why, of course, dear,' she said before returning to her former subject. 'It beats me how a young thing like you passes the time in such a remote place.'

At that moment the door clattered open and they looked up to see Sab stamping the snow off his boots. 'Gosh, it's cold out there. I've cleaned up these big boys, so where do you want them?' he asked, holding aloft the two skinned rabbits.

Fanny looked horrified, then screamed so loudly, Magic bolted from her hiding place under the table and fled up the stairs.

'They're dead rabbits, take them away,' she gasped, frantically flapping her hands.

'Would you prefer to cook them live, then?' Sab

asked, moving closer and swinging them in front of Fanny's face.

Her stepmother screamed again, then collapsed back in her seat, covering her face with her hands. Rowan bit her lip to stop herself from laughing out loud. Some effective cook and housekeeper she was going to be. Well, she'd told Rowan to leave things up to her, so she would.

Chapter 8

Hastily gathering up her mending and placing it on the dresser, Rowan turned to Sab. 'I think we'd better make ourselves scarce, don't you?' she whispered. 'I'll go and draw some water to wash the dishes.'

'And I'd best remove these,' he said, picking up the rabbits. But before they could escape, the door clattered open again and Edward came rushing in, snowflakes fluttering in his wake.

'What's wrong? I heard a scream,' he asked, glancing from the skinned animals in Sab's hand to Fanny, who was now wailing louder than ever. 'Ah,' he said, immediately taking in the situation. 'Best take those back outside, lad,' and he hurried over to his new wife.

Quickly doing as they'd been bid, Sab and Rowan fled to the scullery. Closing the door behind them, they dissolved into hysterics.

'Did you see her face?' Rowan gulped, tears streaming down her cheeks. 'That was really naughty, but the funniest thing I've seen in ages.'

'Well, it was one I owed her,' Sab chuckled, then frowned. 'You two were looking mighty cosy when I came in. What was going on?'

'Don't look like that, Sab. Fanny said she wanted us to get to know one another, whilst you and Father were busy outside. She asked me so many questions.'

'Oh, like what?'

'What goes on around here, how often I go out, and then she asked if I was courting,' she giggled.

Sab's eyes narrowed. 'I don't like the sound of that. You be on your guard, Rowan. I trust that one as far as those dead rabbits can jump.' He nodded towards the inert bodies on the drainer.

'Don't worry, I won't. Her mood's too changeable for my liking. One minute she's all smiley and friendly, the next she's growling and hostile, especially if the answers aren't to her liking.'

'Ah, there you are, you two,' Edward said, pushing open the door. They jumped guiltily, waiting for the telling-off they expected. However, he just stood there shaking his head.

'Fanny's taken herself off to bed with a megrim. I said you'd prepare one of your curatives, Rowan, but that just made her more agitated.' His brow furrowed. 'It appears we are archaic, the farmhouse is antiquated and the animals antediluvian.'

'Ante what?' Sab asked.

'Don't even ask,' Edward said, his hand automatically going to stroke his beard and making contact with his sore chin instead. He grimaced, saying, 'All I know is she wasn't like this when we were courting.'

'What was she like, Father?' Rowan asked. 'We never got to know her before the wedding.'

'She was all sweetness and kind of, well, womanly,' he said, his expression softening as he remembered. Sab glanced at Rowan and raised his eyebrows knowingly.

'Don't worry, lad, you have these pleasures still to come,' Edward said, grinning.

'Not me, Uncle. I'll be steering clear of women if that's what they're like. Apart from you, of course,' he said, turning to Rowan.

'Well, we can't stand here idling the day away. Old Davey's back with the sheep. He's driving them into the barn and needs your help, Sab.'

'Yes, Uncle.' Sab began buttoning his jacket.

Edward turned to Rowan. 'I know you said you were going to leave the cooking to Fanny, but it's still snowing a storm and we'll need a good hot meal tonight, Rowan. Can you turn those into a stew?' he said, pointing to the rabbits.

'Of course, Father,' she answered, eager to appease him.

'Probably be best if you call it meat stew when you serve up, though. That's if Fanny's fit enough to join us, of course,' he added, pulling his cap down over his ears as he went outside.

'Problems in paradise already?' Sab whispered, rubbing his hands gleefully before following Edward outside.

Rowan set about her task, adding onions, turnips and carrots to the pot with the rabbits, for she guessed the shepherd would be staying overnight and would need feeding, too.

She was just hitching the pot of stew onto the arm over the fire when Davey hurried in cradling two of the tiniest lambs she'd ever seen. Knowing from experience that every second counted, she hurried over to the chest and pulled out an old horse blanket. As the shepherd began rubbing the barely breathing bodies with brisk, yet surprisingly tender strokes, Rowan set milk to warm. Moments later, the first one gave a weak, pitiful bleat and Davey turned to Rowan.

'That were close,' he said gruffly. 'I'll leave these two in your capable care, girl. Happen they could use an extra special charm, seeing as they're so frail, like.'

'Whatever is going on?' Fanny demanded, having crept up behind them unheard. 'What are those?' she demanded, sniffing at the tiny bodies.

''Tis a farmhouse, missus, and these here are orphan lambs I've brought indoors so that Rowan can work her magic. It'll be their only chance of surviving, having just lost their mother,' Davey grunted, staring back at her.

Fanny sniffed, glaring down at his frayed trousers and dirty boots.

'Well, you workers are paid to sort out the animals, aren't you?' she asked.

Davey's eyes darkened and Rowan thought he was going to explode, but before he could say anything, a dun-brown collie nudged the door open with its grizzled nose.

'Get out,' Fanny hissed, stamping her feet and waving her hands at the dog.

'No need to vent your spleen on my poor creature, missus. We was just going anyhow,' Davey said, heading towards the door. Then he stopped in front of Fanny and gave her a piercing stare. 'Don't I know you?' he asked.

'I wouldn't think so. I'm not from around here,' she answered, turning away.

'Never forgets a face, doesn't old Davey,' he said, sniffing the air. 'Nor a smell,' he muttered. 'Shouts if you need a hand, young Rowan.'

'You could ask Sab to bring in more wood when he comes,' she replied, noticing the stack by the grate had got low. 'I'll need to keep a good fire going all night for these little ones,' she called after his retreating back.

Her stepmother stood there looking flustered, but quickly turned away when she noticed Rowan staring at her.

'You'd better get this mess cleaned up, my girl,' she ordered, sweeping into the parlour and slamming the door behind her.

Rowan bent over the lambs, her curtain of copper curls adding warmth to their trembling bodies. What were a few wisps of straw on the floor compared to saving these little darlings? Had the woman no heart? Didn't she understand the livestock were her father's living, the means by which they all lived?

Rowan cradled her charges closer, patiently coaxing them to take the milk drop by drop. It took all her powers of persuasion, but eventually she succeeded in getting them to take the minutest amount. Even that exhausted them and as they collapsed against the blanket, she gently tucked it around them, hoping they'd gain strength in sleep. Remembering Davey's words, she kneeled beside them and, placing a finger on each tiny head, whispered:

> *Know me as your healer,*
> *Bestowed with blessed power,*
> *That from these fingertips will flow*
> *The strength to thrive and grow.*
> *So mote it be.*

As energy pulsated from her tingling fingertips to the sleeping forms, she kissed each faintly beating heart in turn. Then staring deep into the heart of the flames she offered up her blessings.

'What on earth are you doing, Rowan?' Fanny asked, suddenly appearing by her side.

Startled out of her trance, she stared up into her step-mother's grey pebble eyes. 'You wouldn't understand,' she sighed.

'I certainly don't understand you muttering nonsense into the fire like that. Whatever next?' Fanny asked, shaking her head. 'It's absolutely freezing in that parlour,' she declared, sinking into a chair beside the lambs, heedless of their sleeping bodies. She wrinkled her nose. 'How long do those things have to stay in here?'

'Until they are strong enough to survive in the barn with the others,' Rowan answered.

'Well, I've never seen anything like it. Animals in my living room, indeed! Your father never told me I'd have to put up with this kind of thing. Of course, he was different before we were married,' she said, glaring at Rowan as though it were her fault. She was just about to say her father had said something similar about her, when the door clattered open and Sab struggled in with an armful of wood, bringing with him a blast of cold air. Fanny shivered.

'Still snowing a storm out there and old Davey reckons it'll freeze solid by morning. Says he'll sleep in the barn in case any of the sheep need a hand,' he said, throwing down his load beside the fireplace. He sniffed the aroma rising from the pot appreciatively. 'That smells right good,

Rowan. Good job you can prepare a nice stew,' he said, staring pointedly at Fanny.

'Rowan won't have to worry about that for much longer,' she said loftily. 'You two are not the only ones who've been busy.' Sab raised his eyebrows in disbelief, but Fanny ignored him. 'I have been preparing a list of the hired help we shall require, along with things necessary to bring this place up to a habitable standard.' She got to her feet, looking around her with disdain. 'It's perishing in that parlour so bring that wood through and get a fire lit, Sab.'

'The lambs . . .' he began, but he was talking to her retreating back. Rowan saw the tic under his right cheek begin to throb, a sure sign he was furious. But as he stared down at the sleeping lambs, his expression softened. 'Think we'll see to you first, little uns,' he said, throwing wood onto the dwindling fire and poking away until it burst into a blaze. Wiping his hand on his trousers, he got to his feet. 'Hired help? Uncle Ted can't afford that,' he muttered.

'I know,' Rowan said. 'And, let's face it, we've always managed before.'

'Sab, I said immediately,' Fanny shouted.

'Blooming woman, doesn't she ever do anything for herself?' he asked, but duly collected up an armful of wood. 'Don't worry, I'll bring in some more after I've seen to the livestock. I'll sleep in here and take a turn tending to these tonight.'

'Are you sure, Sab?' Rowan asked.

'Yes, the warmth will make a nice change after dealing with frosty Fanny,' he said, grinning.

Dinner was a quiet affair. The men, hungry after their busy day, ate ravenously but were too tired to make conversation. Rowan, who'd been careful to announce it as meat stew, watched as Fanny cleared her plate in record time. Tomorrow she would let her stepmother see to their meals and see how she fared.

'That was a lovely meal, Rowan. Just what we need in this bitterly cold weather,' her father said, grinning affectionately at her.

She smiled back and then saw Fanny stiffen.

'All that cavorting around and muttering for the sun to shine didn't work, did it?' she scoffed.

'Sorry?' Rowan said, looking perplexed. 'I don't know what you mean.'

'You told me you were dancing under a full moon to speed up the summer,' her stepmother insisted.

'I think she means Imbolc,' Sab said, laughing.

'That's not what it's about or how it works, Fanny,' Rowan began, but her stepmother had lost interest and was studying her list.

'Talking of the moon reminds me, Uncle. Do you think the snow will clear in time for us to sow the crops on the next quarter?'

'Realistically, I think we'll see at least another moon cycle round before then, Sab.'

'All this talk of the moon and cycles is stupid. Why can't you just go out and plant the crops?' Fanny asked impatiently.

Her husband got to his feet, yawning. 'It's been a long day so let's go up the wooden hill, my dear.'

'Oh, grow up, Edward. We are adults and we go up to

bed, but not yet,' she said, when he looked at her hopefully. 'I haven't gone through my list yet.'

'What list?' he asked, slumping back in his seat.

'You're not the only one who has been busy, Edward. I have spent the afternoon meticulously writing down what needs to be done to make this place habitable. Now as I was saying yesterday . . .'

'Excuse me, missus. I'll just check on those wee ones and then be off to me bed in the barn,' Davey said, scraping back his chair. 'That were a nice bit of stew, my dear,' he added, turning to Rowan. 'I see you enjoyed your rabbit, missus,' he said, nodding to Fanny's empty plate.

'Rabbit?' she said, narrowing her eyes.

'Yes, rabbit, missus. That's what we eat around here, and grateful for it we are, too. There are those upcountry who are quite literally starving,' he said gravely.

Fanny opened her mouth to protest.

'I'll see to the lambs, Davey,' Rowan said quickly, not wishing for any more confrontation. 'You must be tired after driving the sheep down from the hills.'

'Well, really. Is nobody going to listen to the list I've been busy making?' Fanny asked, regaining her composure.

Davey stood in the doorway shaking his head. 'In my experience, there's those who write about the things that need doing and those who actually get on and do them. Night, all. I'll be in the barn with the sheep if you needs help with them little uns, Rowan.'

'Well, how rude,' spluttered Fanny. 'And what's so important about a few shaggy sheep anyway?'

'They bring in a fair proportion of our income,' Edward said wearily.

'Edward, my dear, why ever didn't you say?' asked Fanny, her voice suddenly soft as butter. 'So how do you turn them into money, then?'

'Look, this bad weather means the animals need more tending, so I'll need to be up early. Do let's go to bed, my dear. We can discuss it in the morning,' Edward said, stifling another yawn.

Just then Sab, who'd followed Davey outside, came in staggering under yet another load of wood.

'Good, you can take that upstairs and light a fire up in our bedroom,' Fanny said. 'It's perishing up there.'

Sab looked at Edward. 'It's still snowing and the wood pile's already getting low, Uncle.' Reaching across the table, Edward took Fanny's hand.

'Look, my love, you know I want you to be happy here but we just cannot keep lighting extra fires. This time of year, we all gather around the one in here and when we go to our beds, we hop under the covers, quick as we can,' he explained.

'If only you'd listen to me, Edward,' said Fanny, waving her list in the air. 'I have the very solution.'

'We cannot afford to buy in more wood,' he said, shaking his head. But Fanny was not to be deterred.

'Yesterday, I asked Sab to move the bed so that we can see right down the valley.'

'Yes, I know, and the wind blew over me something chronic all night long,' Edward grunted.

'It occurred to me that if you cut down those old trees beyond the field, we would be able to see right down to the sea. And . . .' she paused, dramatically, '. . . it would mean we'd have a good stock of wood for any numbers of fires.'

The room fell silent, apart from the crackling of the fire. Rowan and Sab exchanged horrified looks.

'But you can't chop down our hangy downs,' Rowan protested.

'Hangy downs? What are you talking about, girl? They're merely old trees,' Fanny snorted.

'Those old trees happen to be our orchard, Fanny, and the hangy downs are the finest apples in the West Country,' Edward said. 'Come on, it's definitely time we went to bed,' he insisted, getting to his feet.

As they made their way upstairs, Rowan and Sab burst out laughing for the second time that day.

'She's priceless,' Rowan said, shaking her head.

'Oh, am I indeed?' Fanny hissed as she peered over the banister.

'Come along, my dear,' Edward said wearily.

'Just coming,' Fanny called in her syrupy voice. 'I was just telling Rowan that we shall have another nice mother-and-daughter chat tomorrow,' she said.

Looking up, Rowan saw the malicious gleam in her stepmother's eye and her heart sank. Not if she could help it, she thought. Tomorrow, she would busy herself in the dairy all day. Heaven knew, there was enough to do and braving the bitter cold would be infinitely preferable to being cooped up in the same room as her stepmother.

'Hard luck,' Sab commiserated, as he went outside to settle the livestock. Rowan settled down beside the fire, cuddling the lambs close.

'Suddenly I wish I was an orphan, too,' she whispered.

Chapter 9

It was several weeks before the weather warmed and the snow had thawed sufficiently for Rowan to take her produce to the market in Sudbury. She'd spent the time she'd been confined indoors experimenting with different herbs, and now had good stocks of flavoured soft cheeses and butter to sell along with her home-baked bread. She'd also perfected her latest curative for pains in the joints caused by wet and cold weather and was hopeful it would prove popular after the prolonged wintry conditions. Although she'd managed to avoid Fanny for most of the time, the strain of being cooped up was beginning to tell and she welcomed the chance to get away from the farm for a day.

Dawn was breaking as the cart slowly crept its way down the Devonshire lanes, the white blanket across the fields deadening the creaking of the axles and the soft plod of Blackthorn's hooves. As they turned to head down the valley, the rising sun bathed the wakening countryside in soft rosy tones. Still hardened snowdrifts were banked up against the hedges, their crystals glistening like stars so that Rowan felt she was in fairyland. Knowing Fanny would still be tucked up in her bed, Rowan and Sab relaxed for the first time in weeks.

'There'll be hell when she wakes up and finds we've gone without her,' Sab laughed. 'I'm in need of new clothes and modern household goods,' he mimicked in a fair imitation of the woman.

'I've never known anyone lie in until the middle of the day before,' Rowan said. 'If we'd waited for her to rise the market would have packed up and gone. I'm surprised she didn't appear, though, after asking me all those questions about where and when it was held. I even had to explain exactly where my stall was located.'

'Maybe she was just being plain nosy. Anyway, she lies abed to avoid doing any household duties. It's a long time since I've not been fed good food regular, like,' he said, looking hopefully at Rowan. Taking pity on him, she took two freshly baked bread rolls from her basket.

'Just one each then or there'll not be enough to sell to make a decent profit,' she said.

He grinned, and then bit into his with relish.

'Gosh, I've missed your baking,' he sighed, munching contentedly. 'Since when did we have to live on porridge and pottage anyway? The pigs get better variety in their swill.'

'I know, but Fanny insisted that as lady of the farm she's in charge of the housekeeping. Thankfully, she never ventures into the dairy so I've been able to get on with the churning, as you well know from your regular forays, Sab Clode,' Rowan admonished.

'Well, a fellow's got to keep his strength up,' he said.

'Needless to say Fanny was still sleeping when I made the bread, so I was able to use the table beside the fire, otherwise I'd still be waiting for it to rise.'

'Uncle Ted looks right miserable these days, doesn't he?' Sab remarked, frowning.

'I know. Father's taken to keeping out of her way during the day. Although she insists he joins her in the parlour of an evening, it being their room now. I must admit I've enjoyed curling up in front of the fire in the kitchen and getting on with my knitting. Oh, that reminds me,' she said, delving into her basket once again and taking out a pair of mittens. 'Here you are, Sab. I've made them with the pop-over tops you like.'

His face lit up in delight and, taking a hand off the reins, he slipped one on, holding it out for her to see.

'Perfect,' he said. 'Thanks ever so much, Rowan.'

'You're welcome, Sab, but I must admit I've missed your company of an evening.'

'Sorry, Rowan, but I've been hiding meself up in the hayloft. I need to keep out of that woman's way. She makes me so wild it's been affecting my speech,' he said, changing the reins over so that he could wriggle his other hand into its mitten. 'These are grand. Have you made any to sell?'

'Yes, and some hats, too. Thought there might be a market for them this weather and I hope to make some extra money. There's nothing wrong with your speech today, Sab.'

'No, I can relax with you. It's Fanny; she says I'm so stupid it's not surprising my mother abandoned me, especially if I stuttered like a starling.'

Rowan gasped. 'That's a terrible thing for Fanny to have said. Surely you don't believe such nonsense? After all, you were only a baby when she gave you up, weren't you?' He nodded. 'Well, babies can't speak, can they? So she wouldn't have known how you talked. Anyway, Mother said it was the rough treatment you got in the foundling hospital that made you stutter.'

Immediately he brightened. 'You're right, Rowan. Gosh, that's a weight off me mind. It's bad enough knowing my mother abandoned me without my thinking it was because I was stupid.'

'You are not stupid, Sab. You are bright, cheeky and my best friend,' she declared stoutly, giving him a reassuring smile. As he turned towards her and grinned back, the cart lurched. 'Look, we've reached the outskirts of Sudbury already, so watch what you're doing.'

Carefully, he guided Blackthorn over the narrow old stone packhorse bridge, then they steadily climbed past the low limewashed thatched cottages up towards the tall square church tower in the centre of town. Opposite the imposing three-storey hostelry, the market square was already bustling with life. Stall-holders called out in greeting as Rowan clambered from the cart.

'I've errands to do for Uncle,' Sab declared, handing her down her baskets. 'I'll be back to collect you midday so make sure you sell everything, then we can treat ourselves to one of Hannah's tasty meat pies.' His eyes lit up at the thought.

Rowan set out her wares, listening to the banter of the other stall-holders. She was pleased she'd managed to produce enough to fill her stall, and was just standing back to admire her handiwork when Timon came over with a mug of tea.

'Here you are, girl; something to warm your insides this raw day.'

'Thanks, Timon, you're a life-saver,' she said gratefully. He gave her his toothless, gummy grin, but before he could answer a matronly woman was asking the price of his candles and he turned away.

'Mornan, Rowan. Get a load of these beauties,' Mabel shouted from her stall opposite. Unable to resist taking a peek, Rowan went over, exclaiming in delight at the pretty emerald ribbon the woman was holding up. 'It'll go beautiful with that copper hair of yours.' Remembering the money her aunt had insisted she take for the socks she'd made, Rowan hesitated. Then, a picture of her wearing muted-coloured homespun alongside Fanny in her finery flitted into her mind, and before she could change her mind, she nodded.

''Ere you are, ducks,' Mabel said, cutting off a generous length and giving her a wink. 'Don't tell no one, mind, or they'll all expect extra measures.'

'Gosh, thank you, Mabel. I'll be able to trim my hat for Easter as well as have some to sew round the neck of my frock. Come over later and I'll let you sample my new chive and nettle cheeses,' she said, handing over her money and making her way back to her own stall.

Business was brisk and Rowan was kept busy dealing with a steady stream of customers, which was just as well, as she didn't have to stand still in the freezing cold. She was just counting her takings when a shadow fell over her nearly empty stall. Looking up, she saw a smartly dressed gentleman with beady brown eyes and slicked-back dark hair under his top hat. He looked quite out of place amongst the market traders and customers with their warm, comfortable woollen coats and cloth caps.

'I see you have just one loaf left, so I'll take it,' he said, pointing to the small cob Rowan had put by for old Aggie.

'I'm sorry, sir, but that one is reserved.'

He peered around. 'I don't see anyone else waiting, young lady, so perhaps you would be so kind as to wrap it for me,' he said, smiling and patting his trouser pocket so that she could hear the coins jangling.

'As I told you, I've put that by for someone,' Rowan said, steadily returning his weasel-like gaze.

'Ah, a girl with a mind of her own, and a pretty one at that,' he said smoothly. 'What's your name?'

'Rowan, sir,' she answered politely.

'Well, Rowan, this is no weather for a young girl like you to be working outside. I could find you more lucrative work in far more comfortable surroundings than this,' he said, gesturing around the market square in disdain. He gave her another of his smarmy grins. 'It looks as if you're finished here so why don't you let me treat you to a hot meal at the hostelry. We could discuss the matter further,' he cajoled, eyeing her in the same speculative way her father used when inspecting livestock at the sales. She shuddered, her hand instinctively going to the red ribbon. Remembering he was a customer, she endeavoured to remain polite.

'Thank you, but I am meeting someone shortly. I'm sorry about the loaf but perhaps I could interest you in some chive cheese instead? I've just the one remaining.' He leaned closer so that she caught a whiff of his cologne. It smelled musky and musty, and involuntarily she took a step back.

'Here, I'll take that cheese,' a young woman said,

pushing past him. She fumbled in her bag for her money and although Rowan took her time serving her, the man still hovered. She was just beginning to feel uncomfortable when Timon appeared at her side.

'Is everything all right, Rowan?' he asked, leaning over the stall. As Rowan turned to answer him, she noticed the gentleman sidling off into the crowd.

'You want to watch gents like him,' Timon said.

'Why, who was he?' Rowan asked.

'Happen he's a rum un. City gents like him don't come here for nothing. Heed a man who knows his sort and steer clear,' he warned. Rowan shivered. 'Don't fret, though. Old Timon will keep his eye out next time you're here.'

'Thank you, Timon, and thank you for the tea,' she said, handing him back his mug. Then quickly placing the cob loaf in one of her baskets, she bade him goodbye.

Trudging through the slush along the cobbled street towards the almshouses, she couldn't help wondering who the slimy gent had been and what he'd really wanted. She was certain that it hadn't been her bread.

Lost in thought, she found herself outside Aggie's front door before she knew it. Carefully, she cleaned her boots on the scraper, for the woman might be old and her eyesight failing but she was as house-proud as ever. Setting down her baskets, Rowan knocked briskly on the door.

'Come on through, Rowan,' a voice called, making her smile. Although she never announced who she was, old Aggie always knew it was her before she'd even stepped inside her low-beamed living room.

As usual, the woman was sitting in her rocking chair beside the fire, a woollen rug over her knees, knitting needles clacking like the clappers.

'Hello, Aggie. How are you? I've brought your loaf,' Rowan said, placing it carefully on the table. Then shrugging off her shawl, she placed it over the back of a chair.

'That's kind, Rowan,' she said, barely looking up from her work. 'Take the money out of my purse, won't you?'

'Now you know there's no need for that, Aggie. I'd die for a cup of tea, though. It's cold and miserable out there. Shall I make us some?' she asked, automatically lifting the kettle from its trivet in front of the fire and pouring hot water into the waiting pot. It was their custom to share a drink and chat whenever Rowan came to market. She knew the old woman had no family, although to look at all the garments she knitted, you'd think she had an army of grandchildren. It was well known that, not having been blessed with her own, she spent what little money she had on buying wool to make clothes for the poor.

'Now come and tell me all the gossip, young Rowan. How's that new stepmother of yours?'

Rowan knew she shouldn't be surprised that Aggie knew of her father's marriage, for talk travelled quicker than time around these parts. Cup in hand, she settled in the other chair and passed the next half-hour exchanging the local news, which was sparser than usual owing to the fact that neither of them had ventured out during the snow. Somehow, though, she didn't feel able to confide in her friend about 'Slimy' as she now thought of the strange man. It was cosy beside the fire but eventually, knowing Sab would be waiting, she reluctantly got to her feet, threw on her shawl, picked up her baskets and bent to kiss Aggie goodbye. Curiously, the woman gripped hold of Rowan's hand and gazed intently into her eyes for a long moment. A shiver stole up the girl's spine and she could feel the red ribbon tightening around her wrist.

'You're a good girl, Rowan, but too trusting, especially for a sensitive. 'Tis a blessing and a curse, so you must treat the gift wisely,' Aggie whispered. 'You can see and hear things for others, but not for yourself. But Aggie sees for ye. Take great care, for I see trouble ahead. Beware she with the forked tongue.' Then, as if she'd exhausted herself, Aggie slumped back in her chair. Before Rowan could ask what she'd meant, the old woman was gently snoring, her knitting falling to the floor.

Hurrying as fast as she could through the slushy streets, Rowan couldn't help pondering on what Aggie had said. Was it connected to her mother's warning that day of the storm? More to the point, was it a warning about Fanny and if it was, what could she do? She shivered and found herself peering down every alleyway she passed. Once she was back in the still-bustling marketplace, where everyone was going about their business, she chided herself for her fanciful thoughts. The appetizing aroma of pie and onions wafted her way and she saw Sab waiting impatiently beside Hannah's stall. As he looked at her hopefully all thoughts of Aggie and her warning went out of her head.

'Fear not, Sab, I sold every single thing so we shall eat today,' she said, pleased to be back in his company.

Grinning, he joined the queue and then, armed with their pies, they took shelter in the shambles.

'That were scrumptious,' Sab declared, licking his fingers. He peered up at the lowering sky. 'But we'd best be getting back before the weather closes in again.'

Fortified by their feast they made their way over to the stables behind the hostelry. Excusing herself to make use of the facilities, Rowan left Sab collecting Blackthorn and made her way carefully along the side of the building. The sounds of revelry coming from inside reminded her of 'Slimy' and his invitation, and she made a note to relay her encounter to Sab. By the time she returned, though, he was laughing with the ostlers and the moment was lost.

Steadily they trundled homewards through the gathering gloom. Weary from her early start and busy day, Rowan fell into a doze. She was woken some time later by Sab cursing as the cart lurched to one side of the track.

'What's up?' she muttered, peering into the darkness. 'Why aren't we home yet?'

'I think Blackthorn must have cast a shoe back along. I've let her go at her own pace but now she's lame,' he said. 'We're nearly there now, but it'll help if I lead her and whisper encouragement.'

'Oh, the poor thing,' Rowan murmured, jumping down from the cart and walking alongside Sab.

'Yes, and poor Uncle Ted. We'll have to call the farrier out and that'll cost.'

Rowan thought of the money she'd made at market. No sooner did she make a profit than it was swallowed up by bills. Sab was right: Blackthorn couldn't go anywhere or do anything until the farrier had seen to her. Remembering the bright green ribbon she'd bought, she sighed. What had she been thinking, frittering money away like that?

By the time they turned into the entrance of Orchard Farm the moon was shining from an inky sky.

'The shippon's in darkness so it looks like Uncle's finished the milking. You go in and get warm while I see to Blackthorn,' Sab said, leading the limping creature away. Rowan sighed. 'Don't look so worried, Fanny will be in her parlour by now, look.' He pointed to the spiral of smoke rising from the chimney.

Quietly letting herself indoors, Rowan threw off her shawl and went over to the fire.

Suddenly the parlour door flew open and Fanny stood there staring at her wide-eyed.

'Whatever are you doing here?' she exclaimed.

Chapter 10

'What do you mean?' Rowan said, staring at her step-mother in surprise.

Her father appeared in the doorway behind Fanny, looking anxious.

'There you are, my dear. Is everything all right? Only it's late and we were quite worried about you.'

'Yes, that's what I meant, of course. Where have you been?' Fanny said quickly. 'We were worried you'd got lost or something.'

'Got lost? We've only been to Sudbury, Fanny. Black-thorn cast a shoe and we had to walk the last half-mile home. Sab's in the stables seeing to her, but I'm afraid we'll have to get the farrier out, Father.'

'Not to worry, my dear, can't be helped. The animal's welfare must come first, you know that. Now come and sit down by the fire; you must be exhausted.'

'But it'll cost extra to have him come here, and I had hoped the money I'd made on the stall would help with the farm's finances.'

'Do you have to pay this man to come out, then?' Fanny cut in.

Rowan nodded and turned back to her father. 'If I'd known Blackthorn was going to need the farrier, I wouldn't have spent the money Aunt Sal gave me on this,' she said, taking the emerald ribbon from her pocket.

'Why, you darling girl, that's just perfect for trimming my lilac blouse,' Fanny gushed, snatching the ribbon from her fingers. Before Rowan could protest, she turned to Edward. 'Didn't I say earlier that you had a delightful daughter, Edward? It's so important that I look my best when you take me out, Teddy,' she crooned, fluttering her lashes at him.

'You always look delightful, my dear,' he said, smiling happily back at his new wife.

Obviously, harmony had been restored whilst they'd been in Sudbury, Rowan thought, wondering if she dare explain she'd really bought the ribbon to trim her own dress.

'Anyhow, I'd best go and see how Sab's getting on,' Edward said, pulling on his cap.

'We really need to go through the farm's accounts soon, Father,' Rowan reminded him, still fretting. 'I noticed the flour's getting really low and we'll need to take more grain to the miller. That'll cost.'

'Rowan, my child, haven't I told you your days of worrying about the farm are over?' Fanny simpered in that false voice she adopted when she was out to get her own way. 'From tonight, I shall take over the accounts,' she announced triumphantly. Rowan stared at her father, willing him to refuse but he was nodding eagerly.

'It does a father's heart glad to hear you thinking of his daughter's welfare, my dear. You're becoming quite the farmer's wife,' he said, kissing her cheek and disappearing outside.

'Did you have a good time in Sudbury?' Fanny asked, eyeing her speculatively. Rowan opened her mouth to explain about her ribbon then noticed the latest orphan lambs were not in their customary place beside the fire.

'Where are the lambs?' she asked, fearing the worst.

'Out in the barn with all the others, where they should be. That shepherd man came in to see to them whilst you were away and said they'd be better off with those who could show them some warmth. I guess he meant with the other sheep and their woollen fleeces.' Knowing just what old Davey would have meant, Rowan smothered a grin. 'Now, dear, you must tell me about your day. Did you meet anyone nice?'

Again she was subjected to a penetrating stare. Not wishing to face Fanny's questioning and with tiredness threatening to engulf her, she shook her head and yawned.

'It's been a busy day, Fanny, so if you'll excuse me, I'll say good night,' she muttered, and, without waiting for an answer, hurried up the stairs.

Although she was exhausted, sleep failed to come and she lay in her bed thinking back over the events of the day. It had been good to get away from the farm, and she'd enjoyed exchanging free and easy banter with Sab and the stall-holders in the market. She was really pleased with the money she'd made, although who that slimy gentleman had been, she'd no idea. There had been something unsavoury about him and she sincerely hoped she wouldn't see him again. Then there was the emerald ribbon. She was furious at the way it had been snatched from her. Why should she let Fanny have it? She'd have it out with her stepmother tomorrow, she decided. Aunt Sal was right; it had taken her a while to make her uncle's socks and she deserved a little something for her hard work.

She must have fallen asleep eventually, for she was woken by the sound of banging. Prising her heavy eyelids open, she could see a faint loom through the window and realized it must be early morning. Then she heard the noise again, only quicker and more persistent. Jumping out of bed, she gasped when she saw her mirror frantically banging against the door. It was warning her someone unwelcome was trying to get in. Sure enough, she saw the latch lift and then heard the thud of a body against wood when it refused to budge.

'Rowan, are you there?' Fanny called. No, I've sprouted wings and flown to the moon, she wanted to cry, not yet ready for another interrogation. She covered her mouth with her hands so that no sound could inadvertently escape. 'Rowan, open the door. I need to speak to you.' Again the mirror clattered its warning and Rowan was thankful for its protection. 'Rowan, either let me in or come out this very moment. Mrs Stokes is here to see to the laundry and needs some wood ash for grease stains. Can you come and show me where it is?' Feeling laughter bubbling up at such a ridiculous question, Rowan bit down on her lip. Didn't the woman know anything? Then she heard her father's step on the stair.

'What's wrong, Fanny?' he asked. 'I could hear you shouting from outside.'

'I'm trying to get into Rowan's room. Mrs Stokes needs wood ash, Edward, and . . .'

'Leave the girl to sleep. She had a long day yesterday. All you need to do is empty the pit out from under the fire.'

'But, Edward, I must keep my hands soft for you, my dearest. Look, this can wait. Why don't we go back to bed and . . . ?' The rest of her sentence was lost as the door to their room was pushed firmly closed. Then she heard giggling and the creak of the bed. Rowan shook her head in disgust. Not for what they were doing, but for the way Fanny used her wiles to get out of the household chores.

Kissing the mirror and giving thanks to it for confusing the enemy, she beseeched it to continue its good work. Then quickly throwing on her dress, she brushed the tangles out of her hair and ran downstairs to find Mrs Stokes. As usual the woman was checking the garments for stains before sorting them into separate piles.

'Morning, my dear,' she said, when she saw Rowan standing in the doorway.

'Sorry I slept in, Mrs Stokes. I was that tired after going to market yesterday. Fanny said you needed some wood ash – oh!' she gasped, seeing the full pail standing in its usual place inside the door.

The woman chuckled. 'Just my little joke. Mrs High and Mighty was getting on my nerves so I thought it'd do her good to get her hands dirty. I never thought she'd bother you, Rowan, girl.'

'You mean Fanny's been out here already this morning?' Rowan asked in surprise.

'Oh, yes. Going on about having to supervise the hired help, she was. I tells you, girl, the day I need someone watching over me's the day I quit,' she muttered, scrubbing the cuffs of Edward's shirts with unnecessary vigour. 'Anyhows, I'll finish this little lot and leave it soaking, then be back on Monday to do the wash as usual.'

'Thanks, Mrs Stokes. I don't know what we'd do without you,' Rowan said.

'I prays you won't have to find out, me dear,' Mrs Stokes answered, grimacing as she rubbed the small of her back. 'There seems to be a lot more for me to do these days, so happen I'll ask Fanny to pay me extra for seeing to her fancy finery,' she chuckled.

Rowan smiled and privately agreed, for the woman did work extremely hard.

As Rowan made her way down to the privy, she saw Sab busy digging.

'Morning, Sab. I thought you'd be preparing for sowing,' she said.

He rested on his shovel and gave a wry grin. 'Fanny told me I had to build this 'ere path like yesterday. Old Davey was saying that whilst we was at market, Fanny got chased by the gander on her way to the privy. Seems the toe of her fancy shoe got caught in the mud and she had to hop back indoors on one foot. Davey said he didn't know who was squawking most, her or the goose,' he said, chuckling. 'She made a right tap and toe, and told Uncle the path's got to be done before the sowing.' He shook his head. 'Uncle said he'd help, but I don't know where he's got to.'

Thinking it best not to mention what she'd heard earlier, Rowan changed the subject.

'How's Blackthorn this morning?'

'Sore, bless her. The tinks was here earlier. Said he had a message for Fanny. Anyhow, he's going to call in at the farrier on his way past and ask him to come over when he can. Probably try and flog him a new pan while he's at it, knowing him.'

'Since when has the tinks been delivering messages to Fanny?' Rowan asked, frowning.

'Don't know. Reckoned he called before the snow to see if we needed anything. Fanny said we didn't, but gave him a note to deliver. Anyhows, I better get back to it,' Sab said, picking up his shovel.

As Rowan hurried into the privy she wondered at her stepmother's cheek. How would she know if they needed any pots or pans? The woman hardly graced the kitchen with her presence, let alone cooked anything. Still, whatever was going on with Fanny and her messages it had nothing to do with her. Or did it? Could Fanny have anything to do with that Slimy? She shivered. She'd be on her guard next time she went to the market, she resolved. Having finished her ablutions, she popped into the barn.

'Come to see the little uns?' old Davey asked, pointing to the corner where the latest two lambs were on their feet, bleating for food. 'Happen that charm worked a treat, along with your tender care. Nearly had another couple for you to look out for earlier. Ewe over there rejected her young uns but no sooner did I show her the dog than she went into protective mode. Now she won't let me anywhere near them, which is as it should be, of course,' he laughed. 'That Fanny's a queer one, though. Only asked me if I knew how many sheep there were on Dartmoor. Told her, if I ever had a spare month of Sundays I'd go and have a count of them.'

Although Rowan smiled, she couldn't help wondering what her stepmother was up to now.

Making her way back towards the farmhouse, Rowan could hear water dripping off the buildings and outhouses. A weak sun was washing the sky, and now with temperatures rising, the thaw had set in. Thoughts of warmer weather and the coming spring lifted her spirits and she felt ready to tackle her bread making. Her mother had always said that a happy heart and warm hands made the best bread. Grabbing an armful of faggots from the rick, she hurried indoors and set about lighting the bread oven. Then, having measured out her ingredients, she set about her task. As ever, the rhythmic kneading soothed her senses and she was just putting the dough to rise when her father crept down the stairs. Seeing her busy at the table, he looked shame-faced.

'Fanny needed me upstairs,' he muttered.

'Sab's been working on that path for some time now, Father, and I reckon he could do with a hand. Now the thaw's set in you'll need to have it finished before the moon's right for sowing,' she pointed out.

'Since when do I need you to tell me what needs doing around my own farm?' he grunted, slamming the door behind him so hard the pots rattled on the dresser. So much for a nice peaceful morning, Rowan thought.

Later, with the bread cooling on the table and Rowan about to go out to the dairy to make more cheese, Fanny appeared.

'Good morning, Rowan,' she chirped. 'I see the weather's improving, so I thought I'd get Edward to take me shopping. Before that, though, I need to see to the accounts. How much did you make at the market yesterday?' Rowan put her hand in her pocket and drew out a handful of coins. 'Is that all?' her stepmother asked, looking suspiciously at her.

'Actually, that's more than we usually make, Fanny. Of course, I did buy the green ribbon but that was with the money Aunt Sal gave me. And, Fanny . . .' she stuttered to a halt as the woman's pebble gaze bore into her.

'Yes, Rowan, do go on,' she said, moving closer so that she towered over Rowan.

'Well, the thing is, I actually bought that ribbon for myself. I was going to trim the homespun I'd dyed with elder,' she said, refusing to be intimidated.

'I see,' Fanny said, silence hanging in the air. Then she gave a brittle laugh. 'Well, I knew that all along.'

'You did?' Rowan asked.

'Yes, of course. It's not as though you particularly like me, is it, Rowan?'

'Well, I . . .' she mumbled, feeling awkward yet not given to lying.

'It's all right, Rowan. I don't particularly like you either. However, for Edward's sake we need to rub along, at least for the time being. But I really like that emerald ribbon so how about we do a deal? I will allow you to continue wearing that red scrap you refuse to take off and in return I will keep the green.' Fanny's eyes glinted as she gave Rowan a supercilious look. Rowan hesitated, her hand instinctively going to her wrist. 'If you insist on having the green one, then you must hand over your red, which if you had an ounce of sense you'd realize would be the better deal. After all, the green is new, the red nothing but a frayed old rag.'

Rowan could feel her temper rising. 'Mine is not a frayed rag, Fanny. It belonged to Mother and is my most treasured possession,' she declared.

'Well, if you will insist, then I will keep the green,' Fanny said, a malicious gleam of satisfaction flaring in her eyes. 'Now, I need to go through the farm accounts, so perhaps you can get them for me.'

Rowan went over to the dresser and took down the well-worn book, placing it on the table. Carefully Fanny counted out the coins Rowan had given her and entered the figure at the end of the last column. Then she totted up the figures so quickly Rowan gasped.

'Is something wrong?' Fanny asked, frowning.

'No. It's just that I've never seen anyone add up so fast,' Rowan admitted. 'It takes me much longer and I've been doing the accounts ever since Mother passed away.'

Fanny sighed. 'I can assure you that keeping tabs on money is something that comes naturally to me, so you can rest assured the farm accounts will be in good hands.'

Forcing a smile, Rowan hurried out to the dairy where she set about making more soft cheese to replenish their supplies. The cool temperature helped calm her temper, and while her hands carried out their task automatically a plan formed in her mind. She would buy more ribbon when she next went to market and justify the extra cost by making more caps and mittens to sell. Fanny might be able to add up quicker than she could, but Rowan knew how to balance the budget.

By the time she'd made the cheese, her stomach was rumbling. Going to the larder, she snatched up the remains of a fitch of bacon and some gherkins, then hurried indoors. The table was littered with crumbs where Fanny had helped herself to some of the freshly baked bread, cutting the tops off and leaving the bottoms, as was her way. Fighting down her irritation, Rowan prepared the men's midday snack and carried it out to them. Her father still looked shame-faced as she approached, but she smiled sweetly and handed over the basket.

'Is there enough for three in there?' he asked.

'There is enough for four, Father,' she said, smiling. 'I'm sure old Davey will be hungry, too.'

'You're a good girl, Rowan,' Edward said, digging his hand in his pocket and drawing out a coin. 'Best get yourself another ribbon next week, eh?'

So he knew, Rowan thought.

With Sab carrying the basket, they made their way over to the barn. Pleased that harmony was restored between them, Rowan linked her arm through her father's. As he smiled fondly back at her, they didn't notice Fanny glaring at them from her bedroom window.

Chapter 11

They perched on hay bales at the far end of the barn and, with the bleating of sheep in the background, tucked into their snack.

'That were a feast, Rowan,' Sab said, finishing his food before the others as usual. 'How is the lambing, Davey?'

'They be coming along, Sab. A couple could be breech so if it's all right with you, Ted, I'll bed down here a while longer?'

'Of course, Davey; you know the animals best. Anyhow, you've no need to ask, you know that.'

'Didn't used to, you means. Things are different now, though, aren't they?' Davey grunted. 'No disrespect, like, but that new wife of yours was asking about price of wool. Mighty unusual thing for a woman to concern herself with, old Davey thinks.'

'That's probably because she's taken over the farm accounts,' Edward replied.

'Why would you let her do that? Bodes bad that, you mark my words,' Davey muttered, shaking his head.

'Well, thank you, Davey. When we need the opinion of hired help we'll ask,' Fanny said, appearing in the doorway. 'Come along, Edward, you promised to take me into Sudbury and I have no wish to be late for my appointment,' she said, adjusting her bonnet.

'I didn't know we were timed, Fanny. I thought you

were just going shopping,' he said, jumping up and brushing the crumbs from his trousers.

'I am, but I also need to see someone about domestic matters. Nothing for you to concern yourself about, though, Edward,' she added hastily, when he looked at Davey in alarm.

'Right, in that case you'd best load the grain onto the cart, Sab. I'll go on to the mill whilst Fanny is about her business. I'll just get Bryony ready, dear. If the farrier should come, show him the problem with Blackthorn, Sab.'

'And make sure he doesn't overcharge us,' Fanny added. 'Now, I'll expect you all to get some work done whilst we are away. Sab, I want to see real progress made to that path by the time I return. Rowan, I have left a note for you on the kitchen table. Please hurry up, Edward; I shall be waiting in the farmhouse,' she called.

They watched in stunned silence as she picked her way carefully back to the farmhouse. Never had they been spoken to like that. Edward shrugged, and Sab followed him out of the barn.

Rowan picked up her empty basket. 'Why would she leave me a note?' she asked Davey. 'Couldn't she just tell me what she wants me to do?'

'Depends if she wants Edward to know what it is,' Davey answered sagely. Rowan frowned. 'You are innocent of guile, young un, but regrettably not everyone is.'

'Well, I'm going to visit Mother first. I haven't been to see her for ages and I've so much to tell her.'

'Aye, good idea, girl, and say hello from old Davey, too,' he said, grinning as he turned back to his beloved sheep.

A breeze had got up whilst they'd been having their noon piece, and Rowan walked briskly through the farmyard, making her way to her mother's final resting place. Daffodils were dancing where the snowdrops had been on her previous visit, their golden trumpets a welcome splash of colour against the dark red Devonshire soil.

Throwing herself onto the ground, Rowan told her mother everything that had been going on at Orchard Farm since her last visit.

'Fanny's horrid, Mother. She says she knows I don't like her and that she doesn't like me either. Apparently we have to rub along for the time being.' She felt the ribbon tighten and automatically her hand went to ease the material. 'Why does that keep happening, Mother? It never used to,' she said. 'Oh, I do miss you and wish you were still here,' she sobbed, closing her eyes to stem the flow of tears.

When she'd got her emotions under control, she opened her eyes and gasped. The daffodils had all splayed out and seemed to be forming the word 'beware'. She blinked in surprise but when she looked again the flowers were bobbing and dancing in the breeze. It must have been her imagination, she thought. Her ribbon tightened.

'I know you're trying to tell me something about Fanny, Mother. I just wish I knew what to do about the woman,' she sighed, getting to her feet and pulling her shawl tighter around her shoulders. 'I'll be back to visit you soon.' *No, you won't*, the breeze seemed to sigh. She shook her head, thinking that was fanciful even for her, and, heart heavy, she made her way back down the path.

Back in the farmhouse, all thought of warning winds and daffodils disappeared as she shrugged off her shawl and saw the note Fanny had left. Beside it lay a lilac blouse and the emerald ribbon.

Dear Rowan,

As your father and I will be back late, please prepare supper for our return.
I'd be obliged if you would sew my new ribbon on to this blouse.
Fanny

Rowan felt her temper rising. Screwing up the note, she flung it into the fire. Really, that woman had the cheek of a thousand devils, never mind one. Well, she knew the men would be hungry so she'd prepare their meal, but there was no way she was going to sew that ribbon on to Fanny's blouse. Going out to the vegetable store, she snatched up some roots from their dwindling supplies then picked herbs from the garden. Back inside, as she prepared a broth she couldn't help staring at the ribbon, a plan forming in her mind. Throwing more wood onto the fire she set the pot to simmer.

After rinsing her hands, she snuggled down beside the hearth with her sewing. Magic appeared as if from nowhere and settled on her feet. Then, in the cosy atmosphere of crackling logs and purring cat, she spent a pleasant afternoon stitching and musing. She couldn't help remembering sitting here with her mother teaching her to sew. Then, after she'd died, Auntie Sal had helped her with the difficult tasks of turning the collars on her father's shirts. Thoughts of her auntie reminded her that she and her uncle hadn't visited in a while, which was quite unlike them. Maybe it was because of the snow. She must ask her father about it when he returned.

Just as the shadows were lengthening and a savoury aroma was rising from the pot, she held up her work and nodded in satisfaction. Skipping upstairs, she laid the lilac blouse on Fanny's bed. Then going into her own room she kissed her mirror and put her handiwork away for later.

She'd just finished setting the table when her father and stepmother clattered through the door. Magic hissed at Fanny and bolted upstairs.

'Something smells good,' Edward said, sniffing the air appreciatively.

'I'm pleased to see you followed my instructions, Rowan,' Fanny said graciously. 'I think we will all eat together tonight.'

Wondering what had brought about Fanny's change of mind, for she knew there must be a reason, Rowan set extra places around the table. She cut bread and was serving up the broth when Davey appeared. Seeing Fanny sitting at the table, he collected his dish and returned to the barn, muttering he had to see to a ewe that was about to give birth. Apart from the scraping of cutlery on plates, there was silence as they all ate ravenously. Finally Edward pushed his empty platter away.

'That were a nice drop of broth, Rowan, my dear,' he declared, patting his stomach.

Sab nodded in agreement. 'Glad you're back to cooking our meals, Rowan,' he said, looking pointedly at Fanny.

She sniffed, but said nothing, just sat there looking smug, like a cat that's cornered a mouse and is waiting to pounce.

Sensing tension, Edward began talking about the warming weather, and when the moon phase would be right to sow the crops.

'Well, we're into March now, so by my reckoning the water table will be right for carrots and tubers soon after next market day,' Sab commented.

'And then we can see about sowing the grain up in Five Acre Field,' Edward said.

'Does this all really take place at night?' Fanny asked, suddenly taking an interest in the conversation.

'No, my dear, we can't broadcast at night, we can only plant the root crops,' Edward told her, smiling apologetically.

'And when will this be exactly?' asked Fanny, looking up from her list.

'Probably at the vernal equinox – or Eostre for you, Rowan,' Sab answered with a grin.

'Do talk English, boy,' Fanny snapped. Silence descended like a blanket of death. 'Well, think how difficult this all is for me, a city girl who has no knowledge of your country ways,' she simpered.

'Sorry, my dear,' Edward said, giving an embarrassed cough.

'And do you have a part in this?' she asked, turning to Rowan and giving her a penetrating stare.

'Oh, yes, I shall be carrying out the ritual Mother taught me to draw upon the earth's natural energies. It will be the time when day and night are of equal length and in perfect balance. We need to ensure the continuum –'

'For heaven's sake, will you stop spouting this mumbo jumbo,' Fanny interrupted.

'Yes, my dear,' Edward muttered. 'Did the farrier come, Sab?'

Sab shook his head.

'Happen he'll drop by tomorrow then. Right, if we've all finished, I'll go and bring in the flour,' he said, rising to his feet.

'Just a minute, Edward,' Fanny said, putting out her arm to detain him. 'Now, Sab, have you finished my path yet?'

'Almost,' he muttered.

'Good. Remember that I decreed it must be done before planting. I cannot afford to ruin more shoes. Now, when I was in Sudbury I engaged the services of a cook-cum-housekeeper, so first thing Monday morning, we will go through her duties together, Rowan. Then you can show her where everything is,' she said, smiling her supercilious smile.

'You didn't tell me about this, Fanny,' Edward said, looking shocked. 'How much is this woman going to cost?'

'Now, my dear, we agreed that you'd see to things around the farm and leave me to deal with running of the household.'

Edward shook his head. 'I'm not sure we can afford . . .'

'Edward, you promised to leave the accounts to me and we did agree that Rowan shouldn't have to cook and clean any more, didn't we?' she said, smiling sweetly.

Feeling there was more to it than this, Sab and Rowan exchanged puzzled looks.

'Well, that's all arranged then,' Fanny said, getting to her feet. 'Mrs Dunmore will be arriving by carter, along with the household items I purchased this afternoon.'

Rowan took special care with her appearance on Monday morning, but waited until she heard the cart arrive before going downstairs. The kitchen was alive with activity as the driver, helped by Sab, unloaded numerous parcels and packages.

'Looks like Fanny's gone crazy with Uncle's money,' Sab whispered as she passed.

Rowan shook her head, wondering just where everything was going to be stored.

Fanny, who'd already shown Mrs Dunmore into the parlour, looked up as Rowan appeared in the doorway. Her eyes widened in surprise, the smile freezing on her lips as she took in the emerald ribbon adorning Rowan's homespun. Involuntarily, she glanced down at the same ribbon, which Rowan had sewn prominently down the placket of her lilac blouse. Rowan grinned to herself. Just as she'd thought, the bright emerald did nothing to enhance Fanny's cold grey eyes. It was only when the matronly looking woman jumped to her feet that Fanny remembered her manners.

'Rowan, this is Mrs Dunmore, who is coming to look after our household matters,' she said frostily.

Rowan smiled at the woman, taking in her meek, accepting eyes, iron-grey hair twisted into a bun and the well-worn, yet clean coat. Nervously the woman nodded back.

'I have already agreed terms of employment with

Mrs Dunmore,' Fanny continued. 'However, I would be pleased if you could familiarize her with what food Edward likes to eat and when. Then I'd like you to show her where everything is kept. When you are satisfied Mrs Dunmore knows what is expected of her you will return. There are things I wish to discuss with you.' Fanny was staring pointedly at the emerald ribbon on Rowan's dress.

It took Rowan only a couple of hours to explain their daily routine and show Mrs Dunmore where everything was kept. Then, to her surprise, the carter returned and the woman bade her farewell.

'But aren't you staying?' Rowan asked.

'Oh, no, dear, I'm to wait until I'm summoned,' Mrs Dunmore replied, climbing quickly into the cart.

Rowan shook her head. The workings of her stepmother's mind were beyond her. Her stomach growled and, remembering she'd had nothing to eat, she hurried back to the farmhouse. She'd just finished her bread roll when Fanny appeared in the doorway.

'Ah, Rowan, I trust everything went well?' she enquired, eyeing her dress speculatively.

'Yes, but I thought Mrs Dunmore would be starting straight away.'

'Well, we have to be mindful of the household budget, don't we?' her stepmother answered.

Rowan stared around the kitchen at the piles of packages. 'Shall I get Sab to tidy these away?' she asked.

'Ah, Sab. Let us go through, Rowan. There are a few things I wish to discuss with you, and he happens to be one of them,' Fanny replied, disappearing back into her parlour.

'Now, first things first. I suppose you found it amusing to trim both our garments with the emerald ribbon?' she said, staring at Rowan with those stony grey eyes.

Rowan swallowed but, determined to stand her ground, she stared boldly back.

'Well, Fanny, although I bought that ribbon for myself, you made it quite plain you wanted it for trimming your blouse. It occurred to me that with careful cutting there would be enough for both of us,' she explained. She waited for her stepmother to explode but, to her amazement, the woman nodded in agreement.

'It makes sense when you think about it, I suppose. In future, though, you will not wear that dress at the same time I'm attired in my lilac blouse. That way, we will not be classed as being from the same stock,' she said, laughing at her own little joke.

Rowan smiled politely but did not answer. It was for her to decide when she wore her green dress, thank you.

'Now, about Sab – such a ridiculous name. Why is he called that?' Rowan stared at her stepmother, surprised at the change of subject. 'Well, Rowan, am I talking to myself?' Fanny demanded.

'Sorry. Sab is short for Sabbath. As he was discovered by the sisters of the foundling hospital on the Sabbath, they named him accordingly. He hated that, so we shortened it to Sab.'

'When was this exactly?' Fanny asked, peering intently at Rowan.

She frowned, trying to remember. 'It must have been about ten years ago, I suppose. Mother couldn't have any more children after me. She was so small, you see . . .'

'Yes, yes,' her stepmother cut in abruptly, her eyes calculating. 'And he's what, about fourteen years old now?'

Rowan nodded. 'Why, has he done something wrong?' she asked, puzzled by the woman's questions and anxious not to get Sab into trouble.

As was her way, Fanny abruptly changed the conversation again.

'You didn't tell me how you got on at the market last Thursday. I expect you saw all the old faces, but did you meet anyone new?' Fanny's gaze bore into her, making her feel uncomfortable. She thought of the slimy man, but some inner sense told her to hold her tongue.

'Well, I expect you will be making more bread and cheese to take to the market on Thursday?' Fanny said into the lengthening silence.

'Oh, yes, I could have sold lots more last week if I'd had the produce,' Rowan said.

'Well, I suggest you spend the next few days making sure you have sufficient for this time,' Fanny said. 'We shall share the household duties until Mrs Dunmore starts.'

As her stepmother smiled graciously, Rowan felt the ribbon tighten around her wrist and a prickle of unease crept up her spine.

Rowan spent the next few days making her produce, but as she chopped herbs for her soft cheese and kneaded dough for her bread, her mind kept going back over the strange conversation she'd had with her stepmother. She wanted to discuss it with Sab, but with the path finished he must have been put to work elsewhere on the farm. Unusually, he hadn't put in an appearance at mealtimes and she'd been so busy she hadn't had a chance to go and find him. Still, they'd have plenty of time to chat on their journey to market. They'd be by themselves and would be able to talk freely.

By Wednesday afternoon, Rowan was satisfied she had enough cheese to meet demand. Wanting to make sure she had more bread than the previous week, she sought her stepmother's permission to make her loaves that evening after they'd finished their supper. Unusually the woman was obliging, and by the time Rowan went to bed that night the kitchen table was completely covered with cooling loaves and rolls. She fell into bed exhausted but satisfied she'd made enough produce to make a decent profit.

Creeping downstairs at daybreak the next morning, she found the kitchen quiet and the kitchen table empty. Puzzled, she hurried out to the dairy, and saw to her dismay that all her cheese was missing, too.

Chapter 12

Thinking Sab might have risen early and packed everything onto the cart, Rowan ran outside. The yard was empty and everything eerily quiet for this time of the morning. With an uneasy feeling uncurling in her stomach, she threw open the shippon door but there was no sign of Sab or her father, and she could tell by the placid way the cows were staring at her that they'd already been milked.

She was just letting the chickens out when she heard the high-pitched squeal of an animal in distress. Hurrying over to the barn, she saw old Davey, hand inside a struggling ewe, shaking his head.

'Lamb's breech and I've been trying to turn it. Can't get me big old hand up far enough, though,' he muttered, and from the beads of sweat running down his face, Rowan could see he'd been trying for some time.

'Here, let me try,' she said, quickly pulling up the sleeves of her dress.

Under Davey's guidance she gently but firmly twisted until finally the lamb was turned the right way. No sooner had she removed her hand than the tiny animal slithered from his mother, landing with a soft plop on the straw at her feet. Immediately, the ewe nuzzled the lamb and began licking away the membrane covering it. Wondering at the miracle of Mother Nature, Davey and Rowan exchanged relieved looks and then went over to the water trough to wash the muck and blood from their arms. Collapsing onto a nearby bale, they watched with satisfaction as the mother completed her job. Tenderly old Davey encouraged the lamb to its feet and directed it towards its mother's teat. As it began to suckle, its midwives gave a triumphant cheer.

'Phew, that were a near thing,' old Davey said, wiping the sweat from his face with his kerchief. 'Thank heavens you was here. I couldn't have managed without you, girl.' His words jerked Rowan back to the present.

'That's just it, Davey, I'm not meant to be here. It is market day and I should be on my way to Sudbury with Sab. I've spent all week preparing my produce. Why, I even worked late into the night baking extra bread as there seems to be a demand for it. I left it cooling on the kitchen table but when I got up this morning, it had all disappeared. There's no sign of Father or Sab either. It's almost as if Fanny's intent on keeping me away from them,' she wailed.

'Are you sure?' Davey asked, wrinkling his forehead. 'Mind you, I vaguely remember hearing the cart rumbling off some time ago, but I was that busy in here, I didn't take any notice.'

'Why would Sab have gone without me? It's not like him. But then he's been ignoring me all week. And Auntie Sal and Uncle Silas haven't visited in ages. It's so unlike them.'

'Happen I agree it's that Fanny who's behind it all. Divide and rule, that one,' he said, scratching his head.

'What do you mean?' Rowan asked.

'That lady will go to any lengths to get her own way. Things is becoming a bit strange all around here. She was even asking if we dealt with them owlers.'

'Surely not. Everyone knows decent folk steer clear of those hoodlums,' Rowan cried.

'Said she'd heard we could get a better price for our wool. Told her, she'd be a right fool to get mixed up with them,' he said, shaking his head.

'But Father would never deal with owlers, Davey. You know how he despises them.'

'True enough, but that woman's got him eating from her hand. Never seen a sensible man change as fast as Edward since her's been here. When I looks in her eyes, all I sees is greed. Don't worry,' he added, seeing Rowan's look of alarm. 'Old Davey will see he stays on the right track, for this year at least.'

'Why only this year?' she asked, looking at him in alarm.

He gave a deep sigh. 'After that it's going to be up to you, little un. Old Davey here won't be seeing another spring,' he said, shaking his head. Rowan gasped. 'Oh, don't worry; 'tis the way of things. The circle of life, as your dear mother used to say. Come next year, old Davey here will be returned to the earth.'

'No, Davey, please don't say that,' she cried, grabbing hold of his arm.

'Don't you fret; old Davey here's had a good life. But you needs to look out for yourself, Rowan. Promise me that, eh?' he begged, staring at her with blue eyes that were surprisingly all-seeing and clear for an old man. Too choked to speak, she nodded. 'That's all old Davey needs to know,' he said, patting her shoulder. 'Now, I expects her ladyship will still be in bed, and I've a feeling she be behind all your problems. Go and speak to her, eh? This be the last of the sheep to lamb this year, so old Davey'll do as he's been told and take himself back to his hut.'

'Do as you've been told? I don't understand,' Rowan said, although she had a hunch.

'The old besom said I'm not welcome to bed here in the barn no more, and old Davey don't stay where he's not wanted. Thing is, I knows I've seen her afore but I'm blowed if I can remember where. It's that smell, you see. Gets right up your nose and stays there.'

Rowan grinned, knowing how true that was.

'Happen I'll remember once I've had a nice long nap,' he said, wincing as he got to his feet.

Rowan stroked the ribbon around her wrist.

'Your mother used to do that when she was worried, too. Said that ribbon would tighten itself around her when she needed alerting to something wrong. You've got her gift, so just you take heed of what it's trying to tell you, young un,' he said, whistling to his dog.

Rowan watched through the open door as, dun-brown collie at his heels, the shepherd hobbled his way across the yard, heading towards his hut in the hills. She was about to call after him and offer him a ride on the cart, then remembered it wasn't here.

Gazing at the new lamb sleeping beside its mother, she thought about what Davey had said about the owlers. Surely even Fanny couldn't persuade her father to deal with the hoodlums he deplored. Those evil men were known to offer higher than the market price for the sheep's wool and then turn on those who'd been tempted by their offers. Often they'd had their farms razed or were found dead in their beds.

The rattling of a cart disturbed her musing and, jumping to her feet, she was just in time to see Fanny, dressed in her finery, climb up beside the driver. Anxious to find out why her father and Sab had left without her, and where her stepmother was going, Rowan raced out of the barn.

'Hey, Fanny . . .' she called, but before she'd got even halfway across the yard, the cart had disappeared in a cloud of dust. Peering through the settling haze, she thought that she recognized the set of the driver, but couldn't recall where from.

It was midway through the afternoon when Fanny came bustling into the kitchen. Rowan finished setting a pot of broth to simmer over the fire, then turned to face her.

'There you are, Fanny. I need to speak to you about . . .' she began.

'Not now, child, can't you see I'm busy?' Fanny snapped, struggling under a load of parcels. As Rowan watched her disappear up the stairs, she heard the rattle of a cart disappearing down the lane at speed. By the time she'd raced outside, she was too late to make out anything other than an outline of the driver before the cart turned the corner and was lost from view. There was definitely something familiar about him, she thought, making her way back inside.

Not long afterwards she heard another cart drawing up and her father appeared, shrugging off his jacket and cap.

'Weather's definitely warming, my dear. Oh, Rowan, it's

you,' he said, looking round from the peg. 'Are you feeling better?'

'Better?' she asked.

'Yes, Fanny said you had a bad stomach. You know woman's . . .' he stuttered to a halt, blushing as red as the flames in the fire.

'Ah, there you are, husband of mine,' Fanny said, appearing at his side and kissing his cheek. 'Don't you worry, my dear, I've been looking after Rowan whilst you've been away. We women have to bear these things stoically, don't we?' she said, throwing Rowan a defiant look.

'But it's not . . .' she began.

'Now don't embarrass the girl, Edward. Let me take care of her,' Fanny simpered. 'Did you do well at the market?'

'Yes,' he said, smiling now that he was on safe ground. 'Sab sold all your bread and cheese, Rowan. He's taken orders for more of those scarves and caps you made, too. Said people were very complimentary about them.'

'Where is Sab?' Rowan asked. At least he'd tell her what had been going on.

'Let Edward sit down before you bombard him with questions,' Fanny scolded, placing a proprietary hand on his arm. 'I'm sure you've been busy and could do with a rest, couldn't you, my dear?' she asked, making to lead him towards the parlour.

'That's very kind of you, Fanny, but I must help Sab with the milking. Did you have a good day?'

'Well, I had Rowan to look after, of course, and, as you can smell, our supper is cooking.'

'But you never —' Rowan began, indignant that her stepmother should lie so glibly.

'Well, you go on out to that cow place and I'll make sure your supper's ready and waiting when you come in,' Fanny said. Edward looked from his wife to Rowan, shrugged, and then in the time-honoured way of men who sense trouble, hastily put his cap back on and disappeared outside.

'What is going on, Fanny?' Rowan demanded. Her stepmother gave her supercilious smile, her eyes remaining cold.

'You'll find out soon enough, Rowan, believe you me,' she smirked, before disappearing into the parlour and slamming the door behind her. Rowan made to follow, then thought better of it. She'd speak to Sab when he came in for his supper.

However, he didn't appear for his meal.

'Said he was still full up from his meat pie,' her father said, when she tackled him. 'Now sit down and have your own meal,' he added. But Rowan had too many unanswered questions to even think of eating.

Deciding she'd have her supper later, she went outside to find Sab. She didn't know what was going on but she intended to find out.

He wasn't in the shippon, and although she searched the barn and around the darkening farmyard she couldn't find him anywhere. It was almost as if he was staying out of her way, she thought. Whatever was going on, she vowed she'd get to the bottom of it.

Over the next few days, though, it seemed as if Sab was playing cat and mouse with her. She'd no sooner catch a glimpse of him than he'd disappear. Or, if she did manage to catch him, Fanny would materialize and he'd scarper so fast, his shadow would have had difficulty keeping up with him. Strangely, he never appeared at meal times. When Rowan asked her father where he was, he claimed Sab was catching up with the chores he'd got behind with when he was laying the path, adding that he'd asked for cold meat or cheese and bread to be left for him to eat in his hayloft.

Deciding she'd had enough of his strange behaviour, and determined to have it out with her father, one morning she waited until he'd finished his breakfast. When he finally pushed away his empty dish, she said, 'Father, I need to speak to you about Sab.'

'Ah, yes. Good job you reminded me, Rowan. Sab said to tell you that he'd be obliged if you could help me turn the cattle out into the field today as he has other jobs to see to,' he said, his weathered face breaking into a smile as he got up from the table.

'But, Father –' she began.

'I know it's early in the season, Rowan, but Fanny's been going on at me something dreadful about needing the shippon for her things, and the weather's warmer now, isn't it?'

Realizing her father's mind was on his beloved cows Rowan knew she'd be wasting her time talking about anything else.

'Do you still want me to switch them?' she asked.

'Why, yes, Rowan. It wouldn't do to turn them out without protection. We don't want anyone putting evil on them, now, do we?'

'Tonight is Eostre, Father, so will you and Sab be up at the top field tonight?'

'Indeed we will, Rowan. Funnily enough, Fanny was asking about that only last night,' he said, getting to his feet and grabbing his cap. 'Happen she'll make a good farmer's wife yet,' he said, chuckling.

'I'll clear these dishes and then collect a fresh bough,' she promised, turning away before her expression betrayed her true thoughts. Anyone less likely to make a good farmer's wife than Fanny she'd yet to meet.

'And I'll get the cows ready,' her father said. 'I don't mind telling you, it'll be a relief not to have Fanny nagging me about it. Once planting and sowing's finished, Sab can swill down the shippon, give it a limewash and then she can move all her blooming stuff in,' he muttered. Before Rowan could ask him about Sab, he'd disappeared out of the door.

Rowan followed, selected her switch from the rowan tree beside the door and stood ready at the entrance to the shippon. As her father drove them out, she struck each beast lightly on the back, saying: *'May the milk rise in the udder as the sap in the stick.'* Then, leaving her father to herd them up to their field, she buried the rowan switch and completed her chant.

As she made her way to the dairy, she didn't see Fanny watching her from her bedroom window.

That night, as Rowan waited for the moon to rise high enough in the sky, she pondered on the strange events of the past weeks, trying to work out how long it had been since Sab had begun ignoring her. After she'd carried out her ritual she would go on up to the top field and have it out with him, she determined. Slipping out of bed, she carefully untied her mirror from the door and tiptoed down the stairs. Although there was little chance of Fanny catching her, for it was nearly midnight and her step-mother would be fast asleep, she didn't want to take any chances.

With her mirror glinting in the moonlight, and dressed only in her nightdress, she made her way up to the old oak. Carefully casting her circle, she placed the mirror in the centre. After giving the tree a greeting hug, she put her back against the trunk and slid to the ground, tapping into the natural energy around her. With her eyes tightly shut, she cleared her mind until she could feel the life rising through its roots, trunk and branches. Then jumping to her feet, she skipped around the huge, old tree, chanting:

> *Daylight and darkness of equal length,*
> *Balance our —*

Suddenly the red ribbon yanked her wrist hard, making her wince and break off the reciting of her charm. Her hand made to soothe it but before she'd even had time to ease the band a sack was thrown over her head from behind. As she gasped for breath she felt herself being lifted roughly into the air and carried over the rutted ground. Desperately, she tried to struggle free, but heard a man's coarse laugh as her captor tightened his grip.

Chapter 13

Rowan opened her mouth to scream but the sour smell of the sacking made her retch. She didn't know what was happening, only that if her body didn't stop jolting up and down soon, she was going to be sick all down this man's back. He came to an abrupt halt, and she felt herself swung into the air before being dropped unceremoniously onto hard bare boards. Momentarily stunned, she lay trying to collect her thoughts. Then, as her strength started to return, outrage burst through her. How dare anyone treat her in such a manner? Anger lent her the determination to manoeuvre herself into an upright position, but no sooner was she sitting up than she was roughly pushed back down again. Feeling a tightening around the hessian, she gasped. Her assailant was tying her up like a parcel.

'You fool, you should have knocked her out,' she heard Fanny whisper. 'You'll need to sedate her or she'll holler so loud Edward and Sab will hear up in the top field.'

'I ain't being responsible for anything like that,' the gruff voice grunted.

'Do it,' she hissed. 'Here's the necessary paperwork, now scarper.' Rowan heard Fanny's footsteps hurrying away.

'What about the rest of my money?' the man called after her.

'You'll get it when I hear the job's been done,' Fanny snapped. 'Now scram.'

Rowan heard the farmhouse door slam. Realizing she was now at the mercy of this man, she began shivering uncontrollably with fear. Then she felt herself manhandled again, the rope untied and the sacking peeled away. A shadowy figure loomed over her and she just had time to register the musty, musky smell of his cologne before a filthy cloth was thrust over her mouth, replacing it with an overwhelming bitter stench. Her last conscious thought was that she was being abducted, and then she knew no more.

She woke to the rattling noise of a wagon being driven at speed over cobbles. Her head felt muzzy and she was incredibly thirsty. What was happening? Where was she being taken? She struggled to sit up but was overcome by a wave of wooziness and slid helplessly back to the floor. She just had time to register the sacking was only loosely tied and that something thick and warm was covering her, before she lost consciousness once more.

Next time she came to, her head felt clearer, but it still took a few moments to register they were stationary. Heated voices were coming from nearby and as she listened it became clear that it was about money for a delivery that needed to be made. As she tried to manoeuvre herself into an upright position the warm cover was suddenly torn away and before she could utter a word she was once again hoisted into the air, tossed over a bony shoulder and dumped unceremoniously onto another hard surface. Then she felt the crackle of an old canvas being thrown over her.

'There you go mate, all yours,' that same gruff voice muttered. 'No helping yourself to any of the goods now.' His coarse laugh was followed by the sound of a horse and cart driving away at speed.

Another man's voice, seemingly softer than the other, called to his horse, and once again Rowan was on the move. Before long the cobbles were replaced by smoother ground but she could tell from the laboured way the horse was plodding that they were climbing uphill. Obviously she'd been transferred to another cart, but where was she being taken, by whom and why? Although her brain was functioning better now, it took her a few moments to remember she'd been snatched from the farm. But why? Was this Fanny's way of getting rid of her? And where was she being taken? By listening carefully, she could pick out muffled birdsong so it had to be daytime, although she couldn't see any light coming through the sacking. She could hear the bleating of sheep all around, so they must be travelling through countryside. This time she had no thick cover to keep her warm and she shivered from the cold air and perhaps, too, from fear.

Someone called to the horse and the cart jolted to a halt, then lurched as the driver leaped to the ground. Wriggling and writhing, Rowan desperately tried to free herself and had just managed to work the rope loose when she heard a scream. The sacking was gingerly peeled back and she found herself staring into the bewildered face of a young lad. Above him mist swirled and she shivered, her breath rising in plumes in the cold air.

'What the . . . ?' he began, looking shaken. 'Who are you?'

It was such an incongruous question, Rowan burst out

laughing. Once she started, she couldn't stop and, realizing she was bordering on hysterics, she pulled herself together. By which time the lad seemed to have recovered his composure.

'I was told this was a delivery of meat,' he said, shaking his head so that his dark, matted hair flapped against his scrawny shoulders.

'Charming,' Rowan spluttered, struggling to sit up. 'Where are you taking me?' she asked, determined to find out what was going on.

The lad shook his head again, his blue eyes wary. 'I didn't know you was alive. I mean I thought you was rations for the asy–' He stuttered to a halt, fearful he'd said too much.

'Asy? What asy?' Rowan asked.

'Look, miss,' the lad said, 'I don't want no trouble. I've to make this delivery or they'll want their money back and then me and my sisters won't have no supper. If they comes after me I'll be the dead meat,' he muttered.

'Who are they? And where are you taking me?' she asked. But the lad, already fearing he'd said too much, wouldn't be drawn.

'Wish I'd never stopped to relieve myself. Look, we're on the moors and if you leg it you'll be lost in no time. We're nearly there now anyway, so if you promise not to try and escape, I won't tie you up again.'

For the first time, Rowan stared around her. She could just make out huge dark rocks looming starkly through the mist, which seemed to be thickening even as she watched. A few twisted, apparently lifeless trees were dotted here and there, but there was no sign of civilization.

Mistaking her look, the lad jumped back into the cart and snatched up the reins, calling over his shoulder, 'Don't you try and jump, miss. The peat bogs here are treacherous. Many a man's been caught bog hopping and been sucked right down till they've swallowed him up whole. Horrible way to go,' he added, shuddering. Then, with a shout to the horse, he drove the cart forward, only to slow a few moments later as he tossed an old blanket back to her.

'That'll keep the worst off yer,' he shouted, before urging the beast to go faster.

Realizing it would be foolish to try to escape, Rowan bunched up the sacking to use as a pillow, then lay back and pulled the cover over her. It was rough and smelled of horse but as the mist enveloped her like a ghostly shroud she was grateful for its warmth. She now knew they were on Dartmoor but had no idea in which direction they were headed. The lad had said they were nearly there, so she would wait until they arrived and then find out where it was. By the way the cart was veering this way and that, he must be carefully picking his way and she didn't want to distract him. She'd heard her father talking about how treacherous the moors could be, and the idea of escaping only to be sucked into a bog seemed sheer stupidity.

Thoughts of her father made her heart leap. He'd be wondering where she was by now. How long would it be before he came searching for her? Then she remembered hearing Fanny's voice when she'd lain trussed up in the first cart. Her heart sank. What treachery had her step-mother come up with now?

She lay on the floor of the cart, watching the grey mist whirling eerily around her until eventually the lad yanked on the reins and the cart rumbled to a halt. Rowan pulled herself up onto the bench, wrapped the blanket tightly around her, then peered into the gloom. Ahead, a forbidding black granite building rose out of the murk. Before she had time to move, there was the jangle of keys followed by a clank, and the huge iron gate in the centre of the edifice squeaked open. There followed a swift exchange between the lad and a guard before the cart rumbled forward again. As they neared the austere-looking building, Rowan eyes widened in horror. It had high slit windows that were fortified by bars.

No sooner had the cart stopped again than two more uniformed figures appeared. One of them inspected the papers the lad was holding out, whilst the other helped Rowan down from the cart. No sooner had her feet touched the ground than the cart moved off at speed, and she could only watch as it was swallowed up by the murky shadows. The gate clanked shut behind her and the second guard, who had a huge moustache, took her firmly by the other arm. Before she had time to ask what was going on, she was marched up some stone steps and through an imposing iron-bound, studded door that was dominated by a huge keyhole.

The stones were freezing cold beneath her bare feet and she shivered. Conscious the men were ogling her body through her white nightgown, she shrugged off their hold, pulled the blanket over her head and secured it in a knot around her neck. As she stood there staring defiantly at them they laughed. Then, taking her by the arms once more, they swiftly marched her down a long, dimly lit corridor. When finally they came to a halt, one of them rapped sharply on a dark panelled door.

'Enter,' a voice boomed. Swiftly she was marched into a room that was dominated by a huge leather-topped desk, behind which another uniformed man was seated. A fire blazed in the grate and Rowan instinctively moved towards it. Immediately, she was tugged back.

'There's no need to be rough,' she said, snatching her arms away.

'Be respectful, woman,' the guard with the moustache barked. 'You are standing before the receiving officer and are permitted to speak only when addressed.'

'Thank you, Jenkins,' the receiving officer said, nodding to the guard. Then he gave Rowan a searching look over his half-moon glasses. 'Now, who have we here?' Before she could answer, papers were passed to him and he sat back in his huge leather-backed chair and studied them. 'Oh, I see,' he said finally. 'You are Rowan Clode?' he asked, peering at her from under his bushy brown eyebrows.

'Yes, but I don't see why . . .' she began.

'Silence,' the guard to her right barked.

'But you said I could speak when I was spoken to, so I did,' declared Rowan. She thought she saw the lips of the receiving officer twitch, but must have been mistaken for he was now staring gravely at her.

'Rowan Clode, it states here that you have been declared insane.'

Rowan gasped. 'Don't be daft,' she said.

'It's you that's daft,' the moustached guard tittered.

'Silence,' the receiving officer ordered, turning back to the paper he was holding.

'Rowan Clode, it has been observed that you are prone to delusions and fantasies,' he read. 'You show abnormal qualities of behaviour, namely that you leap over mirrors in the moonlight, hug trees and talk to them, also by moonlight, plant things in the garden by moonlight, hit cows with sticks, mix magic potions and cast spells on people. Have you done any or all of these things?'

'Yes, I have. You see . . .'

'In that case I must concur with the diagnosis made by your apothecary and clergyman that you are a lunatic suffering with sad mania,' he cut in. 'Are you clean in habits?' he asked, looking her over like she was some animal for auction.

'Of course I am,' Rowan declared.

'And in good physical health?' he persisted. She nodded and he cleared his throat. 'Then by the powers vested in me, I declare that you be committed to this, the Hell Tor Asylum, where you will receive moral treatment until such time as you are deemed cured.' With that, he gave a curt nod to the guards, who once again took her by the arms and marched her out of the room.

'I've never seen any apothecary or clergyman,' Rowan protested. But nobody took any notice. The grip on her arms tightened and she was led along yet another dingy corridor and then down steep, twisting stone stairs to a room in the basement. As another door clanked shut behind her, she felt frightened and began to shiver uncontrollably. Where on earth was she and how would her father ever find her?

'Steeples,' one of the guards barked, making her jump. A woman with fair frizzing hair, whom Rowan deemed to be of middle years, appeared out of a cloud of steam, bringing with her a strong smell of lye and something Rowan couldn't distinguish. All she knew was that it was overpowering and worse than anything Mrs Stokes used on washing day.

'Get this girl cleaned, deloused and into her uniform,' one of the two burly men ordered.

As their footsteps died away, Rowan turned to the woman.

'I haven't got lice,' she declared indignantly. 'And I'm clean, thank you,' she said, looking down and noticing her grimy feet and mud-spattered nightdress. 'Oh, no,' she gasped.

The woman merely smiled back at her. 'Don't worry, dearie. That's not the sort of clean they mean, anyway. Ma here will soon get you organized. Now, where are your things?' she asked, looking behind Rowan.

'I haven't got any,' Rowan said. 'I was snatched from my farm.'

The woman frowned. 'Well, you'd better take off that filthy blanket and nightdress, then we'll set to work,' she said, moving towards a large bowl with a piece of rough cloth lying alongside. Rowan noticed she was dragging her left foot, which was encased in an ugly built-up boot. 'Come along, we haven't got all day,' the woman said impatiently, seeing her look.

'What here, in front of you?' Rowan gasped.

'Tut-tut, dearie. 'Taint nothing Ma Steeples hasn't seen before,' she said, grinning.

'But I don't understand why I'm here. Wherever here may be. They say I'm insane but I most certainly am not,' Rowan declared.

'Course you ain't, dearie. Now hurry up and let me wash you down and then we'll just check your hair. 'Tis the rules,' she said firmly as Rowan opened her mouth to protest.

Whilst Ma Steeples seemed a kindly soul, she had the determined look of someone used to getting her own way. Seeing it was no use arguing, Rowan duly untied the blanket and then stepped out of her nightdress.

'And that ribbon,' Ma Steeples urged.

'No. I never take that off,' Rowan cried.

'But, you must. It's the rules,' the woman insisted, grabbing her by the wrist.

As Rowan snatched her hand away, the room started to spin. Blackness closed in around her and she collapsed in a crumpled heap on the stone floor.

Chapter 14

Rowan struggled back to consciousness, to find icy water dripping from her face and Ma Steeples, empty bowl in hand, glaring down at her.

'What happened?' she asked.

'You passed out, that's what happened. You aren't, you know, in trouble, are you?' the woman asked.

'Trouble? What kind of trouble?'

'You know, you haven't been with a feller?'

'No, I have not,' Rowan denied heatedly, as she tried to struggle to her feet.

'Well, you fainted clean away, so what other reason could there be?' Ma Steeples asked.

Rowan began to tremble uncontrollably, whether through shock from the cold water or anger at the accusations being levelled against her, she wasn't sure. Ma Steeples tossed the blanket at her and she wrapped it around herself.

'If you must know, I haven't had a thing to eat since supper time yesterday,' she muttered, sinking onto the nearby chair.

'Why you poor thing,' Ma Steeples said, her accusing look now replaced by one of concern. 'Dolly, get yourself in here, dearie,' she called.

A sparse woman wearing an ill-fitting dark dress appeared in the doorway, steam billowing in her wake. She had red, work-worn hands and seemed unable to stand still, but it was the vacant look in her eyes that made Rowan shudder.

'Go to the kitchen and ask Cook for a mug of broth. If she asks who it's for, you're to say it's for Ma Steeples. Quickly now,' Ma Steeples urged. 'A right Dolly daydream, that one, and no mistake,' she added fondly as the woman disappeared. 'Now let's get you washed and changed or we'll have Miss Sharp on our backs and that's the last thing we want, believe you me. Sharp by name and sharp by tongue, that one. Now you've stopped shaking, give me that filthy old blanket and take off that red band.'

'You can have the blanket but I'm keeping my ribbon on. It was my mother's and she said I was always to wear it,' Rowan explained, her hand covering it protectively.

'And where is your mother, dearie?'

'She's dead,' Rowan whispered, biting her lip to stop the tears flowing. 'It was the last thing she gave me. It signifies the circle of family life, you see.'

'No I don't, never having been blessed with a family myself,' Ma Steeples said, shaking her head and glaring down at her deformed foot. 'Still, if it means that much to you then I suppose you'd better keep it on. But for heaven's sake make sure you keep it hidden under your uniform. That red will stand out like a ray of sunshine against all the drabness in here.'

Even as she spoke, the woman began giving Rowan a thorough wash down. The rag was rough and the liquid she'd put in the water so noxious smelling, the fumes caught at the back of Rowan's throat. Before long, it felt as if her skin was on fire. Just when she thought she couldn't bear it another moment, Ma Steeples moved up to her head, attacking it with the same enthusiasm. 'Beautiful hair, you got. Better keep it tucked up under your cap or old Sharp will chop it off. She'd enjoy doing it, too. That one gets jealous, although they do say she has a fondness for . . .' her voiced faltered. 'Well, anyway, you just watch out, that's all I'm saying.'

After vigorous drying with another rough cloth, Rowan was pronounced to be clean and louse free.

'Now put this on,' Ma Steeples ordered, holding out a dark dress similar to the one Dolly had been wearing. The coarse fabric chafed Rowan's skin and the garment was so huge, it swamped her.

'I can't wear this,' Rowan protested.

Ma Steeples laughed. 'You'll get used to it, dearie, and at least those long sleeves will hide that ribbon you insist on wearing. Anyway, it's the rules. All females have to wear the same. The rough material and simple design are meant to be a constant reminder to you of your shame of being insane. They call this the uniform stigma of lunacy.'

'But I'm not insane,' Rowan protested.

Surprised by her vehement outburst, Ma Steeples stared deeply into her eyes. 'I have to admit your eyes look spirited to me. Now, you'd better put these on,' she said, holding out dark woollen stockings and a pair of sturdy black boots.

'But I don't wear boots,' Rowan protested.

'Well, you do now, dearie,' Ma Steeples said. 'It completes the uniform.'

Seeing there was no point in arguing, Rowan bent and

did as she'd been told. The boots were far too big and when she went to get up, they almost fell off.

'I need smaller ones, Ma Steeples,' Rowan said, promptly sitting down again. As she went to take them off, Ma Steeples shook her head.

'They are the regulation size. Here, pad the toes out with these,' she said, passing Rowan a couple of old cloths. Sighing, Rowan stuffed the rough material into the boots and then eased her feet in. 'It would be better if they had ties,' she muttered.

'Only step-ins allowed; it's the rules.'

'Why?' Rowan asked.

'No laces, ropes or ties of any kind permitted. People have tried to hang themselves, you see. Ah, there you are, Dolly,' she said, as the woman reappeared, clinging to a mug as though her life depended upon it. 'Right, off you go back to the laundry,' she said, watching as the woman disappeared back through the door of the steam room. 'Now, you sit and sup this whilst I clear away,' Ma Steeples said, turning to Rowan and handing her the mug. 'We can't have you fainting in front of Sharp. You'll need all your wits about you as it is.' She gave a shrill laugh as though she'd made some kind of joke.

Rowan sank back onto the chair, wincing as the rough material rubbed against her stinging skin. She sipped the lukewarm broth, grateful for something to eat even if she couldn't determine what was in it. Ma Steeples moved laboriously around the room, carefully tidying everything away. When all was to her satisfaction, she turned to Rowan.

'Finished?' she enquired, wiping her hands on her apron before taking the mug from her. 'Now let's get all this hair hidden,' she said, tucking Rowan's copper curls under a tight-fitting dark cap.

'So where is this place?' Rowan asked. 'I thought that officer man said something about hell.'

'The receiving officer, you mean? This is the Hell Tor Asylum. Hell by name, hell by nature,' Ma Steeples said, sighing.

'And this Hell place is on Dartmoor?' Rowan persisted, desperate to find out exactly where she was.

'Oh, yes, dearie. High, high up on the moor and as far from civilization as you could ever get,' Ma Steeples said, grimacing.

'If it's that bad then why do you work here?' Rowan asked.

Ma Steeples gave a harsh laugh and pointed to her foot. 'This job provides me with board and lodging. Let's be honest, no man's going to want to marry a cripple like me, now, is he?'

Rowan was about to say she thought a man would be lucky to find someone as kind as her when a thin, severe-looking woman in a black tailored dress marched into the room. The ribbon around Rowan's wrist tightened. Although she was becoming used to its signal, there seemed little she could do about it.

'This the new loon, Steeples?' the woman barked.

'Her name's Rowan, Miss Sharp,' Ma Steeples answered mildly. 'And she's all ready for you.'

'Well, it's lucky I'm ready for her, then,' the woman snapped. 'Come on, loon, follow me.'

As she led the way out of the room, Rowan turned to Ma Steeples.

'Just keep your head down and do as you're told,' the woman whispered, handing her another shapeless garment, this time in a dirty beige colour. 'Here's your nightgown. And for goodness' sake keep that ribbon hidden or we'll both cop it.'

Rowan nodded and hurried after Miss Sharp, trying not to stumble in her boots as she tried to keep up with her fast-paced stride.

They climbed up two steep flights of steps, Rowan holding up the ill-fitting skirt of her dress to save herself from tripping on the jagged flags. Finally, the woman came to an abrupt stop and dramatically threw open a door. Inside ten iron bedsteads lined each wall, with a space barely wide enough to walk between them. Clearly this was a dormitory, and there wasn't going to be any privacy, Rowan thought miserably, longing to be back in her cosy little room at the farm.

'You'll sleep over there, loon,' the woman barked, pointing to a bed at the far end of the room. 'Door is locked sharp at seven p.m. Go to sleep straight away, no dallying. Piss pot under bed. You empty your own filthy mess and will take your turn at slops duty. Rising bell is at six a.m. Make sure you have a thorough morning wash because you will be examined. Only if you are found to be clean will you be permitted down to the breakfast hall. After which, rain or shine, you will exercise in the airing court. Our regime hopes that a healthy body will lead to a healthy mind, but . . .' She let her voice tail off, sneering as she looked Rowan up and down. 'Understood, loon?'

Rowan nodded.

'Right, you're too late for tea, so you'd best change into

your nightdress,' the wardress ordered, leaning back against the wall. 'I said get undressed, loon,' she sneered, looking Rowan up and down appraisingly.

'What, now . . .' Rowan began, not liking the gleam in the woman's eye at all.

'Now,' Sharp confirmed with a grin.

Seeing it would be useless to argue, Rowan bent and pulled off her boots.

'Quicker,' the woman ordered, then cursed when she heard her name being called. 'Go straight to bed. The others will be up shortly. Tomorrow we will discuss your duties.'

'Duties?' Rowan asked.

'This is not a charitable institution, loon. You must earn your keep like all the others,' she barked, before turning smartly on her heel and marching from the room. She was like a drill sergeant, Rowan thought, shivering.

Relieved the woman had gone, but fearful she would return before she was in her nightgown, Rowan undressed with indecent haste. Although the gown smelled clean, the material was stiff from laundering. Sinking into the bed she'd been assigned, she winced. It was rock hard and the sheet felt prickly against her scrubbed skin. She shuddered, hating this place already. Whatever had she done to be sent to an asylum?

Closing her eyes, her thoughts drifted back over the past day – or was it days? With a pang, she realized she had no idea how long it had been since she was snatched from the farm. She'd been carrying out her Eostre ritual. First she'd placed her mirror – Her mirror! Her precious mirror had been left on the grass when she'd been dragged away. Tears welled and she covered her mouth with her hand to prevent herself from crying out. The last thing she wanted was that Sharp woman appearing again. She breathed in deeply, trying to calm herself. It was no good, though, her thoughts continued to race.

She knew Fanny was behind this. Rowan remembered hearing her voice when she was abducted, and hadn't she told Rowan she wasn't prepared to share her father? It was obvious she'd thought him richer than he actually was. Surely her father hadn't led Fanny on? He must have missed his daughter by now. Would he be looking for her or would Fanny have fobbed him off with one of her elaborate stories? With sudden clarity Rowan realized that the father she adored was, in fact, a weak man. She'd never seen it before. Her mother, a gentle, contented soul, had never thought to take advantage of his kind nature. The red ribbon gave a tug, gentle this time, and Rowan smiled into the darkness. At least her mother was with her and understood.

As Rowan lay in the darkening room, her head buzzing with unanswered questions, she heard the door opening. There was the crackling of cloth and creaking of beds as the others got ready for the night. She turned towards the woman climbing into the next bed, but her smile was met with a blank stare. Before she could dwell on it, a bell shrilled, the door clanked shut and Rowan shuddered as she heard a key turn in the lock. That Sharp woman hadn't been joking, then. If it wasn't so ludicrous it would be laughable to think she couldn't take herself outside. Even the animals in the shippon weren't locked in.

At first all was quiet in the dormitory, but after a while

one woman started moaning. Then others joined in and, as the moaning turned to wailing, Rowan sank further under her blanket, covering her ears with her hands. She'd never heard such a din. A key turned in the door and there was the flash of a lantern. Footsteps moved around the room, followed by the sound of muffled voices. Gradually, the wailing ceased, but a figure hovered beside Rowan's bed for some moments. Holding her breath, she kept as still as she could, and eventually whoever it was moved away. She heard the door being locked again, and waited for the echoes of footsteps in the corridor to fade away before gingerly emerging from under her cover. The room was quiet now, but a bitter reek hung in the air. She knew she'd smelled something similar recently. But where, when? Then she realized it was the same pungent odour that had been on the cloth her abductor had smothered her with. Obviously they rendered the patients here unconscious with the same potion. Fearful of being drugged or subjected to any other horrors that might take place under the cover of darkness, Rowan hardly dared to close her eyes.

No wonder this place was called Hell, she thought, as the night dragged interminably on. Still trying to make sense out of what had happened, her thoughts turned to Sab. Why had he been avoiding her? And why had he gone to the market without her? They'd always got on well, and she couldn't think of anything she'd done to upset him. Surely he wasn't party to her being snatched? Thinking of her last visit to Sudbury reminded her of old Aggie's warning. What was it she'd said exactly? *Beware she with the forked tongue.* That was it. Aggie was a respected wise woman and her portents were to be heeded so why hadn't Rowan paid more attention? Obviously she'd meant Fanny, but if her stepmother thought she was going to be rid of her that easily she could think again. There was no way she was staying in this hellhole.

The shrill sound of the rising bell pierced the early morning quietude. Rowan turned towards the slit window set high in the wall and, squinting through the iron bars, could glimpse the cold grey of early morning. Climbing out of bed, she watched in horror as the other women staggered about the room like drunkards, automatically pulling off nightclothes and donning uniforms. Remembering Ma Steeples' warning, Rowan carefully tucked all her hair up under her cap and made sure the sleeve of her dress was covering her ribbon, although that wasn't difficult for the sleeves were so long they almost covered her hands entirely. She heard the click as the door was unlocked and looked up to see Sharp standing there, hands on her hips, sneer on her lips.

'Right, you lot, piss pots at the ready,' she ordered. Immediately, the ladies picked up their gazunders and shuffled into a line. 'Get a move on, loon, or you'll get no breakfast,' Sharp barked, and realizing the woman meant her, Rowan hurried to join them.

Outside they were joined by women from the adjacent dormitory, along with their warder. Then they were marched along a narrow, dingy corridor until they came to the sluice room. Rowan held her breath as the stench of human waste hit her nostrils. Hurriedly she emptied her pot and placed it carefully on the stone floor alongside the others.

Then it was on to the washroom, which looked like the troughs on the farm only not as clean. Gritting her teeth, she put her hands into the icy water, and using the rough slab of lye, which was being passed from woman to woman, Rowan scrubbed vigorously. She was determined to be acknowledged as clean, for her stomach was rumbling and she needed her breakfast. Sustenance was vital if she were to keep her wits about her. Sensing she was being watched, she looked up to see Sharp staring at her in a way that made her stomach turn. Quickly she joined one of the two queues waiting to be inspected. Rowan's heart started beating like the clappers on bells as she stood there, for only now did she notice she was in Sharp's line and could see the woman was being less than gentle. The thought of being touched by that dreadful woman made her feel sick, but the warden was making her way down the line and there was no avoiding whatever she had in store.

Chapter 15

Finally, it was Rowan's turn to be examined. Swallowing hard, she stepped on to the inspection step but as Sharp's hands reached out towards her, another warden appeared and whispered something in her ear. Sharp's face tightened with annoyance and, giving Rowan a malevolent look, she hurried away. Her replacement, a milder woman, merely gave Rowan a cursory glance before nodding and passing on to the next woman.

Letting out a sigh of relief, Rowan followed the file of women down the narrow flight of stairs and into the dining hall. There were two long tables the length of the room with a spoon and basin set at each place. She watched as the others automatically seated themselves in line, and took the next available space on the rough wooden bench. Turning to the woman next to her, she gave a tentative smile. Encouraged when she smiled back, Rowan introduced herself.

'Hello, I'm Rowan. What's the food like here?' she asked.

'Good to meet you, Rowan, but it could be under better circumstances,' the woman quipped. 'I'm known as Simple Susan, and the food here is as dreadful as it looks. If Sharp asks you what you want, say the opposite and you might be lucky,' she whispered.

'What would you like to eat today, Simple Susan?' Sharp asked, materializing behind them.

'Porridge,' Susan answered, only to be passed a slice of bread and scrape.

'What about you, loon?' Sharp hissed in Rowan's ear.

'Bread and scrape, please,' she answered, and sure enough a dollop of porridge was ladled into her basin, just as she'd hoped.

'See what I mean?' Susan whispered. 'It's always the same when she's on duty.' Rowan went to answer, but the stodgy porridge was sticking to the roof of her mouth and she couldn't. She tried to swallow but the lump was stuck fast in her throat. Frantically, she stared around for something to drink, but couldn't see any mugs of water on the table. With tears streaming and her breath coming in gasps, she gripped the edge of her seat. As the room spun around her, no one seemed to notice her distress. Heads bent over their basins, the other women just continued eating.

Suddenly Rowan felt a thump between her shoulder blades and the lump of porridge shot out of her mouth, landing on the table in front of her. Relieved she could breathe again, she looked up to see Susan standing behind her, a worried frown creasing her forehead.

'Thought you was going to pass out,' she said. 'Then you'd have copped it.'

Rowan took a couple of deep breaths, the room stopped spinning and she was able to smile her thanks. Then, as the woman went to sit down again, Rowan noticed the way her dress was straining over her swollen abdomen. A surreptitious glance revealed no ring on her finger, and Rowan realized the stories she'd heard about unmarried mothers being locked away must be true.

'Yeah, I'm a wicked wanton,' Susan whispered, seeing Rowan's look. 'But believe you me, I'm paying for it now. Quick, get that cleared up; Sharp's headed this way,' she hissed. Rowan reached out and scooped up the mess, but as she went to put it back in the basin, Susan shook her head. 'Hide it or she'll force you to eat it in front of everyone,' she whispered.

Rowan had only just covered it with her basin when Sharp peered over her shoulder.

'Not hungry, loon?' she taunted. 'Perhaps you need some help?'

'No, I'm managing fine, thank you,' Rowan stuttered, picking up her spoon.

'Hmm, well, when you've finished here, take a turn about the airing courts and then come and see me. I will then tell you which duties I've decided to assign you to,' she smirked, before moving further down the room and shouting, 'Right, you horrible lot, time to clear away.'

As one, the women rose and began collecting up their basins.

'Lift your bowl,' Susan whispered, then deftly scraped the porridge from underneath it. Flipping it into her own basin, she carefully placed Rowan's on top, then added them to the growing pile on the table. 'Come on, we're not on clearing-up duty so let's scarper while Sharp's not looking,' she urged.

Rowan followed her down a flight of stairs and outside, on to what looked like a rough field. It was enclosed by a grey granite stone wall so high she couldn't see over it.

The sky above and the slight breeze were the only indications they were actually out of doors. Although the day was overcast, it was bright compared to the dingy darkness of inside, and she stood there for a few moments blinking like a barn owl in daylight. Then, as if a signal had been given, the women started marching around the field in a clockwise direction, chanting, '*Healthy body, healthy mind*,' over and over again. Seeing Rowan's bemused look, Susan laughed.

'This is exercise time, the best part of the day. Just make sure you say their blooming mantra of healthy body, healthy mind as you go past the guards. In between, we can get to know each other. What have you been put in here for?' she asked, her blue eyes curious.

'Sad mania, I think the receiving officer said it was,' she answered, trying to remember his exact words.

'Blimey, must be catching. It seems to me nearly everyone here's got that. Apart from me, the wanton one, that is.' They were interrupted by a high-pitched scream coming from the other side of the wall. It sounded like an animal in distress and Rowan's eyes widened in horror.

'What was that dreadful noise?' she asked.

'That'll be from the men's airing courts,' Susan said. '*Healthy body, healthy mind*,' she chanted loudly, digging Rowan in the ribs. 'Keep it up till we're past old Pearce over there,' she muttered, jerking her head to the right.

Peering over, Rowan could see another uniformed woman watching them keenly. There would be no chance of escaping, she thought, her heart sinking. The prospect of spending another night in that dreadful dorm locked up with wailing women sent shivers down her spine. Susan jabbed her in the side again, interrupting her reverie.

'Guards watching,' she hissed.

'*Healthy body, healthy mind, healthy body, healthy mind*,' Rowan chanted.

'All clear,' Susan said. 'Now, what was I saying?'

'You were going to tell me what that dreadful scream was,' Rowan reminded her.

'Oh, that.' Susan shrugged. 'I expect it came from one of the really sick men. Probably one of those who've got syphilis. Sends them right out of their minds, literally. Serves them right; the dirty buggers,' she added with feeling.

Not really understanding, Rowan just nodded.

'Course, there's some who'd say I was just as bad. Except I really love Charles and he loves me too.'

'I didn't know there were men here as well,' said Rowan, her mind still on that terrible scream.

'Oh, yes, and there's more of them than us women. The guards keep us segregated. Probably so they can't get their filthy paws on us. Now my Charles, he's a real gent . . .' she broke off.

'*Healthy body, healthy mind*,' they intoned in unison. They had finished yet another turn of the courts and marched past the guards before Susan spoke again.

'I'm sure they think if we say it often enough, we'll believe it,' she said with a grin.

'You were telling me about your Charles,' Rowan prompted.

'Oh, yes, Charles. I was her lady's maid up at Hattersham Hall. Charles said he fell for me the moment he saw me combing out his mother's hair. Of course, he should never have entered her chamber, but that's Charlie for you. Always ignores the rules. He could charm the bees from their hive, that one. He treated me just like a princess,' Susan said, sighing. 'Trouble was, when her ladyship found I was in the family way, she was furious. She gave me a right dressing-down and accused me of leading Charles on. As if Charles needed any encouragement, the devil. Anyway, when Charles had to go away on business, she arranged for me to be sent here. Still, I know when he returns and finds I've gone, he will come for me.'

Privately, Rowan had her doubts. Were all men weak, she wondered, thinking about her father and the conclusion she'd come to the previous night.

'*Healthy body, healthy mind*,' Susan intoned, digging Rowan in the ribs so hard, she stumbled. 'Careful, girl,' she muttered. 'It don't do to draw attention to yourself.'

'It's these boots, they're far too big,' Rowan protested.

'Well you're only a tiny tiddler. How old are you, anyway?' Susan asked.

'Fifteen.'

'Blimey, didn't think they could commit girls that young. What was it you were accused of exactly?'

'Dancing and digging in the moonlight, making lotions and potions, chanting, that sort of thing,' Rowan said, still not understanding what she'd done that was wrong.

'Well, you'd better get chanting now. *Healthy body, healthy mind*,' Susan intoned in a loud voice.

'*Healthy body, healthy mind*,' Rowan muttered, risking a glance at the other women, but they were all staring at the ground as they marched and chanted in unison. Rowan shuddered. It was unnerving to see the effects institution life was having on them.

'Well, if you can perform magic, Rowan, for God's sake do a spell and get both of us out of this place, will you?' Susan laughed, only half joking. 'I'm that fed up. Every bleeding day's the same.' She was interrupted by the strident jangling of the bell. 'Oh, blimey, here we go, time for work. Don't forget, when you go and see Sharp for your duties, say the opposite of where you want to be. Sewing room's the best but I wasn't given any choice. They put me in the bakehouse saying it will prepare me for motherhood. Like they'd let me keep the baby anyway,' she said with a bitter laugh. 'Still, my Charlie will have come for me by then,' she said, brightening.

'Hurry up, over there,' the guard snapped.

'See you back here this afternoon,' Susan whispered, as they promptly joined the line of women filing indoors.

'There you are, loon,' Sharp said, appearing at Rowan's side. 'Follow me,' she ordered, disappearing along the corridor at her usual fast pace. Rowan tried to keep up but the rigid, ill-fitting boots were rubbing and she could already feel blisters forming. 'Keep up, loon. We haven't got all day,' the wardress called.

Rowan was shown into a small, neat office where Sharp promptly took a seat behind the desk and began sorting through a pile of papers. Rowan stood trying not to fidget as the woman showed no sign of hurrying. In fact, she looked so pompous and full of self-importance that Rowan had a sudden vision of her in an ill-fitting dress, marching around the airing courts chanting, '*Need good manners, need good manners'*. It was such a vivid picture, she felt her lips twitch.

'Finding this amusing, are you, loon?' Sharp asked, looking up suddenly.

'No,' Rowan answered quickly.

'Well, a hard day's work will soon wipe that smile off your face. How does a day of cleaning and scrubbing appeal?' she asked, grinning.

'Actually I would find that very satisfying,' Rowan answered, trying to look as if she meant it. 'There's nothing more rewarding than seeing a lovely, clean room, or a pile of sparkling dishes.'

'Well, hard luck, loon,' Sharp smirked. 'I've decided I'm going to assign you to the sewing room.' Rowan hid a smile, silently thanking Susan for her advice. 'In fact, loon, the hem on my other dress is hanging down so you can start with that,' she said, getting to her feet.

Once again, Rowan found herself following after the straight-backed woman. This time, though, after descending the worn steps, instead of turning left, Sharp turned right. As Rowan hurried to keep up, her boots flapping against her feet, a high-pitched squeal rent the air. Her eyes widened in fear. Someone was in real distress. Abruptly, Sharp came to a halt outside a thick wooden door, bolted both top and bottom. Sure she could hear the clanking of chains, Rowan gulped.

'Take a look in there, loon,' she ordered, pulling back a tiny hatch and shoving Rowan up towards it. Inside, she could just make out the deformed body of a man, writhing in agony, his eyes frenzied like someone with a fever. He was howling in distress and desperately trying to pull away from the chains that were holding him fast to the wall. 'Syphilis,' Sharp spat. 'That's what men get for forcing their lustful bodies on poor defenceless women,' she added, with a satisfied smirk. Rowan swallowed hard and automatically backed away. As Sharp snapped the hatch door shut and turned to go back the way they'd just come, a man's voice boomed out of the gloom.

'Stop where you are.'

'Damn,' Sharp muttered. Rowan jumped as a burly guard emerged from the shadows.

'Sharp, what are you doing here? You know the men's quarters are out of bounds for females.'

'I know that, Tewer, but this loon here took herself off and I've only just found her,' Sharp lied glibly.

'Well, get her out of here or we'll all cop it,' Tewer ordered.

'Come on, loon,' Sharp urged, prodding Rowan in the back. 'If I ever catch you down here again you'll have me to answer to,' she said loudly.

Well, of all the cheek, Rowan thought, but instinct told her to keep quiet.

Back upstairs, Sharp nudged Rowan into another room. This one had been painted white, and housed a single bed with a table and chair beside it. In the corner stood a cupboard from which the guard pulled out a similar tailored dress to the one she was already wearing.

'Sit down, loon,' she said, her voice becoming unusually pleasant. Rowan looked at her suspiciously. 'Come on, we can chat while you mend this hem,' Sharp coaxed, sitting down on the bed and picking up her garment. Although the woman was smiling, Rowan noticed she had that strange gleam in her eye she'd seen earlier. The ribbon around her wrist tightened and she swallowed nervously.

'I see you've become friendly with that Simple Susan. Well, you've seen the shameful state she's got herself in, so just you be careful. Anyway, did you have a beau before you came here?' Sharp asked, watching her closely. Rowan shook her head. 'Ever been with a fellow?' the guard persisted, leaning closer. Rowan shook her head again and this time the gleam in Sharp's eye glittered. 'Well, as you've just seen, men are dirty, despicable things and best avoided. They'll butter you up with their sweet talk and then infect . . .' she stuttered to a halt, jumping to her feet as the door burst open.

Pearce stood in the doorway, eyeing Sharp suspiciously.

'What's going on in here?' she demanded, glancing from Sharp to Rowan and back again. 'You know it's strictly against the rules to have a patient in your room.'

'Loon here's just mending my hem,' Sharp mumbled. Pearce looked at the dress still in her hand and then at Rowan cowering in the chair, and clicked her tongue in disgust.

'Come with me,' Pearce said to Rowan gently. Outside in the corridor, she stopped. 'Did she do anything to you?' she asked, looking worried. Rowan shook her head. 'Thank goodness. Well, I take it you've been assigned to sewing duties, so I'll show you where you should be,' she said, emphasizing the word 'should'.

Although Rowan felt shaky and didn't understand what was going on, she had enough sense to keep quiet. This was her opportunity to get placed in the sewing room, which sounded far preferable to doing the cleaning Sharp had first mentioned.

Rowan was taken into a large room, which had higher windows to let in more light though they were still barred outside.

'This is Ma Robbins,' Pearce said, introducing her to a pleasant-looking woman who had a round face and chirpy smile.

'Come to help us, have you, dear? Good, good,' she said, without waiting for an answer. 'You seat yourself next to the others. I've already cut up some worn sheets so you just need to put the middles to the bottoms and away you go,' she said with a grin.

As Rowan sat at the chair that Ma Robbins had indicated, she saw that there were five other women busily sewing. No one looked up from her work, though, as Rowan picked up the material and began sewing. Turning sheets was a task she'd carried out many times before in the farmhouse, and it was a relief to be doing something familiar. She found the repetitive stitching soothing and, for the first time since she'd arrived, felt the tension easing from her body.

Realizing her ribbon had eased its grip, she sighed with relief. Another danger had been averted, but for how long, she wondered. She didn't really understand what had brought about the change in Sharp's demeanour, but the feverish gleam in the woman's eye really worried her. However, she did know a woman like Sharp wasn't the sort to have her plans thwarted.

Chapter 16

'How are you getting on, dear?' asked Ma Robbins, appearing at her side. Rowan stared down at the pieces of sheeting she'd automatically been sewing together. 'My, my, you are a fast worker,' the woman said delightedly.

Rowan blinked, amazed to see that she had indeed all but finished. Then she looked closer at her work and frowned.

'This needle is too blunt for the thin material. Look at all these holes,' she said, holding up her work. To her surprise the woman laughed.

'You're right, of course. However, we're not allowed sharp needles or pins for that matter in here. Good job you're not stitching fine clothes for fine ladies, eh? ' she said, chuckling. 'Still, you are a bright button to notice that. In all the years I've been here, nobody's ever commented on it before.'

Rowan looked around at the other ladies, but they were just gazing blankly at their work as they laboriously stitched in and out.

'How long have you worked here Ma Robbins?' she asked, hoping she didn't appear rude. Although she was usually self-contained, being in the company of these women who seemed to exist in a trance was unnerving, and she had an overwhelming need to converse with someone who seemed normal.

But Ma Robbins just smiled and thought for a few moments. 'Must be nearly eight years now,' she answered.

'But how did you come to be here?' Rowan persisted, unable to believe anyone could stay in this place voluntarily, let alone be cheerful about it.

'Well, my Bert's in charge of growing the vegetables for the kitchens here, and when we got betrothed the woman in charge of the sewing room announced she was leaving to take up another position. It was like it was meant, so I applied for this job and got it. Wasn't I the lucky one?' she chuckled. Then she saw Rowan staring at her incredulously. 'You must remember jobs around here are few and far between, so we are very blessed. Especially as once we married, we were offered a cottage in the grounds. Made it lovely, we have,' she said.

Their conversation was cut short by the high-pitched ringing of a bell.

'Dinner time, ladies. Off you go now and I'll see you later,' Ma Robbins said, chivvying the women along.

Obediently, they got to their feet and filed out of the room. Rowan followed, wondering what would be on offer this time. She was hungry but the memory of that dreadful porridge at breakfast was still fresh in her mind.

As soon as she took her place at the table, a basin of broth and slice of bread and scrape were set before her. Although she was hungry, she couldn't help staring around the room in case Sharp was hovering. However, there was no sign of the guard and she began to relax. The broth was thin but warm and tasty, even if, just as on the previous day, she couldn't make out what was in it. Of course, the strong smell of lye mixed with something noxious, which pervaded every corner of the place, didn't help her appetite. To her disappointment, she couldn't see any sign of Susan either. Rowan had found it comforting to have someone friendly to talk to, and the woman seemed knowledgeable about what went on in here. There was so much she wanted to ask her. As she mopped up the last drops of broth with her bread she remembered Susan saying she'd see her at the airing courts later and her spirits lifted. Her encounter with Sharp earlier might have left her feeling uneasy, but it had also hardened her resolve to get out of this place.

'Well, did you enjoy your dinner then?' asked Ma Robbins as they filed back into the sewing room. The others just smiled inanely and sat down in the same places they had before. Remembering what the woman had said about her husband being in the charge of the garden, Rowan smiled.

'The broth was really tasty. It must have been those vegetables your husband grows, Ma Robbins.'

The woman chuckled. 'Why bless you, girl. The day that kitchen does justice to my Bert's produce will be a miracle. Usually they manage to boil everything to an unmentionable mush. Still, it's nice of you to say such a kind thing. I'll tell my Bert later, and he'll be mighty grateful. Now, we'd better get you more of those sheets to turn. If you carry on working like you did this morning, our stockpile of sewing will be done in no time,' she said, looking pleased.

By the time the bell rang out to signal the finish of the working day, Rowan had finished turning half a dozen sheets. She still felt unhappy that the blunt needle made such big holes in the worn material, but if they couldn't provide her with a finer one, there was little she could do about it.

Following the line of women shuffling out to the airing courts, she breathed in the fresh air, glad to be outside. How she hated being cooped up indoors, especially as that strong, clinical smell seemed to waft through the corridors, seeping into every room.

To her disappointment, Susan was nowhere to be seen. Resignedly, Rowan took her turn about the courts, chanting the '*healthy body, healthy mind*' mantra each time she passed the guards. Without someone to talk to, even this brief respite from the depressing drabness of indoors seemed monotonous and a complete waste of time. She really didn't see how a few minutes' walking and chanting could make these poor women any healthier. Discreetly glancing at the listless women with their vacant eyes, she couldn't help but wonder how long they'd been in this place.

At last the shrill bell rang out, signalling the end of their outside exercise and the women silently filed back indoors. Rowan duly followed, but as she passed Sharp, the guard leaned towards her, smirking.

'Shame your little friend is suffering those terrible pains. Still, that's what you get for letting a man defile your body. Just you remember that, loon,' she hissed.

'What's wrong with Susan?' Rowan asked, but the guard merely shrugged and quickly moved her on.

Each morning Rowan looked out for Susan, both in the dining hall and airing courts, only to be disappointed when she didn't appear. Although she'd made enquiries, nobody could or would tell her what was wrong with her friend. Seeing her evident distress, Ma Robbins promised she'd try to find out where Susan was, and exactly what was wrong. Every morning, though, as Rowan entered the sewing room and looked at the woman hopefully, she just shook her head. As if that wasn't bad enough, Sharp had taken to smirking and taunting Rowan, reaching out and touching her at every opportunity.

Ma Robbins, sensing Rowan was becoming agitated, produced a roll of black cloth and placed it on the table in front of her.

'As you have made such a fine job of helping to catch up with our sheet repairs, I have brought you the pattern to make some replacement uniform dresses for the asylum. These are desperately required, but as you can see, there is no one else in here capable of this type of work.'

'Thank you,' Rowan said, grateful to be spared the monotony of yet more seam sewing. 'Anything to break the tedium of this gloomy place is more than welcome.'

'Well, it's not much, but I thought it might help take your mind off things a little,' said Ma Robbins.

Rowan busied herself with her new task, only being allowed to cut out with scissors under the direct supervision of Ma Robbins. The coarse material chafed her hands and soon even the novelty of this new task wore off, and she began to wonder about how she was to get out of this hellhole.

Endless day followed endless day, each one exactly the same. The monotonous regime was making Rowan depressed and despondent. Realizing she had no way of tracking how long she'd been in the asylum, at the end of each working day she cut a strand of cotton and hid it in her boot. Each night she took it out and tallied them all up. By the time she'd counted fifteen strands she was ready to climb the walls. Fifteen soul-destroying days of practising the same repetitious routine, followed by fifteen nights of cowering under her bed cover until the guard had quietened the wailing women and was satisfied Rowan was asleep. What she wouldn't give to be sleeping in her own bedroom with the comforting whispering of leaves in the trees and the gentle lowing of cattle for company. Sharing a room with these poor demented creatures was almost more than she could bear and if she didn't get to talk to somebody sane soon, she feared she, too, would go mad.

One afternoon, just when Rowan didn't think she could bear the isolation a moment more, she was overjoyed to find Susan waiting for her by the airing courts. She looked pale but Rowan could see by the swell of her belly she hadn't given birth yet. Smiling at each other, they fell into step, chanting the '*healthy body, healthy mind*' mantra.

'I've missed you. Where've you been?' Rowan asked, as soon as they were past the guards.

'Thought me time had come, early like,' Susan grimaced. 'Luckily it was a false alarm 'cos Charlie hasn't turned up yet. He must still be away, and I do want him to be back in time to wet the baby's head,' she said. 'Lying on a blinking bed, counting me blessings and atoning for my sins is mighty boring, I can tell you. Then I had to recite certain passages from the Bible out loud, over and over again. Suppose they thought I'd come to believe in redemption if I read about it often enough. Anyway, how've you been?'

'*Healthy body, healthy mind,*' Rowan chanted as they passed the guard. 'I've been climbing the walls. This place is unbearable without you to talk to, and nobody would tell me how you were,' she said.

'They probably hoped I'd croak it. The guards may think I'm stupid, but I'm tough as old boots,' she said with a grin. 'God, it's nice to be out in the fresh air again. So tell me what's been going on. Did Sharp set you to work straight away?'

'Thanks to your advice, when Sharp told me I was going to be put on cleaning duties, I said there was nothing I'd find more satisfying.'

Susan laughed, quickly turning it into a cough when Pearce looked their way.

'I'd loved to have seen her face. What duties are you on then?'

'I'm in the sewing room.'

'Good for you, girl,' Susan said. 'It's not so bad in there, is it?'

'No, Ma Robbins is very kind but – *Healthy body, healthy mind,*' she chanted, realizing they'd already finished one turn of the airing court.

'But what?' Susan persisted, as soon as they were safely past the guards.

Rowan shuddered. 'Before we went to the sewing room, Sharp took me to see one of those really mad men. He was chained up and screaming like a wild animal,' she whispered, still shocked by what she'd seen. 'It was ghastly, Susan. That poor man . . .'

'What, she took you to the male wards?' Susan gasped. 'But it's against asylum rules for any female to enter that part of the building, and that includes the guards.'

'Well, this male guard suddenly appeared and shouted at Sharp. She had the cheek to blame me, saying I'd run off and that she'd had to come after me.'

Susan shook her head. 'Sharp may be authoritarian, but she's not usually idiotic enough to break the rules. Wonder what she was up to. I suppose she took you on to the sewing room afterwards?'

'No, she took me to her own room.'

'What!' This time Susan did shriek. As one of the guards hurried over to them, she swore. 'That woman's weird, Rowan,' she whispered. 'You must see . . .' but whatever she'd been going to say was lost as the guard seized them both by the arm and marched them inside. Rowan gulped: now what?

They were ushered into a poky, airless office and given a dressing-down. This guard had slitty eyes, a long beak-like nose and the unfortunate habit of sniffing.

'You two have been committed here to atone for your sins and, as such, are expected to submit to conciliatory and gentle management whilst receiving curative treatments,' she stated pompously.

Susan risked turning towards Rowan and slightly raising her eyebrows. Luckily, the guard was in full flood and didn't notice.

'One such prescribed treatment is for regular exercise around the airing courts. During this time it is expected that you will reflect upon the words of your mantra,' she sniffed. 'You were not out there to have a convivial discussion.' She looked sternly from one to the other, sniffed again and, to Rowan's disgust, proceeded to wipe her nose with the back of her hand. Didn't the woman have a kerchief? She grimaced and the guard, noticing, scowled.

'Your mantra, *"healthy body, healthy mind"* was prescribed by an eminent physician,' the guard continued. 'He is of the belief that regular exercise promotes a healthy body and that repetition of these select words will facilitate the mind to cure itself.' There was another pause as she sniffed once again. 'By combining these two principles, Hell Tor Asylum provides the optimum opportunity for you to be cured,' she said, narrowing her eyes so they reminded Rowan of the slits that passed for windows in this place. 'Any questions?' the guard asked, moving so close that Rowan involuntarily took a step backwards.

'Stay still when I'm addressing you,' she hissed, seizing Rowan by the shoulders and pulling her forward again.

'But you asked if I had any questions . . .' Rowan began, but the guard now had her by the throat and was shaking her violently.

'You are not in here to question me, peasant,' she spat.

Suddenly the door was thrown open and Rowan almost toppled to the floor as the guard abruptly let go of her.

'Everything all right in here, Smart?' a harsh voice enquired.

'No,' shouted Rowan. 'It most definitely is not.'

'Having trouble?'

'Nothing I can't handle,' Smart said, smiling superciliously. The other woman nodded and as the door shut behind her, Rowan, whose anger had reached boiling point, turned to Smart.

'You asked if we had any questions and I want to know who we see about getting out of here.'

The guard sniffed, narrowing her eyes so they almost closed. 'The superintendent is the only person authorized to sign release papers,' she eventually said.

'Well I want to see him,' Rowan stated.

'Impossible.'

'Then how do we get our release papers signed?' asked Susan, who'd finally found her tongue.

The guard stared at Susan's swollen belly and gave a sneer. 'You don't. Women like you, who've shown so little respect for their bodies, can never be cured,' she said with another sniff.

'That's rubbish,' Rowan retorted. 'She's only having a baby.'

'Susan is an immoral woman who is having a baby out of wedlock,' the guard said sharply.

'What about me?' Rowan asked. 'I'm not pregnant. I am, however, quite sane and would like to see the superintendent.'

'It is not your place to ask to see him. Besides, it will be another two weeks before he pays his next visit. He is a very busy man,' she said.

Two weeks! Rowan's heart sank at the thought of being locked up in this hell for another two days, let alone weeks. Never was a place so aptly named.

But Sniffer was still speaking. 'As you both have deemed to abuse our curative treatment, all privileges will be withdrawn.'

'What privileges?' cried Susan. 'We don't get any.'

'Well, you won't miss them, then, will you?' sniffed the guard. 'From tomorrow you will both be put on cleaning duties. You shall scrub the dormitories and corridor floors until they are fit to eat from,' she said, sniffing and wiping her nose with her hand once more.

'But Susan can't scrub floors in her condition, especially as she's been ill,' Rowan protested.

'Then she can clean out the sluice room and you can scrub all of them yourself,' the guard snapped, glaring at Rowan. 'Ah, there's the bell,' she said, looking up as the shrill ring sounded around the building.

Thankful their interview was at an end, they turned to go. 'What a shame you will have to miss your tea,' the guard called after them. 'Go directly to your dormitories and get into bed.' They could hear her cruel laughter following them as they made their way up the stairs.

Susan grimaced at Rowan. 'It's bad enough being in this place without witnessing them enjoying our punishment.'

Rowan nodded.

Then Susan sniffed, making Rowan giggle. Linking arms, together they sniffed their way up the stairs and all the way along the corridor until they came to the dormitories.

'Wish we shared the same one,' Rowan said.

'Me, too,' Susan agreed. 'Oh, well, little un, see you in the morning. What a fun time we're in for, eh?' she said, and then gave a big sniff as she made her way into the room.

Chapter 17

Quickly Rowan undressed and, once under her cover, began pondering how she could get to see the superintendent. First, she needed to find out exactly when his visit would take place. She must have fallen into a doze for the next thing she knew, the others were coming into the room. There followed the usual loud rustle of material as they undressed, and then creaking as they climbed into their beds. Finally, when all had gone quiet, Rowan began to plan. But it wasn't long before a high-pitched wail rent the room, and guessing what was coming, she hid her head under her blanket. Sure enough, moments later, the others joined in and before long the room resounded to their howling and keening. Rowan shuddered. She'd never heard anything like it before she came here, even in the shippon at calving.

As the scenario from previous nights was repeated, Rowan lay still. Then, as the dormitory quietened, she made out the shape of a figure hovering beside her bed. This time, though, she stayed for longer and Rowan just knew it was Sharp. Determined not give the woman any reason to think she was awake, she adopted the tactics she'd used when playing hunter and prey with Sab. Forcing her mind to go blank and her body heavy, she slowed her breathing and counted backwards from 100. Finally, when she'd reached twenty, the woman gave a deep sigh and left the room, locking the door behind her. Rowan lay there waiting for the clicking of her footsteps to die away, wondering what on earth she could have done for the woman to single her out in such a way.

By morning, the effect of Rowan's scant diet and missed meals caught up with her. With her stomach growling in protest, she made her way to the dining hall. She was careful to ask for porridge and was duly given a slice of bread and scrape. It was a different guard serving, but evidently that didn't seem to matter. Obviously, it was some kind of game to them, and they all adopted the same contrary tactics. As she ate, she looked around the room but could see no sign of Susan. However, Sharp was smirking in her direction. A shudder shivered down her spine, and she hoped her friend was all right. Perhaps the baby had decided to come in the night.

Sniffer, as Rowan had named her, was waiting for her as she came in from the airing courts.

'This way,' she ordered, leading Rowan to a storeroom. 'Bucket and brushes in there,' she snarled. 'Follow me,' she barked, leading the way to the sluice and filling the bucket with water. Then she added a measure of vile-smelling solution.

Rowan wrinkled her nose and just had time to register that Susan wasn't there when Sniffer started talking again.

'When you've finished scrubbing the first dormitory, make sure you clean the corridor outside. Do a thorough job because I shall be back to inspect your work, and there'll be trouble if I find one speck of dirt,' she said, her eyes narrowing. Then, with a sniff and wipe of her nose, she strode away.

Rolling up her sleeves, Rowan got on her knees and started to scrub. As she cleaned, she thought, and as she thought, she planned. She needed to find out when the superintendent was due but who would tell her? Perhaps Ma Robbins would, but then it didn't look as though Rowan would be reassigned to the sewing room. Ma Steeples had seemed kind, but how did Rowan find her way back to the laundry room? She remembered when she'd arrived she'd been led along a dingy corridor and down a flight of jagged steps, but then everywhere here was a maze of drab corridors and stone steps.

She did hope Susan was all right. Maybe she'd appear this afternoon for their turn about the airing courts. Sighing as her sleeves fell down over her hands, she pushed them back yet again, and went back to her scrubbing. Working methodically from the back of the dormitory to the doorway, she finally reached the corridor. Getting to her feet, she stretched her stiff back and rubbed her sore knees. Her poor hands were red and raw and she grimaced when she felt blisters already forming. But she knew she'd better get started on the corridor before Sniffer came to find her. She looked along the passage and sighed again. There was a seemingly never-ending length still to scrub.

As she worked, the asylum's mantra came unbidden into her head. *'Healthy body, healthy mind,'* indeed. As if chanting that twice a day was going to make any difference to those poor women with their vacant eyes and pathetic way of doing everything they were told. The repetitive daily regime obviously dulled their already diminished senses, rendering them incapable of having thoughts of their own. And then there were the guards. They seemed to revel in their work, delighting in reprimanding the inmates for the slightest misdemeanour. Rowan thought of Sharp and the mantra that had come into her head whilst she was waiting for the woman to tell her where she was to work. '*Need good manners*' definitely applied to her. Imagining the guard marching around the airing courts chanting that she needed good manners brought a smile to Rowan's lips.

Suddenly a shadow loomed over her and, as if thinking about her had conjured her up, Sharp stood there, glaring down at her.

'Enjoying yourself, I see,' she snapped. 'So, you thought fit to disobey me, did you, loon?'

Looking at the hard set of the woman's face, Rowan felt her heart lurch.

'I thought I said you were assigned to the sewing room,' Sharp snapped. Then her gaze settled on Rowan's wrist and her eyes glittered. Swiftly Rowan rolled down her sleeves before jumping to her feet.

'Sniffer – I mean the other guard, told me I was to clean the dormitories and corridors,' she said.

'Who is this "Sniffer" who dared overrule me?' Sharp asked.

'I don't know her name. She's the guard who sniffs a lot,' Rowan explained, pleased to have diverted the woman.

'I know who you mean, and shall make sure she's reprimanded severely. It pays to remember I am the senior guard here,' Sharp said, drawing herself up to her full height. 'Now, what was that red I saw on your wrist?'

Rowan forced a laugh and held out her work roughened hands. 'Probably blisters. Look, I'm all red and sore after scrubbing the floors with that vile solution,' she said.

Sharp reached out and grabbed hold of Rowan's hands, the gleam in her eyes intensifying. Rowan cringed as the woman ran her thumb along the back of her hand. Then they heard footsteps and saw Pearce hurrying towards them. Abruptly Sharp let Rowan's hands drop. Standing before them, the guard glanced from one to the other, her lips tightening as she took in the situation.

'This will be reported, Sharp,' she said, her voice quiet but firm.

'You've just got your eyes on my job,' Sharp spat.

Pearce turned to Rowan. 'Come on, I'll escort you to the sewing room.'

'But what about the cleaning things?' Rowan said, pointing to where they lay on the floor.

'Oh, Sharp will see to that, if she knows what's good for her,' Pearce said, smiling and giving the bucket a hefty kick. As the filthy water pooled around Sharp's feet, the guard's eyes widened as though she couldn't believe what had happened. She squared her shoulders ready for a fight, but Pearce calmly took Rowan by the arm and led her away.

They'd only gone a short way down the corridor when they saw Sniffer coming towards them. The two guards nodded to each other, but Sniffer carried on walking. Then a commotion behind them caused them to turn. Sharp was shouting at Sniffer as she pointed to the water and then in Rowan's direction. But then Sniffer said something and Sharp's demeanour changed. Gesticulating to the bucket on the floor, she left the other guard mopping up the water and hurried towards them. Seeing the determined look on Sharp's face, Rowan shrank back against the wall. To her surprise, though, the guard ignored her.

'Why didn't you tell me the superintendent was here?' she demanded, glaring at Pearce.

'Didn't know he was,' she answered mildly.

'Take that loon to the sewing room immediately,' Sharp ordered, pointing at Rowan, then disappearing down the corridor at an alarming rate.

'The superintendent's here?' Rowan asked.

'Yes, but that's nothing for you to worry about,' Pearce said, misunderstanding her interest.

'But I need to see him,' Rowan insisted.

'I'm afraid that's highly irregular. He doesn't see patients without an appointment. In fact, he doesn't see them at all, but that's probably because they're usually asleep by the time he gets here. We tend to be on the end of his visiting roster,' she explained. 'Anyway, I shouldn't be standing here discussing asylum business with you,' she added, turning towards the sewing room.

But Rowan had spotted a gentleman sporting a top hat and dark frock coat striding in their direction. By his side, looking all self-important and puffed up like a peacock, was Sharp. She was so busy smiling up at the man that she failed to see them until they drew alongside. Then anger flashed in her eyes, but she made a supreme effort to control herself.

'Pearce, shouldn't dear Rowan here be in the sewing room?'

Pearce spluttered in surprise, but Sharp ignored her. Turning to the superintendent, she shrugged. 'I do try to ensure the asylum's recommendation for conciliatory and gentle management is adhered to, but as you can see, it's not easy,' she sighed. 'Now, Pearce, the superintendent has to continue with his inspection, so I will leave you to take care of Rowan,' she said, her soft voice belying the flinty look in her eyes.

In that moment, Rowan was reminded of Fanny, and all her pent-up anger and humiliation surged to the surface.

'Mr Superintendent, sir, I must speak with you,' she implored. Surprised at being addressed by a patient, the man turned to face her and Rowan saw that although he looked weary, his eyes were kind.

'The superintendent is a very busy man, Rowan, so please go back to your duties,' Sharp ordered.

'But I must speak to you, sir,' Rowan insisted. 'I have been put in here under false pretences and . . .'

'I'm sure the receiving officer would have checked your admission papers thoroughly, young lady. We pride our-selves on running a non-discriminatory asylum here,' he said dismissively, and turned to go.

Panic flared in Rowan's breast. This might be the only opportunity she had to speak with the man.

'If by non-discriminatory you mean even-handed, then wouldn't it be fair to listen to what I have to say?' she insisted.

'Really, this is preposterous,' Sharp interrupted. 'Get

her out of here immediately,' she barked at Pearce, all pretence of civility now gone. Pearce went to take Rowan by the arm, but determination gave the girl the strength to shrug the guard off as the superintendent moved away.

'I can only say, sir, that if you are not prepared to hear what I have to say then you are not the fair man you think you are. Despite your grand words, you obviously don't care that your staff are violent and abuse us,' Rowan screamed after him.

At this, he stopped and walked back towards her.

'Pearce . . .' Sharp called but the rest of her words were drowned by the ringing of the dinner bell.

As women emerged from the workrooms, their blank stares focused on the floor before them, Rowan pointed to her face. 'Sir, look in my eyes,' she pleaded. 'Do they look demented like the poor souls locked in the dungeons, or vacant like those of these poor drugged women?'

'Dungeons? Drugged?' the superintendent barked, staring hard at Rowan.

Relief flooded through her. At last she'd caught his attention.

'Come with me,' he ordered.

As he strode along the corridor Sharp hovered by his side, protesting that Rowan was a habitual liar who suffered delusions. Knowing this might be her only chance to get out of this hellhole, Rowan rehearsed in her mind what she wanted to say.

She recognized the office she was shown into as the one that the receiving officer had used, although he wasn't there. This time she was invited to take a seat. Sharp stood right by her side, bristling with barely concealed anger.

'Now, Rowan, isn't it?' the superintendent asked, taking off his hat and staring at her in a kindly manner across the leather-topped desk. 'Perhaps you'd like to tell me just what it is that I'm not being fair about.' His blue eyes sparked as he sat back in his chair.

'Well, sir, you didn't seem keen to speak with me when I asked for an interview,' she said, deciding to be truthful.

'You are not here to question the superintendent,' Sharp interrupted.

The man leaned forward in his chair. 'I think it would be better if you were to leave us, Sharp,' he said firmly.

'But what about proprietary . . . ?' she protested.

'Thank you for the reminder, Sharp. Perhaps you would send Pearce in. You have no objection to this?' he asked Rowan, his eyes twinkling.

Rowan smiled. 'No, sir, of course not,' she answered.

With a barely suppressed expletive, Sharp stomped out of the room.

'She's right, of course, I shouldn't interview you alone, but I sense there's something going on here that I'm only going to get to the bottom of without Sharp present. Am I right?'

Surprised by his perception, Rowan nodded.

There was a rap on the door.

'Enter,' he called.

'You wanted me, sir?'

'Indeed, Pearce. Please will you bring me the admission papers for Rowan, erm, what is your surname?' he asked, turning to Rowan.

'Clode, sir. I'm Rowan Clode.'

'Right, Pearce, I wish to see the papers for Rowan Clode.'

'Sir,' Pearce said, and promptly left the room.

'Now, whilst we wait I'd like you to explain what you meant about the women in here being drugged. I have to say your statement has come as a great surprise, for I have always found Hell Tor Asylum to be one of the most orderly, well-run establishments that I visit,' he said, his expression becoming serious.

'But I understand you usually visit at night, sir,' Rowan said.

'That is true. Hell Tor is the last on my round, and it is usually evening by the time I arrive, especially if the horses have had to negotiate the peat bogs in the mist,' he said, frowning.

'Well, that explains it,' Rowan said. 'You see, each night since I've been here the women start wailing and moaning after the dormitories are locked, and the guards come in and shut them up.'

'And how do they do that?'

'They drug them. When the room goes quiet again and the guards leave, there's always the same bitter smell lingering.'

There was silence for a few moments as the superintendent sat staring at her.

'That is a serious accusation to make,' he said eventually.

'Well, sir, I can assure you I never tell lies, and as you saw earlier, the women plod around with vacant-looking eyes. They're so meek and biddable all the time. They follow like sheep, just doing as they're told without question.'

There was a knock at the door and Pearce reappeared carrying a file.

'Thank you, Pearce,' he said, taking the file. 'On what duties has Rowan been employed?'

'She's been working in the sewing room with Mrs Robbins,' Pearce replied.

'Please send Sharp to bring Mrs Robbins to me immediately. Tell her she is to stay and oversee the sewing room until Mrs Robbins returns.'

'Yes, sir,' Pearce answered, before hurrying off to find Sharp.

'Well, Rowan, let me look at your details,' the superintendent said, opening the file and studying the papers inside. As Rowan waited, she listened to the crackling of the logs on the fire, thinking how different it was in this office compared to the rest of the building. How lovely it was to smell wood ash instead of the all-pervading lye and whatever noxious substance they mixed with it.

'Right, Rowan,' the superintendent said, breaking into her thoughts. 'It says here that you are deemed to be a wise woman,' and he frowned as he looked up from the papers.

Chapter 18

Rowan couldn't help it, she burst out laughing.

'You find that accusation funny?' he asked, his frown deepening.

'I'm sorry, sir, but a wise woman is an old lady and, as you can see, I am a young girl,' she pointed out.

He scrutinized her, recognition dawning. 'How young? I mean, just how old are you, Rowan?'

'Fifteen, sir.'

He gave a sharp intake of breath and shook his head. 'It states on your admission papers here that you are twenty years old. It is obvious that you are much younger. However, you have been accused of being a lunatic. What say you to that?'

'I say I'm as sane as you are, sir.'

'Hmm. Well, this accusation was made after you were seen chanting and planting by moonlight. Can you tell me these are the actions of a sane person?' he asked, frowning so that his bushy eyebrows met in the middle.

'Mr Superintendent, sir, my family carry out the custom of lunar farming. By using the phases of the moon, we plant and sow when the water table is at its most conducive.'

'I see, and you mean lunar as in the moon?' he asked.

Rowan nodded.

The superintendent looked down at his file again. 'And your family has cows?'

She nodded again, wondering what on earth that had to do with anything.

'And would you profess to like these animals?'

'Of course I do, sir.'

'Well, then, why would you hit every cow with a stick?' he asked, shaking his head.

'Ah, that would be the springtime switching, sir. You see, it is the custom to pat each cow lightly on the back with a rowan twig as it is being let out to pasture for the first time. It bestows a blessing to protect them, and encourages them to give a good yield of milk.'

'Well, not being of farming stock myself I'll have to take your word on that,' he said, glancing down at his papers again. 'But what about the chanting and dancing you have also been accused of?'

'These are the worshipping rituals handed down to me by my mother. She believed in seeking help for a good harvest and then giving thanks for receiving one. It's quite a normal custom in the country. Uncle Silas and Auntie Sal do it, too,' she said.

'And your mother, she still carries out these rituals?'

'My mother is dead, sir,' Rowan whispered, 'so the duty falls to me.'

'You have my deepest sympathy. I would be lost without my mother, although she does fuss sometimes,' he said, giving her a conspiratorial grin, then coughing quickly, as though realizing he'd said too much. 'So, if your mother is dead, who is this Fanny Clode?' he asked, consulting his papers.

'My stepmother, sir. She married my father earlier this year.'

'And you get on well with her?'

'I've tried to, sir, honestly, I have. But she doesn't like me. She told me there wasn't room for both of us and that my father would choose her over me because a man has needs she can . . .' Her voice trailed off and she felt a blush creep up her cheeks.

'I think I get the picture,' he said, coughing again. 'Now, Rowan, think about my next question and promise to answer me honestly, for your future could depend upon what you say. Were you examined recently by an apothecary called Dr Mad and a man of the cloth called Reverend Sin?'

Once again, Rowan burst out laughing.

'I really fail to see what you find so funny,' the superintendent said, puckering his bushy brows.

'Sorry, sir, it was the names that made me laugh.'

The superintendent glanced back down at his papers and a smile twitched his lips. 'Yes, I see,' he said. Then he resumed his former serious manner. 'Now, I repeat, were you examined by either of these men?' he asked.

'No, sir, I was not. I've never even seen these people. One minute I was carrying out my Eostre ritual to celebrate the spring equinox and the next I had a sack thrown over my head and was being dumped onto a cart.'

'What!' The superintendent's bushy eyebrows rose so high they nearly disappeared into his hair.

'Then I had this vile cloth pressed over my face and I passed out. That's how I recognized the same bitter smell in the dormitory.'

The superintendent closed his eyes and shook his head.

There was silence for a few moments, which was broken by a brisk knock on the door.

'Enter,' the superintendent called. Pearce ushered Ma Robbins into the room. 'Thank you, Pearce. Can you please take Rowan and wait outside for a few moments?' he said, at the same time motioning for Ma Robbins to sit down.

After what seemed an age, Ma Robbins reappeared from the office, and said that Rowan and Pearce were to go back in.

'Pearce, I believe that was the dinner bell we heard earlier,' said the superintendent, to which she nodded. 'Perhaps you could arrange for some food to be brought in for the three of us?' he continued.

The guard looked surprised, but nodded and duly disappeared.

Whilst she was away, the superintendent paced back and forth in front of the window, obviously in deep concentration; Rowan thought it best not to say anything.

A few minutes later, Pearce reappeared carrying a tray.

'I've brought mugs of broth and bread and butter, sir. I hope that's all right?' she asked.

'Thank you, Pearce. Please set the tray down on the table by the window. I think we would all benefit from some sustenance, so let's enjoy a late dinner. Come along, ladies,' he said.

To Rowan's surprise, the superintendent walked over to the round table, where he carefully set the plate of bread, glistening with thickly spread golden butter, in the middle.

Then, motioning them to be seated, he proceeded to pass around the steaming mugs.

The broth was thick and delicious, bearing little resemblance to the thin tasteless liquid Rowan had become used to. If Pearce was surprised at the turn of events, she was too polite to show it, but Rowan couldn't help but notice she ate with relish. They finished their meal in silence, the superintendent still staring out of the window as if he was thinking hard. Rowan noticed the window in this room was even larger than the one in the sewing room, and for the first time since she'd arrived she had a view out over the moors. They seemed endless and, strangely, were dotted here and there with huge grey stones. The sun was tingeing the landscape with golden rays, and Rowan felt a yearning to be outside in the glorious fresh air again.

As if he'd reached a decision, the superintendent sprang to his feet. Leaning towards Pearce, he whispered, 'I asked Mrs Robbins to send Sharp back. Is she still outside the door?'

'She was when I brought the tray in, sir.'

He nodded and glanced at Rowan. 'I am about to pronounce my findings on you, Rowan Clode,' he announced in such a loud voice that Rowan jumped in surprise. Supposing he didn't believe her and she was incarcerated here for the rest of her days?

Then he walked over to the door and threw it open so suddenly Sharp toppled into the room, landing on the floor in front of him in a most undignified manner.

'How nice of you to drop in, Sharp. No doubt you have been keeping your ear to the keyhole, so to speak?'

Flustered, the woman got to her feet. 'I pride myself on keeping abreast of things here, sir,' she stated pompously.

'And, no doubt, are waiting to hear my decision about Rowan and whether she should continue to be detained?' the superintendent said, in such a stentorian voice that Rowan realized he was not a person to cross. Oh, dear heavens, she thought, please don't say he's going to put me back in the care of that creepy Sharp. I couldn't bear it.

'Well, Superintendent, I know how you believe in justice, what with you being such a fair man,' Sharp simpered, having now completely regained her composure. 'And of course, as the senior guard here, I can be relied upon to help in any way I can,' she said, smiling up at him expectantly.

'I'm not sure when you elevated yourself to such a position, Sharp, but as it happens there is something I wish you to do.'

'Yes, sir, anything; you know that,' she said, throwing back her shoulders importantly and giving Pearce a superior look.

'In that case, please clear these lunch things away,' he said. Sharp stood there gaping at him like a fish out of water. 'Straight away, if you please,' the superintendent added. Rowan noticed his lips were twitching at the corners. Why, he was enjoying Sharp's discomfort, she thought.

With ill-concealed anger, the guard strode towards the table. 'You heard what the superintendent said, Pearce. He would like the table cleared,' she ordered, glaring at the other woman.

'I believe I asked you to do that, Sharp. Now do get on with it,' he ordered, giving the guard a look that forbade refusal.

Knowing she was beaten, Sharp began gathering up the remains of their dinner things with much clattering and muttering under her breath.

'Pearce, a word if I may?' the superintendent said, nodding towards the corridor. After they'd left the room, Rowan continued staring out of the window. She couldn't believe how the far the moors stretched away below. The mixture of lush greensward, golden gorse and mauve heather, bordered by dry-stone walling, all shimmered in the rays of the bright spring sunshine. She sighed deeply, longing to be outside, breathing in the fresh air. Then Sharp came and stood beside her and the ribbon around her wrist tightened.

'See those dark shapes over there?' she asked, pointing to a row of dark standing stones that rose like sentinels in the distance far below them. 'They were once women patients from the asylum? They tried to escape from here, but the devil chased after them and turned them into stone. So there they stay, in Hell for all eternity, as will you should you ever try and leave this place, loon,' she hissed. 'Can you imagine being out there in the dead of night, not knowing if it's wind you can hear howling or the giant wolves that inhabit the moor on the prowl for their dinner? Besides, it's not as if your family even want you back.' Then, giving a harsh laugh, she picked up the tray and left the room.

Rowan stared down at the stones again and shivered.

Surely her father and Sab would want to see her again even if Fanny didn't?

Before she had time to ponder further, the superintendent strode back into the room. Taking his seat behind the desk, he beckoned to Rowan.

'There are still a few more questions I need to ask, so please be seated.'

With a final look at the stones that now resembled a row of women, Rowan did as she'd been asked.

'Earlier today, I believe you said you had actually seen a madman locked up in his room. Did you take yourself down to the men's accommodation?' the superintendent asked, eyeing her closely.

'Of course I didn't. I had no idea where we were going when Sharp led me down there. It was a dreadful sight,' she said, shuddering at the memory. 'That poor man, he looked like a haunted animal. Sharp said he had syphilis. It must be a terrible disease.'

'It is one of the worst. But let me get this clear. You say Sharp took you to the male part of the asylum?' he asked. She nodded. 'That is strictly against regulations. You have clearly been subjected to a sight you shouldn't have, and on behalf of Hell Tor Asylum, I can only apologize. However, I shall be carrying out a full investigation into that and the other matters you have raised,' he said.

'Am I in trouble, sir?' Rowan asked, seeing the grave look on his face.

He sighed. 'No, you aren't, Rowan, but as regulations have been breached, someone else might well be,' he said, opening a folder of blank paper, picking up a quill and dipping it into the inkwell. He then proceeded to write at great length, the words flowing quickly.

Rowan tried not to fidget, but she was dying to ask what was going to happen to her. Only good manners prevented her from interrupting him. Finally, he put down his pen, carefully blotted the paper and then snapped the folder shut. His chair creaked as he settled back into it and steepled his fingers.

'The question is, Rowan, what are we going to do with you?' he asked so seriously that her stomach churned.

'But now that I've explained everything, surely you can release me and I can go home?' she asked.

He shook his head and her heart sank. Before she could ask why not, there was a rap on the door.

'Enter,' the superintendent called, and then looked surprised as Sharp marched into the room, a triumphant gleam in her eye.

'Excuse me, sir, but the receiving officer has arrived and wishes to see you straight away. I feel I should mention that he was not happy to find his office being used, and then when he heard about . . .' She jerked her head in Rowan's direction.

'Thank you, Sharp,' the superintendent cut in. 'Send him in to see me.'

'Shall I take her back to her room?' Sharp asked, nodding at Rowan.

He shook his head. 'Send Pearce in, too, please, and then return to your duties. If you are as busy as you always profess to be, then you must be behind today.' The woman's lips tightened as she strode from the room.

'Ah, Pearce,' he said as the guard poked her head around the door. 'Take Rowan to the sewing room, please.'

'Sir,' she said, taking Rowan by the arm.

'But what about . . .' Rowan began.

'Please do as I say,' the superintendent said, his attention diverted as the receiving officer arrived. His face was like thunder and Rowan realized it would be futile to protest further.

As she walked down the corridor with Pearce, angry voices followed in their wake. In the sewing room, she could hardly concentrate on her work as her mind went back over the conversation with the superintendent. There was no getting away from the fact that when she'd asked if she could go home he'd shaken his head. She couldn't bear to spend another night in this place, she really couldn't.

It could have been minutes or hours before Pearce returned to say the superintendent wished to see her. Well, she wasn't proud, she'd beg on her knees if necessary for her release.

'Superintendent, sir,' she cried as soon as she was shown back into the office, where he was now alone. 'I beg you, please let me go home.'

'It's not as easy as that, I'm afraid. If a patient does leave here, it's on the understanding they are returned to their family, who will help them be accepted back into the community. From what you have told me, I can't see your stepmother being amenable to having you back. And I'm sure under the circumstances you wouldn't wish to return either.'

Rowan frowned. Of course she would go back to

Orchard Farm. That was her home, where she'd been born. She could feel the tears welling as she thought of her father and Sab. Then, remembering Fanny declaring she was lady of the farm and there wasn't room for both of them, her tears turned to anger. How could one scheming woman ruin so many lives? With a sinking heart she knew the superintendent was right. Besides, her father hadn't come looking for her, had he?

'No, but I'm not staying here,' she burst out. 'Don't worry, Superintendent, sir, I am quite capable of looking after myself,' she declared stoutly.

The superintendent's lips twitched. 'I'm sure you are, Rowan, and Mrs Robbins has said you are industrious and a good seamstress, but I would be failing in my duty if I were to let you just walk away. Oh, don't worry,' he assured her, as she jumped to her feet. 'You will not be staying here. It wouldn't be safe. No, you are coming with me,' he said, picking up the file.

Before she could ask where, Pearce reappeared.

'Sir, Ma Steeples said Rowan's nightdress was in such a state she had to burn it. But she has sent this for her to wear on the journey,' she said, smiling at Rowan as she handed her a thick, woollen shawl.

Journey? What journey? Where was she being taken?

'Thank you, Pearce. I've placed the receiving officer in charge in my absence and will be back first thing tomorrow. Please see that he gets this file straight away, and you are clear as to what else I want you to do whilst I am away?'

The guard nodded.

'Right, put that wrap around your shoulders, Rowan,

and we'll be on our way,' he said, donning his hat and snatching up his cane.

She hurried after him, trying to keep up with his marching stride in her loose-fitting boots. As they approached the thick, wooden front door, it was opened by yet another guard, who saluted respectfully and showed them to a waiting carriage.

Before she knew it, Rowan found herself being helped inside. As she settled back on the plush leather squabs, relief flooded through her. She was leaving this ghastly place at last. But where was she being taken? The superintendent climbed in beside her, called to the driver, and the coach gave a lurch as it pulled away. A couple of minutes later, the driver called to the horses to slow as they approached the guard house, but the gates were opened and they were waved straight through.

'Well, Rowan, how does it feel to be free?' asked the superintendent, turning towards her.

'I am so relieved, I can't tell you,' she said, beaming with delight. Then her relief turned to sadness as she remembered she wasn't returning home. So where was she going? She was about to ask but he was shaking out a copy of the *Exeter Flying Post* and before she could say anything, he'd begun to read.

She stared out of the window at the passing country-side. How different everything looked without mist shrouding it. Inquisitive ponies, still with their long, shaggy winter coats, looked up from cropping the sparse grass as they passed. Rowan didn't think she'd ever seen so many. As the carriage rattled its way further down the moors, passing a profusion of ferns, heathers and multicoloured lichens, she couldn't help thinking what wonderful dyes they would make. A vision of Fanny's bright dresses flitted into her mind. One day, she would wear finer, more tasteful dresses than that, she vowed. Then the landscape changed, and they were passing dark peat bogs with spiky clumps of bright green reeds rising out of their midst. As a line of heavy cloud scudded overhead, she shivered, especially when the carriage swerved and she saw they were nearing the row of dark standing stones she'd seen from the asylum.

'Oh, no,' she gasped, her teeth chattering despite the warmth of the afternoon sun penetrating the window. 'Sharp was right after all,' she cried, pulling her shawl tighter around her.

Chapter 19

'Whatever is the matter, Rowan?' the superintendent asked, looking up from his newspaper and frowning. 'Who was right?'

'Oh, please, Mr Superintendent, sir, don't leave me here for the devil to turn me into one of those big stones,' she cried, cowering down in her seat.

'What?' he asked staring out of the window. 'Don't tell me you believe that old superstition?' The carriage rocked at his sudden mirth. Then, seeing her wide-eyed look, he shook his head. 'Did Sharp tell you that ridiculous story?' Rowan nodded, and the superintendent shook his head again. 'She really has frightened you, hasn't she,' he said, gently.

Rowan nodded again. 'She said the devil turned any woman who escaped from the asylum into one of those stones, and that wolves would prowl and eat . . .' She came to a halt as his booming laughter once again resounded around the carriage.

'Oh my, oh my,' he roared. 'Now, Rowan, do think logically. If you were turned to stone – and I say if – the wolves wouldn't be in the least bit interested in you. As far as I'm aware they don't have a penchant for granite.'

Rowan bowed her head. How stupid of her. Clearly her time in the asylum had addled her brain.

'Besides, you haven't escaped; I released you.'

Happiness surging through her, she sat up in her seat again.

'May I ask where you are taking me?' she asked eagerly.

'Indeed you may. I am taking you to my house.'

'What!' she exclaimed, her eyes widening in disbelief. And she'd thought he was a respectable man.

'Don't look so alarmed. I promise you I am an honourable man,' he said, echoing her thoughts. 'You are right to be wary. However, when I say my house, I really mean the family home. My mother is an agreeable woman and never happier than when she is involved in charitable works.'

'I can assure you, Mr Superintendent, sir, that I am not a charity case. I can earn my living as good as the next person. In fact, I would prefer to,' she declared indignantly.

'I'm sorry, Rowan. In no way did I mean to imply you were a charity case. My choice of words was clumsy. I meant that my mother will be happy to have a bright young woman like you for company. My father's business interests take him away for weeks at a time and my sister, a mantua maker and milliner in Saltmouth, is very busy, so poor Mother doesn't see as much of any of us as she would like. Now, as we are away from the asylum, I think it would be better if you addressed me as Mr Acland. Mr Superintendent, sir, is such a mouthful and much too formal, don't you think?' he asked, with a twinkle in his eye.

'Yes, Mr Acland,' she said, the words sounding strange on her tongue.

'There, that wasn't so hard, was it?' he said, his blue eyes sparkling. 'You will at least be comfortable whilst we seek a suitable position for you. Meanwhile I shall make enquiries about how you came to be admitted to the asylum. There appear to have been irregularities, which I intend to get to the bottom of,' he said, settling back in his seat.

Rowan looked out of the window and sighed. Obviously, neither her father nor Sab had come looking for her.

'Is something wrong, Rowan?' the superintendent asked.

'I had hoped my father would have come for me,' she answered.

'Even if he had wanted to find you, Hell Tor is situated on the most remote part of the moors, Rowan. It is highly unlikely he would think to look there, isn't it?'

'But Fanny would have known where I was being taken,' she protested.

'Ah, but we've already established she was the one who arranged for you to be admitted to the asylum so . . .' He shrugged. 'Still, don't worry, I promise you will be looked after from now on,' he said, giving her a smile. 'And maybe in time, when the dust has settled, you can pay your father a visit. Now, why don't you settle back and enjoy the scenery? The moors are a glorious riot of colour in the spring and, as we are well into April, who knows, we might even be lucky enough to hear the cuckoo.' Rowan looked out of the window and saw they'd left the black forbidding bogs behind; the dark clouds had given way to sunshine and once again they were passing through open moorland. She guessed her father wouldn't have even tried to look for her, any more than Susan's Charlie was likely to go after her. Susan! She did hope her friend was all right.

'Super . . . , I mean, Mr Acland?'

'Yes, Rowan,' the superintendent said, peering over his newspaper.

'Do you know how Simple Susan is?'

'Simple Susan? What kind of a name is that?'

'Well, she's not simple, of course, but that's the name she had in the asylum. We were all given them. Sharp called me "loon".' Rowan saw a flicker of annoyance flash across his face and a tic twitch in his right cheek. 'That's not the important thing, though,' she said quickly, not wishing to upset him. 'Susan was kind to me and was the only friend I made in there. The guards were horrible to her because she's carrying a baby but doesn't have a husband. She was poorly recently and had a false alarm. As I didn't see her before I left, I would like to know she's all right,' she explained.

'I see,' he said. 'When I return there tomorrow, I will ascertain how she is,' he promised.

'Thank you, Mr Acland,' she said, stifling a yawn as the events of the day caught up with her.

'Why don't you lie back and close your eyes?' he asked, disappearing behind the pages of his paper again.

As exhaustion settled over her like a heavy blanket, Rowan did as he suggested . . .

She could hear voices; see a light flickering above her, someone was shaking her.

'Don't touch me,' she screamed, sitting bolt upright.

'Hush now,' she heard a male voice say. Snapping her eyes open, she saw she wasn't in her bed in the dormitory. Disorientated, she looked up to find herself staring into the superintendent's worried face, a lantern swinging from his hand.

'Sorry, I thought I was back in the asylum and Sharp . . .' she muttered groggily.

'You are safe now, Rowan,' he soothed. Although his voice was soft and reassuring, Rowan could see he was frowning. 'Come along, let's go inside and I'll introduce you to Mother.' He helped her down from the carriage.

'Put the horses in the stable, Jenson, but have them ready first thing tomorrow,' he called to the driver.

Rowan became aware of her surroundings. They were standing in front of a large square, red-brick house with bay windows. Shiny green ivy trailed the walls, and the evening air was fragranced with the sweet smell of honeysuckle and lavender. As she felt her spirits rise, the gravel carriage sweep was suddenly bathed in a soft glow. A stylish woman dressed in a pale blue dress, soft tendrils of white hair escaping her bun, was standing in the open doorway.

'Alexander, what a wonderful surprise. I wasn't expecting to see you again so soon.'

As the superintendent bent to kiss the woman's cheek, Rowan smiled. So his name was Alexander. It quite suited the distinguished man, who, judging from the age of his mother, must be around forty, much younger than she'd originally thought.

'And you have brought someone to see me,' the woman said, stepping back from her son's embrace.

'Mother, I'd like you to meet Rowan. She has suffered a wretched experience at the asylum and I've brought her home for some of your loving, tender care.' The woman turned towards Rowan, taking in her ill-fitting clothes and uneasy countenance.

'Welcome, Rowan. It is nice to meet you,' she said, with a warm smile. If she was surprised at her son showing up with a former asylum patient in tow, she was too polite to show it. 'Now come inside, both of you, before we all catch a night chill.' She turned and led the way along the grand hallway, with its floor of highly polished black and white tiles, and myriad candles flickering from their golden sconces on the walls.

Rowan followed her into an elegant, high-ceilinged room, her eyes widening in amazement. She'd never been inside anywhere so grand. The walls were lined with what seemed to her like burgundy velvet, and hung with gilt-framed pictures of wild flowers. Imagine having walls big enough to hang ornamental pieces, she thought, remembering the basic dresser and bacon settle back at the farm. She felt a pang as she thought of her home but Mrs Acland was bidding her to take a seat beside the blazing log fire. Startled, she glanced from the plush upholstery to her dirty black dress and shook her head.

'I think I'd better have a wash first,' she said, fearful of marking the fine tapestry cushions.

'We don't stand on ceremony here at Haldon House. However, I'm sure you would like to freshen up after your journey. Travelling makes one so dusty, I always find,' Mrs Acland said, turning and tugging on the tapestry bell pull by her side. Almost immediately a young girl of about eleven appeared.

'Yous rang, ma'am?' she asked, bobbing a quick curtsy.

'Yes, Daisy, I did, although I don't know how many times I have to tell you that you don't need to curtsy. Rowan here is going to be our guest for a few days. I'd like you to show her up to the Lilac Room and see that she has hot water for washing. Then you can light the fire, turn down the bed and lay out a fresh nightdress. When you've done that, go and see Cook and ask her if she'd kindly heat some of her beef broth. What about you, Alexander? I dare say you are hungry?'

'Beef broth will be fine for me, too, Mother, thank you,' he said, taking off his hat and sinking into the Chesterfield.

'Now, Rowan, you go upstairs with Daisy. She will make sure you have everything you need,' Mrs Acland said, turning back to Rowan, but the warmth from the fire had made her sleepy and she was doing her best to stifle a yawn.

'Thank you, ma'am,' she said.

'You are our guest here, Rowan, so please call me Mrs Acland. You are obviously fatigued so after you have refreshed yourself, I suggest you jump straight into bed. I'll get Daisy here to bring your broth to your room.'

'Oh, I couldn't possibly put you to so much trouble,' Rowan protested.

'It's no trouble at all. Get a good night's sleep and everything will look better in the morning. Alexander and I have a few things we need to discuss, so you would actually be doing us a favour, wouldn't she?' she said, turning towards her son.

'Indeed, Mother. Sleep well, Rowan, and don't worry, I shall remember to ask how your friend Susan is,' he said with a smile.

'Thank you, Super . . . I mean Mr Acland, and you too, Mrs Acland,' she said.

Following Daisy from the room and up the sweeping staircase, she marvelled at its magnificent carved banisters lit by the warm glow from the candles flickering on their brass reflectors.

The room Rowan was shown into was delightful, with pale lilac furnishings and snowy white bed linen. A washstand stood in the corner and a fire in the grate was set, ready to be lit. She shook her head at such luxury but how she wished she was back in her own little bedroom. As Daisy disappeared to get hot water, Rowan went over to the window and looked out across the garden. Even in the gathering shadows, she could see the lawn was superbly manicured and edged with well-tended flowerbeds, bordered by topiary bushes. The contrast with the stark, high-walled airing courts of the asylum was indescribable. It was wonderful to be free but what was to become of her? She couldn't stay here for long, could she?

Her musing was interrupted by Daisy staggering back into the room under the weight of a huge ewer, brimming with hot water. Rowan hurried over to help the girl, but Daisy shook her head.

'I can manage, miss, thank yous,' she insisted, as with great concentration she lifted it on to the washstand.

'Well, thank you, Daisy,' Rowan said, turning and drawing the curtains.

'That's my job, miss,' the little maid stated, her lip quivering.

'Sorry, Daisy, I was forgetting my manners,' Rowan said, anxious not to upset the girl. She waited whilst the maid saw to the fire and then carefully turned down the corner of the bedding. By the time Rowan had washed the smell of the asylum from her skin and combed out her long curls, there was a cheery fire glowing in the grate, and a snowy white nightdress placed to warm on the chair beside it. Feeling human again, Rowan clambered into the soft cotton gown and then climbed into bed. As she sank down into the plush feather mattress and drew the lavender-scented sheets over her, she let out a contented sigh. She watched the flames dancing in the fireplace and listened to the crackling of the logs, thinking she'd never felt so pampered in her life.

Her musings were interrupted by a tap on the door and then Daisy appeared, carefully carrying a tray laden with a mug of the most delicious-smelling soup and a huge hunk of bread glistening with golden butter. Her stomach growled in appreciation and she smiled her grateful thanks.

'Mrs Acland says if there's anything else yous need, yous to ring the bell,' Daisy said, dipping a little curtsy and hurrying from the room. Rowan smiled. Nobody had ever curtsied to her before. Then hunger overtook her and she turned her attention to supper. She'd lost count of the number of pots of broth she'd made since her mother had died, but had to concede this was the most delicious she'd ever tasted. Wiping out the mug with the last of her bread, she set the tray on the table beside the bed. Her head sank into the soft pillows and she drifted off to sleep, thinking she'd never smelled anything as comforting as the lavender that scented the crisp, cotton pillowslips.

She woke with a start, but there were no snores or

grunts coming from other beds. Opening her eyes, she saw the light of early morning filtering through the drapes. As she stared around the room, it was a few moments before she remembered that she was no longer in the asylum but a guest in the superintendent's family home. Feeling invigorated after her night's sleep, and relieved to be free, she jumped from the bed and threw back the curtains. Outside, the lawns were sparkling with dew and she could hear the chirruping of sparrows and the singing of blackbirds. In the fields beyond the gardens she could see cows grazing. Suddenly, she was filled with an overwhelming longing to be outside in the fresh air. There was no sign of her dress or shawl, but a night wrap was draped over the chair beside the fire. Someone, probably Daisy, had evidently been in whilst she was asleep, damped it down and pulled the guard around it as well as removing her supper tray. Goodness, she was being treated like royalty she thought.

Quietly she opened the bedroom door. Then, anxious not to waken anyone, she tiptoed down the stairs and along the hallway. Not hearing anyone moving about, she let herself outside into the crisp morning air. She stood there for a few moments, breathing in the fresh air and marvelling at the wondrous sense of liberty that surged through her veins. Giving in to the urge to feel the grass beneath her bare feet, she skipped onto the lawn and began to dance. Joy flooded through her and she swayed and dipped with gay abandon. She remembered her grandfather saying that freedom never tasted sweeter than when it was restored after it had been taken from you, and that it should never be taken for granted. Now she understood what he had meant. With the first rays of the new day's sun spreading their red fingertips across the eastern sky, she knew what she had to do. Spotting a bird's feather on the lawn, still anointed with the morning dew, she bent and picked it up. Waving it in the air above her head, she chanted:

> *As I feel the wind blow free*
> *And all around me balanced be,*
> *This feather I present to thee*
> *With thanks for all eternity.*
> *So mote it be.*

Plucking a Lent lily from the border, Rowan kissed it, then fell to her knees on the damp grass. Placing the flower and feather in the shape of a V on the ground before her, she closed her eyes.

'Well, well, well. So still you dance and chant, Rowan.'

Springing to her feet, she turned to see the superintendent staring at her in surprise.

Chapter 20

'I'm sorry for picking one of your flowers, sir, but I was just giving blessings for my freedom,' Rowan explained, embarrassed at having been caught dancing on his lawn.

'You were giving blessings? That's remarkable, Rowan. Most people would be bitter at having been locked away unfairly,' he said, shaking his head.

'Mother taught me that it's better to be thankful for the good things in life than to dwell on misfortune. She said bitterness begets bitterness, and that the only person who suffers then is yourself.'

'It sounds as if she was very wise, Rowan. Now I seem to remember one of your other talents was blessing cattle, so tell me, are you going to switch the cows over there, too?' Amusement twitched his lips as he pointed to the field beyond.

'Now I know you mock me, sir.'

'Far from it, Rowan, although I do wish you would call me Mr Acland. Actually, it gladdens my heart to see a young woman enjoying the great outdoors. Some are more concerned about the wind ruffling their coiffure,' he said, his eyes clouding. 'Still, it's a beautiful day, is it not?' His face brightened as he looked about him, breathing in the fresh country air.

'Oh, yes, Mr Acland,' Rowan agreed, and couldn't help thinking how much younger he looked when he relaxed.

'And this is such a delightful garden,' she said, staring at the flowerbeds awash with colourful spring blooms.

'It is indeed. Do you know that the word "garden" comes from the Hebrew, and means a pleasant place?'

'No, I didn't, but it is truly the right word for it, isn't it? And it goes with your glorious mansion,' she said, gesturing to the magnificent building behind them.

'I agree it is a glorious house; hardly a mansion, though. It was originally built as the vicarage. Somewhat ironic, really, considering Father's business interests . . .' Hearing noises coming from the stables, he tailed off and when he resumed it was in his habitual serious manner.

'Rowan, although you look delightful in that white nightgown, with all your glorious hair flowing free, I think you should take yourself indoors before Mother rises and sees you.'

'Oh,' she gasped, suddenly aware she was standing before him wearing only her night attire. 'I'm sorry, sir.'

'Don't be. You look quite charming,' he said. Then, giving a nervous cough, he added, 'Cook and Daisy are already about their business so if I were you I'd sneak in via the French doors over there. It wouldn't do to cause any tittle-tattle, now, would it?' He pointed to a pair of open glass doors behind them. The sound of hooves on gravel could be heard and he became solemn. 'That sounds like Jenson ready to take me to the asylum. I'll remember to enquire about your friend Susan,' he assured Rowan.

As she watched him striding away, she couldn't help thinking what a mixture of a man he was. He obviously loved the garden, and had looked almost boyish when he'd spoken about it, then in a snap he was the officious superintendent. Remembering his advice, she ran towards the open doors, hoping she'd be able to find her way back up to the Lilac Room.

When she had quickly climbed the stairs and entered her bedroom, she found Daisy bent beside the fireplace riddling the ashes. Her eyes widened in amazement when she saw Rowan.

'Have yous been outside like that, miss?' she asked, staring at Rowan's feet. Looking down, Rowan saw they were covered with blades of grass.

'I'm afraid I couldn't resist, Daisy. After being cooped up indoors at the . . .' she stumbled to a halt.

'Lunatic asylum,' the maid finished for her. Rowan stared at her in surprise. 'I recognized the dress when yous arrived, miss. I had a similar brown one when I was at the orphanage. Now I've got a smart uniform,' she said, getting to her feet and smoothing down her white apron. 'I've laid out a dress for yous but I've a feeling it's going to be too big, what with yous being the same size as me,' she said, her eyes narrowing as she assessed Rowan.

Looking at the yellow day dress that was carefully set over the back of the chair, Rowan could see that it was much too long. Still, she was grateful Mrs Acland had thought to provide something for her to wear. Her skin was still chafed from the rough materials of the asylum uniform, and she didn't want to put it on ever again.

'Ma'am said to tell you she'll see yous downstairs in the breakfast room. Do yous need any help, miss, only I'm a bit behind this morning and Cook will have me guts for garters if I don't hurry up?' Daisy asked.

'No, I can manage, thank you, Daisy. Look, why don't you let me finish that before I have a wash?' she asked, pointing to the grate. To her dismay, the girl glowered at her.

'This is my job. I might be slow but I'm learning, so don't think yous going to steal it,' she said, resuming her task with vigour.

'It's all right, Daisy, I was only trying to help, and you can rest assured I have no intention of taking your job. Besides, I'm only here for a few days.'

Immediately the maid relaxed and Rowan chided herself for her insensitivity. If the girl had only just come from the orphanage it was understandable she was feeling insecure about her position.

Going over to the washstand, she saw fresh water had been drawn for her. She busied herself with her ablutions and by the time she'd finished Daisy had disappeared. Carefully pulling the crisp cotton dress over her shoulders, she shook out the folds of material, marvelling at the little white sprigs of flowers embroidered on the skirt. As she'd feared, it was much too long, the sleeves covering her fingertips, the hem trailing on the rug beneath her. She rolled up the sleeves as neatly as she could, then snatched the tie from the night wrap and wound it around her waist, pulling up the skirt until she could see her feet.

Following the delicious aroma of cooked bacon, she made her way to the breakfast room, where Mrs Acland sat sipping tea from a delicate china cup.

'Good morning, Rowan,' she said, replacing it in her saucer and smiling graciously. 'I trust you slept well?'

'Yes, thank you, Mrs Acland, that was the best night's

sleep I've had in ages,' Rowan answered with feeling. 'Thank you for loaning me this dress.'

Mrs Acland looked her up and down, then shook her head. 'I can see it's much too long. I hadn't realized how petite you are, Rowan. We shall have to do something about it after you have eaten.' Then she looked down at Rowan's bare feet and frowned. 'I did ask Daisy to lay out stockings and slippers for you. The silly girl must have forgotten. I'll have words with her when we have finished our meal.'

'Oh, no, please, Mrs Acland. It wasn't Daisy's fault. I prefer to go barefoot,' Rowan replied truthfully.

'That's as may be, but did she put stockings and slippers out?' Mrs Acland persisted.

'I expect I was in a hurry and didn't notice them,' Rowan answered, not wishing to get the little maid into trouble.

'Hmm.' Mrs Acland gave her a knowing look. 'Well, do help yourself from the salvers on the sideboard. Cook likes to indulge Alexander when he visits, so we are spoiled for choice this morning.'

Rowan duly lifted the lids, her stomach grumbling in appreciation at the array of coddled eggs, bacon, kidneys, black pudding, fried bread, tomatoes and mushrooms. After helping herself to some of everything, she took her place at the table and tucked in. It was only when Mrs Acland was pouring tea into her cup that she looked up and saw the woman was grinning. Glancing over at her plate, Rowan saw it was more modestly set with an egg and a single mushroom.

'Oh,' she gasped. 'I'm sorry, Mrs Acland, I'm afraid I've

been rather greedy. You must tell me what chores I can do to repay your kind hospitality.'

'Don't worry, my dear. You need building up after your ordeal. Enjoy your breakfast and then we can discuss what's to be done,' she said, turning her attention back to her food.

Rowan did as she'd been bid, but although the food was delicious, she couldn't help wondering what Mrs Acland had in store for her. Was she going to be asked to become a scullery maid? At least she'd have somewhere to stay, she thought.

'Right, if you're sure you've finished . . . ?' Mrs Acland asked, as Rowan sat back in her chair, feeling replete.

'That was the most scrumptious breakfast I've ever had in my life,' Rowan said, patting her stomach.

Mrs Acland smiled tolerantly. 'Well, I'm sure Cook will be pleased to hear that. Now, I think the first thing we need to do is send for my dressmaker and get her to make adjustments to that dress. We can't have you going out looking like you've donned something from the rag bag.'

'Oh, no, Mrs Acland, there's no need for that. I am quite capable of making the alterations myself, if you don't mind some of this lovely material being chopped off?' asked Rowan.

'Well, if you are sure, Rowan. I know Mrs Pinker is busy making a bridal dress for her daughter at the moment. Now, I have things to attend to this morning, so perhaps you would like to sew upstairs in the privacy of your room. I will get Daisy to light the fire so that you don't catch a chill.'

Rowan was just about to say that she could see to it

herself when she remembered the fear in the young girl's eyes when she'd thought Rowan was after her job.

'That would be most kind, Mrs Acland,' she answered.

'I will send Daisy up with my sewing box, and then she can also lay out those stockings and slippers for you,' Mrs Acland said, her eyes twinkling so that Rowan was reminded of the superintendent. 'Oh, and Rowan,' the woman added as she stood up to leave, 'I think it would be better if we don't mention your stay at the asylum to anyone. Regrettably that place carries a stigma, and if we are to find you a suitable position, that would be sure to count against you.'

'I see,' Rowan replied, nodding her head. 'Yes, I understand. Thank you so much for allowing me to stay here, Mrs Acland. When I've finished sewing, you must let me know what I can do to earn my keep.'

'Rowan, you are more than welcome here, but you are staying as our guest. It's the least we can do after the terrible time you've experienced, and besides, I do enjoy young company,' said Mrs Acland, giving her a gentle smile.

Up in the Lilac Room, Rowan took off the yellow dress and donned the silk night wrap. No sooner had she settled herself at the table in the bay window than there was a knock on the door and Daisy reappeared.

'Here yous are, miss,' she said, placing an ornate sewing box before her. 'Sorry I forgot yous stockings and slippers. Ma'am said I need to pay more attention to detail,' she said, laying the hose on the bed and taking a pair of golden slippers from the walnut wardrobe. Then, kneeling before the fire, she set to work with the bellows. As flames blazed, she carefully placed the guard in front of the fireplace and got to her feet, but instead of leaving the room she stood staring at Rowan.

'Is something wrong, Daisy?' Rowan asked, putting down the needle she'd just threaded.

'Pardon me for asking, miss, but I was wondering why yous always wear a red ribbon around your wrist. I saw yous had it on with your night things and wondered if it was important to you, like.'

'It's the most treasured thing I have, Daisy. My mother always wore it and she gave it to me just before she died. It represents the circle of life, you see.'

The little maid frowned. 'Circle of life, miss?'

'Continuity, Daisy. Although people die, their spirit lives on and is passed down through the family in actions and deeds. My mother passed on her rituals and goodness, and I hope I will pass these on to my daughter, if I'm blessed. There's not a day that passes that I don't look at this ribbon and remember my mother,' she said, rubbing the red band.

'Well, that can't happen to me, can it? Me being an orphan, an' all.' Daisy looked so forlorn, Rowan wanted to put her arms around her. Knowing the gesture was likely to be met with suspicion, however, she cast around for something to reassure her.

'But you can start your own, Daisy. Take your name, for example. Did you know Daisy means a miniature symbol of the sun?'

'Really, miss?' the little maid said, her eyes sparkling in delight. 'They said at the orphanage I was found with a daisy in me hand, so that's what they called me. I ain't got no circle of life, though, 'cos I got no mother, have I?'

'You could be the beginning of one, though, Daisy. Why, you could make a chain from the flowers on the lawn. Create your own circle,' Rowan suggested.

'Blimey, I'd better be quick then. Old Coggins mows the lawns on Tuesdays,' the little maid said, hurrying from the room.

Settling herself back in her seat, Rowan picked up the needle and pulled the dress towards her. If only her problems could be sorted out so easily, she thought. It was very kind of Mrs Acland to say she could stay here, but she needed to find some kind of position to support herself. But what? Her talents were limited. Although she could read and write, her education had been basic. She knew about life on a farm, so maybe she could do some domestic work or even help in the kitchen of a big house. Thinking about farm life reminded her of her father and Sab. Did they wonder where she was or had their lives already moved on? No doubt Fanny would have come up with some plausible explanation about her disappearance. And as for Sab, he'd been so distant latterly.

The harder she thought, the quicker she sewed and it wasn't long before the dress was altered to her satisfaction. Trying it on, she checked her appearance in the gilt-framed mirror hanging on the wall. Looking at her reflection, her eyes widened in amazement. Why, she looked like a lady, she thought, twisting her hair up into a knot and securing it with a couple of pins from the little glass dish on the dressing table. Then, she donned the stockings, climbed into the golden slippers and went downstairs.

'My, my, my,' Mrs Acland said as Rowan hesitated in the

doorway of the parlour. 'Rowan, I can truly say the duckling has turned into a swan. Come in and take a seat, my dear.' She put down her embroidery hoop and indicated the chair opposite her own.

'I don't wish to interrupt you, Mrs Acland,' Rowan said.

'You are not, my dear. I only embroider to pass the time of day. The hours pass slowly when one is by oneself, so come and tell me all about yourself. First of all, though, I must have a look at that dress.' Rowan moved closer. As Mrs Acland inspected her stitching, she fervently hoped everything would meet with the woman's approval for, in truth, she'd done more contemplating than concentrating. 'Well, Rowan, I am truly amazed,' the woman finally pronounced, shaking her head. 'I have never seen such stitching.'

Rowan's heart sank. She should have paid more attention to what she was doing. The last thing she wanted was to upset the woman who had kindly taken her into her home by making a mess of her fine material.

'I'm sorry, Mrs Acland –' she began.

'What for, Rowan? That is the finest sewing I have seen. Why, even Mrs Pinker's stitches are not as fine as these. Now, take a seat and I'll ring for some refreshment,' she said, tugging at the bell pull. But before Rowan had moved over to the chair, Daisy appeared.

'Ooh, miss, you doos look beautiful. You'd never think that was Mrs Acland's old dress – oh, sorry, ma'am,' Daisy said, blushing to the roots of her tawny hair.

'Quite, Daisy,' Mrs Acland said, trying to smother a smile. 'Now perhaps you'd bring some iced tea.'

'Yes, ma'am,' she said, bobbing a curtsy. Then, turning,

she grinned and held up her hand so that Rowan could see the daisy chain around her wrist.

'I'm pleased to see you are looking much happier today, Daisy,' Mrs Acland said, and the maid nodded and disappeared to fetch the tea. 'Well, it seems as if our little maid has settled into her new job at last,' she declared.

Rowan nodded, knowing how important it was to have a sense of belonging.

'I don't know what that daisy chain is about, but she has definitely taken to you, Rowan, and by the way she keeps staring at the ribbon around your wrist, she seems to equate it to that,' she said, giving Rowan a shrewd look. 'Still, if the girl is happier then so be it. Now, Rowan, I'll just finish this, and then we will enjoy our refreshment.' Mrs Acland picked up her embroidery hoop and selected a skein of cerise silk.

'Oh, no, that colour would be completely wrong,' Rowan said before she could stop herself.

Chapter 21

'What did you say, Rowan?' asked Mrs Acland, with a frown.

'I just meant that I thought that the cerise would be too harsh against the soft green you've used for the leaves,' Rowan muttered, wondering how she could have been so rude as to voice her opinion out loud.

'Really? What colour would you suggest I use for this sweet pea instead?' she enquired, staring at Rowan over the rim of her glasses.

'I would opt for the paler powder pink,' Rowan replied. In the ensuing silence, she felt as if butterflies were holding their summer ball in her stomach. Now she'd really overstepped the mark.

'And what colour for this flower, do you think?'

'The light periwinkle,' Rowan said, studying the array of silks.

'And for this one?' Mrs Acland persisted.

'The blush pink,' she whispered.

Carefully, Mrs Acland selected the coloured silks Rowan had suggested, fanning them out on her fabric.

'Unbelievable,' Mrs Acland exclaimed.

'I'm sorry to be so rude,' Rowan said ruefully.

'Rude, my dear? No, you have an amazing eye for colour. I can see now that the cerise would have been much too harsh, whilst these other hues complement each other beautifully. You know, Rowan, usually I find embroidery quite tedious but you have made me see how using the right silks can bring the flowers to life.'

'Oh, thank you –' Rowan replied, feeling relieved.

'Ah, there you are, Daisy,' Mrs Acland said, looking up as the maid entered with their drinks. 'Set the tray down on the table by the window, if you please.'

The maid did as she'd been asked, then with a big grin in Rowan's direction, held up her arm that still bore the chain of flowers.

'Thank you, Daisy, that will be all. Yes, you definitely have a little admirer, Rowan,' she said with a smile, as the door closed behind the maid.

'She's very willing,' Rowan said.

'Indeed. Now let us sit by the window and enjoy our refreshment. I'd hate to spill any tea on my embroidery. It wouldn't do to end up with brown sweet peas after the care we've taken to get the colours right, would it?'

Settled in one of the comfortable chairs with their burgundy brocade cushions, Rowan sipped her lemon tea, thinking she'd never tasted anything so refreshing.

'So how are you feeling after your unfortunate experience?' Mrs Acland said, studying Rowan with her shrewd blue eyes.

'I'm quite well, thank you for asking, Mrs Acland.'

The woman nodded. 'I hope you don't mind, but Alexander has filled me in on some of the detail leading up to your stay on the moors. You must be missing your family, Rowan?' she enquired gently.

Rowan thought for a few moments. 'To be honest, Mrs Acland, I'm not sure I do,' she answered with a sigh.

Her hostess smiled encouragingly. 'Do go on, Rowan.'

'Everything changed when Father married Fanny earlier this year. My stepmother made it quite clear she didn't want me around. She said that if my father had to choose between us, he would choose her.'

'Why would your father have to choose between you?' Mrs Acland asked.

'Because she wanted to take over the running of the household, and did not like the closeness I had with Father. She said she would win, as she could provide the womanly things a man needs.'

Mrs Acland, who was taking a sip of her drink, almost choked at this and quickly placed her cup on the table.

'As he didn't come to find me, I've come to the conclusion that she is right,' continued Rowan. 'He hangs on her every word, doing everything she wants, so I think he must be a weak man with no mind of his own,' she concluded, relieved to have put her thoughts into words.

Mrs Acland sat looking at Rowan for a few moments. 'I do know some men are easily led by the lure of an attractive woman,' she said with such feeling, Rowan stared at her in surprise.

'Mr Acland is away a lot on business,' the woman said by way of explanation. Then she turned to stare out of the window, but not before Rowan had seen the glisten of tears in her eyes. Busying herself with her drink, Rowan looked out over the garden, where the gardener was mowing the lawn. Daisy had made her chain just in time, she thought.

'In many ways, man is the weaker sex,' Mrs Acland said, coming back to the present. 'Therefore it is up to us to steer our lives in the direction we want. Now, Rowan, if going back to your farm is not an option, what position would you like us to find for you?'

'I was thinking about that earlier, Mrs Acland, and I'm afraid my talents are limited,' she said, shrugging, for in truth, although she was being shown nothing but the utmost kindness, she couldn't help feeling like a fish stranded on the shore at low tide.

'Well, that's defeatist talk if ever I heard it. What we need is some fresh air to revive us,' she said, tugging on the bell pull. 'Daisy,' she said, as the little maid appeared, 'tell Coggins to make the carriage ready. When he says it's his day for doing the garden, you may tell him that Mrs Acland has been watching him smoking his pipe behind the potting shed for the past twenty minutes and as he has time to waste, he may switch his duties to the horses.' Daisy's eyes widened in amazement but she scuttled from the room so quickly that Mrs Acland burst out laughing.

'Oh dear, that will set the fox amongst the chickens. Talking of foxes, in the wardrobe in your room, you will find a fox stole, Rowan. You can wear that when we take a carriage ride around the park.' Rowan glanced down at the dainty slippers on her feet and Mrs Acland followed her gaze. 'We shall need to get you sized for some shoes whilst we are out. However, those will suffice for sitting in the carriage.'

Upstairs in the Lilac Room, Rowan stared at the glassy eyes of the dead fox and shuddered. Next to the stole hung a plaid cape and, hoping Mrs Acland wouldn't mind, she wrapped that around her shoulders instead.

'Couldn't you find the fox fur?' Mrs Acland enquired as Rowan descended the stairs.

'I'm sorry, Mrs Acland, but I couldn't bear to wear a dead animal.'

'Oh, well, as long as you have something to keep the chill at bay,' the woman replied.

Sitting opposite Mrs Acland in the fine carriage as they circled the beautiful parkland, Rowan began to enjoy herself. It was such a contrast to the stark airing courts with their towering walls that kept out most of the light. Here, the trees were bursting into leaf and the shrubs were ablaze with colour. They drove past a lake on which mottled, fluffy ducklings were being carried along on their mothers' backs. Further on, a pen swan was sitting on her untidy nest whilst her mate protectively stood guard. Lily pads were floating on the surface, and Rowan laughed as a dog chasing a stick slid from the muddy bank into the water. It gave an outraged yap and then, realizing the lake wasn't very deep, bounded out again, shaking itself all over its indignant owner.

'It's good to see you happy, Rowan,' Mrs Acland said.

'How could I not be when you have been so kind?' Rowan replied, glancing down at the parcel beside her. After having had Rowan sized for shoes in Exeter, Mrs Acland had insisted on treating her to a length of emerald silk from the nearby draper's.

'You will have something to keep you occupied until we find a suitable position for you. I suppose if I were practical we'd have bought some cotton material for you to make another day dress, but it's so boring being sensible all the time, don't you think?' Mrs Acland's eyes twinkled in amusement. 'Oh, there's Verity,' she said, suddenly tapping on the roof with her steel-topped cane. The carriage duly drew up alongside another one, and Rowan saw an elegantly dressed young woman wave her gloved hand in acknowledgement. However, Mrs Acland had pulled down the window and was calling out in greeting.

'Good afternoon, Verity. I trust you are keeping well?'

'Oh, I mustn't grumble, but life can be such a trial sometimes, can't it?' Verity said, giving a sigh. From her expression, you would think she had the troubles of the world on her shoulders twice over, Rowan thought.

Mrs Acland ignored the sighing. 'Verity, I'd like to introduce you to Rowan Clode. She is staying with us for the time being.' The young woman gave Rowan the 'once-over assessing look', as her auntie Sal called it. Obviously, she found Rowan wanting, for her eyes narrowed.

'Is Alexander at home?' she enquired, giving Rowan a dismissive look.

'No, Verity, he is away on his rounds. However, he will be home at the weekend, so why don't you come for dinner on Saturday evening? Shall we say seven for seven thirty?'

The woman nodded and then signalled for her driver to move on. As her carriage drew away Rowan turned to Mrs Acland.

'Is something wrong?' the woman asked, noting her concerned look.

'No, not really, it's just that I thought Alex . . . I mean Mr Acland, would be returning tonight,' she said. She explained all about Susan and how bad she felt at leaving the asylum without her. 'I'm so anxious to find out how Susan is,' she finished.

'Yes, I'm sure you are, Rowan, and don't worry, Alexander will be home either tonight or tomorrow at the latest.

It all depends on how long his business at the asylum takes him. We all know how treacherous those peat bogs are, and I have forbidden him to travel once darkness has fallen. He chides me for fussing, but secretly, I think he's relieved,' she added, with a smile.

'Then why . . . ?' Rowan came to a halt, not wishing to appear rude.

'Why did I tell Verity he wouldn't be back until the weekend?' Rowan nodded. 'Well, the truth is that Verity has set her cap at Alexander and he, naughty boy, is dragging his heels, as it were.' Rowan smiled at the superintendent being described as a 'naughty boy'. 'Of course, it is high time he remarried but Alexander is not a man to be hurried. Understandable, really. He was devoted to his wife. Alas, she died giving birth to their first child. She had a heart condition no one knew about and was just too weak,' she sighed.

'What about the baby?' Rowan asked.

Mrs Acland shook her head sorrowfully. 'Poor Alexander, he withdrew into his shell.'

'Oh, how terrible for him, and for you, of course, Mrs Acland,' Rowan whispered, but the woman merely nodded and gave the roof a sharp tap with her cane.

As the carriage moved on Rowan couldn't help thinking of Susan, and her heart gave a lurch. She crossed her fingers that her friend would be all right, but her ribbon suddenly tightened. As if she'd picked up on Rowan's thoughts, Mrs Acland reached out and patted her hand. 'Don't worry; I'm sure your friend will be fine. She sounds like a robust, bouncy kind of person from what you've told me.'

Rowan watched the scenery gliding by, but her

enjoyment was gone, for she couldn't shake off the feeling of foreboding that had settled over her like a shroud.

Back in her room, she unpacked the beautiful material and laid it out on the table. Then, overcome with restlessness, she went over to the window. The sun had disappeared, replaced now by ominous, lowering clouds. As she watched, one separated then appeared to curl into the shape of a baby, but where the neck should have been, a vortex of mist was spiralling round and round. The ribbon around her wrist tightened, and she tugged at the drapes to blot out the sight. She couldn't help feeling she should have asked for Susan to be released with her, yet she had hardly known she was being freed herself. Shivering, she settled into the chair beside the fire and waited impatiently for Mr Acland to come home. A tap on the door made her jump.

'Come in,' she called, and immediately Daisy appeared.

'Yous shouldn't be sitting in the dark, miss,' she said, scuttling over and lighting the lamp. 'Mr Acland has arrived and said he'll see you in the parlour. He don't look none too happy.'

'Thank you, Daisy,' Rowan said, her heart sinking. She smoothed down her skirts and then she ran down the stairs.

As soon as she entered the parlour, Mr Acland got to his feet.

'Please sit down, Rowan,' he said. His expression was bleak and she sank into the chair beside Mrs Acland. The room was heavy with silence.

'Susan and her baby are dead, aren't they?' she blurted out.

'Yes, Rowan, I'm afraid that is correct,' he confirmed.

'They died this afternoon. The poor little baby had the cord wrapped round and round its neck,' she whispered.

'But how could you possibly know that, Rowan?' Mrs Acland asked, staring at her in surprise.

'I know it's true,' she answered. 'I saw it in the clouds when we got home.'

Mrs Acland and her son exchanged looks.

'I'm truly sorry about your friend,' Mr Acland said. 'I have to return to the asylum first thing in the morning to continue with investigations into that and many other things. However, I promised I would let you know as soon as I found out anything.'

'I should have insisted she came here with me,' Rowan burst out.

There was silence apart from the steady ticking of the grandfather clock in the corner of the room and the crackle of logs in the grate.

'That wouldn't have been possible, Rowan,' Mr Acland finally said. 'An unmarried woman with child would never have been permitted release. And, if by some miracle she had, she would have carried such a stigma she'd never have been able to return home or to her job.'

Rowan nodded, knowing what he said was true.

'At least she still believed that her Charles would be coming to collect her,' she said. 'Oh, I know he would never have had any such intention,' she cried, as he raised his bushy brows, 'but Susan believed it.'

'And that is a comfort upon which you can draw whenever you remember your friend,' Mrs Acland said softly. 'Now, I have kept Cook waiting long enough for dinner, so shall we go in? Oh, and talking of dinner, Alexander, we met Verity whilst driving in the park and I have invited her to dine with us on Saturday.'

As he gave a low groan, Rowan turned to Mrs Acland.

'I really have no appetite, Mrs Acland. Would you mind if I miss dinner?'

'I understand, my dear. You have had a shock. However, you must eat, so I shall send Daisy up with some broth. That at least will warm and sustain you until the morning.' Mrs Acland leaned over and patted Rowan's shoulder.

'I'm truly sorry about your friend, Rowan. Please feel free to pick any floral tribute from the garden. I'm sure you will wish to say a few words for her,' Mr Acland said.

'Thank you, Mr Acland, I would like to do that. Thank you also for travelling back here to tell me about Susan. I appreciate it.'

'Even if you already knew,' he said, his eyes heavy with sympathy.

'Yes,' she whispered.

The air was cool as Rowan hurried out to the garden. The clouds had given way to a clear night, with stars twinkling like the richest diamonds on their velvet blanket and a crescent of silver moon rising in the east. Kicking off her slippers, she selected the brightest flowers to reflect her friend's sunny personality. Then, kneeling on the damp grass, she lifted her face to the moon and gave thanks for Susan and her baby's short lives and blessings for the safe passing of their souls. '*So mote it be*,' she intoned, carefully shaping the flowers into the circle of life.

Chapter 22

Rowan spent a restless night, turbulent dreams of the asylum and Susan dying tormenting her. Despite what Mr Acland had said, she still felt she should have tried to get her friend released as well. Perhaps she would still be alive if she'd had treatment outside of the institution.

To her shame, the sun was high in the sky by the time she finally woke. Groggily, she forced herself to get out of bed. Daisy had laid out clean stockings, chemise and petticoats on the back of the chair, and left a jug of water for Rowan to wash with, although it was now quite cold. By the time she'd finished her ablutions and made her way downstairs, Mrs Acland had gone out. However, she had left instructions for the maid to bring Rowan a tray of tea and toast as soon as she appeared.

'Madam says yous to take it easy today, miss,' Daisy said, carefully setting out a dish of preserve on the table. 'She says if yous wishes, yous can turn that material yous brought yesterday into a dress to wear for the dinner on Saturday.'

'I don't think that invitation is extended to me, Daisy,' Rowan answered.

'Yes, it is. Mrs Acland said it was, so yous to look the part when Miss Verity calls,' the maid said, wrinkling her nose as she tried to remember her employer's exact words.

'Look, me's still wearing me circle of life,' she said, holding up her wrist.

Rowan stared at the dead flowers. 'I think your chain will need renewing every day or so, Daisy,' she said with a laugh.

'Oh, me wondered about that. Dead flowers don't seem right for a circle of life, do they?'

'I think fresh would be better. I suppose Mr Acland has already left?' Rowan asked.

'Yes, he went first thing this morning. He told madam he had a lot to sort out at the asylum 'cos the guards had been negi – negli – or something. Anyway, madam told him he was to be sure to be back in time for dinner on Saturday and he said madam was a right interfering . . .'

'Daisy? Where are you, girl? If I catch you gossiping, there'll be all hell to pay,' a strident voice called.

'Blimey, that's Cook. Better go or she'll have me guts,' Daisy whispered. 'Coming, Cook, and me don't gossip,' she called, scuttling away.

Rowan grinned. It seemed the little maid was gaining in confidence.

Rowan took herself back up to the Lilac Room and stared out over the garden. She could see the flowers still lying in the circle she'd created for Susan and her baby. Thoughts of her friend brought a lump to her throat and she shook her head for the sad loss of life. Then she remembered what Mrs Acland had said about drawing comfort from the fact that Susan had died thinking that Charles was coming for her. She supposed the old saying of living in hope was better than the dying in despair bit.

Shaking her head to rid herself of such depressing thoughts, she picked up the emerald silk and held it up in front of the window. Really it was exquisite, and quite the most expensive material Rowan had ever owned. As the silk shimmered like waves on the sea, she was reminded of the green ribbon she'd bought in the market in Sudbury. That seemed in another lifetime now, she thought with a pang. Forcing her thoughts back to her dressmaking, she knew she'd have to cut and sew carefully and vowed that this time she would concentrate. Mrs Acland had been kindness itself and it wouldn't do to abuse her generosity. Closing her eyes, she visualized the look she wanted to create. Then, spreading out the material on the table, she tentatively made the first cut . . .

By the time Saturday dawned, the dress was finished. She'd even had enough material to make a matching stole to wear around her shoulders and a couple of tiny bows to attach to the front of the golden slippers. Delighted with the results, she skipped down the stairs for breakfast.

'Good morning, my dear,' Mrs Acland greeted her. 'Did you sleep well?'

'Yes, I did, thank you. I trust you did, too?' Rowan answered, helping herself to a slice of toast from the silver rack.

'I did, thank you. Now, as you know, I have invited Verity to dinner tonight. How is the emerald dress coming along?'

'It is quite finished,' Rowan replied with a grin.

'Oh, good, I'm so looking forward to seeing it. You have been busy sewing for days but you are looking much better, so I'm guessing it was good for you to be occupied,' Mrs Acland said.

'I feel very guilty, though, for you haven't let me do a thing around the house,' Rowan said, frowning.

'Rowan, dear, you must remember you are our guest. However, if you wish to help, this morning you may gather and arrange flowers for the house. We must have everywhere looking cheerful for our guest. Of course, Verity's house is much grander than our modest abode, but we strive to keep up standards,' Mrs Acland said with a smile.

Rowan stared around the elegant room with its ornate furnishings and beautifully carved grandfather clock. This was modest?

'But before you do that, I insist on seeing your dress,' Mrs Acland continued.

'I do hope I've done the material justice,' Rowan said, looking anxiously at the kind woman sitting opposite.

'Well, when you've quite finished your breakfast, go and put it on and we'll see, won't we?' Mrs Acland's blue eyes twinkled.

Back in her room, Rowan carefully climbed into the emerald dress, slipped the bows onto the slippers and draped the stole around her shoulders. Then, after a quick look in the mirror, she descended the stairs.

'Oh my,' Mrs Acland said, her eyes widening with shock.

'Don't you like it?' Rowan asked anxiously. 'Have I made a mess of the material?'

The woman shook her head. 'You look quite exquisite, my dear. Like a bird of paradise. That emerald silk brings out the colour of your eyes to perfection and sets off your copper curls magnificently. Why, I'm quite envious of how gorgeous you look,' she said with a laugh. 'Now come closer and let me see how you've worked this magic,' she ordered. 'Hmm. Now twirl around.'

Rowan did as she'd been asked. There was a long silence.

'Is everything all right?' she asked timidly. Again, Mrs Acland shook her head and Rowan felt her stomach sink.

'Don't look so worried, my dear. That dress becomes you; in fact, it's a work of art. The cut is tailored to perfection and as for those stitches . . . Wherever did you learn to sew like that?'

'My mother taught me,' Rowan whispered. 'She made me practise until my stitching met with her approval.'

Mrs Acland smiled. 'In that case, she was an admirable teacher. As for the evening stole and bows to the slippers . . . ! You have created an absolutely stunning outfit. I just hope dear Verity can compete,' she said with a chuckle. 'She's quite possessive of Alexander and can't abide competition. Anyway, that's enough idle chatter. Go and change back into your day dress and create some wonderful floral arrangements for me, will you?'

Relieved her outfit had met with the woman's approval, Rowan did as she'd been asked and then took herself out to the garden. It was a beautiful spring morning and she hummed happily as she gathered armfuls of flowers, breathing in their sweet fragrance. The sun was blazing from a clear blue sky and she noticed the tribute she'd made for Susan wilting under its heat. Picking some golden jonquils with their heady scent, she carefully shaped them into another circle, then laid them in the shade of the cherry tree. 'Sleep sweetly, Susan and baby,' she whispered. Then gathering up her collection of spring flowers, she turned back towards the house.

'Hello. I don't know who you are, but you've certainly enjoyed gathering those, haven't you?' Spinning round, Rowan saw a dark-haired woman smiling at her. She had the same twinkling eyes as Mrs Acland, only these were tinged violet rather than blue and she was stylishly dressed in a lilac dress edged with purple. Her outfit was topped by the most elaborate bonnet Rowan had ever seen.

'Hello, I'm Rowan and I'm staying with Mrs Acland,' she said.

'Then you must be a guest of my mother's. I'm Louisa, her daughter.'

'Louisa, whatever are you doing here?' Mrs Acland cried in delight, appearing through the French doors.

'I've just been fitting Lady Lawton for her new summer outfits, and thought I'd call and see my favourite mother,' Louisa answered. 'And to show off my latest creation,' she added, pointing to her bonnet and giving an elegant pirouette. 'What do you think?'

'It's quite stunning, isn't it, Rowan?' Mrs Acland asked, clapping her hands.

Rowan studied the creation carefully.

'Well, Rowan, don't you approve?' Louisa asked, frowning when Rowan hesitated.

'Erm, well, that is . . .'

'Spit it out, girl,' Louisa persisted, giving Rowan a penetrating stare.

Never one to lie, Rowan took a deep breath. 'I agree it is stunning, but can't help thinking the strong hues of the material overpower your delicate features. You have such beautiful violet eyes and . . .' she stammered to a halt as Louisa's eyes narrowed.

'And?'

'I think that if you were to front the purple with a soft lilac, rather than that strong fuchsia it would enhance rather than drain your natural fair colouring, and would do more justice to the shape of your bonnet. A bluer shade of periwinkle would also work well,' she stammered.

Mrs Acland's tinkling laugh resounded round the garden. 'Rowan's right, you know, daughter. I can see exactly what she means. The bonnet and decoration are a masterpiece but gentler, paler colours would definitely be more flattering on you.'

'But these stronger colours are in the latest mode, and as a milliner I need to make a statement by showing I'm aware of that. People look to me to set an example,' Louisa insisted.

'Of course, and I'm sorry if I've offended you, but . . .' Rowan mumbled to a halt again.

'But . . . ? Come along, you've got this far so you may as well finish what you wish to say,' Louisa said, her violet eyes darkening as they bored into Rowan's.

Rowan took a deep breath. 'If you don't mind me saying, I would be more apt to follow someone who adapted the latest mode to flatter their own colouring.'

There was silence as Louisa stood there taking in what Rowan had said.

'Rowan pointed out how softer coloured silks would work better for the sweet peas on my embroidery,' Mrs Acland said, breaking the silence. I have to admit I was sceptical, thinking it would make the flowers fade into the background. Amazingly, she was right and now all the blooms harmonize and have a vibrancy about them. The whole piece has sprung to life. Come inside and see,' she said, taking Louisa by the hand.

Giving Rowan an unfathomable stare, Louisa let herself be led away. Rowan let out a rush of air. Perhaps she should have held her counsel; she didn't know Louisa, after all. Oh, well, it was too late now, she thought, taking the flowers into the cool of the stillroom where vases had been laid out ready.

As she busied herself arranging the various blooms, she couldn't help noticing the shelves were neatly lined with jars of perfumes, cordials and cure-alls. It was a fascinating array and she could have spent ages perusing the neatly written labels. However, aware that she might have offended Mrs Acland's daughter with her outspoken opinion, she focused her attentions on creating the best floral arrangements she could.

Back indoors, there was no sign of Mrs Acland or Louisa, but she could see the little maid bustling around preparing the dining room. Already the table was laid with silver candelabra, crystal glasses and starched white napkins. Clearly, modest house or not, it was going to be an elaborate dinner. Pleased that she had an elegant outfit to wear, Rowan determined to do something with her unruly curls.

'I've left the vases of flowers in the stillroom, Daisy. I'll be in my room if Mrs Acland should want me,' she called as she made her way upstairs.

'Thank yous, miss,' the maid called back, continuing with her chores.

Rowan spent ages twisting her hair into ringlets, which she curled around her head like a coronet. She'd just finished when Daisy bustled in to attend to the fire, draw the drapes and light the candles.

'Yous looks like a princess,' she cried. 'Cook's having kittens 'cos the jelly that should have set hasn't, and the sauce that should be smooth is curdled. She's in a right two and eight and said me wasn't to be long, so if yous don't need me for anything else me better scootle back to the kitchen.'

'I can manage perfectly, thank you, Daisy,' Rowan said, smiling as the little maid paused for breath. 'You scootle back to Cook.'

As the little maid scurried away, Rowan shook her head. Fancy having someone there to pull your drapes and add fuel to the fire as it burned low. It was so unlike life on the farm, where all these jobs had been hers.

By this time the shadows were gathering in the corners of the room. Carefully Rowan dressed in her silk ensemble, pinched colour into her pale cheeks and, after a final check in the mirror, crept down the stairs.

'You look delightful, Rowan,' Mr Acland exclaimed, looking over his paper as she hovered nervously in the doorway. 'May I get you something to drink?' he asked, indicating the decanters on the sideboard.

'No, thank you, Mr Acland,' she said politely.

'Rowan, dear, how charming you look,' Mrs Acland

said, coming into the room. 'Doesn't she look stylish, Louisa?' she asked, turning to her daughter.

'Yes, indeed she does, Mother,' Louisa answered, moving closer to Rowan and carefully scrutinizing her dress. 'How long did this take you to make?' she asked.

'About three days.'

'What, for the whole outfit?' Louisa exclaimed.

Rowan nodded. Oh dear, she had wanted to get it right, but perhaps she shouldn't have taken so long.

Then they heard the jangling of the front doorbell followed by the sound of voices. Moments later Verity stood regally in the doorway, and as a wave of expensive perfume wafted in her direction Rowan tried hard not to sneeze.

'Good evening, Alexander,' Verity said, kissing his cheek. Rowan saw him turn his head quickly away and guessed he wasn't enamoured by the musky scent either. 'Dorothea, how kind of you to invite me,' she gushed to Mrs Acland. 'And, Louisa, I had no idea you would be here,' she said.

'Nor I, actually, Verity,' Louisa answered.

As Verity deliberately turned her back on Rowan, Mrs Acland took hold of her arm. 'Verity, I believe I introduced you to Rowan when we met in the park the other afternoon,' Mrs Acland said. 'Rowan is here as our house guest, and as she is new to the area, we are doing our best to make her feel welcome,' she added pointedly.

'Oh, is this the girl from your asylum, Alexander? Really, I must say I was surprised when my coach driver informed me of his conversation with Coggins,' she said with a sniff.

'As I said, Rowan is staying here at our invitation. Should I find that Coggins has been divulging private household information, he will be severely reprimanded,' Mrs Acland said sharply. 'Now, Verity, can Alexander get you a drink before we dine?'

'No, thank you, Dorothea,' Verity said stiffly as she turned to Louisa. 'I need a new ensemble, sweetie, so can you pop up to the hall whilst you are here and measure me up, or whatever it is you need to do?'

Louisa smiled politely. 'I'd be delighted to,' she began and then, as Verity grinned in her superior manner, added, 'However, I regret to say my list is now closed for the season.' Verity pursed her bottom lip in a most unladylike manner. 'You could always ask Rowan here if she can help you. Her tailoring and sewing are quite superb.'

Rowan stared at Louisa in amazement.

'And have you been trained as a mantua maker or milliner?' Verity asked, staring down at Rowan, who was some inches shorter than she.

'Well, no,' Rowan stammered.

'In that case, I hardly think a chit of a girl fresh from the asylum can be of any help to me,' she sneered, turning away.

Chapter 23

How rude, Rowan thought, staring at Verity in astonishment. She turned to Louisa, who just shrugged, but Mrs Acland was frowning. Not wishing to upset her hostess who'd had been so kind, Rowan looked around for a means of escape.

'Don't take it personally, Rowan,' Louisa said, as if reading her thoughts. 'It's just Verity's way.' They watched as the woman glided over to Alexander and stood smiling up at him.

'Darling, I haven't seen you in ages,' she gushed, turning so that her back was to the rest of them. Seeing he was cornered, a look of near panic crossed his face and Rowan's heart went out to him. Luckily, his mother had also noticed.

'Well, everyone, I think it's time we went through for dinner,' she announced. Verity uttered something unladylike and Louisa caught Rowan's eye and grinned. Then, as Alexander politely waited for the ladies to lead off, Verity took hold of his arm.

'You may take me in, darling. We'll sit opposite each other and then we can catch up on all our news,' she purred, her amber eyes glinting so that Rowan was reminded of a tiger with its prey in sight.

'Perhaps you would pour our wine, Alexander,' Mrs Acland said, smiling graciously at Verity as she tugged on the bell pull. Daisy appeared almost immediately, trundling in the soup tureen on a trolley.

'What on earth is that monstrosity, girl?' Verity asked, pointing to her wrist.

''Tis me circle of life,' Daisy answered proudly.

'Since when do servants wear daisy chains, Dorothea?' Verity enquired.

'I wears me circle like Rowan does,' Daisy whispered.

'Oh, I see; it's an emblem of servitude, is it?' Verity sneered, staring pointedly at Rowan's ribbon.

As the room fell silent, Rowan made an effort to smile. Verity wasn't a tiger at all, she thought. That was far too grand an animal to liken to a woman with such appalling manners. No, an alley cat would be far more appropriate. Daisy, not knowing what to do, hovered uncertainly, then turned to her employer for guidance.

'You may serve us now, if you would be so kind, Daisy,' Mrs Acland said, smiling at her encouragingly.

The little maid nodded, carefully lifted the tureen and took it over to Verity.

'The other side, girl,' the woman snapped.

Daisy's lip wobbled. 'But if I go over to the other side of the table me arm won't reach yous,' she said.

'Not the other side of the table, you fool. To my right; you serve from my right,' Verity said, shaking her head in exasperation. 'Really, Dorothea, surely your servants should be properly trained before they come to you. Not that you need worry, my dear,' she said, turning to Alexander and placing her hand on his arm. 'When you make me your wife, I shall ensure our servants behave impeccably,' she said, and although Alexander smiled in response, he remained silent.

Rowan couldn't believe it. This man, who had been so

self-assured at the asylum, wasn't saying anything. Was he was merely being polite at his mother's dinner table? Or was he a coward like her father, acceding to his woman's whims? As that unwelcome thought flitted into her mind, she forced herself back to the present.

'Daisy is new here and she is doing very well,' Mrs Acland said mildly, turning to the maid. 'If you would kindly see that Miss Landsdowne is served from her preferred right, Daisy, I would be most grateful.' The little maid did as she'd been asked and then looked askance at Mrs Acland. 'You may serve the rest of us in the normal way, Daisy. It is the food and company that are important to us here.'

Seeing Verity's mouth tighten, Rowan smiled. It would appear that Mrs Acland was the tiger, after all. Although a true lady, she had clearly put the woman in her place without seeming in the least bit rude.

'Of course, things would be very different if your father were here,' Verity said to Alexander. He smiled uncomfortably.

'Indeed they would be,' Mrs Acland agreed. 'Now shall we eat before Cook's delicious white soup goes cold?'

They concentrated on their food and an appreciative hush descended. Despite the earlier confrontation, Rowan found to her surprise that she was hungry. After a quick glance at Mrs Acland to ensure she was using the correct spoon, she ate her soup with relish. The table was beautifully set, but never had she seen so many glasses or so much cutlery laid out for one meal before. How glad she was that it wasn't up to her to do the washing up, although she would offer to help, of course. Alexander finished his soup first and carefully placed his spoon on the side of the plate beneath his bowl.

'That was delicious, Mother. Cook at her finest, I think,' he said, giving Mrs Acland a conspiratorial grin. 'The flowers in here are beautiful, especially those Lent rosums. Who arranged them?' he asked, gazing at Rowan expectantly.

'Ah, roses, I just adore them,' Verity cut in, fluttering her eyelashes at him.

'Actually, I arranged the daffodils,' Rowan explained, emphasizing the word 'daffodils'.

'It is lovely to see them displayed in their own golden glory instead of being mixed with other flowers, although those are beautifully arranged as well,' he said, ignoring Verity and smiling at Rowan. The woman glared down the table at her with such vitriol, Rowan almost expected her to hiss as well.

'I understand their sap can be poisonous to other blooms,' Rowan said quickly.

'A bit like some people, then,' Louisa said with a pointed look in Verity's direction.

'Well, I hate flowers being brought indoors. They carry insects and creepy crawlies and should remain in the garden where they belong,' Verity said, giving a dramatic shudder.

Alexander raised his eyebrows at Rowan, and she quickly raised her napkin to her lips to stop herself from laughing out loud.

As the fish course was placed before them, Rowan glanced at Mrs Acland, noting which cutlery she picked up. Louisa noticed and smiled at her encouragingly. She seemed as nice as her mother, Rowan thought.

'Have you given any thought to what you will do when you leave here, Rowan?' Louisa asked.

'I have been thinking of nothing else. Of course, I am really grateful for the kind hospitality I have been shown,' she added quickly. 'I am good at household chores and willing to help.'

'Indeed,' Verity agreed. Then her amber eyes gleamed with mischief. 'Alexander, I have just had the most marvellous idea. Rowan could come and work for us when we are wed. I'm sure with the correct training she would be able to manage the duties of a parlour maid satisfactorily,' she said, shooting a triumphant look in Rowan's direction.

Alexander frowned.

'Goodness, Rowan, there seems to be quite a demand for your services this evening,' Louisa said quickly. Rowan looked at her in surprise. 'I also have a proposition for you, but thought it only polite to leave talking about it until we have finished our meal,' she added, with a smile.

'You mean you wish to have Rowan as your maid?' Verity asked, raising her eyebrows. Rowan looked at Louisa but she was busy answering Verity.

'I'm afraid my premises in Saltmouth aren't large enough to warrant that,' Louisa replied.

'Oh?'

'No, Verity, my living quarters are above my shop, as you would have seen had you taken the trouble to visit me.'

'Ah, yes, I'd quite forgotten you are trade now,' Verity said with a sniff. 'Of course, I get my business people to call at the hall whenever I require anything. Now,

Alexander, I really feel we need to do some serious planning about the future,' she continued.

'Oh, do you?' he asked, glancing in his mother's direction before turning back again. He really did seem uncomfortable, Rowan thought, and what had Louisa meant about having a proposition for her?

She had no opportunity to ask, though, for Verity monopolized Alexander throughout the rest of the meal. Mrs Acland and Louisa caught up with local affairs, leaving Rowan to her own thoughts, for which she was grateful. Savouring the delicious food, she mulled over her own prospects. What was she going to do? And where could she go? Returning to the farm was not an option, and although Mrs Acland hadn't been anything other than hospitable, Rowan knew she couldn't stay here indefinitely.

'Well, if everyone has finished, I think we shall take our coffee in the drawing room,' Mrs Acland announced, getting to her feet. No sooner had they settled themselves into the comfortable chairs than the maid appeared with the tray. 'Thank you, Daisy. We can pour our own drinks so you may leave us now. Please convey our compliments to Cook for providing such a splendid meal.'

The little maid beamed, began to bob a curtsy and then remembered it wasn't necessary and scuttled from the room.

'Oh dear, dear, dear,' Verity sighed. 'Much training still needed there, Dorothea, I think. Why don't you pour our coffee?' she asked, turning to Rowan, amber eyes glinting.

'Yes, of course,' Rowan answered, getting up and walking over to the table that was set in the bay window.

'Oh, what dinky little bows on your slippers,' Verity said. 'Of course they were the height of fashion last season.'

'And this one, in fact,' Louisa said.

Verity stared at her in disbelief. 'Surely not?'

'Why, yes, Lady Arlingham ordered some only yesterday,' Louisa added.

'Rowan, what are you doing?' Verity's shrill voice cut across the room, making her jump so that she almost spilled hot liquid onto the embroidered tray cloth. Coffee pot in hand, she turned towards the woman. 'You are putting the coffee in before the milk,' Verity said in a horrified voice. 'Are you completely ignorant? The hot liquid will crack Dorothea's delicate china.'

Rowan's eyes widened in horror. 'I'm sorry, Mrs Acland, I didn't realize. At home we always put the milk in afterwards.'

'Well, in that case you must use thick earthenware mugs or something equally basic. Those beautiful Royal Worcester cups and saucers are family heirlooms, Rowan,' Verity snapped.

'And as such, you are obviously hoping they will be passed down the line, Verity,' Mrs Acland said, in a much harsher voice than Rowan had heard her use before. 'Please don't concern yourself, Rowan. It is the coffee we shall enjoy drinking, not the vessel it comes in.'

'But I could have broken them,' Rowan said, shaking her head.

'That would hardly have been the end of the world, Rowan,' Alexander said, smiling at her across the room.

'Well, I was only protecting your interests, Alexander,' Verity said with a pout.

'I'm sure you were, Verity. Now, instead of waiting for your carriage to return, why not let me take you home? There's something important I feel we need to discuss,' Alexander said, looking very serious.

'Really?' Verity answered, her eyes lighting up. 'Goodness, I hardly dared hope, but then you have been gazing at me most intently tonight,' she gushed.

'You can be sure I have certainly seen you in a different light this evening,' he answered, getting to his feet.

'Well, thank you for a wonderful evening, Dorothea,' Verity said, bending and kissing the woman's cheek. 'It appears we shall have lots of planning to do. Exciting, what? Goodbye, Louisa. It seems I shall be putting business your way very soon. Oh, and that reminds me, Mother said the peacocks are moulting if you would like their feathers?' she added, grimacing.

Louisa smiled graciously. 'Please thank the Dowager. I would be delighted to accept her kind gift.'

Verity looked put out for a moment and then turned to Rowan. 'Perhaps you could ask Dorothea for some advice on the duties of a perfect maid. If Alexander is going to propose what I think he is, I could provide the solution to your predicament. Good night,' she purred, and with a covetous look at the Royal Worcester china, glided from the room.

'I trust this won't take long,' Alexander whispered, grimacing at his mother.

'Well!' Mrs Acland said, collapsing back in her chair as soon as the door shut behind them.

'Indeed, Mother. Still, I do believe Alexander has seen the light at last,' Louisa giggled. 'How I'd like to be a fly on that carriage wall tonight. You are looking very thought-ful, Rowan.'

'I'm very sorry. You have all been so kind and I don't wish to appear ungrateful, but I do not think I would be good enough to work for you,' Rowan answered, staring at the patterned rug.

'Why ever not?' Louisa asked.

'Why would you want me to be your maid in your posh business when Verity . . .'

'Oh, you chump. Even if Alexander were going to pro-pose marriage . . . which judging by the set look on his face he isn't . . . we couldn't possibly expect you to work for her. Perish the thought. Your talents would be quite wasted in that department. No, Mother and I were talking earlier and we agreed you would be ideal. Rowan, I would like to offer you a position as my apprentice,' Louisa said.

Rowan stared at her in surprise. 'As your apprentice?'

Louisa laughed at her shocked expression. 'Does that sound such an outrageous idea?'

'But I don't really know anything about dress or bonnet making,' Rowan gasped.

'You could soon learn. You have a wonderful eye for colour and style, combine that with your beautiful stitch-ing and, *voilà*, you have the makings of a fine mantua maker and milliner. I feel with the right training, you could be a valuable asset to my trade. What do you say?'

Rowan stared from Louisa to Mrs Acland, who was nodding her head encouragingly.

'Louisa runs a first-class business, my dear, and I can see you fitting in very well with the fashionable ladies of Saltmouth.'

'Yes, if you can handle Verity, then you can certainly deal with the most demanding of my clients. And as for your little *faux pas* with the coffee cups, there's nothing you can't learn about etiquette,' Louisa said, her eyes twinkling with amusement.

Rowan shook her head at the memory.

'Besides, I haven't forgotten how you pointed out the colouring of my bonnet was too strong. Oh, in a most tactful way, of course,' she added, as Rowan made to protest. 'The fact is, I shall be returning to Saltmouth first thing in the morning, and if you decide to become my apprentice, you may accompany me on the daily coach.'

Rowan's heart leaped. What a wonderful opportunity to make a new start and learn a trade. She would be foolish not to accept. Then thoughts of her father crept into her mind.

'I would love to accept, Louisa. However, there is just one thing,' she said, turning to Mrs Acland.

'Yes, my dear?'

'If I were to write a letter to my father, could you see that it gets delivered?'

'Indeed. In fact, it would put Alexander's mind at rest. He feels terrible about the way you've been treated. Apparently you were subjected to behaviour that contravenes the asylum regulations and he is carrying out an investigation to ensure it can never happen again. I understand one guard in particular is to be reprimanded severely.'

'I would be obliged if you could ask him to ensure my note gets delivered to my father personally. I know that if it is intercepted by my stepmother, he'd never get to see it and I'd like him to know where he can find me,' Rowan said.

'Leave the note with me before you leave, Rowan, and I shall see that Alexander receives it with those very instructions,' Mrs Acland assured her.

'Thank you very much, and thank you for making me so welcome here.'

'It's truly been a pleasure, my dear. In fact, by the way Alexander was looking at you tonight, I think it is you who has done us the favour,' Mrs Acland said.

'Me? I don't understand,' Rowan said, frowning.

'Your kind and attractive nature may just have reminded him of his first wife.'

'But Mr Acland is much older and . . .' Rowan stuttered to a halt, not wishing to appear rude.

'Don't worry, Rowan, we merely mean you have made Alexander see the light and saved him from the jaws of madam predator,' Louise added with a laugh.

'Right, on that note, I think it's time we turned in,' Mrs Acland said. 'Rowan, I wish you well for the future. Please remember, though, that on no account must you mention your stay in the asylum to anyone. Although we here know your incarceration was a terrible mistake, there will always be those who prefer to think the worst, especially of a pretty young girl like yourself. Alas, in this society, once a stigma has been placed on someone, it is virtually impossible to remove. Which reminds me, I must ask Alexander to speak with Verity's driver. We must be assured of his discretion.'

Chapter 24

As Louisa had promised, the coach picked them up from outside the Aclands' house just after they'd broken their fast. Rowan stared down at her shiny new shoes, thinking how kind Mrs Acland had been. She'd quite refused to take any money for them, insisting Rowan should wear the cotton dress and cape for travelling and take the silk outfit and slippers with her. 'You can make me a hat when you have completed your apprenticeship,' she'd said, kissing her goodbye.

What would her new life in Saltmouth hold for her?

Almost as if she'd picked up on her thoughts, Louisa smiled, looked around at their fellow passengers and then leaned forward in her seat.

'You know, one thing puzzles me,' Louisa said, staring at Rowan with those beautiful violet eyes.

'What's that?' Rowan asked.

'How are you so knowledgeable about colours? You said you were brought up on a farm, so I don't suppose you frequented the draper or haberdashery shops.'

'No, that's true,' Rowan said, laughing. 'The nearest we got to that was Mabel's stall at Sudbury market. She stocked ribbons, gewgaws and gimcracks. It was Mother and Auntie Sal who taught me about dying wool and clothes. They showed me which plants to collect and how you could vary the depth of colour by using either the leaves, stems or flowers.'

'Fascinating, and I love the way you call them by their botanical names. "Periwinkle", for example, sounds much more exotic than "light mauve", and I fully intend to make use of these descriptions of yours,' Louisa said, her eyes alight with plans for the future.

'Well, Mother always said that for putting colours together, you can't beat Mother Nature's good eye,' Rowan said, her heart jolting as she thought about the kind gentle woman.

'I knew you were going be an asset to my business,' Louisa cried, clapping her hands excitedly. The gentleman opposite frowned over the top of his newspaper and the woman seated beside him had given up all pretence of knitting and was listening avidly to their conversation. 'We'll talk more later on,' Louisa whispered, sitting back in her seat and staring out of the window.

As the carriage rumbled along, Rowan noticed the trees were in full leaf and feathery blossoms festooned the orchards. Later in the year the boughs would be laden with fruit, she thought, remembering with a pang the fragrant spicy apple cakes her mother had made. Then her attention was caught by the bluebells spread out like luxury carpeting under the trees, and campions blazing pink among the nodding creamy froth of cow parsley. She sighed with pleasure, knowing she'd never take her freedom for granted again.

Her thoughts turned to the new life awaiting her in Saltmouth and happiness bubbled up inside. Never in her wildest dreams had she thought she'd become apprenticed to a mantua maker and milliner. Louisa had already explained what her duties would be, leaving Rowan in no doubt she was expected to do as she was instructed, willingly and without question. In return, Louisa had promised to train her to the highest standard and provide a room in the attic along with her board.

The coach lurched to a sudden halt, sending Rowan sliding down the seat to the woman sitting by the opposite window. She smiled apologetically then hastily resumed her position as more passengers clambered into the carriage, only just managing to snatch up her neatly wrapped parcel before a rotund gentleman with a florid face sat on it. However, her discomfort was soon forgotten when they turned down the Saltmouth Road and she saw the iridescent shimmer of the sea in the distance. The coach carefully made its descent towards the town, throwing up dust in its wake. They clattered over a bridge spanning a little river, passed houses with castellated roofs, first-floor balconies and tent-shaped canopies, and slowed down beside an imposing old stone church. Rowan stared towards the marketplace where water carts stood beside the pumps, and men were working the handles to wash down the streets. She gazed up at the tall, ornate buildings and shook her head in wonderment.

'Well, here we are, Rowan,' Louisa said, as the coach pulled up outside the church, where Sunday worshippers stood putting the world to rights after morning service.

As they crossed the street, a little woman with a birdlike appearance broke away from the throng.

'Good morning, Madame Louisa. I don't believe I have met your companion before,' she said, her beady eyes boring into Rowan.

'Mrs Parker, allow me to introduce you to Miss Rowena. She has kindly consented to become my apprentice, so no doubt you shall be seeing more of her when you pay your next visit to my humble establishment. For now, I hope you'll excuse us. We have spent the morning travelling by the staging coach and are quite in need of refreshment,' Louisa said, taking Rowan by the arm and leading her towards the entry set to one side of a bay-windowed shop.

Madame Louisa? Rowan wondered. Was her new employer married then? She'd never mentioned having a husband. And why had she called her Miss Rowena? Her mind was buzzing with questions, but then the creation set on a stand in the centre of the little bay window caught her eye.

'Do you approve of my latest design, Rowan?' Louisa asked. Staring through the little panes of glass, she saw a pink and white bonnet adorned with toning ribbons that interlaced as they trailed down from the stand.

'Why, it looks just like a maypole,' Rowan answered.

'I'm pleased to hear that, Rowan. It is my May Day frontispiece.'

Rowan turned her head this way and that, then frowned.

'Is something wrong?' Louisa asked.

'I was just wondering why there is only one bonnet in the window. I was expecting to see a display of them.'

Louisa gave a tinkling laugh. 'Look behind the bonnet and tell me what can you see.'

Rowan duly stared into the shop. Her eyes widened as she saw the room beyond was festooned with every bonnet, hat and trimming imaginable.

'More bonnets, hats, parasols and lots of other pretty things,' she gasped.

'The idea is to excite the clients' interest. Whet their appetites. If they can see only one creation, they think it must be exclusive and stop to look. Then their attention is attracted by the others inside. It's an idea I copied from Paris and I have to say it works perfectly. Now let's go in. We'll have some luncheon and then I'll show you around.' Louisa led the way down the entry and unlocked a side door.

Rowan followed her into a little kitchen area, which led through to a larger room furnished with a Pembroke table around which four tall-backed chairs were set.

'Do make yourself comfortable, Rowan,' Louisa said, taking off her bonnet and placing it carefully on the little chiffonier. 'There's a pump and privy in the yard outside if you need to refresh yourself. I'll go and see what Maria has left for me. She's a treasure and sees to all my household needs. Alas, I can only afford her services on a shared basis, so she is often working next door.' Louisa bustled back through to the kitchen.

Rowan stared out of the little window, delighted to see that the yard was bordered by lavender, myrtle and hydrangeas. Placing her parcel beside Louisa's bonnet, she took off her cape and was folding it over the back of a chair when Louisa reappeared carrying platters of bread, ham and cheese. She really had landed on her feet, Rowan thought, eyeing the food hungrily.

'Luckily for me Maria, who has a handsomely rounded shape herself, thinks I need feeding up and leaves enough food to feed the proverbial five thousand. From tomorrow, business will dictate we take our refreshment at different times as I keep the shop open throughout the day. I find that luncheon time can sometimes be the busiest.' Her smile turned to a frown, as she looked at Rowan's appearance. 'This afternoon we will attire you with apparel suitable for a milliner's apprentice. Now do help yourself,' she said, pointing to the food on the table.

They ate in companionable silence, but Rowan's mind was buzzing with a thousand questions. Finally, when the platters were cleared, Louisa turned to Rowan.

'Your brain's been ticking louder than my mantel clock, so fire away.' Rowan stared at her in surprise. 'Go on, ask me anything you want and then I'll take you on the grand tour.'

'I was wondering if you were married,' Rowan said. 'Only Mrs Parker called you "Madame".'

'I shall never, ever marry,' Louisa burst out so vehemently that Rowan shrank back in surprise. 'Mrs Parker is renowned for being the Saltmouth tittle-tattle. She is a frequent visitor to my establishment, but alas her tongue wags far more often than she opens her purse. You must watch out for her, Rowan. Be polite, of course, but wary of what you divulge, for her ears can grow by at least two inches if she gets a whiff of gossip.'

Rowan gulped and vowed to watch the woman's ears next time she encountered her.

'Madame Louisa is my trade name, Rowan. It's all about respectability, and as such I have decided Miss Rowena will be the perfect title for you. If you have no objection, that is how you will be addressed during business hours which, as I have already said, are from seven a.m. to eight p.m., or later if the season requires.' Louisa looked at Rowan expectantly and she nodded.

'It will be your duty to sweep the pavement outside the shop each morning and whenever any dirt accumulates, which it does frequently from passing carriages and the staging coach, of course. You will also ensure the glass of the window is kept sparkling. There is nothing more off-putting to a prospective client than not being able to see for grubby windows. Now, unless you have any more questions, we will go through to the workroom and I'll show you where everything is,' she said, smiling as she got to her feet.

Rowan's eyes widened in amazement as she stared around the workroom, its high-rise shelving stacked with seemingly every colour of ribbon, feather and trimmings imaginable. The huge table running the length of the room was laden with the most peculiar tools and gadgets Rowan had ever seen. There were big wooden blocks in various shapes and sizes, irons and cutting tools, measuring tapes, needles and pins of all sizes. As she shook her head in bewilderment, Louisa gave her tinkling laugh.

'Don't worry, Rowan – or should I say, Miss Rowena – you will soon learn what everything is for, and who supplies what. Come through to the shop itself and I'll show you some of my creations.'

The first thing Rowan noticed was the heavenly fragrance that wafted around the room. It was similar to the floral scent that Louisa wore but lighter.

'What is that delightful smell?' she couldn't help asking.

Louisa smiled. 'That, Miss Rowena, is my establishment's signature fragrance. It is called Madame L and is made in Paris to a secret receipt. It is another little sales ploy I learned from my stay in France. You will find that all my robes, wrapping papers and hatboxes are impregnated with the same scent. The idea being that whenever a client smells it, they associate it with Madame Louisa's. Rowan stared from Louisa to the colourful bonnets and shook her head. Would she ever be half as clever?

'Now, if you've no more questions, we'll go upstairs. I will show you which will be your room, and then we must see you correctly attired for business tomorrow.'

The room she showed Rowan was up two flights of stairs and nestled under the eaves. It was cosy and had a multicoloured coverlet over the bed, and a tiny window with a curtain to match. She could hear sparrows chirruping in the thatch, and the bells from the church summoning worshippers for evensong made everything feel homely.

'Mixed blessings, being here,' Louisa said, grimacing. 'On the one hand all those passing on their way to church can't resist glancing in the window of the shop. It is an excellent time for ladies to point out their hearts' desires to their husbands. On the other hand, the bell ringers are so earnest in their work, one can hardly hear oneself think, let alone try to have a decent conversation. Leave your things and come down to my dressing room,' she said. Then, seeing Rowan's look of surprise, added, 'Well, it's just a spare room full of fabrics and whatnots from the shop, but it serves a useful purpose.'

Rowan stood in Louisa's dressing room and tried not to shudder when she held up a bolt of black bombazine.

'I think this would be admirable for an apprentice, don't you?' she asked. Then she saw Rowan's expression. 'You don't agree?' she asked, frowning.

'It's not for me to disagree with you,' Rowan murmured, remembering the woman was her employer.

'But . . . ?' Louisa persisted.

'Well, it is so dull and funereal, and besides . . .'

'Please speak your mind, Rowan. If we are to work together it's essential we understand each other.'

'Well, the uniforms in the asylum were black dresses and . . .' Her voice trailed off as she remembered the feel of the rough materials chafing her skin. 'I don't mean to be awkward,' she said, as the woman turned away.

'No, I quite take your point. How about this, then?' she asked, holding up a swathe of fabric in a French navy. Rowan smiled and nodded.

'We'll make a dress out of this and trim the collar and cuffs with lace. That will make a smart outfit suitable for a milliner's apprentice, I think. You will also need petticoats to support the full skirts and a boned corset.' Rowan grimaced; she hated being trussed up. 'Oh, don't worry, this one is lightly boned,' Louisa said, handing over a corset and petticoats. 'It is imperative we both set an example and are dressed *à propos*.'

Rowan looked askance at her employer, but she was already heading out of the door. She supposed she must mean she needed to be properly attired for her duties.

Down in the workroom, Louisa measured Rowan. 'My, you're a minikin and no mistake,' she said with her tinkling laugh. 'There'll be enough material here for at least a couple of dresses. I think we'll trim a bonnet with lace to match. Oh, what's that red ribbon around your wrist?'

'That's my ribbon of life, given to me by my mother. I never take it off,' Rowan said, staring Louisa in the eye.

'Well, if you could ensure it is kept hidden by your sleeve during working hours, I'd be obliged, Miss Rowena,' Louisa said with a wink.

'Gosh, you have everything to hand,' Rowan said admiringly, as Louisa produced a template.

'I'd surely be a poor mantua maker if I didn't. Of course, skirts have become fuller so I'll need to make a bit of an adjustment,' Louisa answered as she began cutting the material. 'You can select matching thread for sewing.'

They had almost finished when they were disturbed by a noisy jangle of bells.

Louisa sighed. 'I've a feeling I know who that is. You finish off the dress and I'll be back as soon as I can. If it becomes too dark to see, light the candles,' she said, pointing to the glass candlesticks on either side of the work table.

As the door closed behind her, Rowan continued sewing. She was excited, yet nervous about the next day. Would she ever learn what all these mysterious-looking instruments were for? In the growing shadows, the wooden blocks seemed to take on sinister faces. It was enough to give her nightmares, she thought, wondering if it was too early to light the candles.

The sound of a man's angry shout made her jump, interrupting her musing. Should she go and make sure Louisa was all right? She was just wondering whether it would be prudent to intrude, when angry voices sounded in the hallway. There followed the slamming of a door, the man's voice snapping to a driver in the street, and then a carriage being driven away at speed.

Chapter 25

As Rowan sat shivering in the ghostly shadows, Louisa appeared in the doorway.

'How are you getting on?' she asked, and although her voice was calm Rowan noticed two angry red spots burning her cheeks.

'I've almost finished sewing the lace onto the cuffs now,' Rowan answered.

Louisa nodded. 'Well, I'm going to make us a hot drink. When you've finished, come through to the living room,' and she disappeared before Rowan could answer.

Louisa had made a pot of strong coffee, and as Rowan joined her at the table, she gave a groan. Without thinking, Rowan patted Louisa's hand and asked what was wrong. The woman stared at her in surprise and Rowan wondered if she'd been impertinent. Louisa was her employer, after all.

'You probably heard the commotion?' Louisa finally asked. Rowan nodded. 'That was my father. He visits sometimes to ensure his investment, as he likes to call it, is showing a profitable return. Tonight, though, he had a different reason.'

'His investment?' Rowan asked.

Louisa gave a deep sigh. 'You remember me saying I shall never marry?' Rowan nodded. 'Well, that's because of him.' Louisa's voice was now unusually hard. 'I shall never, ever allow myself to become an object of ridicule like my mother. I expect you've realized my father is away from home a lot?'

'Yes, Mrs Acland told me that his business interests keep him away,' Rowan replied.

'Pah,' Louisa spat. 'They are merely a foil for his dalliances. He has mistresses, you see,' she growled, shaking her head.

'Poor Mrs Acland, she is such a wonderful woman,' Rowan said.

'Yes, she is, and she deserves to be treated better. A while ago, I was visiting a friend when I saw Father being nice, as he likes to calls it, to one of Mother's friend's daughters. He begged me not to tell her. I told him my silence would come at a price. He would have to facilitate my visiting the Grands Boulevards and the Opéra in Paris, to see the great milliners and *modistes* there, pay for my training, then set me up in my own establishment. He blustered about but, like all weak men when they are cornered, he buckled. Of course, I'd never hurt Mother by telling her, and he knows it. However, he couldn't take the risk,' she finished, taking a swallow of her rapidly cooling drink.

'But she knows about his dalliances, doesn't she?' Rowan said, recalling the woman's sad face.

'She suspects, but all the time nobody actually says anything she can pretend to herself. It wouldn't do for me, I can tell you, but that's her way.'

Rowan remembered about her own father and thought perhaps he wasn't so bad after all. He was weak, yes, but he had loved her mother and never cheated on her. Suddenly she was gripped by an overwhelming longing to see him again. Then she realized Louisa was still speaking.

'The real reason for his visit tonight was you, Rowan.'

'Me?'

'Yes, he'd heard I had engaged a pretty young apprentice, and called by to be introduced.' For the first time since Rowan had left Mrs Acland's house, the ribbon tightened around her wrist. 'Now, you must go and get some rest, for you will have a busy day tomorrow.'

Rowan went up to bed with her head full of her impressions of the day, but despite her excitement she immediately fell into a deep sleep.

First thing the next morning she jumped eagerly out of bed, rinsed her face and brushed her hair until it gleamed. Donning the boned corset, she grimaced, but as she climbed into her petticoats and new dress, carefully smoothing out the folds of her full skirts, she felt elated. Why, I feel like a lady, she thought, pinning up her copper curls under the lace-trimmed bonnet and giving a twirl in front of the tiny glass on the dressing table.

She made her way downstairs and, mindful of Louisa's instructions, snatched up the broom and hurried out to sweep the walkway in front of the shop. Staring up at the tall, regal-looking buildings with their leaded windows, she couldn't help smiling.

What a contrast to her previous rural surroundings, she thought. The sudden memory of her old home tugged at her heartstrings but she shook herself, for wasn't she lucky to be working in this smart Regency town? As the tang of salt carried by the onshore breeze wafted towards her, she inhaled deeply. Exhilaration tingled in her veins. Although she couldn't actually see the sea, it was only at the end of the road, and she fully intended to promenade beside it on

265

her half-day. Unbidden, memories of collecting seaweed with Sab on the beach at Saltcombe sprang into her mind, but she firmly pushed them away. This was her life now, and her father and Sab would soon know where they could find her if they had a care to.

People were already bustling about their business, some looking at her curiously, others calling out in greeting. Noticing there was a patina of dust on the windows, she hurried back inside for a cloth. As she gave the panes a vigorous polish, her gaze was drawn to the pretty May Day bonnet with its candy-coloured ribbons elegantly presented on its stand. It was a masterpiece and she couldn't help wondering who would buy it. Beyond that, the other bonnets were displayed artistically, and she had to agree that not quite being able to see them from the pavement certainly made one inclined to enter the shop and view them properly. It was indeed a shrewd sales ploy, and Madame Louisa was obviously a good business-woman as well as a creative milliner.

'Good morning, Miss Rowena.' Spinning round, Rowan saw Mrs Parker beaming at her.

'Good morning, Mrs Parker,' she replied, before hurry-ing back down the entry. However, no sooner had she disposed of her cloth and walked through to the shop to turn the sign round to open, than the doorbell tinkled and the woman entered. Rowan watched her employer, bright smile on her face, briskly step through the curtained door-way from the workroom and greet the woman.

'Good morning, Mrs Parker. How kind of you to pay my establishment such an early morning visit,' she said. 'I trust you are quite well?'

'Indeed, Madame Louisa.' There was a slight pause. 'I couldn't help noticing you had a visitor last night. Your father, I believe?' Mrs Parker said, looking at Louisa expectantly.

'Your acute powers of observation never fail to amaze me, Mrs Parker,' Louisa answered smoothly. 'Now, how may I be of help?'

'Madame Louisa, I feel it is I who may be of assistance to you and, as such, have come to offer my services. You see, it occurred to me only last evening that your new apprentice might well be in need of a person to practise upon, someone discreet, like myself,' Mrs Parker said, giving a little cough.

Remembering Louisa's words of the previous afternoon, Rowan stared hard at the woman's ears.

'Well, how kind of you, Mrs Parker, and should I require such assistance for Miss Rowena then you can be sure it will be you I think of. This morning, however, I shall be busy instructing my apprentice in the procedures of the workroom and familiarizing her with the tools of our trade. Now, perhaps I may assist you? You are in need of a new bonnet, perhaps? Maybe ribbons or feathers for trimming your current one?' she asked, all the while carefully edging the woman towards the door.

'No, no, I merely came to offer my services,' Mrs Parker said quickly. 'You know how I deem myself to be a pillar of the community.'

'Indeed you do, Mrs Parker, and appreciating how busy you are, allow me to open the door for you. Thank you so much for calling,' Louisa said, the little bell tinkling again as she pushed it firmly closed behind the woman.

'Well, Miss Rowena,' Louisa said. 'Come through to the workroom and we shall begin your instruction. Rule number one: always be pleasant to your client, even when you know they have no intention of buying,' she said, indicating for Rowan to take a seat.

'But isn't that a waste of time? I mean, if you know she isn't going to buy anything . . .' Rowan began.

'Ah, but we do not know how many people Mrs Parker will speak with today,' Louisa cut in. 'If we give her any reason to spread gossip, believe you me, she will.'

'I didn't see her ears grow.'

Louisa laughed. 'Well keep looking and maybe you will be lucky on her next visit which, I feel, will surely be tomorrow. Now, rule number two is to make each and every client feel valued. Pay close attention to everything they say, and respond as if it is the most interesting thing you have ever heard. Even if they tell you it is raining and every other client before them has said the self-same thing, it is news to you. That way, they will leave feeling respected and treasured and, one hopes, vowing to return again soon. Keep the client happy and our business will be happy too. Memorize those rules, and I shall tell you the rest tomorrow. May I say how smart you look in your apprentice outfit? Do you find it comfortable to wear?' Louisa asked, looking Rowan up and down.

'Oh, yes, the material isn't scratchy at all,' she answered, thinking it prudent not to mention how restrictive she was finding the new corset. 'I was amazed how quickly you were able to turn it into this lovely dress.'

'Well, I wouldn't be a very good mantua maker if I couldn't. Time is money, as they say, and most people don't have either to waste. Now let us take a look at the tools of our trade,' she said, turning her attention to the work table.

By the time Louisa told her she could take her break for luncheon, Rowan's head was swimming with strange images and peculiar names. There were wooden blocks and sparteries for moulding, boisiers, singalettes, *camions*, umpteen pins of varying lengths, chalk markers, hammers, irons, *coqs*, stretchers and reels of wire. As for the trimmings, apparently, feathers were ordered from the plumassier, flowers and foliage from *feuillagistes* or veruriers. She'd never dreamed there were so many different fabrics. Why, she'd never remember half of them, she thought, supping the broth Maria set before her.

'You look like you've lost a shilling and found a farthing,' the maid of all work said.

'I'll never learn everything I've been shown this morning,' Rowan sighed.

'You wait till ma'am starts you on that fancy French talking,' Maria said, looking at her knowingly.

'French talking?' Rowan gasped. 'I don't know any of that.'

'Me neither, but it's ma'am's way. She trained in Paris and some other French place I can never remember. Anyway, when she uses these hifalutin words, she waves her hands around like this.' The maid giggled, putting her nose in the air as she demonstrated. 'Don't worry, Miss Rowena, you'll soon get the hang of it all. When me and my follower, Jem, do marry you can make me one of those fancy bonnets. It would be nice to have something prettier to wear than this,' she said, taking off her maid's plain cap and grimacing at it. 'Well, better get over to next door. They share me, you see,' she added, placing the cap back on her halo of curls.

'Isn't it time you weren't here, Maria?' Louisa said, coming into the room.

The maid's eyes widened and she scuttled out of the door as fast as her ample frame would allow. Rowan sprang to her feet.

'I'll get back to the workroom,' she said.

'Before you go, I feel I should finish our conversation from last night. I was angry and upset and I thank you for listening. Should my father visit here whilst I am out on business, please tell him to call another time. Say that is your employer's instruction,' she said, as Rowan frowned. 'Maria is right when she says Father will only pay for a maid of all work, and for the minimum of hours he can get away with,' she said with a sigh. Feeling uncomfortable at her employer's disclosure, Rowan turned to go.

'Father and I are both victims of our own actions, I'm afraid,' Louisa continued, seeming not to notice. 'He presumes I won't tell Mother about his philandering, but can't be certain. I, on the other hand, am on tenterhooks in case he withdraws his allowance and closes my business. So there we are, Rowan, both of us trapped. I wouldn't normally talk about my private affairs but as my apprentice you are my responsibility and should be aware of how things are, especially as my family visit from time to time. My web gets ever more tangled than old Mrs Willett's lace,' she said, shrugging her shoulders.

Not knowing what to say, Rowan just smiled politely.

'Now . . .' her employer said briskly. 'We shall spend

this afternoon in the shop itself. I will talk you through the bonnets, their shapes, fabrics and trimmings. It will be a chance for you to see how much you have remembered from your lesson in the workroom.'

Rowan gulped.

'It is the best way to learn, so don't look worried. Whilst I have my luncheon, please ensure the fitting area is neat and clean. I have seen a couple of clients this morning, and the room needs tidying and refreshing with my signature scent.'

Rowan hurried through to the shop where there was a fitting area partitioned by another white and blue curtain. As she tidied and straightened the chairs, she noticed they were also covered in the same material, lending the whole place an aura of sophistication. She'd just finished refreshing the dressing area with Louisa's fragrance, deliberating whether the floral undertone could be lilac or peony, when the shop door tinkled and an elegantly dressed lady of middle years stepped daintily inside.

'Good afternoon, madam,' Rowan said politely. The woman inclined her head and then walked over to the bonnet in the window.

'I would like to try this, if I may?' she asked.

Rowan gulped. Was she permitted to take it out of the window? Louisa had said she must keep the client happy.

'Mrs Crawford, good afternoon. I do hope my new apprentice, Miss Rowena, has been attending to you?' Louisa said, coming into the room with a rustle of skirts.

Rowan gave a sigh of relief. She would have to find out what exactly she was permitted to do.

'I have only this moment stepped inside, Madame Louisa,' the woman said with a smile. 'I happened to be passing by when my eye was caught by that delightful creation in your window. It would be perfect for Lady Arlingham's May Day celebrations. If the weather is clement, she is hoping to hold it in the open air,' she said, eyes bright with anticipation.

'Allow me to put it on for you,' Louisa said, carefully lifting the bonnet from its stand. 'Do come through to the fitting room,' she said, sweeping back the curtain. 'Miss Rowena will be on hand with the looking-glass so that you may see how the back looks.'

With a swish of the curtain, the two ladies disappeared. As Rowan stared around the shop, she spotted the plain hand mirror lying on the counter. Picking it up, she couldn't help remembering the beautiful one of her mother's. With a dreadful pang she recalled how it had been left behind in the copse when she'd been snatched. As if that wasn't bad enough, Fanny would now be able to access her room without the mirror there to guard it. She wondered if anyone had found it.

Another swish of the curtain brought her back to the present.

'Looking-glass, please, Miss Rowena,' Louisa called. Hurrying over, she held it up so that the woman could see the back of the hat in the ornate standing mirror before her.

'Oh, that is quite exquisite,' Mrs Crawford trilled.

'It's as if it has been especially made for you, madam,' Louisa flattered.

'What do you think, girl?' the woman asked, giving Rowena the full force of her stare.

Rowan's heart sank. Should she say what the woman wanted to hear, or what she honestly felt?

Chapter 26

'Well, Miss Rowena? Won't you please share with us your humble opinion,' Louisa said, frowning at her hesitation.

'It is indeed the perfect shape for madam's face,' she stuttered. But the woman was staring at Rowan.

'You are not totally convinced, my dear, I can tell,' she persisted.

As her employer shot her a warning look, Rowan thought quickly.

'I just wondered what colour dress madam would be wearing with it,' she said.

Mrs Crawford considered. 'Purple, dear. I shall be wearing purple silk.'

'Perhaps Miss Rowena would care to give us her considered opinion on the match,' Louisa said, throwing Rowan a challenging look.

'Oh, yes, please do, dear. I do like a person who is not afraid to say what they really think,' Mrs Crawford said, staring at Rowan, reflected in the looking-glass.

Rowan glanced around, her eyes lighting on the myriad ribbons adorning the shelf above the counter.

'I feel that perhaps if the bonnet were trimmed with contrasting lilac, deep rose and perhaps buttercup, it would complement madam's dress better. The bonnet should be your crowning glory and the pale pinks and whites would fade into the background,' Rowan said. As the little fitting room fell silent, Rowan swallowed hard. Had she been too impertinent?

Then the woman turned to her and smiled. 'Would you hold them up against the bonnet, please?' Rowan turned to Louisa, who nodded, so she duly draped the ribbons over the bonnet.

'Well, well, well,' the woman said, turning this way and that in front of the mirror. 'Madame Louisa, you have a *modiste* in the making. These colours completely transform the bonnet and yet they are still the perfect colours for May Day. If you can have them changed and the bonnet delivered tomorrow, I shall purchase.'

'Of course, Mrs Crawford,' Louisa said. 'Rest assured, I will see Miss Rowena makes the changes herself.'

As the little bell tinkled behind the woman's retreating back, Louisa turned to Rowan and quirked an eyebrow. Rowan's heart thumped in her chest. Had she gone too far? Would she be sacked?

'Well, Miss Rowena, that was diplomatically handled, for of course I could see the pink and white ribbons were *en mésalliance*,' her employer said, waving her hand theatrically in the air.

'Pardon?' Rowan said, her eyes widening.

'It means an inappropriate match. They would have done her dress no justice,' she said briskly.

Well, if her employer knew, why hadn't she told the woman herself?

'Now,' Louisa said, placing the hat on the counter, 'please see that the fitting room is tidied and refreshed.'

'Of course,' Rowan said, letting out a silent breath of

relief. 'I do like this material,' she added, pointing to the curtain.

'That is toile de Jouy and I would be pleased if you would familiarize yourself with these names. Clients expect to deal with people who are knowledgeable,' she added. 'And on that subject, when you have finished tidying, we will go through the names and types of bonnets on display. Then, should you feel the need to suggest alterations to another client, as least you will know what you are talking about,' she said, shaking her head as she disappeared through to the workroom.

Oh dear, Rowan thought. It appeared she had offended her employer after all. She picked up the May Day hat and carefully replaced it on the stand in the window.

As Rowan tidied the fitting room, her mind was in turmoil. Had she been wrong to tell Mrs Crawford the truth? Perhaps she should have followed her employer's lead and flattered the woman. But Louisa had said they had a duty to the client, and surely that meant ensuring they looked their best. Oh, it was all so confusing. Perhaps she should go back to milking cows. At least she knew where she stood with them.

'Miss Rowena, if you've quite finished, we will continue your instruction,' Louisa said coming through to the shop.

Quickly pulling the curtain back into place, Rowan nodded.

'First, we will go through some of the basic shapes of bonnet. I have on display examples of each model, covered in different fabrics and trimmings. These can be altered to suit the client, or purchased as they are,' her employer said.

Rowan stared at the bonnets on the stands and frowned. 'How do I know how much they are? They haven't got the prices on,' she said.

Louisa arched an eyebrow. 'One never flaunts prices, Miss Rowena. That is a vulgar custom practised by lower trades. However, should a client enquire, and most simply request their purchase be charged to their account, then you refer to this,' she said, bending to retrieve a gilt-edged book from a drawer beneath the counter. 'I must stress the importance of keeping this discreetly concealed at all times. The client must never see it. Of course, until you are more familiar with the business, you will refer to me before dealing with financial affairs. You understand, Miss Rowena?'

Rowan nodded. That suited her fine.

'Now you will find that most bonnets are constructed in a similar manner. It is the shape and fabric that differentiates them. This one, for example, is wired buckram, which of course can be covered with material of the client's choice. Each bonnet is customized to the individual's requirement, and I hardly need tell you that it would be *mal à propos* to sell two clients identical ones.' From the grave look her employer was giving her, Rowan gathered it was something she mustn't do on any account. Well, it made sense to her, for didn't all ladies have different colouring?

'This is the *bavolet*, or curtain,' Louisa continued, pointing to the frilled fabric at the back. 'Then you have the outer brim, the under brim, which is usually best lined in a toning material, the crown and the ties, which in this case are silk twill.' Louisa ran her hand gently over the materials as she spoke.

Rowan gulped. 'I had no idea bonnets were made up of so many bits,' she said.

'It is indeed a misconception that a simple bonnet is easy to make. But then, Miss Rowena, I pride myself on creating *les pièces de résistance* and not run-of-the-mill. I encourage clients to make their own selections from the material here,' she said, indicating the bales neatly lined along the shelves. 'Then I adorn that with the ribbons, feathers, flowers or trimming they desire. These examples here are merely to give them an idea. Taking into account their face shape, age, colouring and, in some cases, budget, it is your job to ensure they make the best choices. Although their means are never discussed, of course,' she said, turning to look directly at Rowan. 'That would be infra dig,' she added in a hushed voice.

Rowan gathered that she meant it was something she mustn't do. But if she wasn't told how much they had to spend how could she know what to suggest?

Her employer had already moved on to another stand and Rowan had to admire her energy.

'This we call the coal scuttle bonnet,' Louisa said.

Rowan laughed. 'I can see why. It's because of its shape, isn't it?'

'Indeed,' Louisa said. 'This example is covered with geranium silk twill and lined with a paler pink cotton bobbinet. The inner brim is covered with black silk and has matching black ties, also in silk twill.'

'You'd have to have strong colouring to get away with that, wouldn't you?' Rowan observed.

'You would,' Louisa agreed. 'As I have said, though, these are examples and all the bonnets can be customized to suit the clients' requirements. We are here to invoke their desires,' she said.

'You mean like a charm. Assemble the ingredients, add some magic and . . .'

'*Voilà*,' supplied Louisa, waving her hand like a wand and smiling for the first time since Mrs Crawford had left. 'I think we understand each other perfectly and as I have said before, I will be incorporating your idea of using flower names for the colours. I could see Mrs Crawford was really impressed when you mentioned lilac, rose and buttercup. It conjures up delightful images, reflecting perfectly the ambience I strive to portray. Now, back to bonnets. This one I have named Little Miss and, as you might suppose, it is designed for the younger ladies in our society. Then, of course, there are bonnets covered in black crepe for mourning, and calashes, which are hoods with hoops, old-fashioned but very useful for keeping caps and bonnets dry during inclement weather.' Louisa turned to check that Rowan was taking in everything.

'I have so much to learn, don't I?' Rowan said, shaking her head.

'Yes, there is certainly more to it than one would suppose. Of course, as a mantua maker, I also visit ladies' homes to measure and fit them for their dresses. Usually they purchase their own materials for that, so it is merely a case of sewing that up and adding any trimming they want.'

The little bell tinkled, and a woman of senior years stood on the step looking furtively around, before entering the shop. Louisa turned to Rowan, whispering,

'Observe and learn. Good afternoon, madam. How may I be of assistance?' she asked, smiling in welcome.

'Good afternoon. I am new to the district and wondered if you . . .' She stuttered to a halt, glancing nervously in Rowan's direction.

'Miss Rowena, perhaps you would be good enough to attend to materials in the workroom,' Louisa said quickly.

'Of course, Madame Louisa,' she replied, and disappeared through the curtain separating the two areas. She watched as the older woman bent closer to Louisa and whispered urgently. Her employer smiled reassuringly and wrote something in another little book. As the woman hurried out of the shop, the little bell tinkling in her wake, Rowan rejoined her employer.

'She didn't buy anything, then?' she asked, in surprise.

'Miss Carruthers placed an order. You will sometimes find that ladies of a certain age can be nervous of discussing their requirements in public. She is urgently in need of a new mantua and I have promised to call upon her first thing in the morning. Luckily she requires one in the traditional style, which, being straighter and narrower, will take minimal material and less time to make up,' Louisa said, smiling. 'I wasn't intending to leave you alone so soon, but I'm sure you will manage. It will give you time to finish retrimming that bonnet for Mrs Crawford if you don't manage to get it done tonight.'

Rowan gulped, but before she could voice her fears of being left alone, the room went dark as a carriage drew up outside the window.

The bell gave its little tinkle and a tall, regal-looking

lady swept into the shop, her silk skirts rustling in her wake.

'Good afternoon, Lady Arlingham. What a lovely surprise,' Louisa greeted her.

'Madame Louisa, I was passing by your shop when my eye was taken by that magnificent bonnet in the window, and knew I just had to have it. I am hosting a little soirée on May Day and that will be quite perfect. Please have it delivered tomorrow. Good afternoon.'

Before Louisa could open her mouth to answer, the woman left. Horrified, Louisa stared at the bonnet in the window but the carriage was already drawing away.

'How did that get there?' she asked, turning to Rowan. 'I left it on the counter ready for the trimmings to be changed for Mrs Crawford.'

'I placed it back on the stand when I was tidying away,' Rowan murmured.

'How could you? Once a hat is sold it is never left on display,' her employer berated.

'I'm sorry, I didn't realize,' Rowan said, her knees trembling.

'Whatever shall I do? I've already promised the hat to Mrs Crawford, yet Lady Arlingham is a woman of great standing here in Saltmouth. My reputation will be ruined,' she whispered, sinking onto the chair.

Aware that she'd committed a cardinal sin, Rowan thought hard.

'Perhaps if you explained to Mrs Crawford, she would be happy to choose another one,' she ventured.

'I suppose I could call and see her, offer her a more

expensively trimmed bonnet for the price of the original. But, no, that would never work. It would be *mal à propos* if she were to appear in public more handsomely attired than her hostess.'

'But who would know?' Rowan asked, frowning.

'I would know and Lady Arlingham would see from the trimmings . . .' Louisa's protests were cut short as the little bell tinkled once more and Mrs Parker stepped through the door.

'Good afternoon, Mrs Parker,' Louisa said, getting to her feet and forcing a smile.

'Madame Louisa, I am most perplexed,' the woman said, her beady eyes brimming with curiosity.

'Indeed, Mrs Parker, and why might that be?' Louisa asked, with a barely suppressed sigh.

'Earlier this afternoon I was taking tea with Mrs Crawford when she told me she had purchased that beautiful new bonnet you have had on display, for Lady Arlingham's May Day gathering. She was in such a state of excitement. Well, imagine my surprise when I just happened to be passing your shop and saw it still displayed in the window. I know you have only made one, as you told me yourself. I also know it is your policy to remove a bonnet once it has been sold, so I wondered if my dear friend might have been mistaken about her purchase. She is getting on in years and prone to forgetfulness,' Mrs Parker said, with a shake of her head.

Rowan heard Louisa smother a very unladylike exclamation.

'Don't worry, Mrs Parker. Your powers of observation are as acute as ever, as is Mrs Crawford's memory. I think you will be suitably reassured when you see them both at the party. I take it you, too, have been invited?' Louisa asked solicitously. In a snap, Mrs Parker's gleeful look was replaced by a scowl.

'I merely wished to acquaint you with my findings in case a mistake had occurred,' the woman muttered, giving an indignant sniff as she hurried from the shop.

'If only you knew, Mrs Parker, if only you knew,' Louisa whispered, flopping back down on the chair.

'She only came in to make mischief, didn't she?' Rowan asked.

Louisa nodded.

'And you knew she wasn't invited to the soirée, didn't you?'

Louisa nodded again. 'She is a nosy woman, inclined to spite. For obvious reasons, her presence is hardly ever requested at social gatherings. Still, that doesn't solve our problem, does it?'

'I'm really sorry . . .' Rowan began, but Louisa interrupted.

'No, it's my fault for not ensuring the bonnet was placed in the workroom ready for the ribbons to be changed. Well, it is time to close the shop for today. Let us go through and have something to eat. Maria will have left something ready. We can ponder a solution whilst we eat. If, indeed, there is one,' she said, looking despondent.

Rowan felt a pang when she saw how ashen her employer looked. Although she had been quite reasonable under the circumstances, Rowan was mortified to have caused her such anxiety.

The little maid had left a rabbit stew simmering on the open range and, despite her anxiety about their predicament, the smell made Rowan's mouth water. There were freshly baked rolls to mop up the rich gravy, and although they ate in silence she felt her spirits reviving. Her imagination went into overdrive as she strove to find an answer. As her mind went over all the bonnets displayed in the shop, a vision of the two women popped into her head. Excitedly, she jumped to her feet.

'That's it!' she exclaimed, making Louisa jump. 'They're both so different.'

'Sorry, Rowan, do you think you could elucidate?' Louisa asked, quite forgetting to call her Miss Rowena.

'Mrs Crawford is quite petite, like me, while Lady Arlingham is tall and, well, a bit on the large side,' she said. 'So I think I have the answer to the problem.'

Chapter 27

'Miss Rowena, just because you are the cause of this trouble, I don't think there's any need to be rude,' Louisa protested, looking aghast.

'Oh, I'm not, Madame Louisa. Truly I'm not,' Rowan cried. 'I merely meant that as Lady Arlingham is quite, well, regal, that bonnet would get lost on her head. The other one with the bigger crown – sorry, I've forgotten its name – would suit her better,' she said breathlessly.

'You mean the Lady Anna cottage bonnet? Yes, I can see that its height and wider brim would be more appropriate for Lady Arlingham's stature. However, the one displayed in the window was the Lady Rachel model,' Louisa pointed out.

'I know, but when she came into the shop, she only pointed to the window. She didn't actually look at the bonnet, did she?'

'I'm sorry, Rowan, I'm not sure I take your point,' Louisa said.

'If she only spotted it from her carriage, she would have seen just the front view. She didn't study it closely or try it on, did she? Were you to cover the Lady Anna bonnet in the same colours and trim it with those pink and white ribbons, it would look suitably like the one in the window. Mrs Crawford tried hers on so she knows what hers will look like, but with the change of ribbons we discussed. If we were also to change the colour of that bit around the face on hers, they'd look completely different from the front, wouldn't they?'

'The underbrim, you mean? Yes, I can picture what you say. Well, that might just solve our problems,' Louisa said, giving Rowan a warm smile. Relief flooded through her but her employer was already back in business mode. 'Come along, Miss Rowena, I fear we have a long night ahead of us.' Louisa was already getting to her feet. 'You are about to get an instant master class in millinery.'

Throughout that long night as the candles burned lower in their sticks, they sewed, pleated and frilled until finally the two bonnets were completed. As Louisa sat back and studied them carefully, Rowan held her breath. After all the trouble she'd caused, it would be dreadful if her employer found her stitching wanting.

'Well, Miss Rowena,' she finally proclaimed, with a weary smile. 'I think we have created two suitably diverse May Day bonnets that I hope will pass muster. Fingers crossed we get away with our little subterfuge or my reputation will be in shreds.' She stifled a yawn, as she carefully packed them into two hatboxes lined with the softest tissue paper. As her signature scent wafted around the workroom, Rowan tried not to yawn herself. 'Right, I'm going to snatch a few hours' sleep before our work is put to the test,' Louisa announced, getting to her feet.

'I'll clear up in here,' Rowan said, pointing to the table, which was strewn with scraps of material, ribbons and equipment.

'One thing I feel I have to say before I go,' Louisa said, her voice so stern Rowan's heart lurched. Was she going to be fired for her mistake, even after working so hard tonight? 'What is the one thing you must never forget?'

'Never place a bonnet that has been sold back in the window,' Rowan said.

'Yes, and you must also remember the secrets of the milliner stay in the workroom. With any luck, both ladies will be so delighted with their creations it will never occur to them they have had the material pulled over their eyes,' Louisa said, her own eyes twinkling with amusement. 'Now you go and get some rest, too. You can clear this little lot away whilst I am out on my appointments. That's after you've made a replacement hat for the window.'

'What?' Rowan shrieked.

'Just my little joke, Miss Rowena,' Louisa said, laughing as she left the workroom.

Despite not getting to bed until the early hours, Rowan was up at first light. A legacy from her life on the farm, she thought, wondering how her father and Sab were faring. Father should have received her letter by now and she hoped she'd receive a reply soon. Splashing her face with water from the jug Maria had left on the washstand, she dressed quickly and hurried downstairs and out to the yard. The privy was clean and quite serviceable, but as she watched the huge dark spiders scuttling up the walls to their webs that festooned the corners, she was glad she wasn't afraid of them.

Snatching up the broom, she hurried through the entry to sweep the pavement outside. Louisa was placing another elegant bonnet, this one of rose and gold, on its stand in the window, and she nodded in greeting. Obviously, Rowan was forgiven for her *faux pas* of the previous day. Goodness, she was beginning to think in French like her employer now.

'Good morning, Miss Rowena,' her employer trilled as she appeared in the shop. 'Have you eaten yet?'

'No, I thought I'd better tidy up the workroom first,' Rowan said, although her stomach was rumbling like a cart over cobbles.

'I appreciate your diligence, but after your long night's work your body needs sustenance. Maria has made a pot of porridge so go and help yourself. When you've eaten, I will instruct you on what's to be done in my absence.'

Feeling better after breaking her fast, Rowan hurried back to the shop with renewed energy and enthusiasm.

'Now, Miss Rowena,' Louisa said, 'whilst I am out I would like you to tidy up the workroom and then label the ribbons with your flower names. It's occurred to me that we need to ensure we always call them by the same name, or confusion could occur.'

'How shall I know what names you want to use?' Rowan asked, eager to get everything right today.

'As you are familiar with the vernacular names, such as you have been using, I will be quite happy to go along with those you choose. It will be good for you to assume responsibility from the beginning of your apprenticeship, Miss Rowena, and I have the utmost faith in your abilities,' Louisa said, smiling.

'What, after my *faux pas* yesterday?' Rowan asked.

Louisa gave one of her tinkling laughs. 'I'm impressed by the way you're using French expressions. I think it lends an air of sophistication and we should work well together,' she said.

Rowan smiled, not feeling it necessary to let on she only knew what Louisa had taught her.

'As for yesterday, well, we all make mistakes. The thing to do is learn from them and move on. Now I shall deliver Mrs Crawford's bonnet and then call upon Miss Carruthers. If I have time to deliver it before noon, I will call back to collect Lady Arlingham's bonnet. Otherwise, it will have to wait until later this afternoon, after social visiting has finished.'

'Social visiting?' Rowan asked.

'Yes, between the hours of noon and three the ladies of Saltmouth pay their daily visits. Call upon their neighbours and friends,' Louisa elaborated, seeing Rowan's blank look.

'You mean they stay for three whole hours?' she asked.

Louisa laughed. 'No, silly. They stay for precisely fifteen minutes per visit and then move on to their next point of call.'

'But supposing they are halfway through a sentence when their time is up?' Rowan asked, frowning.

This time Louisa's laugh was louder. 'That would hardly be socially acceptable. No, these ladies have got their etiquette down to a fine art. I understand they merely pass the time of day with small talk.'

'Well, it sounds stupid to me. Why don't they all get together in one house and save all that moving around?'

'I can't say I disagree with your sentiment. However, that's how society works in Saltmouth, and it pays our business to respect this. Personally I find these quiet hours the perfect time to catch up on my bonnet making. Now, whilst I am away, please deal with any client politely and efficiently. Take a note of their name, address and requirements in that red book on the counter. Tell them Madame Louisa will call upon them to fulfil their order as soon as she returns,' she said, gathering up her workbag and hatbox. Rowan hurried to open the door for her employer, nerves flitting like butterflies in her stomach. Did Louisa really think she could manage the shop in her absence?

She busied herself tidying the workroom and then, in her neatest handwriting, began penning the labels for the ribbons, as Louisa had instructed. Gradually, as she became absorbed in her task, her nerves subsided and she began to enjoy herself. She was just deliberating between buttercup and primrose for the shiny yellow, when the shop bell tinkled. Smoothing down her apron, she hurried through the dividing curtain.

'Well, hello there. And who do we have here?' a smartly dressed gentleman boomed in a voice far too loud for the small room. He stood there for a full moment, blatantly eyeing her up and down. With his brown hair, short legs and portly stomach protruding from his waistcoat, he reminded Rowan of a weasel from the woods.

'Good morning, sir. How may I be of help?' Rowan asked, willing her own voice not to squeak.

'Amos Acland at your service, my dear,' he boomed, doffing his top hat. 'I have called by to see that daughter of mine, Louisa.'

'I'm afraid Madame Louisa is out visiting a client. May I give her a message?' Rowan enquired, hoping to keep his visit as short as possible.

'Madame Louisa, eh?' he laughed. 'And what may I call you, young lady?'

'Miss Rowena, sir,' she said. 'Madam is likely to be some time so if you'd like to state your business, I shall, of course, see that she gets your message.'

'If I were to tell you what I'd like my business to be, it would bring a blush to that pretty little face of yours,' he smirked.

Rowan shuddered and took a step backwards. Surely sweet Mrs Acland couldn't be married to this insidious little creep? But then, he had said he was Louisa's father. With great difficulty, she fought down the urge to slap the sickly smile off his shiny face. Taking a deep breath, she forced a smile.

'Your message, sir?' she asked, pleased to hear her voice sounded firmer this time.

'Don't worry, Miss Rowena. I shall call again – very soon,' he added, his grey-blue eyes glittering. Then, with another doff of his hat, he went out to his carriage, which was drawn up outside.

With her legs trembling, Rowan collapsed on to the chair. What a truly obnoxious man. She couldn't believe he was married to the refined Mrs Acland, or that he was father of the gentlemanly Alexander and ladylike Louisa. Then she remembered what Louisa had said about his philandering ways and shuddered. The tinkling of the bell roused her from her reverie. Jumping to her feet, she pasted on a smile and then nearly groaned aloud when she saw Mrs Parker bustling through the door.

'Was that Mr Acland's carriage I saw leaving?' she asked, her eyes bright with curiosity.

'Good morning, Mrs Parker, how may I help you?' Rowan asked, ignoring the question.

The woman glanced around the shop. 'Is Madame Louisa not here?'

'Not unless she's hiding in a hatbox,' Rowan said. Then, not wanting the woman to think she was being rude, she smiled. 'Sorry, Mrs Parker, just my little joke.'

'Well, I'm not daft, dear. She would never fit inside one, would she?'

Rowan raised her eyebrows. It was going to be a long morning.

'Anyway, not to worry, I'll call another time,' Mrs Parker said, pausing to look at the bonnet in the window. 'I think that one is far more tasteful than the one Mrs Crawford has purchased. All those pink and white ribbons will do nothing for her complexion,' she said, grinning gleefully, as she bustled out of the shop again.

Clearly Mrs Crawford hadn't chosen to share the fact that she was having the colours of her ribbons changed, Rowan thought, smiling as she took herself back to the workroom and resumed her task. Having neatly labelled the rolls of ribbons, she then arranged them on the shelves in their colour bands. She had just finished and was admiring her handiwork when Louisa appeared in a rustle of petticoats. Placing her workbag on the work table, she turned to look at Rowan.

'Everything all right, Miss Rowena?' she asked. Rowan thought again how elegantly presented her employer was in her sapphire dress with its pin-tucked bodice and dome-shaped skirts. Her bonnet, with its toning ties and single egret feather, tastefully completed the ensemble.

Rowan wondered if she could ever achieve such a sophisticated appearance. Probably not, with her mop of copper curls to manage, she decided.

'Has anything upset you, Rowan? You look, I don't know, quite remote somehow,' her employer said, forgetting her shop title as she gave her a searching look.

'Everything's fine,' Rowan reassured her.

'I see you have taken it upon yourself to rearrange my ribbons as well as labelling them,' Louisa frowned.

'I just thought they looked more harmonious arranged in their contrasting colours but I can change it back if you don't like it,' Rowan replied quickly.

'No, it's all right. I agree they are far more pleasing to the eye like that. Obviously, I need to get used to someone else having a say around here,' Louisa said with a laugh that didn't quite reach her eyes. 'Now then, have we had any clients this morning?'

'Only two ... well, that is, not clients exactly. There was Mr Acland and then as soon as he left, Mrs Parker came in.'

Louisa raised her eyebrows. 'Did Father leave a message?'

Rowan shook her head.

'And did, by some miracle, Mrs Parker decide to purchase anything?'

Rowan shook her head again.

'Well, I have had a productive morning. I am pleased to report that Mrs Crawford was delighted with her bonnet. She was singing your praises, I can tell you. Miss Carruthers, being of the old school, requires a mantua in a traditional style. I have measured, cut and pinned it, and brought it back for you to sew up,' Louisa said, drawing out a length of drab from her bag.

'What a dreadful colour,' Rowan said, grimacing at the dull yellow-brown material.

'It's what the client wants, Miss Rowena, and probably more to the point, what she can afford. It's not for us to question, and it is business, after all,' her employer pointed out. Rowan nodded and pulled up the high stool. 'As you can see from the shape, Miss Carruthers wanted it fitted above the waist with the open front and draped skirt,' Louisa continued, raising her eyebrows. 'You merely need to follow the pins and use this matching thread,' she added, holding up a reel. 'I did have the temerity to suggest a bow on the front but was met with a stony glare.'

Rowan laughed. She could just imagine the timid woman's reaction to even the tiniest show of frivolity.

'Now, if I hurry, I shall just have time to see if Lady Arlingham approves of her bonnet,' she said, picking up the other hatbox.

As the workroom fell silent, Rowan bent her head over her work. Although the drab was dull in the extreme, it was at least softer than the material of the uniform dresses in the asylum. Glancing around the well-equipped workroom, she couldn't help contrasting it to the sewing room in that dreadful place. She thought of Susan and her baby, and hoped they were at peace. Her fate was a tragic thing to have happened to such a vivacious girl in the prime of life, but at least, as Mrs Acland had pointed out, she had died thinking her Charlie was coming for her.

Carefully, she followed the line that Louisa had pinned, and before long was absorbed in her sewing. If she concentrated she would have it finished before her employer returned, she thought, finishing one seam and picking up the scissors to snip off the thread.

'Well, hello there!' a loud voice boomed, making her jump, so that instead of merely cutting the thread she sliced clean through the material.

As she stared from the ruined mantua up into the florid face of Mr Acland, the ribbon around her wrist tightened.

Chapter 28

'Oh dear, oh dear, oh dear,' Mr Acland's voice boomed so loudly the hand glass on the shelf vibrated. 'It would appear you've got a problem, Miss Rowena,' he smirked, moving closer.

Her ribbon gripped her wrist even tighter.

'But you frightened me half to death,' Rowan sobbed, staring down at the ruined material in dismay. As luck would have it, she'd cut right through the front of the mantua. Why couldn't it have been at the bottom? she thought. It was the first sewing job Louisa had entrusted her with and she was bound to be furious. Would she deduct the money for the material from her wage? Or worse still, sack her so she had no wage at all? Her employer had been quite tolerant of her mistake yesterday, but then no actual damage had been done.

'Don't look so worried, my lovely,' Mr Acland crooned, sidling right up to her. 'You are young and inexperienced. Why don't you let me show you . . .' he began.

Unable to bear his close proximity, she jumped to her feet. 'Please leave me alone,' she cried. The smell of his heavy cologne was overpowering and she glanced around, seeking some way to escape.

He gave another smirk, his glassy eyes boring into her as he placed a hand on her shoulder and pushed her back onto her seat.

'Now then, whatever would dear Madame Louisa say if she found out her apprentice hadn't heard the bell? After all, she did leave you in charge of her shop in her absence, didn't she?' he asked, his eyes narrowing. 'Still, there's no need for her to find out if you . . .' He stuttered to a halt as a figure appeared in the doorway.

'Father,' Louisa spat, two red spots burning her cheeks.

'Louisa, my dear, what a lovely surprise. I thought you'd gone out,' he said smoothly.

'Luckily for Rowan, I had to return for something,' she said, placing the hatbox on the work table. 'When I saw your carriage outside and nobody in the shop, I guessed you were up to no good. What do you think are you doing here in my workroom, Father?' As she stood there, hands on hips, staring glacially at him, he gave a little laugh and edged away from Rowan.

'I was protecting your interests, my dear. You want to be more careful; a thief could have crept in and stolen all your beautiful bonnets. Your new little apprentice here failed to hear the shop bell. When nobody came to attend to me, I came through to make sure everything was all right. Miss Rowena was obviously daydreaming,' he said, smirking at Rowan.

Her heart plummeted. It was true. She'd been so engrossed in her work she hadn't heard the bell tinkle.

'Rowan, it's time for your luncheon. Go and see what Maria's made for us today,' Louisa ordered sternly. With a last glance at the ruined material, Rowan got to her feet and fled the room.

'Blimey, girl, you looks like you seen a ghost. Why, you're shaking,' Maria said when she saw Rowan standing in the kitchen doorway. 'Go and sit at the table and I'll bring you in a bowl of hot broth. That'll put some colour in you.'

For the second time in as many minutes, Rowan did as she'd been told, and moments later the maid appeared carrying a tray. Giving Rowan a searching look, she set the steaming bowl and a plate of bread on the table.

'Want to talk about it?' she asked, pulling out the chair next to Rowan and plonking her generous body on it.

'I think I'm going to lose my job,' Rowan whispered. 'I've cut right through the material I was sewing. It was that Mr Acland, he crept into the workroom and made me jump,' she continued, the words coming out in a rush.

'You want to keep away from him. He's a right dirty old man, that one. Always creeping in through the entry and frightening the living daylights out of me. Only last week, I was bent over the range and he crept up and pinched my behind,' Maria said with a shudder. 'If my Jem finds out, he'll use old Acland's guts for sweeping his chimneys. He's very protective, is my Jem,' she said proudly, puffing out her ample chest.

'Thank you, Maria,' Louisa said, coming into the room.

The maid jumped to her feet. 'Sorry, ma'am, only Miss Rowena here was all upset and I was trying to cheer her up,' she explained.

'That was kind of you, Maria. But I think you should leave her to her luncheon, don't you?'

'Yes, ma'am. I was just saying how a drop of hot broth would put the colour back in her cheeks.'

'Very true. Now if you don't mind I'd like to speak to Miss Rowena in private. I expect Mr Ware is waiting for his luncheon, and we don't want that delicious-smelling broth going cold, do we?' Louisa said firmly.

The maid nodded and scuttled away.

'I'm sorry, Madame Louisa. I'll pay for the damaged material,' Rowan offered.

'There's no need to apologize,' Louisa said.

'But I was so engrossed in what I was doing I didn't hear the shop bell.'

'That's because it didn't ring. I understand Father came in via the entry. Apparently, it is one of his little tricks,' Louisa said.

'Oh, that explains it,' Rowan cried, her heart lifting. 'I'm so glad it wasn't my fault.'

'Don't worry, I will ensure the entry door is kept locked in the future,' Louisa said.

Then Rowan remembered the drab and her heart flopped again. 'But I've still made a mess of the mantua. I was being careful to follow your line of pins,' she said with a sigh.

'Believe you me, there's nothing that can't be rectified. Eat your broth and everything will look better. Now, I really must get back to the shop,' her employer said, patting her shoulder. 'Come through when you've finished.'

Rowan stared down at her bowl, not feeling the least bit like eating, but knowing she must do as her employer instructed. After a few spoonsful, though, the tasty broth warmed her insides and she felt her spirits revive.

Returning to the workroom, she found Louisa sitting on her stool, studying the mantua.

'Feeling better?' she asked.

Rowan nodded.

'Good. I'm pretty certain you won't be bothered by my father again. Now I have had a good look at this, and with a bit of judicious alteration it can be saved.' She unrolled another length of drab. 'Although as Father has kindly insisted that Miss Carruthers have a complimentary one made as well, we will have more work to do.' As Rowan stared at Louisa in surprise, her tinkling laugh filled the room.

'Well, maybe he did take a bit of persuading to open his wallet. Luckily, when I visit a new client, I always take their measurements and then make a pattern,' she said. Rowan watched as Louisa took a shaped sheet of paper from her bag and pinned it on to the material. 'Now, I'd like you to cut this out and begin sewing, whilst I'm at luncheon.'

Rowan stared at her in surprise. 'But I messed up the other one,' she murmured.

'And we all know why that happened,' her employer said briskly. 'You are quite capable, Miss Rowena. When I return I will show you how we can adapt the original garment. Don't look so worried, Miss Carruthers will have her traditional mantua plus an extra one, slightly embellished. When she protests she has only commissioned the one, I shall assure her she will be doing me the utmost kindness in trialling my new design. The poor woman exists on such modest means it will be a wily way of increasing her apparel without compromising her pride.' Getting to her feet, she gestured Rowan to take her place.

As the door shut behind her, Rowan thought what a kind woman her employer was. Who would believe she had such a repulsive man for a father? The vision of her own father's gentle face swam before her, but she forced herself to concentrate on her work, picked up the scissors and nervously made the first incision. Soon she was engrossed in the task and her confidence returned. By the time Louisa reappeared the mantua had been cut out and the first seam sewed.

Louisa took a look and nodded. 'Just like falling off a horse, you have to get straight back in the saddle,' she said with a smile.

Rowan nodded, not liking to say she had always ridden bareback on the farm.

'Let me show you what I propose doing with the other one and you can finish them both off whilst I deliver Lady Arlingham's bonnet,' her employer said. At the thought of being left along again, Rowan's heart sank, but she duly moved her sewing to one side.

'Now, I propose we cut the front into a V to incorporate your little nick,' Louisa said, pointing to where the cut should be made.

'But won't that make the neckline too low?' Rowan asked, remembering the timid little woman.

'Yes, I know what you mean, but we could inset this triangle of contrasting material behind it, thus preserving Miss Carruthers' modesty,' she said, holding up a piece of pale buttermilk cotton. 'Of course, if we were dealing with a less modest person we could really go to town and add a sprigged piece of cotton or a silk bow.'

Rowan stared at her employer in admiration. She would never have thought of such an ingenious solution.

'That should keep you busy for the rest of the day, Miss Rowena,' Louisa said, getting to her feet and throwing a soft lacy blue shawl around her shoulders. 'If you finish before I return, please place Miss Carruthers' pattern in the bottom drawer over there,' she said, indicating the chest in the corner of the room. 'That's where I keep the patterns for all my clients. It saves so much time if I don't have to keep remeasuring them. It also gives me an advantage over the competition.'

'You have competition?' Rowan asked.

'Oh, yes, there are quite a few milliners here in Saltmouth, which is why I also make mantuas. I pride myself on providing the best service possible, and by having my ladies' patterns to hand I can sew them a dress, just like that.' Louisa snapped her fingers. 'I also keep a note of their bonnet size as well. Talking of which, I really must be on my way to Arlingham Hall to see if her ladyship's discerning eye will approve our *pièce de résistance*,' she said, gathering up the hatbox and bustling through to the shop.

Rowan heard the tinkle of the bell and settled down to her sewing. Luckily, this morning's mishap seemed to have turned out all right. Thoughts of the repulsive Mr Acland made her stomach turn and she hoped Louisa was right when she said he wouldn't turn up again.

She had just finished the first mantua and was stretching her back before making a start on the adaptations to the other, when she thought she heard someone outside the workroom. Opening the door, she nearly jumped out of her skin when she saw Maria hovering in the hallway. To her surprise, the maid coloured up and quickly thrust her hands in her apron pocket.

'Is something wrong, Maria?' Rowan asked, frowning.

'Oh, no, Miss Rowena, I was just checking the shop to

make sure madam was out. I came to see if you'd like to go to the May Fair on Monday. My Jem's calling for me. Have you got a follower? Only you can come with us if you haven't. It's being held on the field in front of Curzon Crescent. Jem's promised to try and win me a twit,' she added.

'A twit?' Rowan asked.

'It's a baby goldfish,' Maria said, nervously hopping from one leg to the other.

'That's kind of you, Maria. I'll have to check with Madame Louisa, though. She hasn't told me which is to be my half-day off yet.'

'I could get Jem to bring one of his friends along, if you like,' the maid called, as she hurried back to the kitchen.

Rowan shook her head as she returned to the workroom. The maid had seemed on edge. Surely she hadn't been worried in case Louisa caught them talking? Her employer didn't appear to be a snob. Shaking her head, she picked up the mantua and resumed her sewing. It would be fun to go to the fair. She hadn't had time to explore the little town yet, and it would be lovely to be free for a few hours. Although it was kind of Maria to offer, she really didn't fancy having to spend the afternoon with a man she'd never met. On the other hand, she did want to make new friends.

The shadows were creeping into the corners of the workroom by the time Louisa returned. She walked into the room sniffing the air and frowning.

'Have you refreshed the fitting area this afternoon?' she asked, setting down her bag.

Rowan looked up guiltily. 'No, I haven't, Madame Louisa. Sorry if I was meant to, but I've been so busy sewing the time ran away with me. I'll do it straight away,' she said, jumping to her feet.

Louisa shook her head. 'No, that's all right. Have you had any clients whilst I've been out?'

'No, but I did keep my ears peeled for the bell.' Realizing what she'd said, Rowan burst out laughing.

Louisa smiled. 'I could do with a little light relief after the afternoon I've just experienced,' she said, collapsing onto a chair. 'Lady Arlingham is satisfied with what she is to wear, at last,' she added, with a shake of her fair head. 'She was in a very particular mood, but the funny thing was, she never once said anything about the bonnet not being the one she saw in the window.'

'What was the matter, then?' Rowan asked.

'First of all she queried that it would go with the dress she proposes wearing for her soirée. She then summoned her maid to lay out her full ensemble. She changed into it, wondered if it was grand enough for the occasion, then changed into another. By the time she'd tried on another half-dozen, she decided her original choice was actually the best. Her poor maid was going frantic tidying everything away. Then her ladyship began fussing about which was the best way to wear the bonnet.'

'But surely there is only one way,' Rowan asked.

'Of course there is, but the client is always right, so another half-hour was spent assuring her she looked regal enough to host her party, and would surely be the belle of the ball. In the end, she conceded the bonnet was the *crème de la crème* and I was dismissed. Now let's take a look at your handiwork,' she said, lighting the candles and then picking up the mantuas. Rowan held her breath. She'd taken great care with her stitching for she did so want to do something right for her employer.

'Well done, Miss Rowena,' Louisa pronounced with a smile. 'When I left Arlingham Hall, I took a stroll in the fresh air to clear my head and as I was passing Curzon Crescent, Esther Elliot beckoned to me.' Curzon Crescent? Hadn't Maria said the May Fair would be held in the field by there? Rowan was just about to ask Louisa about her half-day, when she realized her employer was still speaking. 'Anyway, it will be a rush to get it done in time, but she is a valued client and I can't let her down. It will be quiet on Monday with everyone celebrating May Day so I've decided to shut the shop at noon and you can help me make it,' Louisa said, looking at her expectantly. 'You have no objection to your first real instruction on bonnet making being then, have you, Miss Rowena?' she asked, frowning.

'No, of course not,' Rowan said, her heart sinking. She'd have to ask about her half-day another time. After the mistake she'd made putting the bonnet back in the window yesterday and then cutting into the mantua today, she really didn't have any choice in the matter, did she?

Chapter 29

On Monday afternoon, Rowan hurried back to the work-room ready for her first bonnet making instruction. Maria had left for the May Fair in a flurry of excitement at the prospect of spending the rest of the day with her fol-lower. When Rowan had seen the maid dressed in her finery, eyes bright with excitement, she'd experienced a fleeting stab of envy.

Telling herself it was more important to make the most of the opportunity she'd been given, and that she'd have plenty of time to socialize once she'd learned her trade, she began setting out the ostrich feathers she'd spent the morning cleaning. The powder mixture in the bag she'd had to shake them in had smelled so noxious it had got right up her nose, making her eyes water. As soon as she had completed her task, she'd hurried out to the yard to get some fresh air. Still, the feathers were in pristine con-dition now, she thought, setting the tray to one side.

'Right then,' Louisa said, coming into the workroom and interrupting her musing. 'Are you ready for your initi-ation into the world of bonnet making?' Rowan nodded enthusiastically but her employer was frowning down at the ostrich feathers.

'Have I done something wrong?' Rowan asked.

'They look clean enough, but are you sure you took them all out of the bag?'

'Yes, I checked before I went outside to clear my lungs,' Rowan said. 'Why?'

'Well, I could have sworn I unpacked eight this morning but there are only seven here now,' Louisa said, shaking her head. 'Oh, well, not to worry, we'll sort it out later. Now, let's make a start.' She laid out various pattern pieces on the work table. 'I have already measured Esther for her bonnet. So first of all we will trace out the main shape and crown panel, which is the round piece for the back,' she added, seeing Rowan's puzzled look. 'Now we carefully cut out this buckram exactly to the line traced. Sometimes we use a double layer of fabric called willow, a type of grass, but this is so much more convenient.'

Rowan watched her employer's deft movements closely, determined to commit them to memory.

'Pass me some of those pins, please,' Louisa asked, pointing to the little jar, but in her haste to appear willing, Rowan sent it spinning and watched in dismay as pins scattered all over the work table. Louisa clicked her tongue impatiently.

'Sorry,' Rowan gabbled, hurriedly collecting them up, and passing the jar to her employer.

'Right, now we pin the two ends of the main bonnet together. Got that?' she asked, after a few moments. Rowan nodded vigorously. 'Now you sew where you have pinned, using strong thread. I find blanket stitch works best. This is reinforced by the ends overlapping, so there are three rows of stitches. It's really quite straightforward.'

Is it? Rowan thought. She swallowed nervously, feeling hopelessly out of her depth.

Louisa cut a length of wire. 'Right, now bend this gently around the wooden block to form a circle for the crown panel,' she said, handing the wire to Rowan.

'Me?' she squeaked.

'Yes, you, Miss Rowena. How else are you going to learn?' Tentatively, Rowan started to bend the wire. 'I said gently. We don't want any kinks, or the shape will be ruined.'

Rowan tried but it was no good, her hands were shaking so much she couldn't make the wire form into a circle. Silently, Louisa took it from her and moments later the job was done. 'Now we overlap the ends of the wire here and bind them together to the exact size inside the crown.' Although Louisa said 'we', Rowan was relieved her employer did it herself. 'Have you any questions?' Louisa asked, staring at Rowan.

Yes, please can I go home? she pleaded silently and then remembered, this was her home as well as the place she worked in. Wordlessly, she looked at her employer and shook her head.

'It's important to say if there's anything you don't understand,' Louisa said, cutting another length of wire. 'This is for the peak and body of the bonnet. You form the shape around the wooden mould and finish it off by bending gently, using both thumbs, to frame the peak just so. Now join both ends together so that it will be hidden at the back. It all makes complete sense, doesn't it?' Louisa gave Rowan a smile.

No, it does not, the young apprentice wanted to scream.

Completely absorbed in her task and oblivious to Rowan's discomfort, Louisa proceeded to sew the wire into the crown. 'Always make sure the join is at the bottom,' she instructed. 'Nearly there now . . .' She finished sewing the wire into the main part of the bonnet and peak. 'Again, make sure the join is at the bottom. Sew the round piece of buckram to the crown over the back of the bonnet here and *voilà*, we have the finished shape.' She threw her hands in the air in a gesture of artistic triumph.

'I'm not sure I'll ever remember all that,' Rowan said, shaking her head and collapsing onto the stool.

'Of course you will. With the basic frame formed, all we have to do now is select the materials for the covering, lining and trimmings. That is the fun bit, and as you will find, it is all about balance and flow.' The only thing that was flowing was her attention, Rowan thought, but her employer was off again, and making a supreme effort, she turned and faced her, with what she hoped was some semblance of intelligence.

'Before we can go any further, I need to consult with Esther,' Louisa said. 'So I'm afraid that is the end of your lesson today, Miss Rowena.' Thank heavens, Rowan thought. 'I shall pay her a visit later and take some samples for her to choose from. She isn't able to walk very far these days, so I like to make it as easy as I can for her,' Louisa got to her feet. 'I hope you aren't too disappointed,' she added, mistaking Rowan's silence.

'No, of course not,' Rowan said as her employer slipped through the dividing curtain and into the shop. Her head was spinning. Whoever would have thought so much went into the making of a bonnet? Louisa had also said the shape was evolving with new hats already coming into mode in Milan. All she could think was it was a good thing the shop had been closed so they'd had no interruptions.

'Miss Rowena?' Louisa said, coming back into the workroom. 'We haven't had any clients today, have we?'

'No, Madame Louisa,' she replied.

'I thought not. And as such you have had no reason to freshen the fitting room?'

Rowan shook her head. Either her employer was becoming forgetful or obsessed with the freshening process. That was the second time she'd asked, and the shop had been closed since noon.

'Is there a problem?'

Louisa thought for a moment, as if she were weighing up her words. 'I have noticed that the level of scent in the bottle seems to be going down at an alarming rate recently and I wondered . . .' Her voice trailed off as she looked at Rowan speculatively.

'You mean you think I've been stealing it?' she asked, her eyes widening in dismay.

'No, of course not,' her employer said quickly. 'It occurred to me that perhaps you were being a little over-zealous in your duties.'

'I am most careful, Madame Louisa,' Rowan assured her.

'Yes, of course. It's just that my signature fragrance doesn't come cheap. Look, let's forget it. Why don't you see what Maria has left you for supper?' she said, smiling apologetically.

Rowan couldn't forget it, though. Surely Louisa didn't think she was helping herself to things that weren't hers? That thought preyed on her mind all evening, so that she couldn't relax. Deciding she needed some fresh air, she took herself out to the yard. It was still warm, with the scent of lavender and myrtle wafting on the night air. Spirits lifting, she wandered over to the small area of lawn beyond the privy where the wild flowers grew, and threw herself down onto the cool grass. Seeing the daisies, their petals tightly closed for the night, reminded her of Mrs Acland's little maid. As she wondered if Daisy still wore the chain of flowers, her hand went to the ribbon on her wrist.

Staring up at the silvery moon, she shivered. Her future seemed uncertain and she wished her mother was here to advise her. 'So much has changed in the years since you've been gone, Mother, but I do remember what you taught me. Please show me how to prove to Louisa I'm not a thief,' she whispered to the darkening sky. She felt a gentle tug on her ribbon and warmth flooded through her. Mother had heard, and Rowan knew without a shadow of doubt that all would be well.

Reassured, she jumped to her feet. What a numpkin she'd been. Of course, she had a lot to learn about her new trade. Things that mattered never came easily, and tomorrow was another day. She would pay close attention on her next instruction and then persevere until she had mastered the art of bonnet making. And hers wouldn't be just ordinary bonnets. They would be the finest bonnets in the town of Saltmouth, or even the whole county of Devonshire. Giggling at the thought, she let herself in through the entry and was about to return to her room, when she heard a movement in the workroom. Heart thumping louder than the clappers on the church bells, she gingerly pushed open the door.

'Who's there?' she asked, trying to keep her voice steady.

'Golly, girl, you made me jump like a frog,' Maria exclaimed.

'I've just been doing a spot of tidying up. Oh, I've had such a lovely time, Rowan,' she rushed on. 'I'll tell you all about it tomorrow, but now I'm away to my bed to dream.'

Watching as the maid skipped down the corridor, Rowan caught a whiff of floral perfume. Madame Louisa's signature fragrance! Surely the maid hadn't refreshed the fitting room at this time of the night?

'Maria,' she called, but the maid had already disappeared. She'd speak to her in the morning she resolved.

When Rowan woke, she felt rested and eager to get on with the day. The best thing she could do was forget everything else. She couldn't have Louisa thinking she was a thief, but on the other hand, it wasn't in her nature to tell tales. Remembering how kind the maid had been to her after Mr Acland's visit, she sighed. She was still undecided as to what to do, as she turned the little sign on the shop to 'open' the next morning. The one thing she was sure about was that she would master the art of making a bonnet.

'Good morning, Miss Rowena,' Louisa said, appearing through the curtain. 'I trust you slept well?'

'Yes, thank you, Madame Louisa, and I am ready for more instruction,' she answered cheerily.

'Well, I'm glad someone is bright and breezy this morning for I fear I am going quite mad.' Rowan stared at her employer in surprise. 'It was those ostrich feathers. They were expensive and the loss of one preyed on my mind all night, so first thing this morning I went into the workroom and what did I find? Only that they were all there!' Louisa exclaimed. 'It is most unlike me to make a mistake, but then I was eager to begin your instruction. Let that be a lesson to you, Miss Rowena: concentrate on only one thing at a time.' She paused and looked at Rowan speculatively. 'Unless by chance you borrowed one?' she asked. As Rowan opened her mouth to protest, the little bell gave its tinkle and they looked up to see Mrs Parker bustling into the shop.

'Good morning, Mrs Parker. Don't tell me. It is a blue moon occasion and you are in need of a new bonnet,' Louisa quipped.

The woman stared at her in surprise. 'A blue moon occasion?' she asked. 'Is someone having a celebration I haven't heard about?' As the woman stood there looking indignant, Rowan had to turn away to stifle a giggle.

'Just my little jest, Mrs Parker. Now, how may I help you this morning?' Louisa asked, assuming her normal professional manner.

'Well, it wouldn't surprise me if that snooty lot around here were planning something without telling me. The way they treat me, you'd think I couldn't keep a secret,' she said with a sniff.

'Oh, surely not,' Louisa said soothingly. 'Now, do tell me what brings you into my humble establishment this morning.'

'It's like this,' Mrs Parker said, brightening. 'Now you mustn't let on I've spoken to you, but Mrs Elliot is going to ask you to make her a new bonnet,' she gushed.

'Is she now?' Louisa asked, keeping her face deadpan. 'And would it be for some special occasion?'

'That's just it. She wouldn't say. Anyway, I thought if I gave you prior notice, tipped you the wink, so to speak, you could find out and tell me. One favour for another, so to speak,' she said, giving Louisa a wink.

'I see. Well, that is most thoughtful of you, Mrs Parker. Thank you so much,' Louisa said, opening the door for her.

'My pleasure, Madame Louisa,' she said, beaming as she scuttled away.

As her employer shut the door with a sigh of relief, Rowan burst out laughing. 'I don't know how you do it. You never tell her anything and yet she leaves here thinking you're party to her playful games.'

Louisa laughed. 'It comes with practice, Miss Rowena. Keep the client happy, remember. Talking of which, I need to gather more samples for Esther to see, and then there is a gown to deliver to Lady Beliver. She lives in Honeysuckle House, which is a beautiful cottage orné, a short walk from there. I do so love visiting her.'

'A cottage orné?' Rowan asked.

'It's a fairy-tale style of architecture,' her employer explained.

'Obviously one you particularly like,' Rowan said.

'Yes, I do, but I like her cook's lady's finger biscuits even more,' she said, with a grin. 'However, it does mean postponing the next stage of your bonnet instruction.' To her surprise, Rowan felt quite disappointed for she'd woken feeling cheerful, certain this was going to be a positive day.

After Louisa had left, Rowan checked the fitting room was tidy, and saw that the level in the bottle of Madame Louisa's signature fragrance had got down alarmingly. She was just debating what she should do about it when the little bell tinkled and a lady in a green dress, toning wide-shouldered cape and bonnet entered, followed by a tall, dark-haired young man wearing a top hat and flared frock coat. The woman smiled, and Rowan took an instant liking to her.

'Good morning, my dear. I'm Camilla Richmond and this is my nephew, Jack Carslake.'

The man doffed his hat as he removed it, and gave Rowan such a dazzling smile that her heart jumped. As his piercing blue eyes stared directly into hers, she swallowed hard.

'Would Madame Louisa be free to attend to me?' Camilla Richmond enquired, seemingly unaware of Rowan's inner turmoil.

'I'm afraid madam is out this morning. I am her new apprentice, Miss Rowena. May I be of assistance, or maybe take a message for her?' she asked, endeavouring to concentrate on the client.

'Well, unusually for one paying a visit to a milliner, I require a new bonnet,' the woman said, her eyes twinkling with mischief. 'Perhaps you would be kind enough to show me some of your examples?'

'Yes, of course, madam,' Rowan replied, acutely aware of the man's gaze on her.

'Jack, I fear you will be bored to tears watching me trying on these creations, wonderful though they look,' Camilla Richmond suggested hastily. 'Perhaps you'd like to take a walk and return in an hour or so.'

'Your wish is my command, Aunt Camilla,' he teased, giving Rowan a wink before striding out of the shop. Despite herself, Rowan couldn't help watching after him.

Chapter 30

Seeing Rowan's interest, Camilla laughed.

'Forgive that nephew of mine. Jack is cheeky, and no mistake. Mind you, I'd be lost without him,' she added. 'He's just started work at the Preventative Station here and is staying with me until he finds his feet. Now where was I?'

Flustered at having been caught out, Rowan turned her mind back to her duties.

'Did you have anything particular in mind, madam?' she asked, hoping her voice sounded normal.

'I require a new bonnet for my great-niece's christening,' the woman said.

'Something special then, madam?' Rowan enquired, glancing at the examples on the stands.

'It is actually Miss Richmond but please call me Camilla. I absolutely hate the title "Miss".' Rowan stared at the attractive woman in surprise, but she was still talking. 'Now, I assume you need to know what I propose wearing. As it will be midsummer by then, I have a mind to shock Mother and appear in bright yellow,' she said, laughing. 'However, my sister would kill me if I turned up looking like a canary, so I'll content myself with a more acceptable ensemble in mid-blue.'

'Your sister?' Rowan asked, her mind still on the cheeky young man.

'Yes, Jack's mother,' the woman explained, with a frown.

'Forgive me, I was just thinking what we have that would

complement your face shape and wonderful dark hair,' she said, improvising quickly and forcing herself to concentrate.

Together they walked around the shop discussing the merits of each bonnet on display.

'Of course, once you decide on the shape you prefer, we can customize the colours to suit your requirements, perhaps add a flower or two,' Rowan suggested.

'To be honest, I think flowers should be fresh and left to grow in their natural environment. Now, I'm quite useless at this kind of thing. Perhaps you could make a suggestion?' After another appraisal of the woman, Rowan lifted a coal scuttle design from the stand. It was covered in mid-blue taffeta with a black velvet bow.

'This shape would be perfect for you,' Rowan said, lifting it from the stand.

The woman frowned. 'It's a bit, well, dare I say, old hat,' she said, bursting into peals of laughter.

Rowan smiled. 'I agree it is a bit conventional, but if you'd like to try it on, I can talk you through some suggestions for personalizing it to go with your outfit without any artificial flowers,' Rowan said, leading the way into the fitting room. When Camilla had donned the bonnet, Rowan stood holding the hand mirror so that Camilla could see the back in the wall glass.

'I was thinking that if the bow was replaced with an iris-blue silk frill and toning ribbons it would give a more celebratory look. Of course, it would be important to see your outfit first to get a match. There are so many different blues and the whole effect could be ruined by the wrong tone.'

'I'm impressed, dear. You have made what I thought was going to be an arduous task most enlightening.'

The little bell tinkled, and Rowan excused herself to see who had come in. When she saw the handsome man she now knew to be Jack, her heart began hammering in her chest.

'Hello again,' he said. 'I hope my aunt has been behaving herself. She hates shopping, you know.' He gave a conspiratorial grin and Rowan couldn't help smiling back. Clearly aunt and nephew were close.

'I heard that, young man,' his aunt chided, emerging from the fitting room. 'Now, here is my address,' she said, handing Rowan a little silver card. 'If you could call, shall we say, at ten o'clock tomorrow morning, I shall have my outfit ready and we can discuss those trimmings.'

Just then the little bell rang again as Louisa returned.

'Good morning, madam,' she said. 'I do hope Miss Rowena has been attending to your needs?'

'It's Miss Richmond, Camilla Richmond, and Miss Rowena has been most helpful. I have ordered a bonnet and asked if she will bring it over tomorrow morning so that she can advise me on trimmings to match my outfit. It is for my great-niece's christening, therefore imperative I get it right,' she said.

'For such a special occasion, it will be my pleasure to call upon you myself,' Louisa said. The woman and her nephew exchanged looks.

'I have already arranged for Miss Rowena to visit at ten o'clock. She has been most obliging and knows exactly the look I wish to achieve,' Miss Richmond said quickly.

Rowan saw Louisa stiffen but, as ever, she maintained her decorum and continued smiling.

'As you wish, Miss Richmond, ten o'clock tomorrow it is then.'

'Thank you, madam. We will see you tomorrow then, Miss Rowena,' Camilla said.

Aware that Louisa was less than happy, Rowan's heart sank. But as she hurried to open the door, Jack gave her a wink, sending her emotions soaring once more.

'If it's not beneath you now, Miss Rowena, perhaps you would see the fitting room is tidied and refreshed,' Louisa said stiffly, going through to the workroom. 'And please remember my signature fragrance does not grow on trees,' she added haughtily.

Well, that depended upon what it consisted of, Rowan thought, but refrained from saying so. Obviously Miss Richmond had ruffled Louisa's feathers, she mused as she tidied the little room.

'I wouldn't have thought you had enough *savoir-faire* yet to call upon clients this early in your training, Miss Rowena,' Louisa said coming back into the shop. 'However, as you have seen fit to offer your services, I shall just have to trust you know what you're doing. Put that bonnet in a box ready to take to Miss Richmond tomorrow, and then go for your luncheon. Never let it be said I don't treat my staff fairly. This afternoon we will see how much you've remembered of your bonnet making instruction, and for your sake I hope it's most of it,' she added in a stentorian voice Rowan had never heard before.

Her heart sank and she prayed she could recall what she'd been taught, for Louisa really was not in the best of moods.

'He was a good-looking one,' Maria exclaimed, as Rowan went through to the kitchen. 'I clocked him as I came down the entry. He had his eye on you and no mistake. Staring through the window for ages, he was, before he came back inside the shop.' At the mention of the tall, dark man with the piercing blue eyes, Rowan felt her cheeks growing hot.

'Madam has accused me of being heavy-handed with her fragrance when I refresh the fitting room and . . .' she said quickly.

'Oh, don't worry about that. She's always moaning about it going down too fast,' the maid muttered.

'Is something wrong?' Louisa asked, appearing in the doorway.

'No, Madame Louisa, I was just talking to Maria whilst she was dishing up my luncheon,' Rowan said.

Hastily, the maid of all work began ladling hot pease pudding into a bowl.

'I came to enquire whether you'd had the nous to write down Miss Richmond's details, only they don't appear to be in the book. Or did the position of advisor go to your head?' their employer snapped, in the clipped voice Rowan was coming to dread.

She gulped. 'Miss Richmond gave me this,' she said, putting her hand in her pocket and pulling out the silver card. 'I'm afraid I forgot to transfer the details to the book.'

With an exasperated click of her tongue, Louisa took it and disappeared back to the shop.

'Blimey, she is in a bad mood and no mistake. When she said about the position of advisor going to your head, I was going to say, as well as the bonnet,' Maria said. 'But seeing the look on her face, I didn't think I dare.'

'No, Maria, I don't think that would have been a good idea today,' Rowan agreed.

'Don't worry, Miss Rowena. Like I said, she blows hot and cold all the time,' she added, thrusting a tray with her lunch on it into Rowan's hands.

As Rowan sat at the Pembroke table eating her meal, she couldn't help thinking once again how much easier it had been dealing with the placid cows back on the farm. She wondered if her father had written back yet, but decided she'd better wait until Louisa's mood had improved before asking her.

No sooner had Rowan gone through to the workroom than Louisa began firing questions at her.

'What's the name of this material?' she asked.

'Buckram,' she answered.

'And what can be used instead of it?'

'Double layer of willow.'

'Which is . . . ?'

'A type of grass.'

And so it went on until Rowan thought her head would surely burst.

Finally, apparently satisfied with her answers, Louisa said, 'Right, you can spend the rest of the afternoon making a bonnet yourself. When, and only when, I am satisfied, we will proceed to the next stage. Of course, you will need to spend this evening preparing the items to take to Miss Richmond. I cannot help because I was not privy to the discussion,' she said, as with a rustle of petticoats she swept through the dividing curtain and into the shop, only to reappear a few moments later, holding a swathe of dark blue material. 'May I enquire what you propose wearing to call upon Miss Richmond?'

Rowan looked down at her work dress and frowned. 'Well, my uniform dress, of course,' she answered.

'And what do you propose to wear over it?' her employer said sternly.

'Oh, don't worry, Madame Louisa, it is lovely and warm so I won't need anything,' she said.

There was a long-drawn-out sigh. 'Miss Rowena, I would remind you that when you call upon clients, you are representing my establishment. As such, it would be *mal à propos* to visit without an outer garment covering your day dress. Use this to make yourself a cape this evening,' she ordered, putting the material down on the work table with unnecessary force. 'If you have time, you may use some of the lower-grade silk material to line it. Oh, don't worry,' she said, seeing Rowan's surprised look. 'I will deduct the cost from your wage.'

As she disappeared through the curtain once more, Rowan breathed a sigh of relief. It was obvious her employer wasn't pleased Miss Richmond had insisted Rowan call upon her. Well, she'd been told to keep the client happy and that's what she'd tried to do. Then, as the image of the dark-haired Jack and his cheeky grin swam before her, she couldn't help wondering if he'd be there when she called.

She looked at the material Louisa had left on the work table. It was of good quality and Rowan could easily turn it into a stylish cape, though she still didn't understand why one was necessary when the weather was so clement.

*

As soon as Rowan had completed her early morning duties, she straightened her bonnet, and donned the cape she'd spent half the night sewing. Then checking her bag had everything she needed, she picked up the hatbox containing the coal scuttle bonnet and, with the shop bell tinkling in her wake, went outside.

It was a beautiful morning, with the sun shimmering on the sea and the gulls wheeling on the thermals. How she'd love to linger and promenade along the Mall, but Louisa had instructed her to go directly to Miss Richmond's. As her destination lay just off the main Saltmouth Road, she left the seafront behind and hurried through the bustling little town. She went back over the bridge they'd crossed in the coach, and turned into the lane where grand houses lay secluded amongst open fields. It didn't take her long to find Poppy Cottage, a mellow red-brick building with tall chimneys, which had a veranda running all the way around it. Obeying Louisa's other instruction, she went round to the back entrance. The door was opened by a tiny young maid, who scarcely reached even to Rowan's shoulders.

'Let me take your cape, miss, then I'll show you through to the drawing room,' she lisped.

'Thank you,' Rowan said, putting down her things and handing her cape to the maid. Following her along the carpeted hallway with its impressive sweeping staircase, and into a high-ceilinged room, she couldn't help marvelling at the cottage's stylishness, although anything less like a cottage she'd yet to see. To her surprise it was Jack who greeted her. Jumping to his feet, his grin warm and welcoming, he took her bag and the hatbox from her.

'Miss Rowena, how lovely to see you again. Please sit

yourself down,' he said, his velvety voice sending shivers down her spine. 'Forgive my aunt's tardiness. She is running a little behind this morning, and has asked me to entertain you in her absence.' He turned and pulled on the tapestry bell rope.

'Sarah, please could you bring a pot of coffee and some of Cook's excellent lady's finger biscuits?' he said as the little maid appeared. 'Our cook makes the best ones I've ever had,' he said, turning back to Rowan.

She smiled politely, wondering if she would dare share this later with Louisa, who enjoyed Lady Beliver's lady finger biscuits so much. Jack sat looking at her quizzically, and she smiled politely.

'This is a lovely room,' she said.

'It is, and it seems even lovelier now that you are sitting in it,' he quipped with his cheeky grin.

Her heart lurched. Careful, Rowan, she cautioned.

'Tell me, have you been working for Madame Louisa long? I'm sure I wouldn't have forgotten if our paths had crossed before. Not that I make a habit of visiting milliners' shops, of course,' he added.

'I've only recently become apprenticed to Madame Louisa, sir,' she answered.

He roared with laughter. 'Sir? Oh, please, Miss Rowena, you will give me ideas above my station,' he exclaimed.

'And that would never do, nephew,' Camilla Richmond said, coming into the room. 'Miss Rowena, it is lovely to see you again. Do forgive my reprobate of a nephew, and for heaven's sake take everything he says with a pinch of salt,' she warned, giving him a fond look.

'Ha-ha, very funny, Auntie. Miss Rowena and I have

merely been getting acquainted. I, too, have started a new position, Miss Rowena, mine as a Preventative, stationed on the sea front. Hence my lodging with good old Auntie here,' he quipped.

'A situation that can soon be remedied if I have any more of your cheek, young man,' Camilla chided. 'Ah, coffee, lovely,' she added as the little maid struggled in under the weight of a laden tray.

As Jack jumped to his feet and took it from her, Rowan thought that underneath his jesting exterior he was obviously a considerate man.

Camilla poured coffee and, having carefully placed a biscuit in the saucer, handed it to Rowan.

'You can take yours in the other room, Jack,' she said. 'I mustn't keep Miss Rowena too long or madam will be gunning for her.' As Rowan stared at her in surprise, she gave a loud laugh. She waited whilst Jack picked up his cup, placed two finger biscuits in the saucer, and with a resigned sigh left the room. 'Oh, yes, I saw the look on your employer's face when I insisted you call instead of her,' she continued, then, leaning closer, added in a whisper, 'Jack would have killed me if I'd done otherwise.' Rowan's eyes widened. 'Now, let's enjoy our coffee and then I will show you my outfit. You can tell me if you think it will be suitable.'

Rowan's eyes widened even further. The woman wanted her advice on her ensemble? She crossed her fingers and hoped she had enough of that *savoir faire* Louisa had mentioned.

Chapter 31

As Rowan followed Camilla up the stairs and into her elegantly furnished dressing room, she was convinced all the butterflies of Saltmouth were having their annual ball in her stomach. She stood watching nervously as the woman pulled a beautiful pale-blue day dress from her closet and held it up against her.

'Well, what do you think, Miss Rowena? Will this pass muster?' she asked.

'It's an exquisite gown, Miss ... sorry, Camilla,' she amended as the woman gave her a look. Rowan's mind was buzzing like a bee around a rosebud. Dare she say that she felt the colour was too pale and would make the woman look washed out?

'But ... ?' Camilla persisted, giving Rowan the same penetrating stare her nephew had earlier.

'I think perhaps it would suit you better if a stronger coloured trim were added around your neck and down the front.' To her surprise the woman clapped her hands delightedly.

'Jack said you wouldn't be afraid to speak your mind. I'm quite hopeless at knowing what looks good on me, and tend to wear safer colours, like this,' she said, pointing to her grey dress. 'Jack says I need to brighten myself up.' Privately Rowan agreed with him.

Camilla continued, 'To be honest, I feel more

comfortable in less formal clothes these days. I find solace in my garden, you see. It drives old Simms wild when I mess with his shrubs but . . .' Her voice trailed off and she shrugged. 'Now, let's see what you have come up with for the bonnet, and this idea for trimming my dress.'

Carefully, Rowan took the bonnet from its box, along with the samples of materials and ribbons she'd brought with her.

'You see, I thought if we added a frill in a stronger iris blue around the outer brim, lined the inner brim in a softer bluebell material and added brighter ribbons, say, in speedwell, it would all tone beautifully,' Rowan explained. 'It needs a stronger colour than this ribbon I have here, but I could dye some for you.'

'You don't think it would all look a bit, well blue?' Camilla asked. 'Shouldn't we add some white or pink?'

'With respect, I feel too much contrast would detract from your natural colouring. And with that in mind, we could trim the front of your dress in the stronger iris blue as well,' she couldn't resist adding.

Camilla stood in front of the long mirror reflecting. When she didn't say anything, Rowan's heart began beating as strongly as the clock on the dressing table. Had she been too outspoken, she wondered. Anxiously, she moved over to the window and stared down at the sweeping lawns, bordered by brightly coloured rhododendrons and camellias. A movement on the grass below caught her eye and she saw Jack throwing a ball for a lively young Labrador. As she stood watching, Camilla came up behind her and chuckled.

'Good looking, isn't he?' Rowan spun round and caught

Camilla looking at her speculatively. 'I think you'd make just as good a match as those trimmings you've recommended for my bonnet and dress. The question now is, whether your employer will allow you, as her apprentice, to have a follower.'

Rowan stared at Camilla in astonishment. 'But . . .'

'Oh, I know he hasn't asked you yet, but he will. He offered to work the late shift in order to be here this morning.' She smiled warmly. Then seeing Rowan's embarrassment, asked, 'Do you have family in Saltmouth?'

Rowan shook her head. 'We lived on our farm in Sudbury, but my mother died and then Father remarried . . .' she replied, hastily gathering up the ribbons and trimmings.

Sensing she'd touched on a sore subject, Camilla held out her dress.

'I can see what you mean about this material being too pale, Miss Rowena. Oh, I know you didn't say it outright but that's what you meant. However, if you are to dye my trimmings you'd better take this with you to get the right match. Please tell Madame Louisa I concur wholeheartedly with all the recommendations you have made, and wish for you to call and fit the finished ensemble. Now, I really mustn't keep you, or I shall have your employer after me. You have been most helpful, Miss Rowena, and I look forward to seeing you again soon,' she said, pulling the bell rope. 'And be prepared, for I'm sure my nephew will just happen to appear as you leave,' she chuckled.

'Oh, I'm sure he won't be interested in someone with a past like mine,' Rowan said, then, remembering Mrs Acland's words, could have bitten her tongue.

Camilla stared at her in surprise. 'Living on a farm is nothing for you to be ashamed of, my dear.'

Rowan smiled and quickly bade the woman goodbye before she could put her foot in it even further.

She was making her way down the path when she heard footsteps hurrying after her.

'Would you do me the honour of permitting me to walk you back to your shop, Miss Rowena?' Jack asked, beaming at her.

Her heart was thumping so loudly, she could only nod as he reached out and took her bag and hatbox from her.

'It is a beautiful bright morning, isn't it?' he declared. Trying to stop her voice from trembling, she nodded and then cast around for something to say before he thought her as wooden as one of Louisa's bonnet blocks.

'I couldn't help admiring the wonderful shrubs and flowers in your garden. Those poppies make a vivid splash against the green grass, don't they? Do you know, I was looking out at the rhododendrons and camellias earlier, and couldn't help thinking how beautiful your aunt would look in those colours. She would suit a bonnet trimmed with bright poppy, too. It would quite match her bright nature.' Realizing she was rambling, she stumbled to a halt but Jack chuckled.

'Do you always think in colour, Miss Rowena?'

She reflected for a moment, and then nodded. 'Yes, I believe I do. Forgive me if I have been outspoken. The trouble is I always tend to say what I think.'

'And an admirable quality that is, too. One knows where one stands with candid people. I remember my aunt was always attired in vibrant clothes, until her betrothed was killed near Shanghai during the Opium Wars with the Chinese. After that she retreated into herself. Now she spends most of her time in her beloved garden, saying she finds it comforting.'

'That's sad. That she lost her betrothed, I mean. I can understand her finding comfort in shrubs and flowers, though. Do you know the word "garden" comes from the Hebrew and means a pleasant place?' Rowan asked, reminded of her conversation with the superintendent.

'No, I didn't, but that is most appropriate, isn't it?' Jack replied. 'And Auntie is truly pleasant herself.'

What a lovely thing to say, thought Rowan, thinking again how close they were.

They continued their way through the town and along the Mall. Rowan found Jack easy to talk to and conversation flowed, so that before she knew it, they were standing outside Madame Louisa's.

'Miss Rowena, if you are new to Saltmouth, I dare say you haven't had time to explore the area yet?'

'No, indeed. I must confess I can't wait to walk all along the Mall and see what's around,' she answered.

Jack cleared his throat. 'I was wondering if you would care to walk out with me on your half-day? I could show you all the best sights.' He turned and stared at her with those piercing eyes that seemed to see right into her soul.

'Oh, but I don't know when that is yet,' she said, realizing how foolish she must sound.

'Well, in that case, would you permit me to check with Madame Louisa? It would be courteous to ask your employer's permission, provided you are agreeable?

Perhaps I should ask Madame Louisa if I may step out with Mademoiselle Rowena,' he quipped.

'Oh, heaven forbid,' she shuddered. 'Louisa has enough fancy ideas as it is. My name is really just Rowan, you know.'

He turned and smiled at her. 'And a very beautiful name it is, too. It suits you with all those copper curls.' She grimaced, pushing an escaping tendril back under her bonnet. 'Well, come along, Mademoiselle, let us see if we can gain permission from the formidable Madame,' he said, giving a low bow as he pushed open the door.

'Is everything all right?' Louisa asked, looking up in surprise as they entered the shop together.

'Good morning, Madame Louisa, Jack Carslake at your service,' Jack said, removing his hat politely. 'My aunt sends her regards and wishes me to convey to you that Miss Rowena has been most helpful,' he continued.

'I am very pleased to hear it,' Louisa said.

'Madame Louisa, I am a respectable man, working at the Preventative Station here and would like to walk out with Miss Rowena. I have offered my services in showing her around the area but as you are her employer, I feel it important to seek your permission.'

Louisa turned to Rowan and studied her for a long moment. Rowan felt her heart jump into her mouth. Please say yes, she wanted to shout.

'If that is Miss Rowena's wish, Mr Carslake, then permission is granted,' Louisa said.

'Thank you, madam. May I enquire as to when her half-day will be?' Jack continued.

Louisa raised one perfectly arched eyebrow and there

was a moment's silence. Rowan lowered her eyes in embarrassment.

'Sunday afternoon, Mr Carslake, and if it is what Miss Rowena wishes you may call for her at two o'clock,' she finally announced.

'Thank you, madam. I will see you then, Miss Rowena, and rest assured, I shall be counting the hours,' he added cheekily. Then he stepped briskly out of the shop, raising his hat in his hand in farewell. As Rowan watched him go, her employer cleared her throat.

'I can see you have had a very productive morning indeed, Miss Rowena,' Louisa quipped, and Rowan was pleased to see the woman was back to her usual pleasant self.

Picking up her things, Rowan was about to make her way through to the workroom, when Louisa said, 'I, too, have had a busy morning and the fitting room requires refreshing. I trust you will take care to use my signature fragrance sparingly; it is still disappearing at an alarming rate,' she added with a frown.

Not wishing to have her happy mood spoiled, Rowan quickly placed her things in the workroom and set about freshening the fitting room. She'd just finished when the little bell tinkled and Mrs Parker bustled into the shop.

'You are a dark horse, Miss Rowena. There I was, walking through the town earlier, minding my own business, you understand, when I saw you being escorted by the new Preventative. Naturally, I had to come and make sure you were delivered safely back,' she said, her eyes bright with anticipation.

Staring at the woman, Rowan thought if she were to

have a signature fragrance named for her, it would surely have to be called Eau de Gossip.

'As you can see, Mrs Parker, Miss Rowena's follower did, indeed, deliver her safely. Now how may I be of help today?' Louisa asked.

The woman's eyes widened. 'Her follower, did you say? Oh, I never realized. In that case, I shall bid you good morning,' she said, bustling from the shop as quickly as her little legs would carry her.

Louisa laughed. 'By this afternoon the whole of Salt-mouth will know you are walking out with the new Preventative.'

'But I haven't even been out with him yet,' Rowan chuckled, shaking her head.

'Never mind that, you will be the talk of the town. Consider it your good deed for the day, for you have just given a lonely old woman a good excuse to speak to people,' Louisa said. 'Now, come through and show me what it is Miss Richmond requires.'

As Rowan shook out Camilla's dress and sat the bonnet beside it on the work table, she saw Louisa frown. Quickly, she went through the recommendations she'd made, adding that she was happy to dye the ribbons in her own time.

'Let me get this straight, Miss Rowena. You not only brought a client's dress here to make adaptations,' she asked, 'you also offered to dye some of my ribbons?'

'The ones we have aren't quite the right colour for what I had in mind . . .' she stuttered to a halt as her employer clicked her tongue.

'Don't you think that was presumptuous of you with-out consulting me?' Louisa asked, looking affronted.

'I'm sorry if I spoke out of turn, Madame Louisa, but I only did as you said, and recommended what I thought was best for our client,' she protested. As Louisa stood studying her for a long moment, Rowan felt her heart sink to her shoes. Surely, she wasn't going to lose her job? Then, to her surprise, her employer smiled.

'I have to admire your spirit, Miss Rowena, and also your imaginative flair for colour. Having seen the woman in question, I agree that gown is far too light for her. Now you have explained, I can visualize exactly how she will look. For that I commend you, and will permit you to make the adaptations.'

'Thank you, Madame Louisa,' Rowan replied, her spirits lifting. It seemed she'd got it right after all.

'No doubt Miss Richmond has asked for you to deliver the work personally?' Louisa asked.

Rowan nodded.

'Well, it seems you are going to be busy then.'

'Oh, I don't mind hard work, Madame Louisa,' Rowan replied happily.

'Good, because when I saw the mess you'd made of that bonnet yesterday, I was not best pleased.'

Rowan's stomach churned. 'Surely it wasn't that bad?' she protested.

'It was atrocious. In fact, I would go as far as to say I have never seen such a dismal effort. I intended to make you revisit it before we moved onto your next instruction. However, as this task is for coverings and trimmings, and you have seen fit to make those recommendations to Miss Richmond, I think we'd better move on. I have my reputation to think of, and her bonnet will need to be finished to my exacting standard and in a timely manner.'

Feeling relieved, Rowan smiled. She was finding the actual bonnet making harder than she'd imagined, but the trimming would be fun.

'It's no good thinking you're getting away with it, though, Miss Rowena. You still need to master the art of bonnet making or you'll be no use as a milliner. However, my business must come first, so go and have your luncheon and when you return, we will proceed with your next instruction.'

Hurrying from the workroom, Rowan shook her head. Why did she get the distinct impression Louisa was pleased she'd had difficulty mastering the art of bonnet making?

'I'm in madam's bad books 'cos she caught me laughing with Jem over the fence this morning,' Maria told Rowan as she entered the kitchen. 'Went all la-de-da, she did, and said I was on my honour to conduct myself *comme il faut*, which apparently means I got to be prim and proper,' she laughed. 'Anyway, I got back in her good books by offering to make a fruit crumble for supper. It's her favourite, see.'

'Oh, Maria, you're incorrigible,' Rowan spluttered.

'What about you? I saw your admirer following you into the shop. You walking out with him, then?'

Rowan nodded, her heart soaring at the thought. 'He's offered to show me the sights.'

'I bet he has,' Maria chuckled. 'He looks right dandy and if I hadn't got my Jem I'd have given you a run for your money there.'

Rowan grinned. The maid might be hopeless, but she did make her smile.

'So you'll be busy making us a fruit crumble this afternoon,' she countered.

'Well, it was a sop for madam and I managed to get hold of some nice fruit,' she said, giving Rowan a broad wink. 'Anyway, as my Jem says, it's all good practice for when we're wed. Can you cook, Rowan?'

'Yes, I used to cook all the time at home.'

'That's good. 'Tis the best way to keep your man happy,' Maria said, ladling out the broth. 'Or one of them, anyhow,' she added, giving a raucous laugh.

That afternoon, Rowan found her instruction on linings and coverings far more interesting than the one in the actual bonnet making. When Louisa left her to trace out the crown panel and the main bonnet shape for the inner lining, she found herself humming happily. By the time she'd sewn the rest of the inner lining into the buckram and over the wire at the edges, she felt she'd made good progress.

'Well, you got to grips with that bit easily enough,' Louisa said, nodding in approval. 'Let's see how you do with the outer coverings. Trace out the main bonnet shape and crown panel on this material for the outer covering, allowing two inches all round for seams,' she instructed.

Rowan did as she'd been told and then, under Louisa's guidance, cut it out. By the time she'd double folded the edge of the material for the outside of the crown and ironed it flat, she again began to realize that millinery was an art in itself. Louisa returned, nodded her approval again, and then proceeded to show her how to do herringbone stitch for the outside of the bonnet. Then, as she demonstrated how it was necessary to allow sufficient material to cover the join with half an inch on to the body of the bonnet, Rowan found herself stifling a yawn.

'Is there much more?' she couldn't help asking, for the room was growing darker and her eyes were gritty with having to concentrate so much.

'No, we'll call it a day,' Louisa said, stretching her back. 'Don't worry, you have done well. If you can master the actual construction of the bonnet, we might make a milliner of you yet,' she said. 'The secret is to imagine the person wearing your creation.'

As a vision of the dark-haired Jack sporting the half-finished bonnet flashed before her, she grinned. She couldn't wait to see him on Sunday.

Chapter 32

Promptly at two o'clock on Sunday, the little bell rang and Rowan, wearing the yellow dress Mrs Acland had let her keep, and a bonnet she'd trimmed with a matching buttercup ribbon, hurried to open the door.

'Enjoy yourself, Miss Rowena, and remember not to say anything about your stay in the asylum. It would do neither your reputation nor my business any good whatsoever if that got around, unfortunate mistake though it was. Now off you go and have a pleasant afternoon,' Louisa said with a smile.

'Yes, Madame Louisa,' Rowan replied, remembering her near miss with Camilla and vowing to be more careful. Then she saw Jack smiling at her through the window and hurried outside.

'You look stunning, Miss Rowena. That colour really suits you. Now, where would you like to explore first?' he asked.

'It's such a lovely afternoon, why don't we wander along the Mall? No disrespect to Madame Louisa, but I'm going crazy as a caged cat being cooped up indoors all the time.'

'What an interesting notion,' he said, quirking his eyebrow. 'Let us release you from your cage and promenade along the Mall then. I understand the band will be playing this afternoon, and we could stop for refreshment at the coffee shop. How does that sound, Miss Rowena?'

'It sounds heavenly, apart from one thing,' she said, staring up at him.

'What's that?' he asked.

'Please can you call me Rowan whilst we are out?' she ventured to ask.

'Whatever the lady wishes,' he declared gallantly, giving a little bow.

They'd only gone a few paces when Jack turned to her and whispered, 'I think someone is trying to attract your attention.' Looking up, Rowan saw Mrs Parker crossing the road and she stifled a groan.

'Good afternoon, Mrs Parker,' she called, quickening her step so that before long they'd left the woman behind.

Jack stared down at her quizzically. 'Not someone you wanted to encounter?'

'I'm afraid Mrs Parker is renowned for being the Salt-mouth tittle-tattle. Madame Louisa says her ears grow by at least to two inches when she hears something salacious,' Rowan said, and grinned up at him shyly.

Jack threw back his head and laughed. 'I think it might be her nose that grows, too.'

'Yes, nosy Parker, very good,' she said, grinning up at him.

'Well, here we are with the sparkling waters of Lyme Bay spread out before us, so let's enjoy our promenade,' Jack said as they reached the sea front. 'Although I dare say you will be busy studying the ladies' fine bonnets to see how you could make better ones.'

Rowan sighed. 'To be honest, I don't care if I never see another bonnet again,' she blurted out.

Jack stopped walking and turned to face her. 'All not well in Milliners' Row?' he enquired.

'I had no idea there was so much to it. Madame Louisa was not at all impressed with my first attempt, although she said I did better with the linings and coverings.'

'Well, that's good, is it not? We all have to learn from our mistakes so don't be too hard on yourself. Do you know, on my first day at the station here, the others sent me out for a pint of elbow grease. They said it was for waterproofing the boats. The ribbing I got as I trailed around Saltmouth asking for some.' He looked so affronted, Rowan burst out laughing.

'I don't believe that for one moment. You just said that to make me feel better.'

'And it worked, did it not?' he said with a grin. 'Now let's enjoy our stroll; we have precious few hours off to waste them.'

As they continued their walk along the Mall, mingling with the other elegantly attired ladies and gentlemen who were taking a stroll, Rowan felt happiness bubble up inside her. It was so good to be out in the fresh air again, and the recent high tide had swept the beach quite clean. The sun was glinting on the imposing red cliffs that enclosed the bay, and she could hear lively music coming from the bandstand. She stared at the little cottages with their backs to the sea and shook her head.

'What a waste of a view. If I lived in one of those, I'd have my windows facing the water like those Regency houses we just passed, so I could watch the waves dance,' she said.

'It might seem idyllic now, but come the winter storms, which sweep water right over their roofs, you would soon change your mind,' Jack pointed out, as they turned off the Mall. He stopped outside a handsome three-storey Regency building on which was a sign advertising 'Free Library and Coffee House'. Through the open doors to the balcony Rowan could see people sitting taking refreshment and Jack proposed that this seemed the ideal place to have a rest.

'Tell me about yourself, Rowan,' Jack asked as they enjoyed their afternoon tea and scones spread with cream and jam. 'What did you do before you came here?'

Rowan's heart sank. Mindful of Louisa's warning, she gave him a sketchy description of life on the farm but she found the memories painful and her voice tailed off.

'Is something wrong?' he enquired solicitously.

'Talking about the farm reminded me of my step-mother. She took a real dislike to me and – well, it's probably best that I'm away from there.'

Jack frowned. 'I can't imagine anyone not liking you, Rowan. You're such a warm person, and Aunt Camilla thinks you're quite lovely. She said you had the most open face she'd ever seen.'

Rowan swallowed hard and, in an attempt to hide her emotions, picked up her scone. It wasn't a patch on her auntie Sal's splitties, although she was too polite to mention it. Still, it was no good dwelling on her past. Having ascertained from her employer that no letter had arrived from her father, she had to come to terms with the fact he didn't want to contact her. She would concentrate on the here and now, she thought, turning her attention back to Jack. Sensitive to her mood, he smiled.

'Well, if you've been used to roaming wide open spaces it's not surprising you hate being cooped up indoors,' he said, then began regaling her with tales of his training until she found herself relaxing once more.

'Like you, I much prefer the great outdoors. Yesterday we rowed out to intercept smugglers returning from France, their luggers laden with booty of brandy, baccy and spices. Do you know how they hide it?' Rowan shook her head. 'They weight down the barrels, throw them overboard and then mark where they've hidden them with a row of corks to make out they've set fishing nets. They call it "sowing the crop". Well, Jack Carslake is wise to that, and when they go back to reap their crop – that's lifting it up again – I shall nab them,' he vowed, rubbing his hands together vigorously.

'All by yourself?' she couldn't resist teasing.

'Well,' he said, having the grace to look abashed, 'the other Preventatives will help, of course. There's still a lot to learn, yet already I feel I'm making a difference. You wouldn't believe how much revenue these scoundrels avoid paying.' She smiled at his earnest expression and picked up her teacup. The walk in the salty air had made her thirsty and she sipped her drink gratefully. Glancing over at Jack, she saw him staring at her wrist, where the cuff of her sleeve had risen.

'I can't help noticing you always wear that red ribbon around your wrist. Is it for decoration or does is have some special significance?' She gave him a calculating look and was just wondering if she should be truthful and risk him asking her more questions about her family, when he added, giving his cheeky grin, 'I only mention it because if it was some fashionable accessory, I can't help feeling, with your passion for matching colours, you would have chosen to wear a yellow band today.'

He was certainly observant, Rowan thought, placing her cup back on its saucer.

'This ribbon represents the circle of life and was the last thing my mother gave me before she died,' she whispered. 'She always wore it, believing that when we depart this world, our spirit stays within the family, gently guiding us. In that way we are never forgotten.'

Jack reached over and gently patted her hand. 'What a wonderful sentiment. She sounds a remarkable person, and I can tell you loved her very much,' he said, his penetrating gaze holding hers.

'Yes, and I do sense her presence guiding me sometimes. I suppose you think that's farcical.'

'Far from it, Rowan, it must be reassuring to feel she is still with you. You know, you and Auntie have quite a lot in common. She is convinced she can feel the presence of her betrothed in her beloved garden, or even when she is flicking through the pages of her *hortus siccus*.'

'Her what?'

He laughed at her bemused expression. 'It's an album with dried flowers in,' he explained.

'Oh, I should love to see that,' she cried, then could have bitten her tongue in case he should think her forward. But his eyes lit up.

'Then I shall ask Auntie to invite you to tea so that she can show you,' he replied, getting to his feet. 'Now, I really must escort you safely back to the shop, or Madame

Louisa will be on the war path. I don't want to spoil our first time out together by blotting my copybook.'

She smiled. How considerate he was or maybe he'd had enough of her company and was merely being polite, she thought with a pang. But his next words allayed her worries.

'I have enjoyed this afternoon and trust we can do it again soon?' He stood looking down at her hopefully, and although her heart was beating like the clappers on the church bells, she strove to keep her voice casual.

'That would be nice,' she replied, getting to her feet and brushing down her skirts.

'I shall forever think of this as our place now, Rowan.'

She looked at him, not sure if he was jesting but he seemed perfectly serious.

As they were making their way outside again, Rowan felt a burning sensation in her back. Certain someone was watching her, she glanced round to find herself staring into the blue-grey eyes of Louisa's father. His companion was a flaxen-haired young girl, beautifully attired in the latest mode. He lifted his glass in greeting but the look on his face made her shiver.

However, as they walked back along on the Mall, Jack regaled her with yet more of his amusing anecdotes and she soon forgot about Louisa's father.

'Thank you for a lovely afternoon, Jack,' she said, as they reached the shop.

'I'm sure by the time we next meet you will have mastered the art of bonnet making,' he gallantly assured her.

'And you will have found that elbow grease,' she

grinned, letting herself in through the entry as the church bells began ringing for evening worship.

'Did you have a good time, Miss Rowena?' Louisa asked, coming out of the workroom, dressed in her Sunday best. 'Although that question is superfluous as I can tell by the flush to your cheeks you have. Maria has saved some of her wonderful crumble for your supper and when you have eaten that, I suggest you get an early night. We need to go through the first stages of bonnet making again, so I'll see you in the workroom first thing in the morning,' she said, pulling on her calfskin gloves.

'I'm happy to make a start after supper, Madame Louisa,' Rowan offered, anxious to please her employer.

'Judging from the stars in your eyes, Miss Rowena, you will be in no fit state to concentrate. Now, I shall be late for the service if I don't get a move on. Good evening.'

As she bade her employer good evening, Rowan wondered if she should mention seeing her father in the Coffee House, then dismissed the notion. She might ask if he'd been alone and Rowan wouldn't wish to lie. Then she realized that her seeing him out with his companion was probably the reason for him giving her that strange look.

'Well, what was he like?' Maria asked eagerly, as Rowan went through to the kitchen. She thought she'd be too excited to feel hungry but the delicious aroma of the fruit dessert and custard made her stomach rumble.

'Who?' Rowan teased.

'That posh Preventative, of course. Did he take you anywhere nice?' The maid was all agog.

'We went for a stroll along the Mall and took afternoon tea in the Coffee House.'

'Ooh, you took afternoon tea,' Maria teased. 'I hope you remembered to raise your little pinkie,' she giggled, holding up her little finger.

Rowan smiled. 'What about you? Did you have a good time with Jem?'

'We went for a walk up Pyke's Way. And very productive it was too,' she giggled, pointing to the broad beans in the sink.

'Oh, Maria, you didn't filch them?'

'There's so many there, no one will notice a few missing,' the unrepentant maid said, grinning.

'It's a shame it's the wrong time for elderberries. They would be perfect for dying Miss Richmond's ribbons.'

Maria's face brightened. 'Now it just so happens I got some preserved,' she said, opening a cupboard door and pointing to a large jar. 'As you've seen, madam loves a crumble so I always bottle what fruit I can. Pays to keep in her good books, like.' She winked at Rowan, conspiratorially.

'Could you spare some with their juice?' Rowan enquired.

'Don't see why not.'

'And some salt?'

'Crikey, what do you want that for?' Maria asked, wrinkling her nose. 'It won't taste nice with berries.'

Rowan laughed. 'I can use it as the mordant,' she explained.

'The mordi what?'

'Mordant. It's what sets the dye into the material so it doesn't run out when the material's washed.'

'Well, love a duck, if that ain't the daftest thing I ever heard,' Maria said, shaking her head.

'I'll go and get the ribbon, then you can see what I mean. While it's steeping I can eat my crumble,' she resolved, hurrying down the passage to the workroom. Having already worked out the length she would need, she carefully cut the ribbon and took it back to the kitchen.

Rowan strained some of the fruit from the bottle and placed it into a square of muslin. She poured juice into a pan, then squeezed the bag to bruise the berries and release their seeds. Placing it in the juice, she added a little salt and gently stirred until the mixture came to the boil.

'You looks right spooky stirring that pot like that. You ain't going to cast a spell, are you?'

Staring at Maria's incredulous face, Rowan couldn't resist asking, 'Did you say you gathered these from the woods?' When the maid nodded, Rowan stirred the mixture faster and faster, and then as it swirled, she removed the spoon, closed her eyes and chanted:

> *Spirit of the woods*
> *Turn this black into blue,*
> *Fast it deep to the ribbon*
> *Til it turns the right hue.*
> *So mote it be.*

'What happens now?' Maria gasped, staring at Rowan in trepidation.

'I have my crumble while the spell gets to work, of course,' she quipped. With trembling hands, the maid served up the crumble and custard. Rowan moved the pot half off the fire so that the heat in the dark mixture died to a simmer. 'As madam is out, I'll stand and eat this here, and then I can watch in case any bad spirits jump out of the pan.' Maria's eyes widened even further. 'Don't worry, I'll bash them on the head with my spoon if they do,' Rowan joked.

'I'm off to the privy,' Maria muttered. As she hurried out of the door, the ribbon around Rowan's wrist tightened. 'Sorry, Mother, I was only teasing,' she murmured. After finishing her crumble, she went over and moved the pan from the range.

By the time the maid returned, the mixture had cooled enough for the ribbon to be added.

'Do you want to stir?' Rowan asked.

Maria shook her head. 'Did any spirits jump out?' she whispered, eyeing the pan warily.

'That was only a joke, Maria.' Seeing how pale the girl had gone, Rowan felt guilty for playing such a mean trick. 'Why don't I make us a cup of tea? By the time we've drunk it the ribbon should be the right colour,' she said, eager to make amends.

'No, thanks. I'm away to my bed,' Maria muttered, giving Rowan a suspicious look before hurrying out of the door.

Rowan felt dreadful. She'd have to think of something she could do to make up for her stupid prank. Going over to the cooled pan, she fished out the ribbon on the spoon and saw to her delight it had reached the desired colour. Carefully she carried it all out to the yard, where she tipped away the liquid, discarded the bag in the waste and poured cold water from the pump onto the ribbon. As she rinsed the excess colour away, a tingle of excitement ran up her spine. The ribbon was now the vibrant colour she'd envisaged. She could just imagine Miss Richmond's face when she saw her outfit transformed. And if she was pleased she would be bound to tell Jack. Thoughts of him made her heart soar and she was overcome with an irresistible urge to dance.

Kicking off her shoes, she skipped over to the little patch of grass and then, heedless of anything or anyone, bent and removed her stockings. The feel of the cool grass beneath her feet was exhilarating. It was ages since she'd felt so happy, so alive, so free, she thought as she leaped into the air.

'Miss Rowena, whatever do you think you're doing?' shouted Louisa.

Chapter 33

Rowan entered the workroom to find Louisa had laid out the patterns ready for her to sit her test in bonnet making. She was under strict instructions to show her employer each piece as she completed it before going on to the next stage. After the dressing-down she'd received last night, and having had her failings pointed out in no uncertain terms, Rowan knew she had to complete the bonnet to Louisa's exacting standards or her apprenticeship would be terminated. What a comedown it had been after her exciting afternoon with Jack. As the image of his handsome features swam before her, she pushed it firmly away. Nothing or nobody must be allowed to interfere with her concentration.

By the time she'd traced out the main shape and crown panel, then cut out the buckram precisely, Louisa was hovering at her side.

'That's slightly better than before. You may begin pinning and sewing, but see me before you cut any wire,' she said tersely, before disappearing back through the curtain. Obviously her employer's mood hadn't improved since she'd returned the previous evening to find Rowan dancing on the lawn.

As Rowan endeavoured to follow the instruction precisely, the little shop bell tinkled and she heard someone enquiring about the new bonnet Louisa had placed in the window. Rowan had seen the new creation when she'd been outside sweeping the pathway earlier. It was covered in brown silk; the brim interlined with beige and the ribbon ties the colour of eggshells. She thought it looked dull and quite unlike the brightly coloured May bonnet. She couldn't imagine who would want to wear something so sombre. Moments later, she heard the jangle of the bell and surmised the client couldn't have been impressed either.

She worked hard all morning, only stopping to eat her broth while Maria skirted around her warily. Hurrying back to the workroom, she found Louisa waiting for her, a box packed and ready for delivery beside her.

'Take this bonnet to this address,' she said, handing Rowan a gilt card. 'Give it to the maid and come back directly. You still have your work to finish.'

'Yes, Madame Louisa,' she replied, taking it from her and making for the door. Then, seeing the space in the window, she exclaimed, 'Don't tell me someone's bought that dull brown bonnet?'

'Now you are showing just how little you know about this business, Miss Rowena. And surely I don't have to remind you again about being suitably attired when you are about my business,' Louisa snapped. Smothering a sigh, for the day was warm, Rowan snatched up her cape and hurried outside.

Having duly delivered the bonnet, she was making her way back to the shop when a carriage pulled alongside and she saw weasel-faced Mr Acland grinning at her. Her spirits dropped. Could this day get any worse?

'Miss Rowena, allow me to offer you a lift,' he suggested.

'Thank you, Mr Acland, but that won't be necessary,' she replied, quickening her step.

'Oh, come along,' he insisted, calling to his driver to keep pace with her. 'Come for a little ride with me. We can stop for some refreshment.' She shook her head and continued walking. 'Now don't be so hasty, my dear. I am a generous man and could provide all manner of finery for a pretty young girl like yourself. Why, if you were especially nice to me, I could arrange it so you wouldn't have to continue working for that bossy daughter of mine.'

Rowan shook her head. Putting up with Louisa's haughty manner was infinitely better than listening to his sickly suggestions, she thought, deliberately crossing the street and trying to lose herself among the crowd.

But if she thought she'd shaken him off, she was mistaken, for moments later the carriage veered across the road and stopped beside her. The window snapped down and Mr Acland leaned out.

'Well, Miss High and Mighty, let's see what that young Preventative has to say when he finds out he's walking out with a loon from the asylum,' he hissed, his eyes narrowing menacingly.

Shocked, Rowan stood frozen to the spot but before she could think of an answer, Mr Acland had shouted to the driver to move on smartly and she was left staring at the dust settling in the wake of his carriage.

Fear gripped her heart. Surely he wouldn't tell Jack? It was an empty threat he'd issued, wasn't it? By the time she reached the shop she'd convinced herself he was blustering because she'd refused to ride with him.

Back in the workroom, she forced herself to concentrate on her bonnet. In her efforts to please Louisa, she continued with her handiwork well into the evening.

Finally, as the shadows crept into the corners of the room, bleary-eyed, she left the finished shape, now ready for covering, on the work table. She sincerely hoped it would pass her employer's inspection.

That week crawled interminably by and despite Rowan's best efforts to please Louisa, the woman continually found fault with her work, seeming to take delight in pointing out the minutest of defects. She'd been given strict orders to stay in the workroom and practise her bonnet making until it was deemed passable, and with so much time to herself, her thoughts ran wild. One minute she was convinced Mr Acland would carry out his threat, the next she was certain he wouldn't. She even toyed with the idea of telling Jack about the asylum herself before remembering Mrs Acland's advice. Despite Louisa's coolness, Rowan didn't want to risk losing her job. And, as if things weren't bad enough, she found being cooped up indoors almost unbearable.

One day towards the end of the week, Louisa had grudgingly informed her a client was specifically asking for her. When it turned out the woman wanted her bonnet trimmings dyed to match her dress, her employer hadn't been pleased at all.

'What led her to believe we provided such a service, Miss Rowena?' she exclaimed when the woman had left. 'I assumed when you took it upon yourself to offer to personalize Miss Richmond's trimmings, it would be a single occurrence.'

Rowan didn't know what to say and, since she could obviously do nothing right at the moment, kept quiet.

'And now you've promised to dye Mrs Pickering's ribbons to match the pale lemon of her dress. I just hope you can, for if you don't meet her exacting standards my reputation will be ruined. Not everyone is as easy-going as I am, Miss Rowena.'

Rowan bit down the retort that sprang to her lips. If her employer was easy-going, heaven help her.

When the church clock rang two o'clock on Sunday, Rowan ran outside, relieved to escape the confines of the workroom. Jack sat waiting in a pony and trap. He smiled his easy smile and her spirits lifted. To hell with it, after the dreadful week she'd had, she was going to relax and enjoy her afternoon. She'd just have to trust Mr Acland had been bluffing.

'I thought we'd take a ride along the Mall and Auntie has invited us to tea afterwards, if that is agreeable with you. She can't wait to show you her *hortus siccus*,' he said, jumping down to assist her into the little cart. Her heart leaped, but whether it was the thought of spending an afternoon in the outdoors, or the touch of his hand on hers, she wasn't sure. Leaning back in the seat, she enjoyed the feel of fresh air on her face.

'Have you had a good week?' Jack asked solicitously, as the pony trotted along the seafront.

'No, I have not,' Rowan answered so vociferously, he turned and stared at her in surprise.

'I thought you seemed preoccupied. All not well in Milliners' Row again?' he asked, patting her hand.

'Oh, Jack, I thought I was making good progress with my bonnet making, but Madame Louisa still seems displeased with me. I can't do anything right at all.'

'Surely it's not that bad? Auntie has been singing your praises to all and sundry this week. The girl with the red ribbon, she calls you. Look, I can see you are jittery so why not settle back and enjoy the ride? We can talk later, when you have had a chance to relax.'

As they trotted along the seafront, she watched a group of barefoot urchins splashing stones into the blue water while Jack regaled her with stories of yet more antics he and the other Preventatives had got up to. Rowan was sure they were highly exaggerated, but found his light-hearted banter especially entertaining after the strained atmosphere in the workroom.

'Of course, the job has its serious side, too. Those owlers, for example. We've had a tip-off they're trading close to here and have been tasked to catch them red-handed with their fleeces.'

Rowan thought of her father, and Fanny's insistence he did a deal with them, and her hand flew to her mouth.

Mistaking her concern, Jack reached over and patted her hand. 'What a worrier you are. Fear not, Rowan, I shall take the greatest of care,' he assured her and, as was his way, began telling her about yet another prank they'd pulled. It was impossible not to join in his laughter and by the time they reached Poppy Cottage, her spirits had fully revived.

'Miss Rowena, how lovely to see you,' cried Camilla, tearing off her gardening gloves as she came round the side path to greet them. 'Please forgive my not having changed, but the time always seems to run away with me when I'm outside. Do come indoors.'

'Tut-tut, Auntie, taking afternoon tea in your gardening dress, whatever will Rowan think?' Jack scolded.

'I think you look wonderful, Camilla,' Rowan said

sincerely, for the woman appeared younger and softer in her brightly sprigged cotton.

'Thank you, my dear. What a sweet girl like you sees in that naughty nephew of mine, I fail to see.' But her fond grin in his direction belied her words, Rowan thought, watching as she tugged on the bell pull.

The atmosphere was convivial as they sat enjoying their refreshment in the bright, airy drawing room, which looked out over the magnificent gardens.

'How are the trimmings for my dress and bonnet coming along?' Camilla asked. 'For the first time in a long while, I'm actually excited at the prospect of having a new outfit to wear.'

Rowan put her cup down on the table. 'I'm afraid I haven't been able to do much to them. Oh, I've dyed the ribbons and they've turned out beautifully,' she reassured, as Camilla frowned. 'It's just that I've been having trouble with my bonnet making and have had to spend all week in the workroom practising until I got it right.'

'You had to spend all week indoors? Sounds ghastly to me,' Jack said. 'No wonder you looked like a dormouse coming out of hibernation when I called for you. I did mention you seemed preoccupied, are you sure there isn't something else worrying you besides your bonnet making?'

She looked at him in alarm.

'Jack, that's very rude,' Camilla chided. 'Have you mastered the art now, my dear?'

'I think so, but getting Madame Louisa to admit it is another matter,' Rowan answered, glad the conversation was back on safe ground again. 'Then yesterday, a client came in requesting I dye her trimmings to match her dress.'

'Well, Madame Louisa must be pleased you are drawing in business for her, surely?' Camilla asked, studying Rowan closely. Rowan shrugged and Camilla, raising her eyebrows, turned to her nephew. 'Rowan has finished her tea so why don't you both take a stroll around the gardens whilst the sun is still shining? We can save the album for another day.'

Suddenly anxious to be outside again, Rowan nodded gratefully.

Fortified by her refreshment, Rowan wandered around the grounds with Jack, marvelling at the beautiful shrubs and flowers.

'You're not worrying about your job, are you, Rowan? Only you still seem rather subdued,' he asked, stopping and focusing his sharp gaze upon her.

'I'm sorry, Jack. I hope you are not finding me a miserable companion.'

'Of course not,' he assured her. 'I was merely thinking that you seem quite unlike yourself this afternoon. I can take you back if you've had enough.'

'Oh, no,' she said, quickly. 'I've been looking forward to seeing you all week.' Then, fearing she'd been too forward, she stared down at the ground.

'I'm pleased to hear you say that, Rowan, for you have been in my thoughts since we parted last Sunday evening. I hope you won't think it presumptuous of me to tell you I have never before met anyone as sweet and charming as you. You are not like other women, who think it clever to play cat and mouse. I find your honesty quite refreshing.'

Rowan felt a tug on her wrist. Glancing down at the red ribbon, she sighed. She knew she should tell him about the asylum. Although Mrs Acland had been adamant she should keep quiet, relationships were meant to be built on trust, weren't they? And there was always the risk Mr Acland might carry out his threat.

Mistaking her silence, Jack gave a self-conscious grin.

'I'm sorry if I've made you uncomfortable. Auntie warned me against saying too much too soon. Let's resume our walk, or we'll take root and Auntie will think she's grown a new species of plant. Talk of the devil,' he grinned, as Camilla appeared.

'Well, my dear, I hope Jack is behaving himself.'

'Auntie, please. My manners, as always, are impeccable, are they not, Miss Rowena?'

'Of course they are, Mr Carslake,' she said, bobbing a curtsy.

He chuckled. 'You do wonders for my self-esteem.'

'I hope I'm not in the way,' Camilla teased.

Rowan smiled. 'You have the most delightful garden, Camilla. If only . . .' she stuttered to a halt.

'If only what, my dear? You have impeccable taste, well, apart from in the beau stakes perhaps,' she teased. 'So if you think something could be improved upon, feel free to say. I commented to Jack only the other day that you are like a breath of fresh air with the way you are not afraid to say what you think. Your frankness is quite refreshing.'

'That's kind of you to say, especially as I was going to beg a favour of you. May I take some of those rhododendron leaves back with me?'

Camilla stared at her in surprise. 'Surely you mean the flowers?'

'No, the leaves would make the perfect pale yellow pigment for dyeing my client's ribbons.'

'How very interesting. I'd have thought they'd come out green.'

'You can use them for that, too. The colour depends on whether you steep the flowers or the leaves and which mordant you use to fix it,' Rowan explained, relieved to have found the solution to one of her problems. 'The only thing I need now is time to get everything done. I fear if Madame Louisa continues to keeps me this busy bonnet making, I will never have time to do anything else. I might even have to work my next half-day off.'

As Jack frowned, Camilla eyed her speculatively.

'Auntie, you're giving Rowan one of your scheming smiles,' Jack cried.

'Yes, I do believe I am,' Camilla agreed. 'Leave it to me, my dear.'

As Rowan let herself in through the entry, Maria eyed the rhododendron leaves she was carrying.

'You're not doing more hocus-pocus, are you?'

Rowan laughed then stopped as she heard voices coming from Louisa's private parlour on the first floor.

'Madam's got visitors and said you was to go up as soon as you got in.' Before Rowan could ask any questions, Maria hurried through to the scullery.

'Come in,' Louisa called, in answer to her tap on the door. 'I trust you have had a pleasant afternoon?'

Rowan nodded and couldn't help smiling when she saw who the visitors were.

'Rowan, its lovely to see you,' Mrs Acland cried. 'And

judging by how radiant you look, I'm guessing you have spent the afternoon in the company of some handsome beau.'

'Mrs Acland, it is lovely to see you, too,' Rowan said, going over and kissing the woman's cheek.

'You are indeed looking well,' Alexander confirmed, rising to his feet. 'I am pleased you have returned in time. Jenson will be returning with the carriage shortly and I have something I wish you to know.'

'Shall we go and find that material you wanted, Mother?' Louisa said. 'We can leave Alexander and Miss Rowena to have their discussion.'

As soon as the door closed behind them, Alexander smiled at Rowan.

'I can't quite reconcile "Miss Rowena" to the same little pixie who still loves to dance with gay abandon on the grass.' Seeing Rowan's look of surprise, he laughed. 'Yes, Louisa spilled the beans as to your antics, but to more serious matters. As promised, I have carried out a thorough investigation into the affairs of Hell Tor Asylum and frankly what has transpired is worrying in the extreme. First, you were right in the assumption that the patients were "knocked out", as you put it, at night.'

'Yes, I shall never forget that smell; it was quite vile.' Rowan shuddered at the memory.

'The cleaner used to keep the premises sanitary contains an active ingredient which, if not diluted, gives off a noxious chemical sufficient to overcome a human being. Naturally, the cleaner was only distributed to our establishments on the strict understanding it be diluted before use. In this case its use was abused. I'm afraid Sharp was

359

the chief perpetrator. She was also proven to have, shall we say, unsavoury desires and delusions. She is already in the best place for a person suffering from her condition, except now she is on the other side of the system, having herself been certified of lunacy.'

'That's appropriate. She was evil and I'd hate to think of anyone else suffering because of her,' Rowan said.

'I'm pleased to say that the final outcome of the investigation is more positive. Hell Tor is to follow the guidelines set out at the Model Institution, which will bring about constructive changes to the welfare of our patients. For example, women like your friend Susan will receive better health care and guidance. I know it can't help your friend, but it would be a comforting tribute to think her death will assist others who find themselves in a similar position to be better cared for.' Rowan nodded. 'Well,' Alexander said, as the clock struck the hour, 'I mustn't keep Jenson waiting. It's really good to see you looking so well, Rowan.'

'Thank you, Mr Acland, and thank you for telling me about the asylum. I'm pleased things will be better for the patients now. May I ask if you were able to deliver that letter to my father?'

'It was delivered by one of my assistants. Have you not heard from your father?'

Rowan shook her head. 'It was handed to him personally?' she persisted, hurt to think he had chosen to ignore it.

Alexander frowned. 'That was certainly my instruction,' he confirmed.

Rowan's heart sank.

'Come along, Alexander,' Mrs Acland said, popping her

head round the door. 'Goodbye, Rowan. I do hope you will visit us soon. Don't forget you promised me a new bonnet,' she teased, her eyes alight with mischief.

'I'm sure Louisa has told you my bonnet making leaves much to be desired,' Rowan sighed.

'I don't believe that for a minute. Why, she was telling me earlier how talented you are, and that she has plans to expand her business by dyeing trimmings to match dresses. Now that is a clever idea, is it not?'

Before Rowan could answer Alexander said, 'Don't worry about Louisa. My sister can be very exacting and bossy, but I can guarantee she would be keeping you employed only if she was satisfied with your work.'

As she heard their voices disappearing down the stairs, Rowan collapsed back in her chair. She was pleased that depraved Sharp had got her comeuppance, and that Susan hadn't died in vain. It was a relief to know that Louisa was pleased with her work after all, and surely if she was intending to expand her business, then that must mean her apprenticeship was safe. Perhaps Mrs Acland would get a new bonnet after all. Mr Acland was a truly nice man. As was Jack, she thought, her pulse racing as she remembered the time they'd spent together earlier. She would tell him about her time in the asylum when next she saw him, she vowed.

The only fly in the liniment was the fact that now she knew for sure her letter had been delivered to her father, his failure to reply obviously meant he wanted nothing more to do with her.

Chapter 34

'Good morning, Miss Rowena,' Louisa said, as soon as Rowan entered the workroom the next morning. She was studying the bonnet Rowan had made, and although her voice sounded pleasant, Rowan could sense an underlying current.

'Good morning, Madame Louisa,' Rowan responded, nervously.

'When I went to give Maria her instructions earlier, I noticed some ribbons steeping in a pot beside the range. As the liquid is yellow, I presume they're for Mrs Pickering?'

Rowan nodded. 'Miss Richmond kindly let me have some rhododendron leaves.'

'Well, the dyeing process isn't something I'm familiar with, and that is why we need to discuss the terms of your apprenticeship. When I engaged you, it was to learn the art of bonnet making, was it not?' Louisa asked, tapping the untrimmed bonnet.

Rowan's heart sank. 'Is there something wrong with it? I felt sure it would pass your inspection.'

'And it did. However, there is the question of this personalizing facility you have presumed to offer. That didn't form part of our agreement, did it?' Rowan shook her head. 'The matching of trimmings to ensembles will encroach upon bonnet making time, and it is imperative I continue to provide a timely service, especially as this is the season for visiting, our busiest time of year. I shall continue advising and fitting clients with bonnets and mantuas, whilst you concentrate on the dyeing and colour matching. Will this be agreeable to you?'

'Oh, yes, Madame Louisa. I find it really rewarding matching trimmings to outfits,' Rowan cried.

'As Mother pointed out, we will provide a service other milliners do not. However, it is imperative the colours are of first-rate quality. Our bonnets must continue to be *haute volée*, the *crème de la crème*,' Louisa said, waving her hands theatrically.

They were interrupted by the tinkling of the bell and Louisa hurried through to the shop. Rowan heard her greet Mrs Parker and hoped the time-wasting woman wouldn't sour her employer's mood. Then the bell gave another jangle and she hurried through to see if she could be of help.

'Good morning, my dear,' Camilla Richmond greeted her.

'Miss Richmond, how may I help you this morning?' Rowan enquired.

'I was wondering if those trimmings you were personalizing for my outfit were ready yet, Miss Rowena.' As Rowan stared at her in surprise, Camilla gave her a surreptitious wink. 'When Madame Louisa is free, I should like a word, if I may?'

Mrs Parker's head snapped up from the bonnet she had been studying. 'I am merely perusing, Madame Louisa, so please attend to Miss Richmond,' she said, clearly eager to find out what the woman wanted.

'If you are sure, Mrs Parker,' Louisa said. She turned to Miss Richmond. 'Is something wrong?'

'Quite the reverse. Madame Louisa, may I compliment you on the exemplary service I have received from your apprentice, Miss Rowena. You have obviously trained her to your own very high standard.'

Louisa looked pleased and surprised at the same time. 'Why, thank you, Miss Richmond.'

'Credit where credit is due, that's what I say. Now, I wonder if I may procure her services again. I am to be godmother at my great-niece's christening shortly and, as the family live some distance, shall be staying for some time. My mother and sister move in élite circles and I shall be expected to attend all manner of soirées, garden parties and other social events during my time with them.'

'That will be pleasant, for you,' Louisa said.

Camilla shrugged. 'I am at a loss as to how to match my bonnets and outfits, and it would be infra dig not to be dressed appropriately. I wonder, therefore, if Miss Rowena might visit and advise me. Obviously I would pay an additional amount for the short notice and,' she lowered her voice, and Rowan smiled when Mrs Parker move closer to hear, 'I realize once word of her excellent dyeing skills becomes common knowledge, they will be in demand.'

Rowan saw Mrs Parker's eyes gleam and had to bite her lip to prevent herself from laughing aloud. Clearly Camilla was a superb actress.

'When do you wish Miss Rowena to call upon you?' Louisa asked.

'Tomorrow morning, if you can spare her, Madame Louisa.'

'Shall we say ten o'clock?'

'That would be perfect. Thank you so much, Madame Louisa,' Camilla said, turning to go, and then hesitating.

'Was there something else, Miss Richmond?' Louisa enquired.

'Well, yes. I am seeking the services of a stalwart member of our community.'

At this, Mrs Parker positively sprang to attention. 'May I be of help, Miss Richmond?'

'How kind. I am seeking to help those unfortunate souls in the Poor House.'

Mrs Parker sniffed. 'Being a woman of limited means, I find I am unable to open my purse.'

'How true,' Louisa muttered under her breath.

'I fear you misunderstand me, Mrs Parker. I am looking for a person who knows the people of Saltmouth, someone who could spread the word that I am collecting good clothing, eggs, spare vegetables from the kitchen gardens, that kind of thing. Of course, it would need to be someone who is known and respected around here.'

'Well, I think I can safely say there is no one in Saltmouth who does not know of me,' Mrs Parker declared.

Rowan turned away to hide her smile.

'How kind you are, Mrs Parker. I shall leave you to spread the word, then. Good morning to you.'

No sooner had Miss Richmond left than Mrs Parker, puffed up like a peacock, strutted out of the door.

Louisa laughed. 'Well, you'd better get dyeing, Miss Rowena. I have a feeling that Mrs Parker will be gossiping to all and sundry this morning, and not just about donations for the Poor House either. I fear Miss Rich-mond didn't realize what a tittle-tattle that woman is.'

Rowan wasn't so sure. She had a feeling Camilla knew exactly what Mrs Parker was like.

Promptly at ten o'clock the next morning, Rowan was shown into Camilla's dressing room.

'Tell me, Rowan, did you get many clients yesterday perchance?' she asked with a grin.

'Poor Madame Louisa was rushed off her feet, and I now have a list of clients to visit. Apparently everyone wants their trimmings dyed to match their outfits. Madam is convinced it will soon become *de rigueur* to wear complementary colours,' Rowan said.

Camilla chuckled. 'I see you have managed to trim my outfit and bonnet.'

'Madam insisted it be done before I visited today. Shall we see how they look?'

Politely she went and looked out of the window whilst Camilla disrobed, and her heart gave a leap when she saw Jack striding towards the house. Seeing Rowan's smile, Camilla grinned.

'Jack was delighted when he heard you were visiting this morning. He is working the later shift again today,' she said, her eyes sparkling with mischief.

Rowan shook her head. The woman was incorrigible. Forcing herself to concentrate, Rowan checked the newly trimmed ensemble was hanging correctly and then adjusted the bonnet.

'Well, what do you think, Rowan? Will I pass muster?' Camilla asked, twirling around in front of the looking-glass.

'You look delightful,' Rowan answered truthfully, for the iris and bluebell hues livened up her complexion and made her eyes sparkle like sapphires. 'What else did you want me to look at?'

'Don't worry, I won't keep you long. If you could think of a suitable way to liven up these outfits here, I'll be happy.' Whilst Camilla changed out of her dress, Rowan studied the other ensembles. They were too dull for this vivacious woman. However, they were of good quality and it would be easy to transform them.

'Would you like me to get out my samples and make some suggestions?' she asked, once the woman had changed back into her sprigged cotton.

Camilla grimaced. 'You've made such a good job of this outfit I shall leave it entirely up to you. Now, I am due to visit the Poor House, and Jack is waiting for you in the garden, so off you go. Not a word to Madame Louisa, though,' she said, putting a finger to her lips.

Rowan's heart gave a flip and she needed no second bidding.

Jack's eyes lit up when he saw her walking towards him.

'Rowan, what a lovely surprise,' he exclaimed. She shook her head. He was as incorrigible as his aunt.

'Well, it was a surprise for me when I heard you were working the later shift today.'

'A wonderful coincidence, is it not?' he asked, grinning. Then his expression changed and he cleared his throat. Before he could say anything, though, they saw Camilla making her way towards them.

'I'm off now. Visit whenever you wish, Rowan. I believe I have given you the perfect excuse, but, of course, you may need to collect extra plants and flowers from the garden,' she said with a wink. As she disappeared through the gate, Jack turned to Rowan and grinned.

'Crafty old Auntie, didn't I say she was planning something? There was no way she was going to let you escape from us. She thinks you're quite special, you know,' he said, looking serious. 'As do I, Rowan. Knowing how important honesty and straight-talking are to you, I wish to make my intentions clear. I know we have been walking out but a short time, but I truly feel as if I have found my soul mate in you.'

The ribbon around her wrist tightened. 'But you don't really know much about me,' she whispered.

'Then, I shall enjoy finding out,' he said, the twinkle in his eye returning.

Her heart lurched.

'Of course, I have my training to complete, and you have to finish your apprenticeship, which means our time together will be limited. However, I don't want to run the risk of someone else running off with you so, if you are agreeable, perhaps we could make our relationship exclusive, if you get my meaning?'

She stared at him in surprise. 'You mean, not walk out with anyone else?'

'That's exactly what I mean and then, if all goes well, in the course of time we can – but forgive me, I'm getting ahead of myself.' He shook his head, then grinned. 'Now, my girl with the red ribbon, would you care for something to drink before I walk you back?'

With a start, Rowan realized the sun was high in the sky, meaning she'd been here for some considerable time. She jumped to her feet. 'Thank you but I really must get back or madam will be cross.'

'I'll run you back in the trap. It will be quicker,' he said, understanding.

Pulling up outside the shop, Jack patted her hand and promised to call for her on Sunday afternoon.

'Goodbye, dearest Rowan,' he called softly as he picked up the reins.

With her blood singing in her veins, she let herself into the shop, relieved to find Louisa busy discussing the merits of various bonnets with a client. Needing time to compose her thoughts, Rowan took herself through to the workroom. Her insides felt fluttery, and she was all fingers and thumbs as she fumbled with her cape.

She could hardly believe Jack had suggested that they should, as he put it, make their relationship exclusive, she thought, dancing happily around the room. If only her mother were here to share her happiness. And she would stop worrying about Mr Acland for he obviously hadn't said anything yet so perhaps he never would.

The warm glow stayed with Rowan all week, despite the fact she was rushed off her feet. Word of her dyeing services flew around Saltmouth faster than the pigeon post, and she took so many orders she went to bed dreaming of the materials she needed to make her various pigments. Good relations had been restored with Maria after Rowan had turned an excess piece of trimming into a flower to trim the maid's Sunday bonnet. She'd been delighted and had offered to help Rowan by furnishing her with gleanings from her regular sorties to the kitchen gardens. She'd even offered to stir her colour concoctions, as she called them, as long as there was no more mumbo jumbo!

Despite her hectic schedule, Rowan managed to complete Camilla's ensemble with days to spare before she was due to leave for the christening.

On Sunday, as Jack pulled up outside the shop in the pony trap, she snatched up her bag and bonnet boxes and ran outside.

'Rowan with the red hair and ribbon, it feels an age since we last met,' he quipped, reaching down to take her things from her. His fingers brushed against hers and she felt a tingle shiver up her spine. During the long hours she'd spent sewing, thoughts of him had continually buzzed around her head, the wooden blocks on the work bench taking on his cheeky grin. Settling back in her seat, she lifted her head up to the sun.

'It feels so good to be out in the fresh air,' she said, as the pony trotted towards the seafront.

'I would prefer it if you said it felt good to be sitting beside your beloved,' he said, staring at her mournfully.

'Fool,' she said, tapping his arm playfully. 'I hope your aunt will be pleased with the way I've trimmed her ensembles and bonnets. She left the colours and trimmings up to me, you know.'

'No disrespect to good old Auntie Cam, but that can only be a good thing. You've already made her see she needs brightening up. Now I wish to spend some time alone with my beloved, so shall we take the scenic route along the Mall? I shall slow down as we pass the Preventative Station so you will be able to think of me whilst I'm away.'

Her heart turned over. 'You are going away? When?'

'Tonight, so I'm afraid we won't be able to spend long with Auntie. I did tell you we'd had a tip-off about owlers further along the coast, didn't I?'

Her heart lurched. In all the recent excitement, she'd quite forgotten. She thought of greedy Fanny and hoped the woman hadn't persuaded her father to get involved with those men of the night.

Chapter 35

Rowan missed Jack more than she could have imagined but had little time to dwell on his absence. The shop's reputation for providing the new personalizing service was spreading rapidly, and she was rushed off her feet from the time she got up to the time she went to bed. Louisa, thrilled with the way her business was thriving, was even talking about expanding into larger premises. Telling Rowan she was pleased with her progress, she assigned her more responsibility, sending her to call upon some of the more influential ladies of Saltmouth.

One afternoon, Rowan was returning from measuring up a client, when she caught a glimpse of corn-coloured hair ahead of her. She looked away for a second, puzzled as to what it was about the hair that had caught her attention. Then she felt a jolt of recognition. It couldn't be, she thought, pushing her way through the crowds to get a closer look.

'Sab?' she called tentatively. He turned, looking startled for a moment, and she waved excitedly, unable to believe it really was him.

'Rowan?' he gasped in surprise, stopping dead so that the people around bumped into him. But he seemed oblivious as he stared at the girl hurrying towards him.

'Oh, Sab, it really is you,' she cried, throwing her arms around him in delight.

'Hey, look at you, dressed up like a grand lady,' he said, holding her at arm's length and studying her. 'Your fellow must be doing well.'

She frowned. 'Pardon me, Sab, but I'm sure I don't know what you mean,' she protested, wondering how he could have heard about Jack. 'What are you doing here? I thought you hated towns.'

'I do but I'm here on a spot of business,' he said.

'How's Father and the farm?' she asked. 'And why were you so distant before I was ab–' A passer-by jostled her arm, interrupting their conversation.

'Look, there's lots I want to ask you, too, but we can't talk here. Got time for a walk?'

She stood dithering for a moment, knowing she should return to work. Yet she so wanted to catch up with her dear friend. Pushing her guilty feelings away, she nodded. It was wonderful to have met up with the man who'd been like a brother to her, and she had so much she wanted to ask him.

'Let's walk along the Mall. It'll be quieter there,' she said. 'Oh, Sab, I have missed you. You look all grown up.' She smiled up at him and he grinned back.

'I've missed you, too, little sister, though you haven't grown any these past few months, have you?' She punched him playfully, then noticed they were passing the Free Library and Coffee House.

'How about a quick cup of tea?' she asked, keen to find out more about what Sab had been up to. He stared at the building uncertainly. 'Oh, come on, my treat,' she insisted, taking his arm and leading him inside.

'Now you must tell me how Father is and how

everything is at the farm,' she insisted, once they were seated and their order had been taken.

His eyes clouded. 'Wouldn't know, would I?' he muttered, shifting in his chair.

'Whatever do you mean, Sab?'

'After you scarpered with your fancy man . . .'

'But I didn't have a fancy man, Sab.'

'But Fanny said you'd run off together whilst we were sowing up in Five Acre Field.'

'I didn't run away, Sab, I was abducted.'

His eyebrows rose, almost disappearing under his corn crop of hair.

'I was kidnapped whilst I was carrying out my ritual up at the oak. A man came up and threw a sack over me, dumped me in a cart and took me to the asylum on Dartmoor. Fanny arranged it all.' She blinked as the terrible memories came flooding back. 'Anyway, that doesn't explain why you were ignoring me before all this happened, Sab.' He stared out of the window, but she didn't think for one moment he was seeing the boats bobbing on the water.

'Fanny said I had to. Said if I didn't, she'd tell Uncle we was carrying on together, you know, having rela—' His voice trailed off.

'That's disgusting! Father would never have believed it,' she protested. Turning, he gave her a level look and she sighed. 'He believed everything she said, didn't he?'

'Yup. She had him well and truly in her clutches. Put me off marriage for life, that did. She even threatened to shop me to the authorities. Said as I'd been over four when I left the orphanage, they were morally obliged to make sure I was an obedient citizen, and that I'd be taken to a boarding house and made ready for the army. Wasn't having any of that so I up and left. It were only when I found work on the other side of the valley that Farmer John told me as I'd been trained as a labourer, it wouldn't have applied to me.'

'Oh, Sab, that's terrible,' Rowan murmured, reaching out and patting his arm.

'Joe. I'm called Joe now,' he said. 'And what about you? I gather you must be working here in Saltmouth now,' he said, nodding towards her bag.

'Yes, I'm apprenticed to Louisa Acland, milliner and mantua maker. And I'd better go or I won't have a job,' she said, gathering up her things. 'Why don't you come back with me? The shop will be closing soon and we can catch up with the rest of our news?'

He shook his head. 'Got to get back or I'll not have no job either. Only came to bring something in to one of the shops. I'm labouring at Pear Tree Farm, beyond Saltmouth. Just for the summer, mind. Funny, eh, when we was at Orchard Farm before?' They laughed, sharing the joke, happy their easy relationship was established once more. 'You passing by before autumn, call in. Farmer John's wife's the welcoming type and happen I wouldn't mind seeing you again meself,' he said with a grin.

'I'd love to,' she said, delighted. 'And if you're in Saltmouth, you know where you can find me. I'd love you to meet my follower. He's called Jack and works at the Preventative Station. You'll like him, Sab. He's kind and cheeky. A bit like you, I guess.'

They got up to leave, hardly noticing their untouched drinks cooling on the table. Laughing and joking, they walked back along the Mall but as soon as they reached the town, Sab turned to Rowan.

'Best hurry now,' he said and, waving his hand in salute, disappeared into the market.

As she watched him weaving his way through the rapidly emptying stalls, Rowan was reminded of the last time they'd been to Sudbury Market. If only she'd heeded old Aggie's warning to *beware she with the forked tongue*. But then never in her wildest dreams had she imagined Fanny would turn out to be such a malevolent woman. Surely her father loved them too much to believe the woman's sick allegations? But then if he loved Rowan as much as she'd thought, he would have responded to her letter, wouldn't he? Although it had been good seeing Sab again, it had brought bad memories of the past flooding back.

Preoccupied with her musing, she found herself back outside the shop before she knew it. Seeing the smartly dressed gentleman hovering impatiently outside, her pulse began to race.

'Jack,' she cried. 'When did you get back?'

'Boat landed further along the coast this morning and we rode the rest of the way but it was a futile mission. Reckon someone had tipped off those owlers.' Rowan thought of her father and breathed a sigh of relief. 'Had to come and say hello to my favourite girl, although I can't stay long,' he added, giving her his winning smile.

'Favourite girl!' she squeaked. 'I should hope after what you proposed last time we met, that I am your only girl.'

'Indeed you are, Rowan.' The clock on the church struck the hour and he frowned. 'Shame you weren't here when I arrived as I've to report back for our debrief session. May I call for you on Sunday?'

She nodded, her heart leaping at the prospect. He'd been away so long and she'd missed him, although she knew better than to tell him that.

'Auntie will still be away, so I'd better behave correctly and take you out for tea. Shall we go to the Free Library and Coffee House?' he suggested, grinning at her roguishly. Her heart began doing the weird dance it always did when he stared at her like that. She smiled and then noticed Louisa peering at them through the bowed window.

'I'd like that, Jack. Better go in now, though.'

'Until Sunday then,' he said with a bow. 'Parting is such sweet sorrow, Rowan,' he called after her.

'I thought you'd got lost, Miss Rowena. It is not my policy to encourage followers to call upon my staff during working hours,' Louisa admonished as Rowan entered the shop.

'Sorry, Madame Louisa. Jack's only just returned and he called to see if I'd walk out with him on Sunday afternoon.'

'I saw him loitering outside,' she said disapprovingly. 'It doesn't look good for business so perhaps in future you'd ask him to wait down the entry. Now what orders did you take today?'

By the time Rowan had gone through them all, her employer was mollified. 'Goodness, you are going to be busy with all this extra work, but I have to say I am getting nothing but compliments about your ingenuity. It appears we have started the fashion for personalization and now are clearly heads ahead of our rivals, if you'll excuse the pun. Of course, with you using more ribbons, the orders to the plumassier and veruriers have declined, but that's not my concern.' She waved her hand, as if batting a bothersome fly. 'One must move with the times. With that in mind, I am designing a new style of bonnet. As we both need to focus on our work, I have engaged a girl from the Poor House. She will sweep the pathways, dust the windows, keep the shop and workroom tidied and the fitting room refreshed.'

'That will make a huge difference, Madame Louisa. I was wondering how I was going to get everything done in the timely manner you insist upon.'

'I can't deny we will both have to work even harder, but we mustn't grumble. This is the season for visiting, when we would expect to be at our busiest. However, I pride myself on being a fair person and will ensure you receive a Christmas box worth opening.'

'Thank you, Madame Louisa,' Rowan cried. Compliments and money, what more could she ask for?

'In the meantime, take yourself up to my spare room and choose some material with which to make a new work dress. That one is looking decidedly the worse for wear,' she said, nodding to the one Rowan had on.

'But it is only a few months old,' Rowan pointed out.

'And it has seen much heavy use. It's no good us encouraging the good ladies of Saltmouth to be dressed *à propos*, if you go around looking *passé*,' she declared. 'As you have worked so hard, you may also choose a length of something summery for your Sunday jaunts. We need to set an example when we are out.'

Rowan's eyes lit up, for although she'd been grateful for Mrs Acland's generosity, it would be wonderful to have a dress of her own to walk out in.

'That will be all for today, Miss Rowena. I believe Maria has made a hearty vegetable stew for supper. How that girl manages such bounty on the money I give her, I really don't know.'

Rowan smiled but said nothing. It wasn't her place to spill the beans.

Hoping Maria had kept her promise and saved her the carrot tops and onion skins, she made her way upstairs. Her stocks for making dyes had dwindled alarmingly and with the new orders she'd taken today, she urgently needed to replenish her supplies. Rummaging through the bales of materials, she settled on a smart *mousseline de laine* for work and a length of bright green cotton for her Sunday gown. If she worked late into the nights, she might just have enough time to have it finished before she next walked out with Jack, she thought, her heart racing. She could trim both her dress and bonnet with moss-green ribbon as well.

By the time Sunday came, the weather had turned inclement with light drizzle falling from a leaden sky. Oh, well, Rowan thought philosophically, summer or not, the sun couldn't shine all the time. Excitedly changing into her finery, and then parting her hair down the middle in the style she'd seen the ladies of Saltmouth now wearing, she carefully donned her newly trimmed hat and ran down the stairs.

'You may borrow a calash to protect your bonnet,' Louisa called from the workroom, where she was working on her new creation.

'Thank you, but it's merely a mizzle,' Rowan said, then felt guilty her employer was still working. 'Would you like me to stay and help?'

Louisa laughed. 'I need this to be finished by the time we open tomorrow, Miss Rowena, not next week.' Then seeing Rowan's crestfallen look she smiled. 'Thank you for the offer, but I do believe your beau is waiting.'

Outside, Rowan felt her heart jump when she saw Jack seated in the pony cart, but instead of his usual cheeky grin, his smile seemed strained. No sooner had she climbed up beside him, than he flicked the reins.

The wet weather meant everyone was travelling by carriage or cart and she saw Jack frowning, but put this down to him concentrating. The cloud was hanging heavy over the bay, making everywhere grey and dismal, and it was difficult to differentiate between the sea and the sky. The ride seemed endless and by the time they entered the Coffee House, Rowan was relieved to be amongst the cheery chatter and laughter. They busied themselves ordering and then an awkward silence fell between them. Rowan began telling Jack how Louisa was allowing her to call upon the grander houses and how, with new orders to fulfil, she had more dyes to make. He nodded politely but his look remained set and he was clearly distracted.

'Is something wrong, Jack?' she asked, stumbling to a halt.

He shook his head. 'It would appear you have been busy whilst I've been away. No time for any recreation then?'

'Oh, no, I'm afraid it's been all work, but Madame

Louisa said I would be pleased with my Christmas box,' she enthused.

'So you've not had any time for promenading then?' he asked, looking at her closely.

'Gracious, no. What about you? That dog of yours looks a lively fellow. I expect he takes a lot of exercising,' she said, trying to inject some lightness into the conversation.

'Yes, he does. But you know where you stand with animals.'

Rowan shook her head. What a strange thing to say. Then she was struck by a terrible thought. Had Mr Acland carried out his threat? Could that be the reason for Jack's coolness towards her? Should she mention the asylum? But if he didn't know, would she be risking their relationship? The ribbon tightened.

Fumbling to find the right words, she stared around the room, taking in the smiling faces, animated chatter, tinkling of glasses, chink of china and the lively background music coming from the pianist in the corner. The overall happy atmosphere of the place contrasted starkly against their awkward pauses, and she couldn't help thinking how much easier conversation with Sab had been when she'd last visited here. She was about to mention her old friend when Jack fumbled in his pocket and took out a soft leather money bag.

'We are very busy at work and I need to be getting back as soon as we've finished,' he muttered, throwing some coins beside the bill and getting to his feet.

'But we've hardly . . .' she began, looking at their untouched scones and still steaming cups of tea.

'Whenever, you are ready,' he said politely but she

couldn't stand the strained atmosphere any longer and got to her feet.

'Clearly you are anxious to be away,' she said stiffly. 'And I have more dyes to make.'

'So you said.' He waited whilst the cape was placed around her shoulders and then strode out of the Coffee House.

By the time he drew up outside the shop, Rowan could have screamed. She stared at Jack for a long moment but he refused to meet her gaze. Whatever was troubling him, he wasn't going to share it with her.

'Goodbye, Jack,' she finally said, climbing down from the cart.

He nodded and she'd barely alighted when he called for the pony to walk on. Stamping down the entry, she threw off her cape and, deciding she needed a cup of tea she could drink, went through to the kitchen. This being Maria's afternoon off as well, the place was empty. Rowan set the kettle on the range, snatched up the maid's apron and began preparing the carrot tops and leaves for her dye. By the time the maid returned, she was vigorously stirring the pot.

'Jem loves me flower,' Maria said, taking off her bonnet and pointing to the trimming Rowan had made.

Rowan grunted.

'My, my, someone's in a moody. Hope you're not going to do more of that weird mumbo jumbo stuff, 'cos if you are, I'm off.'

'No, I've almost finished. I just need to steep these ribbons overnight. Can I leave the pot here or will it be in your way?'

'No, it'll be fine. Madam's going to evening service, so she had a hot meal lunch time. Do you want anything? You're looking right peaky, if you don't mind me saying.'

'I've got a bit of a head so I'll get an early night,' Rowan muttered, taking off the maid's apron and returning it.

Up in her room, she tore off her new dress. All those nights she'd spent stitching whilst the candles had burned low, and what for? It had been a complete waste of time. Jack had hardly glanced in her direction, let alone noticed what she'd been wearing. Why, he hadn't even commented on her new hairstyle. What a waste of effort. She'd been so excited at the thought of spending time with him again. Clearly he didn't find her attractive any more, she thought. Or had he found out about her past? Burying her head in the pillow, she let the hot tears fall.

Chapter 36

Although she felt drained after her restless night, Rowan was up at first light. After bathing her swollen eyes with cold water, she dressed carefully and made her way down to the yard. The mizzle had cleared and a fresh sea breeze was carrying the tang of salt on the air. Returning from the privy, she smiled at the timid young girl who was hurrying out to sweep the pathways. Well, at least that was one job she didn't have to worry about any longer, she thought, stepping back indoors to see how her ribbons had turned out.

'Good morning, Miss Rowena,' Louisa said, as Rowan carried them through to the workroom. 'I see you have plenty of work to do here today, so I shall leave you in charge of the shop whilst I deliver this new bonnet to Lady Arlingham. She is becoming quite a regular client and, as you know, where Lady Arlingham leads the ladies of Saltmouth follow.' She paused and stared at Rowan, her violet eyes clouding. 'Are you quite well this morning?'

'Yes, I'm fine, thank you, Madame Louisa,' Rowan assured her employer.

'Ask Maria for some beef tea later. It will do you the power of good. I can't have a wet blanket seeing to my clients.'

Rowan watched as she gathered up her things and

bustled out of the door. Resting her throbbing head in her hands, she prayed the shop would remain quiet for a while. Jack's strange behaviour had played on her mind all night, and she'd tossed and turned, worrying what could have been wrong. Perhaps he really had been busy, or maybe something had gone wrong with one of his jobs. Of course, the covert nature of his work meant he could never discuss it in detail with her. Or was it that Mr Acland had carried out his threat? No doubt it would all come out in the wash, as her auntie Sal used to say.

Forcing herself to concentrate, she spread out the ribbons on the work table and began measuring. But as she reached for the scissors the blocks seemed to spring to life, glaring at her with Jack's angry eyes, snarling with his tight lips. She blinked and looked again, but the blocks were devoid of anything other than their wooden shapes. Chiding herself for having fanciful thoughts, she shook her head to clear it and resumed work.

She was just thinking she should stop for some nourishment, when the little bell tinkled. Before she could get to her feet, Louisa appeared at her side, eyes glowing with excitement.

'Look, Miss Rowena. Is this not the most beautiful looking-glass you have ever seen?' she said, placing a parcel down on the work table and pulling back the soft cloth. As Rowena stared at the bronze mirror, its trumpet scrolls decorating the grip, her heart began thumping. She'd know that design anywhere.

'Where did you get it?' she whispered.

'Why, at the local repository. The old fool sold it to me for a song, but I think it could be valuable.'

'It's priceless,' Rowan whispered, tracing the engraved scrolls with her finger. Immediately, she felt the energy flow through her body, and couldn't help smiling.

'Of course, I shall have it valued properly, but if it's worth what I think, then my prayers have been answered and I can start searching for larger premises straight away,' Louisa continued.

'But you can't sell it,' Rowan said, looking up in alarm.

'I beg your pardon, Miss Rowena,' Louisa remonstrated. 'I can and I will.'

'But you don't understand. This mirror belonged to my mother and has magical properties. It passed to me when she died,' she said, snatching it up and hugging it to her chest.

'Rubbish. This is a Celtic mirror from a burial ground, of that I am sure, for I remember reading about one in the paper some time ago. Now, please give it back, Miss Rowena,' Louisa ordered, holding out her hand. As Rowan hugged it tighter, her employer's eyes narrowed.

'I can prove it's mine,' Rowan exclaimed, turning the mirror upside down. 'See, the face looks like a grinning cat.'

'I agree it does. However, that in no way proves it is yours.'

'I wouldn't have known that otherwise, would I?' Rowan persisted, staring down at it.

In an instant, Louisa reached out and snatched the mirror from her hand. 'It is mine, Miss Rowena. Bought and paid for by me this morning. Now I suggest you go and have your luncheon and we will say no more about this unfortunate confrontation.'

'Madame Louisa, please listen. I promise you this is my mother's mirror. She found . . .'

But she was talking to Louisa's back, for the woman had turned and was rewrapping it in the soft cloth. Instinctively, Rowan reached out to snatch it back, but Louisa was too quick for her, moving so that she was between Rowena and the mirror.

'I have had my suspicions about you for some time, young lady.'

'Suspicions? What suspicions?' she asked, in surprise.

'That you take things that don't belong to you,' she said slowly, emphasizing every word. Rowan gasped. 'Oh, you may well look innocent, but no sooner had you arrived than my signature scent started to disappear at an alarming rate.'

'I knew you thought I was taking it, but I can assure you I am not the thief,' Rowan protested, her face growing hotter by the minute.

'Well, how do you explain the ostrich feather then? One went missing after you'd cleaned them, only to reappear the next morning.'

Rowan stared at her employer in disbelief. 'What would I want with an ostrich feather? I didn't go anywhere.'

'Well, who else would have taken it?' Louisa asked.

'I can't stay here if that's what you think of me . . .' Rowan began, but Louisa cut in.

'No, I agree you cannot stay here. Pack your things and leave immediately.'

The ribbon around Rowan's wrist tugged so tightly that she cried out.

'Oh, please, Louisa.'

But the woman was adamant. 'I cannot have someone of dubious behaviour in my employ. Neither can I furnish a thief with a character.'

As the air crackled between them, Rowan squared her shoulders.

'I repeat, I am not, and never have been, a thief. That was my mother's mirror, and I shall return and prove it to you,' she vowed, turning on her heel and running up to her room.

Taking off her uniform dress, she donned the yellow dress and cape Mrs Acland had given her. Carefully ensuring she gathered only her own possessions together, she tied them into a bundle and stole down the stairs and out of the entry.

How had her beloved mirror come to Saltmouth, she wondered as she stormed along the street. The last time she'd seen it had been the night she was snatched. She'd been carrying out her Eostre ritual, and it had been left on the ground when she'd been abducted. So how had Louisa come to find it in the local repository? As her feet pounded the ground, questions pounded her brain. Who could have found it and brought it here?

She walked another mile or so before remembering her chance meeting with Sab. He had known how much the mirror meant to her and would never have sold it. But then he had thought she'd run off with a man. What a ridiculous notion, she thought, stamping even harder. Then she remembered Sab saying he'd come to Saltmouth on a spot of business. What was it he'd said exactly? She thought hard. He'd had to bring something in to one of the shops. Yes, that was it. So he must have had something to sell, mustn't he? Clearly no one could be trusted, she thought, coming to a halt as exhaustion overtook her. Overwhelmed with misery, she leaned against a nearby fence and sobbed. Finally, when there were no tears left, she wiped her face with her kerchief. What should she do now, she wondered, and it was only when she looked up that she realized she was standing outside Poppy Cottage.

She wasn't sure if Camilla had returned from her visit to relatives but, before her courage left her, she opened the gate and defiantly marched up the front path. Just as she reached the door, it opened and Jack stood there, smartly dressed in his uniform.

'What on earth are you doing here?' he asked, staring at her in surprise.

Remembering his cool manner from the previous afternoon, she hugged her bundle closer and stuck her chin in the air.

'I merely came to enquire if Camilla had returned yet.'

Eyeing her warily, he shook his head. She waited a moment and when he didn't say anything, turned to leave.

'What did you want her for?' he said finally.

She thought quickly. 'I just wanted to say farewell and thank her for her kindness,' she replied.

'Oh.'

'Is that all you can say, Jack Carslake?' she burst out. 'You invited me out for tea then spent all afternoon ignoring me. Despite your proposal for our future, you clearly couldn't care a tinker's cuss about me.'

'That's not true,' he sighed. 'I rather think it's the other way around.' Anger blazing in his blue eyes turned them to navy.

'What?' Rowan asked.

'Come along, Carslake. You haven't got time to spend chatting up a lady, however pretty she might be.' They looked up to see a uniformed man, grinning as he walked towards them.

Jack muttered an expletive under his breath. 'You go on, Crawton, I'll catch you up,' he called, straightening his hat. 'Look, Rowan, I must go, we've got wind of a big movement of wool from a farm up Sudbury way. Word is it's to be transported to Saltcombe Regis, then shipped out sometime in the next few days.'

'What?' she asked, her mind ticking back to old Davey's words. 'You don't mean owlers?' He nodded and her heart sank.

He sighed again. 'I don't like leaving you like this, Rowan, but I must obey orders. We're trying to catch the farmer red-handed as he hands over the wool to the owlers. If we can do that we'll be up for promotion and that means a pay rise. Look, as soon as I'm back, I'll call by the shop and we'll talk. Something's been on my mind that I need to ask you about.'

'But . . .' she started, but he interrupted.

'This job is rumoured to be of great magnitude, and I really shouldn't have said anything, so not a word about this to anyone,' he ordered. Before she could answer, he was running down the path to join the other Preventative.

Could this day get any worse, she wondered. She had no job, no home, no mirror, no explanation from Jack for his strange behaviour, and now this. Collapsing on the lawn, she put her head in her hands. Even Camilla had deserted her. What was she going to do now? The red ribbon jerked and, as if her mother had spoken the words, her question was answered. 'Sorry, Jack, but I must warn Father, just in case he's involved,' she whispered, and as the words came back to her on the freshening breeze, she got wearily to her feet. Her father was basically an honest man. Whatever he had or hadn't done, he was still her father and she couldn't wait to see him and her old home again. After all, she had nowhere else to go, she thought miserably. The ribbon loosened its grip.

Clutching her bundle to her, she trudged up the hill, trying not to think of the long walk ahead of her before she reached Orchard Farm. The lowering cloud grew even blacker, and before she'd got to the top of the road, the rain was coming down in stair rods. Pulling her wet cape tighter round her, she took shelter under a tree until the worst had passed. The time dragged on, and she was just wondering whether to risk continuing on her journey, when a cart drew to a halt.

'Be likin' a lift, little un?' the carter called.

Hardly able to believe her luck and for the first time in her life grateful for her petite stature, Rowan nodded.

'Where you be goin' to?' he asked.

'Sudbury, sir,' she replied, taking in his friendly smile and gentle eyes.

'Well, ain't you the lucky one. I be goin' near there myself. Hop in.'

Climbing up, she stared around for somewhere to sit, for every surface was piled high with odds and ends of furniture. 'Reckons you'll have to find somethin' to perch on, but it'll be better than walkin', eh?' he chuckled.

She couldn't argue with that, she thought, upturning an old box and making herself comfortable. He looked at the bundle on her lap and frowned.

'Not runnin' away, are you, little un?'

'No, returning home,' she answered, feeling a mixture of excitement and trepidation.

'Why, you ain't no little un at all,' he said, assessing her with his shrewd eyes. 'Sorry, maid. On we go, Jess,' he called to his horse.

They'd been travelling some time when the cart suddenly lurched off the main road and onto a rutted track. Startled out of her musing, Rowan looked sharply at the carter.

'Where are we going?' Thoughts of being kidnapped ran through her head. Had she been foolish taking a lift from someone she didn't know?

'Calm yourself, maid. 'Tis a short cut I know. Want to be in Sudbury before sundown,' he answered, looking up at the sky and chortling. 'Not that we can see it. Here, you hungry?' He bent and took a package out of a knapsack. 'Missus always packs me a feast.' He handed her a chunk of bread and a wedge of cheese. Her stomach rumbled in appreciation, and she remembered she'd missed her luncheon.

They continued on in companionable silence as they devoured the home-baked bread.

'Your wife's a good baker, sir,' Rowan said when she'd eaten, brushing the crumbs from her lap.

'She is that, and rain's stopped. See yonder,' the carter replied, pointing ahead. A beautiful rainbow arched the rolling hills beyond. ' 'Tis lucky. Have a wish, maid.' She grinned at his optimism, knowing full well it was merely a sign of more rain to come.

Soon the rutted track widened and her heart leaped as the cart began climbing the familiar lane to Sudbury. As they approached the sprawling hamlet, her heart lurched. How would her father greet her? What would Fanny say when she saw her?

When they reached the market square opposite the church, the carter turned to her.

'Where be your home, maid?' he asked, breaking into her thoughts. She pointed up to the hills.

'Orchard Farm's up there. You can drop me off here.'

He snorted. 'I may not be a toff, but I do know me manners.' He yanked on the reins and the horse obligingly moved on through the village, over the humped-back bridge and turned onto the familiar track that led to the farm. She smiled gratefully, for truth to tell she was feeling quite exhausted. Settling back in her seat again, she stared around at the familiar scenery then squinted through the trees as she noticed a plume of smoke rising from an old caravan. She didn't remember that being there.

'There we are, my dear. You'll be glad to be home, I'm sure,' the carter said, interrupting her musing as he pointed towards the farmhouse. 'And before sun's set as promised,' he laughed.

'Thank you so much, sir,' she said, fumbling for her purse.

'Get away with you, maid. Been a pleasure having your company,' he called as she clambered down. With a quick wave, he turned the cart and was soon lost to view.

Rowan stood looking around at the farmyard. Although it was strangely empty and had an air of neglect, she couldn't help the feeling of excitement that bubbled up inside her. She took a deep breath of the country air, with its distinct smells that were so different from the salty tang of the seaside town. She could hear the dogs barking, but they didn't come to see who was there. Clutching her bundle, and suddenly feeling nervous, she made her way towards the house that had been her home for so long. Should she knock, she wondered. Before she could decide, the door was thrown open and Fanny stood there glaring.

'What the hell are you doing here? Be off with you,' she snarled, as though Rowan was some stray.

'Who's there?' her father called. Fanny made to shut the door but Rowan was too quick for her and stuck out her foot. Then her father appeared, his eyes widening as if he'd seen a ghost.

'Rowan, is it really you?' he gasped, then peered around. 'Where's Sab?'

'Sab? Why should he be here?' she asked.

'Oh, stop mithering and get inside, Edward. You're letting all the heat out,' Fanny whined, but to Rowan's surprise he ignored her.

'Come in, my dear, and let me look at you. How have you been? Is Sab treating you well?' he gabbled, leading Rowan towards the fire.

'Why do you keep asking me about Sab, Father? And why should he have been treating me well or otherwise?' she frowned.

'Let me take that wet wrap,' Fanny butted in, her eyes

gleaming as she held her hands out for the soft cape. Rowan ignored her.

'How have you been, Father? I was right sorry you didn't reply to my letter.'

'Letter? We haven't had any letter, have we, Fanny?'

The woman turned away but not before Rowan had seen the flush that swept over her cheeks.

'I suppose you're in trouble,' she spat, nodding towards Rowan's stomach. 'Well, let me tell you . . .'

'You be quiet, Fanny.' Both women turned to stare at Edward in surprise. 'Now, Rowan, sit yourself down and tell me what's been going on. I couldn't believe it when Fanny said you and Sab had run off together.'

'What?' she cried. 'But I was kidnapped, Father.'

'Now don't you come here telling your father a pack of lies . . .' Fanny began.

'I said quiet, Fanny, and I meant it,' Edward ordered. 'If you had any manners, woman, you'd be offering the girl a cup of tea or bowl of broth, not berating her. Now, I want you to go into the parlour whilst I speak to Rowan.'

Fanny stared at him in amazement. 'But . . .'

'''Tis you who insist on keeping the fire going in there, so go and make use of it.' There was a moment's silence. 'I'm waiting, Fanny, and don't come back until I call for you.'

Chapter 37

As Fanny slunk from the room, Rowan turned to her father in surprise. 'Gosh father, that was quite a speech for you. I've never heard you talk like that before, especially not to Fanny.'

'I know. Should have put me foot down from the start. Guess I was a bit infatuated. Being lonely after your mother died, I think the attention went to my head.'

'Yes, Fanny did say she could provide your creature comforts and . . .' Seeing her father looking uncomfortable, she stuttered to a halt. 'So how have you been?'

He shrugged. 'Truth is, after you and Sab ran off, Fanny began lording it over me.'

'Father, as I said, Sab and I never ran off together. I was kidnapped, and Fanny threatened to tell the authorities where Sab was if he didn't ignore me. He was scared of being sent to train for the army, that's why he disappeared.' Edward stroked the beard, which had regrown since she left. He was also in need of a haircut, she noted, taking in the wiry locks curling over his shoulders.

'I had a feeling Fanny wasn't telling me the truth when I asked where you were, but when I never heard anything from either of you what was I to think?'

'Look, Father, let me start from when you and Sab were sowing Five Acre Field. I was carrying out my Eostre ritual as usual when a man came up and threw a sack over my head.'

'What?' he cried, reaching out and patting Rowan's hand. 'My poor little girl. What happened next?' He put his pipe to his mouth, but did not light it.

Without sparing any detail, Rowan related the events of that terrible time in Hell Tor Asylum. Then she told him about her apprenticeship, meeting up with Sab, and finally about the mirror and losing her job. Exhausted, she stuttered to a halt. Her father sat staring into the flames in the fireplace as he digested everything she'd told him.

'Fanny, get yourself in here this minute,' he barked suddenly, making Rowan jump.

'Did you want me?' Fanny simpered, appearing in the doorway.

'Not particularly, no,' he muttered. 'Come here so I can see your face.'

'Why, Edward, dearest,' she gushed, rushing over to him.

Seeing her father's set look, Rowan gulped. Couldn't this stupid woman read her husband after all this time?

'Now, Fanny, I need to ask you a question, and I want a truthful answer. Was a letter from Rowan delivered to this address?'

'Well, yes, but I didn't want to worry you.'

'And did you sell Rowan's mirror?' he cut in, stopping the woman's excuses mid-flow.

'Oh, that old thing. Davey found it in the field a while back. When the pedlar called and asked if I'd any trinkets to sell, I thought the money would buy us a few luxuries, Edward, dear.'

'The only luxuries around here are those you've bought for yourself. Now go,' he ordered. As Fanny stood gaping like a goldfish, he pointed to the stairs. 'Pack your things and be gone. I can't bear you near me a moment longer.'

'Edward, my dear, I was only thinking of you,' Fanny said, rushing over and throwing her arms around him. Silently he moved away, his eyes glittering.

She stood staring at him in surprise as it finally dawned on her he wasn't going to be swayed.

'Give me a chance, Edward. I can change. I'll be a good . . .' she began.

'Be gone now, Fanny, or I'll get the dogs.' The woman hovered a moment longer, but when Edward remained silent she shot a malevolent glare in Rowan's direction and stomped up the stairs.

As drawers slammed and footsteps thundered overhead, Edward just sat staring into the fire, the set look remaining on his face. Finally, Fanny came back down the stairs, staggering under the weight of two enormous bags.

'Edward . . .' she simpered.

'Be gone,' Edward shouted, without turning away from the fire.

'I'll take the trap then, shall I?'

'You're taking nothing more from me. You can walk.'

'But it's a long way and my bags are heavy,' she said, dropping them theatrically onto the floor.

'Should have thought of that before you packed so much stuff,' he said mildly. 'Anyhow, you've put on so much weight since you've been here, you look like a barrel. Some exercise will do you good.'

'Well!' Fanny gasped. She looked so indignant Rowan

had to hide a smile. Finally, realizing Edward wasn't going to be swayed, the woman picked up her bags and stormed out, leaving the door swinging in her wake.

Edward got to his feet. 'And good riddance,' he called, slamming the door behind her.

Rowan stared at her father as if she'd never seen him before. Unaware of her scrutiny, he crossed to the dresser and poured two jugs of cider.

'Guess we need something after that performance,' he said, handing her one before sinking back in his chair and taking a long drink. 'I'm sorry about that letter, Rowan, but it's really good to see you again. Tell me, did you just decide to pay your old father a visit after all this time or was there some other reason?'

Her father knew her too well, she thought wryly.

'Actually, Father, I came to warn you.'

He looked at her sharply. 'What about?'

'Father, I'm walking out with a Preventative officer who is stationed in Saltmouth where I've been working.'

'You're what?' her father cried.

Intent on telling her story, Rowan ignored his outburst.

'Jack, that's his name, let slip they'd had a tip-off that owlers will be moving wool in this area, and I thought . . .' she stuttered to a halt.

'You thought I might be involved?' he finished for her. 'Well, you can rest assured I'm not.' Relief flooded through her. Her father took a long pull of his cider. 'I might well have been if I'd listened to Fanny, though. She tried her best to get me to deal with them, but dear old Davey, God rest his soul, said your mother would turn in her grave.'

Rowan gasped and he reached over and patted her hand. 'Sorry, my dear, you wouldn't have known about poor Davey.'

'But I did. Well, that is, he told me he wouldn't see another spring,' she said, tears welling as she remembered. How she'd loved that wise old man.

Her father nodded sagely. 'He knew his body was wearing out. Said it was like the seasons and his had reached the final days of winter.' Rowan smiled sadly; she could imagine him saying that. 'Offered him a bed in the farmhouse, but he was having none of it,' he continued. 'Helped with shearing as usual then went back to his hut. I went and found them, dog and man together, dead to the world.' He covered his face with his hand.

'You all right, Father?'

He nodded. 'Just something in my eye,' he insisted. 'Anyhow, old Davey's words stayed with me. The thought of dealing with those hoodlums never sat easy with me, you know. I sold my wool straight after shearing, the way I always have in the past. It saddens me to think you thought so badly of me, but I guess I haven't done much to earn your respect recently.'

She looked at him forlornly. It was the truth and there was no good denying it. Lost in their thoughts, they sat staring at the dying fire, neither having the energy to prod it back into life.

Then she realized her cat wasn't curled up in her usual place.

'Where's Magic?' she asked.

Her father looked uncomfortable. 'I caught Fanny kicking her once too often.'

'What! Why, that old besom. Magic's not . . . ?' She could hardly voice her fears.

'No, she's all right. Auntie Sal took her to their farm.'

'Oh, Father . . .' She shook her head.

'That was when I first began having my doubts about the woman; can't abide cruelty.'

Rowan nodded, then stifled a yawn, as the traumatic events of the day caught up with her.

'Can I sleep here tonight, Father?' she asked, breaking the silence.

'This is still your home, Rowan. Stay as long as you like. And I am grateful that you thought to come and warn your old father, after all that's gone on this past year.'

'I'm glad it wasn't necessary, though,' she said, getting to her feet and kissing his cheek. 'I'll see you in the morning.'

To her surprise, no sooner had she climbed into her old bed than sleep overtook her and she knew nothing until the cold light of dawn crept through the window. For a moment she wondered where she was and then, as her mind cleared, she lay there, thinking back over the past few days. So much had happened, she thought, her hand automatically going to her wrist. Stroking the red ribbon, she reflected on how her life had turned full circle. Through a strange chain of events, she was back where she'd been born. Except now she wasn't the naïve country girl she'd been when she left.

Her musing was rudely interrupted by the frenzied barking of the farm dogs. Then she heard the shout of voices and hooves thundering over the cobbles in the yard. Jumping out of bed, she peered out of the window, just in time to see two uniformed riders dismounting. One of them was Jack! Hastily throwing on her dress and running her fingers through her tousled hair, she ran down the stairs. The senior Preventative officer was talking to her father.

'Edward Clode, we have a warrant to search your property,' he said, holding up a card for her father to read.

Jack was peering over the officer's shoulder and into the room beyond.

'But Father hasn't done anything wrong,' Rowan cried.

Hearing her voice, Jack's eyes widened and he stared at her in horror.

'Carslake, you search the house with the girl. I'll take the farmer and have a look around the outbuildings. If you find anything, blow on your whistle.'

'Sir,' Jack responded, giving a smart salute.

'It's all right, Jack,' Rowan said, as the men disappeared across the yard. 'Father isn't hiding anything. He sold his wool in the usual way, he told me so last night.'

'Miss Clode, I'd be obliged if you would allow me to carry out my duty,' he said stiffly, ignoring what she'd just said. As he began rifling through their cupboards and the bacon settle, she followed after him, explaining about her father and Fanny, but he took no notice. Then without even glancing in her direction, he bounded up the stairs. Seeing he had no intention of listening, she sank onto the chair beside the fire, and idly prodded the wood.

When he came down the stairs again, she jumped to her feet, determined to make him understand her father was innocent.

'Jack, please listen. Although Fanny wanted Father to deal with the owlers, his principles wouldn't let him. He listened to his conscience.'

'And you, Rowan, did you listen to your conscience? Or doesn't betrayal count?' he asked, his cold stare sending shivers down her spine.

'Betrayal? What do you mean?'

'What I told you about our movements was in confidence. I expressly asked you not to tell anyone. Yet I arrive to find that you hightailed it here and tipped off your father. You might have thought you were being clever trying to pull the wool over my eyes once again, Rowan, but believe you me, it will be the last time.'

'Come along, Carslake, there's nothing here,' the officer called from the doorway.

'Yes, sir,' Jack said as, with a final glare at Rowan, he turned to go.

'Please don't leave like this, Jack,' she cried, grabbing his arm.

'Don't touch me,' he hissed, trying to snatch it away. Determined to make him see sense, she hung on, and in the ensuing tussle her ribbon caught on the button of his sleeve. With a final yank, he freed himself from her grasp and strode from the room, too wound up to notice the red material dangling from his cuff.

'Jack,' she shrieked, hurrying after him. But he'd already mounted his horse and was galloping away, kicking up red dust in his wake. She stared down at her bare wrist, its band of white skin gleaming up at her. 'Oh, no,' she whispered.

'Well, that was a bit of excitement,' her father said, as

she went back indoors. Then he saw the tears coursing down her cheeks. 'Whatever's the matter?' he asked.

'He didn't believe me, Father, and now I've lost everything, including my ribbon,' she sobbed. Drawing her close, Edward waited until the storm of anguish had passed. When her sobbing had turned to hiccups, he sat her down beside the fire and handed her a glass.

'Drink this. It'll make you feel better,' he urged. As the water hit the back of her throat, she spluttered. 'Best thing I know for curing hiccups. Now, you'd better tell me what you meant about losing everything.'

She held up her wrist. 'My ribbon's gone. It caught on Jack's button and he never noticed,' she wailed.

'Well, it was always just a piece of ribbon, in my book. Oh, I know your mother thought it had some magical power,' he said, as Rowan opened her mouth to protest, 'but let's be honest, it's just a tatty bit of ribbon really.'

'No, you're wrong, Father,' she cried. 'It warns me when things are about to happen. Or it did,' she muttered, stroking the naked flesh where it had been.

Her father shrugged. 'You're just like your mother, and there was never any point arguing with her, she always maintained she was right,' he said with a grin. 'I take it your Jack was one of those Preventatives, then?'

'Yes, and he thinks I betrayed him.'

'Ah, I see now. He told you about the raid, you came here to warn me, then he turned up, saw you here, and went mad. Well, girl, that is a bit of a mess and no mistake. Never mind, we'll think of how to square things.'

She looked at him hopefully. 'Do you think we can?'

He nodded. 'Of course. Everything sorts eventually.

He was looking mighty mad when he left. I reckon you'll need to give him time to cool down and sort his head out. Chances are he'll come to his senses, and it will give you time to think about what you want, too. Meantime, why not stay here with me? It would be lovely having you round the place again, and Lord knows it needs some attention. Fanny was never one for housekeeping, that's for sure.'

'What happened to that Mrs Dunmore? I thought she was meant to be helping, and wasn't she going to cook for you as well?'

Edward shook his head. 'Turns out she was an old crony of Fanny's. All they did was blether. Not a jot of work got done between them, nor any meal cooked neither. Off they'd go each morning to the market or Honiton, spending, spending, spending! Chatting, chatting, chatting! Couldn't afford it, or stand the noise, so Mrs Dunmore had to go.'

'You mean you actually put your foot down, Father?'

'And not before time, I can tell you. I'd have been bankrupt if I hadn't. Old Davey had a hunch what Fanny was up to. Told me I should insist on seeing the accounts. I nearly blew my haystack when I did. Been a right old fool one way or another,' he said, looking so forlorn that Rowan smiled.

'I guess you missed Mother after she passed away.'

He nodded. 'Silly to think I could ever replace her. Fanny was just an aberration and could never hold a candle to my Hazel.'

Insistent lowing from the shippon pulled him from his reverie. 'Better get milking or those poor cows will be busting. If you're staying, our Rowan, happen you'd best change into something more suitable.'

Staring down at the yellow sprigged dress, Rowan grimaced.

'You're right, Father, or by the time I've got this place anywhere near clean, it would be black as the chimney. Do you need help with the cows first?'

'No, that's all right, Rowan. I've pretty much got used to dealing with them myself. I miss young Sab, though. Couldn't believe it when I came down for me breakfast that morning and Fanny told me you'd run off together. She was so plausible, even dabbing her eyes with her handkerchief, and then she put a plate of bacon and egg in front of me ... Of course, that should have been a warning in itself.' He shrugged and pulled on his cap. 'Oh, well, the cows won't wait while I stand here mithering.'

'I'll have breakfast waiting when you've finished,' she promised. 'Then I'll go and tell Mother what's been going on.'

'Well, you'll have to tell old Davey too; he's laid alongside her.'

'I'll do that,' Rowan said.

Chapter 38

Although Rowan put an appetizing plate of bacon and eggs in front of her father, he seemed distracted throughout their meal. Glancing at him across the table, she saw that he had dark shadows under his eyes and was sure he'd lost weight. Obviously the past few months had taken their toll, and she was alarmed to see how old he looked.

'Thanks, Rowan, that were right nice,' he said, pushing his empty plate away. 'I haven't had a decent spread like that since you left.'

'Sorry there was no bread, Father. I guess Fanny didn't make any yesterday.'

He shook his head. 'Nor the day before that, nor the week before, come to that. If your auntie Sal hadn't met me regularly in the village with some of her baking, I reckon I'd have starved.'

Rowan frowned. 'Why did you meet her in the village?'

'Fanny were so rude to her, Silas forbade her to set foot inside here. Still, they'll be able to visit again now,' he said, his face brightening. 'I'll let them know her majesty's left when I go out later.'

'You're going out?'

'Yes, got a spot of business to see to whilst you visit your mother. No doubt it will take you all morning to tell her what you've been doing,' he said, smiling as he donned his cap, then lifted the latch. The dogs heard him and began barking.

'They'll be able to come indoors again now, won't they, Father?' she called.

His answering grin lit up his face, making him look younger again.

Deciding to leave the clearing up until later, Rowan snatched her shawl and basket from its nail and made her way outside. The sun had risen, and the chickens clucked around her bare feet as if they were pleased to see her again, although she knew they were really after scraps.

'Well, look who the cat's dragged in,' a kindly voice called.

Looking up, Rowan saw Mrs Stokes standing in the doorway of the wash house. The woman seemed to have aged considerably since she'd last seen her, and was looking dishevelled.

'Mrs Stokes, what are you doing here?' she cried, her heart lifting at the sight of the charwoman. 'I thought you usually came in on a Monday, or at the weekend if the clothes were stained.'

'No, Mrs Stokes has to call upon request, if you please,' she intoned, in a fair imitation of Fanny's faux posh voice. 'In other words, every other blinking day. Couldn't be fashed to do nothing herself, that one. Old Davey was right, that woman's naught but a slut, if you'll pardon my French.'

'I was sad to hear of his passing away, Mrs Stokes, but it wasn't like him to speak ill of anyone,' Rowan said, looking puzzled.

'Well,' the woman hesitated, 'I suppose I can tell you

now he's gone. Davey knew he'd seen her majesty somewhere before. It was that smell, you see; got right up his nose. Said she had a face like a fusty ferret. Racked his brains for weeks till he remembered. It were last year when he'd been in Exeter for supplies. Saw her touting for trade outside one of those dens of iniquity, you know, them places where men go when they want a bit of young flesh.'

Rowan raised her eyebrows. 'You mean she . . .?' Rowan gasped, hardly able to put it into words. Luckily Mrs Stokes understood her meaning.

'No, dear, and she'd never dirty her hands doing anything herself. Lured the young girls, she did, promising them big money and fine clothes, all for a few minutes being nice,' she said, wrinkling her nose in disgust. 'When Davey realized who it was your father had married, he didn't know whether to tell him or not. He was fond of Edward, thought of him like a son. Anyhow, he confided in me, and we decided he probably wouldn't believe it anyhow, him being that smitten.'

'Yes, he certainly was,' Rowan replied, thinking back to when Fanny had first arrived at the farmhouse. 'Well, Mrs Stokes, you'll be pleased to know Father sent her packing last evening.' She laughed as the older woman look incredulous and then gave a whoop of delight.

'I knew this day was going to be good. Anyway, where's young Sab? Place has gone to racksitts since you two left. Must admit, it shocked me to me core when Fanny said you'd run off together.'

'But we didn't, Mrs Stokes. It was a story she hatched up. Look, I haven't time to explain now,' Rowan said, seeing the woman's eyes widen with curiosity. 'One day, when you've time, drop by the kitchen for a cuppa and I'll tell you all about it.'

The woman looked disappointed for a moment and then nodded.

'Guess, I got too much to do this morning anyhow,' she said, pointing to the dirty laundry piled high on the floor. 'You anything for laundering?'

Rowan thought of the clothes she'd worn on her journey back from Saltmouth. 'Oh, yes, I have stockings, petticoat and a yellow dress that need seeing to. They're up in my room so I'll go and get them.'

'No need, I've got to get the bedding anyhow. You know, Miss Rowan, although you look the same, you're kind of different, like you're all grown up.'

'That's exactly how I feel, Mrs Stokes,' she said, shrugging.

As she continued on her way, she stared down at her homespun. It was cheap and thrown together compared with the fine dresses she'd been wearing these past few months. Still, Madame Louisa would have to agree she was dressed *à propos* for the farm, she thought, picking her way through the yard, which needed a good swilling down.

She walked on past fields that were filled with crops needing harvesting, ditches that required clearing and overgrown hedges that needed trimming. Nearing the old oak, she quickened her pace and couldn't help shuddering as she remembered the night she'd been snatched. Still, it was broad daylight and Fanny had gone for good. A skylark's happy trill sounded nearby, lifting her spirits, and the feel of warm earth beneath her bare feet gave her the sense of connecting with nature in a way she hadn't for a long time.

She wasn't going to let one woman's vindictiveness spoil her life. After all, if she hadn't been snatched she wouldn't have become an apprentice milliner, or met Jack, would she? Except she no longer had a job and probably no follower either, she thought, carefully picking her way through the overgrown brambles. Everywhere was a shambles, just like her life.

Finally reaching her mother's resting place, she was pleased to see it had been tended and looked as tidy as the new one alongside. She didn't think she could bear it if this special place had been neglected like the farm. Throwing herself down on the grass between them, she rolled onto her stomach.

'I'm home, Mother,' she whispered. 'Hello, Davey and dun collie. You'll all be pleased to know Father has sent Fanny packing.' The branches above rustled, sounding like a sigh of satisfaction, she thought. 'So much has happened since I last visited you, Mother. Good things and bad. Let me tell you . . .'

It took her some time to unburden her soul. The words came out hesitantly at first then, like a dam bursting, all her pent-up emotion came flooding out. 'It's lovely seeing Father again, but my coming here to warn him angered Jack. He accused me of betraying him, and rode away without giving me back my red ribbon. How will I know what to do without it?' she cried.

But there was no answering breeze, only the stillness of silence. 'Perhaps you can't hear me without it? I couldn't bear it if you're no longer with me, Mother,' she sobbed.

'Please send me a sign to show you are listening.' This time there was a faint, answering ripple. The grasses round her mother's resting place parted, and there in the centre lay one perfect four-leaf clover. Rowan's heart lifted and warmth coursed through her veins.

'Thank you, Mother.' She gently plucked the tender stem, then leaning forward, kissed the spot it had sprung from. 'I'll be back soon,' she promised, placing it tenderly in the pocket of her apron.

Her steps lighter now she knew her mother was still listening, she hurried back towards the farmhouse. Passing the fields with their abundance of crops, she stopped. A vegetable broth would make a welcome supper, she thought, pulling up carrots, turnips and onions and placing them in her basket. There wouldn't be time to make any bread today, but she could put a couple of potatoes to bake. Seeing the profusion of vegetables and the brightly coloured flowers that covered the hedgerows, she excitedly began planning the dyes she would make. Then her heart sank. She was no longer an apprentice milliner, was she?

The sun was overhead by the time she got back to the farmhouse. Quickly, she cleared away the dishes and set about preparing the vegetables. The pot of broth was soon simmering over the fire, and she looked around the room, wrinkling her nose at the patina of grime and dust that covered every surface. She would give everywhere a much-needed clean.

It was late afternoon before she heard Blackthorn's hooves clattering into the yard. A few moments later the door rattled open and her father stood there with a bundle in his arms. He sniffed the air appreciatively.

'My, I haven't smelled anything this good since . . .' he shook his head.

'Breakfast?' Rowan teased.

He laughed, then looked around the room, taking in the gleaming surfaces and scrubbed table set ready for their meal.

'Everywhere looks grand, Rowan. You've obviously been busy and I've had a fruitful journey. Look what I found strewn along the track.' He held out the bundle, which Rowan could now see were clothes. 'It seems Fanny's greed was greater than her strength,' he said with a chuckle. 'I'll get Mrs Stokes to wash them and then you can see if the Poor House can make use of them. Can you imagine her majesty's face if she sees them folk wearing her finery?'

Rowan giggled at the thought. 'You're wicked, Father,' she teased.

'I'm sure the Good Lord will forgive me after what I've been through these past few months. Now, I must see to the stock, and then we'll eat. Afterwards, I've got a nice surprise for you, my girl.'

'What's that?' she asked, looking at him curiously. He grinned boyishly, but wouldn't be drawn. 'Do you want any help?'

'No, that's all right.'

'Well, I'll take those clothes over to Mrs Stokes's cottage, shall I?' she asked, anxious to be doing something.

Her father's face dropped. 'She's not there. Fanny turfed her out so Mrs Dunmore could have it.'

'What!' Rowan shouted, remembering the woman's dishevelled appearance. 'Oh, Father, how could you?'

'Fanny insisted, said as it was a tied cottage I should have asked her to leave when Mr Stokes passed on,' he said, looking shamefaced. 'I did let her have the old shepherd's caravan, so she had somewhere to live.'

'Well, now Fanny's gone, Mrs Stokes can have her cottage back, surely?'

Her father brightened. 'You can go and tell her the good news first thing in the morning,' he said, and disappeared outside again.

When he returned, the dogs scampered in behind him, barking joyously and circling Rowan's feet for petting, before settling contentedly in their old places beside the fire.

'Feels like a home again, doesn't it, Father?' Rowan exclaimed, ladling out their broth.

'It certainly does, and will feel even more so soon. I called to see Sab down at Pear Tree Farm.'

'Sab? How is he?' she asked, anxious to hear how her friend was faring.

'He's grand. When you told me his work there was only temporary, I thought I'd see if he wanted to come back here permanently. I'm desperately in need of help here and I miss the young fellow. Of course, I had to clear it with Farmer John. He was surprisingly agreeable, although obviously Sab'll have to stay until he finds a suitable replacement. Seems he knows of a young lad nearby looking for work. Be quite like old times again, with the three of us, won't it?'

Rowan nodded, but couldn't help wondering if she wanted to remain on the farm.

Unaware of her doubts, her father continued, 'It was

always my intention to leave the farm to Sab and the house to you, and these past few months set me thinking.'

She looked at him in surprise. 'You're not ill, are you, Father?' she asked, looking at him anxiously.

'No, but I'm not getting any younger. Supposing I'd died and the farm had passed to Fanny? It was probably why she married me, anyway. She'd have sold it to strangers. I had nightmares thinking about it.' He shuddered. 'Any road, after that narrow escape, I decided to get things sorted straight away.'

'But Fanny is still your wife, Father,' Rowan pointed out.

'Not in the true sense. The marriage was never consummated, see,' he muttered, staring down at his dish.

'But she said . . . I heard . . .' Rowan stuttered to a halt, remembering the noises she'd heard coming from their bedroom.

'Fanny was very good at flirting and promising, but not delivering the full works, if you get my meaning. Said she wouldn't risk getting in the family way,' he explained, keeping his eyes averted. Seeing the flush spreading across her father's cheeks, Rowan stayed silent. Well, well, so the fabulous Fanny was full of hot air. Could the day hold any more surprises, she wondered. Her father took another spoonful of broth and seemed to recover his composure.

'Anyway, I saw my solicitor on the way back, filed for an annulment on the grounds of non-consummation and changed my will. Everything's signed, sealed and settled. My, but this baked spud's grand. It's ages since I had anything so tasty,' he said, pushing aside his empty dish and biting into the soft potato.

Knowing it was her father's way of changing the subject, Rowan turned her attention back to her own food. Then she had a thought.

'Did you mention the mirror to Sab?' she asked.

'No need, was there? We know Fanny sold it to that pedlar. Sab being in Saltmouth around the same time must have been coincidence.'

Rowan smiled, relieved her dear friend need never know of her ill-founded thoughts. Still, it didn't help her get it back, did it? And get it back she would, she vowed, gently stroking the clover in her pocket. Then, there was her ribbon . . . Her head throbbing, she bade her father good night and went up to her old room.

Carefully she placed her clover between two books, then throwing herself down on the bed, thought back over the past few days. It seemed she'd lost everything she held dear: Jack, her ribbon, her job and her mirror. Whilst it was lovely to be back with her father, she knew in her heart farm life was no longer for her and she couldn't remain here. What a tangle she found herself in.

Through the window filtered the silvery light of the moon. 'Please help me solve my knotty problems,' she whispered up at it. Knotty! Why, that was it. Quickly, she rummaged in her chest until she found a length of string. Carefully placing a candle in each corner of the room, she cast her circle and made her acknowledgement. Seating herself in the centre and drawing energy up from her toes, she stared hard at each flickering flame in turn. Then holding the string tightly, she closed her eyes.

Ye, who kens the mystery of the unhewn stone,
Banish my darkness, light my way.

Carefully she tied four knots, one for each of her problems. Intoning, after each one:

One for the sun who brings the light,
Two for the stars that shine so bright,
Three for the moon who silvers the sky,
Four for the clouds that shield her by.
Answer the questions on my tongue,
Share your secrets yet unknown.
So mote it be.

Sending her thanks soaring to the skies and moving widdershins, she carefully blew out each flame. Then placing the knotted string under her pillow, she climbed into bed and closed her eyes.

Chapter 39

Next morning Rowan helped Mrs Stokes move her piti-
fully few things back into her cottage.

'There's nothing like being home,' she cried, and
although Rowan was pleased for the woman, she couldn't
help wondering what the future held for her.

The next few days passed in a frenzy of cleaning, cooking and helping her father harvest the crops that were
ready. But no matter how hard she tried to settle back into
farm life, her heart wasn't in it, and her spirit was restless.
Jack was constantly on her mind, and she found herself
staring down over the valley, willing him to appear. Many
times she went back over the conversation they'd had at
the Coffee House, yet she could find no reason for his
sudden coolness towards her.

She really missed the bustling atmosphere of the shop,
calling upon the ladies of Saltmouth and personalizing
their dresses and bonnets. The abundance of colourful
flowers and herbs in the garden was a constant reminder
of the job she now realized she'd loved so much.

To her consternation, her charm showed no sign of
working. Every night she'd taken the string from under
her pillow, untying one knot every time, but nothing had
happened. Now there was only one remaining. Staring
down at the white skin around her wrist, she sighed. Had

it been the ribbon that made things happen, or perhaps her beloved mirror?

'Well, hello there, stranger.' The familiar voice interrupted her musing and she spun round in surprise.

'Sab, I didn't expect you so soon,' she cried delightedly. He smiled his lopsided grin, hefting his bundle higher onto his shoulder.

'Well, that's a fine way to greet your old friend, and after I pleaded with the carter to hurry so as to be here in time for luncheon,' he said, his eyes twinkling.

'Sorry, Sab – or should I say Joe now – Father didn't know when you'd be arriving,' she answered.

'Think I'll revert to Sab. Seems right now I'm coming back. Got to help Farmer John finish harvesting, then I'll be home for good. I was that pleased when Uncle told me he'd sent the old crone packing. Going to be quite like old times, isn't it?'

Rowan nodded, trying to ignore the sinking feeling in her stomach. Was she destined to stay here? Then, realizing she was being churlish, she grinned.

'Welcome back, Sab,' she said, injecting more enthusiasm into her voice. It wasn't his fault he wasn't Jack.

'Any grub going? I'm starving.'

The sight of the familiar cheeky face lifted her spirits and she smiled. 'Funny you should say that. I baked this morning, so there'll be fresh bread and cheese for your meal.'

Sab rubbed his stomach appreciatively. 'Farmer John's wife is a good cook, but her baking isn't a patch on yours.'

'And I suppose you think flattery will get you bigger portions?' she quipped.

'But, of course. That and my fatal charm. I've brought some of my things with me, so I'll take them up to my room, then go and find Uncle,' he announced, then frowned. 'That is, if my room is . . .'

'Don't worry, Sab, the shippon and your room are just as they were. Seems Fanny never got round to changing anything there.'

He grinned in reply and she watched him head towards the farmhouse before returning to her weeding. His light-hearted banter would lighten things up, and her father would certainly benefit from some male company. Digging the fork into the tilth, she wondered if she'd been wrong to assume Jack would return her ribbon. Maybe he no longer cared. Perhaps she should go to Saltmouth and ask him what was wrong. But that would hardly be *comme il faut*, as Louisa would have said.

The clatter of hooves on the cobbles in the yard interrupted her musing. She jumped to her feet, staring in amazement. For there, as if she'd conjured him up, was Jack sitting on a horse alongside another Preventative, who saluted.

'Good day to you, Miss Clode. We've called by to let your father know we intercepted owlers at Saltcombe Regis where the boats were waiting to take the fleeces to France. Perhaps you could tell him he is no longer implicated and has no need to worry.'

'Thank you, I will,' she said. Feeling Jack's gaze burning into her, she turned and stared at him. As he gave a tentative smile, warmth flooded through her, melting the ice that had encased her insides.

'You all right, Rowan?' Sab called, hurrying towards them.

In an instant Jack's expression changed to one of dismay. 'Is that him?' he asked, in a tight voice. The senior officer nodded.

Jack turned and spoke to the other officer, who nodded and, with a salute in their direction, rode away.

Rowan watched as Jack dismounted and tied his horse to the post. He looked so stern her stomach turned right over.

'You are Sab?' he asked.

Sab frowned. 'I am, but I've done nothing wrong.'

'I have a message for Edward Clode. Perhaps you would immediately convey to him that we have apprehended the owlers and he has been absolved of any blame.'

'That's wonderful news, isn't it, Sab?' Rowan said, but Jack continued staring at Sab until he finally nodded and made his way back to the farmhouse. Only then did he look at Rowan. She stared back and silence stretched before them until she couldn't bear it a moment longer.

'I told you Father was innocent, didn't I?' He nodded and, when he still didn't say anything, she cried, 'He is a fine, honest man.'

'But what about his daughter?' Jack asked. Rowan felt sick. So Mr Acland had carried out his threat. 'I couldn't believe it when Vaughan told me,' he continued. Rowan frowned. Mr Acland wasn't called Vaughan. 'Why didn't you tell me yourself, Rowan? I would have been hurt but I'd have tried to understand. As Auntie says, you are very young and if someone paid you attention whilst I was away . . .'

'Paid me attention? Whilst you were away? Jack Carslake, what are you on about?' she cried.

'That Sab. Vaughan saw you walking along the Mall with him. Said you were laughing and joking and clearly knew each other extremely well. Now I see only too well, and I can't deny I was hurt at the thought of being cuckolded,' he laughed coarsely, jerking his thumb in the direction of Sab's departing back. Relief flooded through her and she burst out laughing.

'Oh, Jack, of course I know Sab very well. We were brought up together on the farm here.'

'What?' he exclaimed.

'Yes, we bumped into each other when I was returning from delivering a bonnet. We hadn't seen each other for so long we went for a walk to catch up.'

'But why didn't you tell me?'

'I intended to but when you picked me up you were as prickly as a hedgehog.'

He threw back his head and laughed. 'Oh, Rowan, you do tell it like it is. I'm so pleased the air is clear between us. I can return to my duties with a lighter heart knowing we no longer have any secrets between us. Although next time I tell you about a tip-off I'll expect you to be more discreet. Can't have my intended ruining my career chances, can I?'

His intended? Her heart leaped. But, as he stood there grinning at her, Rowan knew she had to tell him about her past.

'Before you go, Jack, there's something you need to know. Something that might affect our future relationship,' she whispered nervously.

He frowned and gestured to the fallen tree trunk nearby. 'Sounds serious,' he said. 'Shall we sit for a moment whilst you tell me?'

She nodded and when they were seated, took a deep breath and told him about her time in the asylum.

'So you see, Jack, you might not wish to continue our relationship now. Especially if someone like Mr Acland does tell,' Rowan finished up.

There was silence save for the rustling of leaves and the lowing of the cattle in the nearby field.

'Well, I can't deny this has come as a shock, Rowan. If it's any consolation I don't think you have anything to fear from Mr Acland. He sounds like a bully who uses what he can to get his own way. Once he finds out I know your secret he'll have no hold on you and will move on to his next target.'

Rowan smiled at him, grateful for his reassurance. But he didn't smile back. Getting to his feet, he stared at her gravely, his next words sending her spirits diving to the depths.

'I must get back to the station now or they'll be wondering where I am. Thank you for telling me, Rowan, although I cannot deny I'm hurt you haven't felt able to open up to me before about such an important part of your life. It is abundantly clear we don't know each other as well as I thought we did,' he said, giving a tight smile.

She watched as he mounted his horse, desperation spurring her on to call, 'But, Jack, you must understand that I had my future to think of.'

'As do I, Rowan. As do I.' With a nod, he picked up the reins and galloped away.

She stood watching until the dust had settled and then threw herself to the ground. That was that, then, she thought, dashing the tears from her cheek. So much for the truth, Mother, she sobbed.

Finally spent, she picked herself up and made her way back to the farmhouse where her father and Sab, having finished their midday meal, were deep in conversation.

'Conscience wouldn't let me deal with them owlers, however much Fanny pleaded. To thy own self be true. Isn't that what your mother used to say, Rowan?' Edward said, looking up as she entered the room.

She nodded and forced a smile. If only she'd trusted her father, Jack wouldn't have found her here.

'You not having anything to eat?' Sab asked.

She shook her head. Even the thought of food made her feel sick.

'Well, come along, Sab, we'd better get on if we're to get the ditches cleared before you return to Farmer John tomorrow morning,' her father said, getting to his feet.

'I know, Uncle Ted,' Sab replied. 'Wish I could stay here but he's been good to me and I can't let him down. I'll be right glad to be back here permanent, like. I was telling Rowan earlier, nobody bakes like she does.'

Rowan smiled and started clearing their platters away, but in the privacy of the scullery, she leaned against the sink and wept. Clearly Jack couldn't bring himself to forgive her. Was she destined to stay here for ever? She couldn't just leave the men. They needed someone to cook and care for them, didn't they?

That night, she took the string from under her pillow and, gripping it tightly, intoned:

Let me now regain true harmony,
Oh blessed one.
So mote it be.

Then slowly and deliberately, she untied the final knot. Replacing the now smooth length under her pillow, she pulled the bedcover over her head and willed the charm to work.

Visions of Jack haunted her dreams. In the first, he came to her wearing a green bonnet and holding out her mirror. In the second he was wearing a red one and waving her ribbon. The third time he appeared in a black mourning bonnet, his eyes and nose the colour of jet. Then everything changed. They were standing facing each other, separated by streams of ribbons.

She woke feeling drained, but knowing that whatever happened, she couldn't remain here. Mrs Stokes was right, she had changed. Life on the farm was no longer right for her. She'd so enjoyed her job in Saltmouth, dealing with the ladies' requirements. Her thoughts turned to Louisa and that horrible confrontation. She could see now that she had acted hastily when she'd seen the mirror. Had she been rude to Louisa? She really couldn't recall but she did remember being accused of theft. Should she return and try to clear her name? In all fairness, although she didn't think he would say anything, she needed to warn Louisa that Jack knew about her past, and sooner rather than later.

Who would look after the men, though? They might have been pleased they'd fed themselves but that was only because she'd made the bread, butter and cheese!

Perhaps she'd ask Mrs Stokes if she had any ideas who could look after them in her absence.

Jumping out of bed, she stared out over the yard, where her father and Sab were already carrying pails of milk to the dairy. Her arm knocked against the books on the windowsill, reminding her she'd placed her clover between them. Pulling out the now perfectly pressed specimen, she smiled, remembering the first time she'd found one. She'd been deliberating on what she should wish for, when her mother had, in an unusually serious moment, told her it was up to folk to make their own luck.

'That's what you were trying to remind me, Mother,' Rowan whispered. 'I understand what to do, but need to know if this is the right time.' Throwing on her homespun, she raced down the stairs and there on the back of the chair lay her freshly laundered yellow dress, stockings and petticoat. Her heart leaped, for if she was to return to Saltmouth, she needed to be smartly attired.

Before she could change her mind, she ran over to Mrs Stokes's cottage and banged on the door.

'Mrs Stokes, I wonder if you could help me?' she asked.

'Come away in, Rowan,' the charwoman greeted. 'Make yourself comfortable. Can I get you a drink?'

'Thank you, but no,' she replied, then sat bunching her apron between her fingers.

'What's up, girl? Spit it out,' Mrs Stokes encouraged.

There in her cosy kitchen, Rowan began telling her about her dilemma. She was only going to mention her father and Sab needing someone to look after them, but the woman was so understanding, she found herself blurting out about Louisa and Jack as well.

'Well, it seems you have a lot to sort out, Rowan, and it sounds like it's going to take some time. Why don't I take care of your father and Sab until you return?'

'Would you?' Rowan exclaimed. 'It would mean higher wages and meals for you in the farmhouse.'

Mrs Stokes gave her gap-toothed grin. 'A new life for both of us, eh?'

'You mean you'd take it on permanently?' Rowan asked, her hopes rising.

'Why not? Tell your father I'll get cooking later. Good luck, girl. You deserve it.'

Rowan could have hugged the woman. Hurrying back to the farmhouse, she ran up to her room. By the time she'd washed and changed into the smart clothes, her father and Sab were sitting at the kitchen table, breaking their fast.

'Well, look at you,' Sab whistled appreciatively as she came down the stairs.

Her father looked at her bundle and frowned. 'You going then?' he asked, shrewd as ever.

She nodded. 'If it's all right with you, I'll cadge a lift with Sab as far as Pear Tree Farm.'

'No, you won't,' her father grunted.

'But, Father . . .'

'You'll sit and have a bite to eat and then Sab will take you right into Saltmouth. I guess that's where you're headed?'

'Thank you, Father,' she cried, going over and throwing her arms around him. 'I will be back to see you soon, and Mrs Stokes is going to cook for you.'

Her father stroked his wiry beard and nodded.

'If I'm to take you on to Saltmouth, Rowan, we need to be heading off straight away. Farmer John won't be happy if I'm late,' Sab said, jumping to his feet. 'See you tomorrow, Uncle Ted.'

'I'll take some bread and ham with me,' Rowan said, snatching up her basket. 'Goodbye, Father. You will look after yourself, won't you?'

'Course I will, stop flapping like some mother hen, girl. Just remember, you always have a home here.'

Blinking back her tears, she nodded and followed Sab outside.

'This takes you back, doesn't it?' Sab said as the trap rattled its way towards Sudbury. 'Do you think Fanny will have gone back to London?'

'She never came from London. Mrs Stokes told me she was born and bred in Exeter.'

'But I thought she said she'd looked after young girls?'

Rowan shrugged, thinking it prudent not to divulge everything the charlady had told her. 'It seems an age since we last travelled together,' she said instead. 'I don't know about you, but I've certainly changed since then.'

'Good thing too, or I wouldn't be sitting this close,' Sab jested, pretending to pinch his nose. She gave him a playful punch. 'Well, you didn't wear such fancy clothes then, Rowan. Hope that young Preventative's worth it.' She turned and gave him a sharp look, but he just grinned knowingly.

The church clock was chiming eight as she climbed down from the trap.

'Thanks, Sab. I'll see you again soon, I'm sure.'

'Look after yourself, Rowan. You know where I am if

you need me.' Serious for once, Sab stared at her for a moment, then turned back the way they'd come.

Rowan stood outside Louisa's shop, butterflies churning in her stomach. She noticed the bonnet in the little bow window was the same as when she'd left, but the window and pathway were spotless. Obviously the young girl from the Poor House was doing her job well. Come along, Rowan, you won't achieve anything by standing here, she chided. She was making her way towards the entry when she stopped and, taking a deep breath, pushed open the door to the shop instead. As the little bell gave its familiar tinkle, Louisa came hurrying through from the workroom. Seeing Rowan standing there she arched an eyebrow.

'Good morning, Madame Louisa,' Rowan said, forcing a smile to her lips. 'I wonder if I might have a word with you.'

Louisa stared at her for a moment then nodded.

'First I should like to apologize if I was rude to you,' Rowan said.

'Apology accepted,' Louisa answered graciously. 'And I owe you one, too. I regret I falsely accused you of theft. After you left, I caught Maria helping herself to my signature scent. It would appear her follower likes her to smell like a lady when she goes out with him, would you believe. The silly girl also admitted to wearing that ostrich feather in her bonnet when she went to the fair,' she added, shaking her head. 'She is on her absolute honour not to take anything again or I have told her she will be dismissed. Between you and me, if I didn't know she had a widowed mother and seven siblings to provide for, she'd have been gone in an instant.'

So Louisa did have a softer side to her nature, Rowan thought, relieved she had been cleared of blame.

'I was wondering if you'd sold my mother's mirror yet?' she enquired.

Louisa sighed. 'No, Rowan, I haven't.'

Rowan felt her heart lift. 'In that case, I wonder if I might come to some financial arrangement with you,' she said, making her voice as businesslike as she could.

Louisa's lips twitched. 'And what do you propose?'

'As I left here without collecting any wages, I thought perhaps you would offset them as a deposit.' Louisa's eyebrows rose higher. 'Naturally, I wouldn't expect to take ownership of my, er, the mirror until it was completely paid for. However, in order to finance this, I need to find employment and was hoping you might reconsider providing me with a character. After all, I did work hard and really can't believe you had any cause to complain about my efforts.'

'I agree you did work hard, but what about your attempts at bonnet making?' Louisa asked, her lips twitching again.

'Well, I admit the first was abysmal, but the second one passed muster with even your exacting standards,' Rowan protested.

'None the less, I'm not sure about providing a character . . .'

'But you have just said it was Maria who helped herself to your things so . . .'

She was cut short by the tinkling of the bell. 'Good morning, Mrs Parker,' Louisa said stiffly, as the birdlike woman bustled through the door. 'Now, why am I not surprised to see you this morning?'

'Well, I was just passing, Madame Louisa, when, as usual, I looked in through your window to see if you had any new creations and, to my surprise, I noticed Miss Rowena. Ah there you are, dear. Are you back for good?' the woman asked, turning to Rowan.

'Miss Rowena and I were just in the middle of a business discussion when you came in, Mrs Parker. Is there something you wish to purchase today?' Louisa enquired.

'I have just come in to browse, thank you, madam, so please carry on with your conversation. I won't listen,' she added primly.

Louisa looked at Rowan and shook her head. 'Mrs Parker, I don't wish to appear rude, but I must finish my discussion with Miss Rowena. If there is nothing I can help you with, I'll bid you good morning,' Louisa said, ushering the woman towards the door.

But the gossip wasn't to be fobbed off.

'You have been sorely missed, Miss Rowena. Have you been on vacation, or was there some family crisis perhaps?'

'Miss Rowena will tell you all about it later, Mrs Parker. Good morning.' Louisa almost pushed the woman out of the door. Closing it firmly behind her, she dropped the latch and turned the sign round to show 'shut'. Rowan's eyes widened in amazement; never had she known Louisa to close during working hours.

'Come upstairs where we can talk in private. We'll never get anything sorted out here,' Louisa said, heading down the hallway. 'Maria, please bring a tray of tea for two up to my parlour,' she called.

'Well, Miss Rowena,' Louisa said when they were sitting

in the comfortable chairs that looked down over the yard to the little back garden beyond. 'Firstly, I must tell you that I am not prepared to furnish you with a character.'

'But why not?' Rowan cried. 'As I said, I did work hard.'

'Yes, and that is why I'd like you to return to your position here, Miss Rowena.'

'You would?' gasped Rowan in amazement.

Louisa nodded. 'Mrs Parker was right when she said you have been missed. Even in the short time you have been away, I have been inundated with requests for your services.'

Rowan's heart soared. This was going better than she'd hoped. Then the door opened and Maria clattered through.

'Coo, look what the wind's blown in,' she said, putting the tray down on the table.

'Maria, please,' Louisa reprimanded.

'Sorry, madam. I already poured it to save bringing up the pot,' she replied, unrepentant as ever.

'Thank you, that will be all, Maria,' Louisa said, though as the maid retreated she continued staring at Rowan as if she had something she wished to say.

Chapter 40

'Now about the mirror,' Louisa said as the door closed behind the maid. 'I have considered your proposition and am happy to accede to it.' She handed Rowan a parcel.

Rowan recognized it immediately and her heart leaped. Placing her cup on the table, she eagerly folded back the soft material and lifted out her most treasured possession. As she sat tracing the etched scrolls tenderly with her finger, warmth flooded through her, bringing life back to her body which had felt numb since Jack had left her standing in the farmyard.

'Thank you,' she said, smiling at Louisa.

'I knew as soon as you'd left that I'd been hasty. Forgive me, Rowan, but I was excited at the thought of being able to expand my business. However, if the mirror was your mother's then I have no right to hold on to it.'

'Thank you, Madame Louisa. You have no idea what this means to me,' Rowan said, hugging it to her.

'I take it you are agreeable to returning to your post?'

Tearing her eyes away from her beloved mirror, she smiled at Louisa. 'Oh, indeed. I will work hard and try to master bonnet making.'

'Good. I've had so many requests for our personalizing service that I was going to get your address from Alexander in order to call upon you.' As Rowan stared at her in surprise, Louisa smiled. 'You have a real talent, not only for assessing what suits the ladies of Saltmouth, but getting along with them as well. As I mentioned once before, some of them are not the easiest to deal with.'

'But they are all happy with the service you provide, Madame Louisa,' Rowan assured her.

'Just as well or my business wouldn't last long. Now as you know, it is imperative we move with the times. Only yesterday I was asked to call upon Lady Beliver. She recently had visitors staying with her from London, where apparently, a colour called magenta is what anyone who is anyone is wearing.' Louisa leaned forward in her chair. 'Would you believe, it is our dear Queen Victoria who started this mode. Of course, Lady Beliver wants her bonnets trimmed in this purple pink as soon as possible. I showed her the ribbons I had in stock, but they were nowhere near bright enough. Knowing you have such a good eye for colour, I wondered if you would know how to make this particular hue?'

Rowan thought for a moment. Rhododendrons! The flowers would be perfect for creating the right colour.

'I think I know how to achieve that,' she replied.

Louisa clapped her hands delightedly. 'In that case, I shall arrange for you to call upon Lady Beliver. She is so well esteemed that if we can pull this off we will have clients queuing all down the street. You will find your room just as you left it, so I suggest you go and put your things away, then change into your apprentice attire.'

'Thank you, Madame Louisa,' Rowan said, gathering up her bundle and basket.

'By then you will be ready for some nourishment, so ask Maria for a bowl of her broth. I don't know how she's managed it, but she's made the most delicious one filled with all manner of different vegetables.' Rowan grinned inwardly, thinking that despite her recent telling off, the maid must still be making her forays to the kitchen gardens in the area.

'Now the shop has been closed for too long as it is. I shall go and reopen and see you downstairs when you've eaten.' Louisa swept from the room in a rustle of petticoats.

Suitably attired in her working outfit and feeling revived from her broth, Rowan went through to the shop.

'I have just taken an order for a new bonnet. The client would like it to be ready for collection tomorrow, so whilst I work on it this afternoon, I would like you to . . .' Louisa was interrupted by the tinkling of the bell. She smothered a sigh.

'Verity, how nice of you to call,' she said graciously. 'You remember Miss Rowena, of course.'

'Darling, I have just heard about your new enterprise,' Verity purred, ignoring Rowan completely.

'And what might that be?' Louisa asked.

'That you are offering bespoke colouring, silly. I said to myself, Verity you really must call upon darling Louisa and offer your support.' Rowan stared at the woman, wondering how word of their service could have reached as far as Exeter.

'That is most kind, Verity. However, it is Miss Rowena who offers this particular service.' In a flash, Verity's attention was transferred to Rowan. 'In that case, you may measure me for a new bonnet directly.'

'I'm really sorry, Verity, but Miss Rowena's service has proved so popular, her list is already closed for the season.' As the woman's face turned from pink to puce, Rowan had to bite her lip to stop herself from laughing.

'However, I would be happy to put your name down for the next available appointment,' Louisa offered.

'That won't be necessary,' Verity said stiffly. Then, nose in the air, she turned towards the door.

'Do give my love to Alexander, won't you?' Louisa called as the bell tinkled behind her.

'I didn't know Alexander was still seeing her,' Rowan said.

'He isn't, thank heavens,' Louisa replied, giving a wicked grin. 'Now I want you to give priority to the magenta dye. I assume you'll need to collect some plants or flowers before you can start?'

'Yes, but . . .' Rowan was about to say she didn't know if Camilla had returned home yet, but Louisa interrupted.

'As I said, making the dye is your most important task. I will keep an eye on things here whilst working on this new bonnet, so go and obtain whatever you need straight away. When you return, I shall inform Lady Beliver we can supply her with the magenta ribbons she requested. This is such good news for the business, Miss Rowena.'

Having secured her job and not wishing to prejudice her new position in any way, Rowan gathered up her cape and basket.

As she made her way to Poppy Cottage, her thoughts ran amok. Supposing Camilla wasn't there? Would it be all right to pick a few flowers and leave a note explaining what she'd done, or would that be infra dig? Camilla was such a lovely woman, not like that awful Verity, who couldn't abide flowers indoors. She was glad Alexander was no longer walking out with her. He would be much more suited to the gentle Camilla, she thought. They shared a love of gardens and plants and would get on well together.

Her thoughts, as she headed towards the seafront, turned to Jack. Now that she'd had time to think, she understood his being hurt she hadn't confided in him about her past, but she was angry at the way he'd jumped to conclusions. How dare he presume she'd been walking out with someone else whilst he'd been away? Anger quickened her steps. She couldn't believe he'd thought so badly of her. She was better off without him, wasn't she? Her question hung on the salty air but her musing was interrupted by a carriage drawing up alongside her.

'Rowan, how are you, my dear?' Camilla was smiling at her.

'Camilla, I was on my way to see you.'

'Well, it's a ood job I spotted you then. I have an appointment in to and your journey would have been in vain.'

'Oh, r Rowan cried, imagining Louisa's disappointed look if e returned without the wherewithal to make the new e.

' as it a social call or did you want me for something in p ticular? Having recently returned from my vacation, I feel hopelessly out of touch with everything here. Even that reprobate nephew of mine is monosyllabic at the moment. Getting more than two words out of him is harder work than digging up bindweed. It was a relief when he went out earlier.' She drew to a halt, then, seeing Rowan's crestfallen look, called to her driver, 'Wait here, please, Perkins.'

'You look dreadfully pale, Rowan. Has Louisa been overworking you?'

Rowan shook her head. 'I only returned to work this morning and if I don't get my new dye made, Louisa will tell me to leave, I know she will.'

Camilla stepped out of the carriage and studied her closely. 'Come along, sea air is the best tonic there is to soothe the soul. We can talk whilst we walk. And don't worry about Louisa,' she said, as Rowan made to protest. 'I will speak to her if necessary. Now tell Auntie Cam what's wrong.'

They strolled along the front and Rowan began telling her about the magenta dye and how she'd been on her way to ask permission to pick some rhododendrons.

'How clever of you to know that you can make this new purple pink colour from the flowers when you made yellow dye from the leaves,' Camilla said. 'But if you don't mind my saying, you were sporting that long face before you knew I wouldn't be at home.'

'It was walking along the Mall that upset me,' Rowan sighed.

'Poor old Mall, what did it do, then?' Camilla teased. When Rowan didn't answer, she turned towards her, studying her intently. 'I have to ask myself if the fact my favourite nephew and his intended are both unhappy is coincidental.'

Seeing the woman's sympathetic look, Rowan's pent-up emotion burst forth and she found herself pouring out everything that had happened. Camilla was quiet for a few moments.

'When you really love someone there's no room for pride,' she finally said, before signalling to her driver. 'Now I can easily walk to my appointment from here so Perkins will take you to Poppy Cottage. Collect as many flowers as you want, my dear, and let me know how you get on. It sounds an exciting venture.'

'But . . .' Rowan began.

'In you get,' Camilla ushered. 'Everything will sort, it

always does, one way or another.' Before Rowan could answer, she called to the driver and the carriage began to move.

As soon as Rowan saw the profusion of beautiful mauve and red rhododendron flowers, her heart lifted. Eagerly she began gathering the brightest blossoms but, as ever, the best ones were just out of her reach. Determined not be beaten, she threw off her cape and climbed into the bush. Its boughs shook and wavered, but she clung on tightly, her eye on the prize blooms above. Then, she saw dark two eyes staring up through the bush at her, and froze.

'What the heck . . . ?' the faceless voice shouted, making her jump so that she lost her grip and fell to the ground. Stunned, she lay on the grass, her head violently spinning. Wildly reaching out, her hands made contact with some coarse material, and she grasped it tightly until the spinning began to subside. It was only then she realized that she was hanging on to a coat sleeve and, looking up, saw those same two dark eyes staring down at her.

'Rowan, are you all right?' a voice asked. It sounded like Jack, she thought, but he was out; Camilla had said so. Then she felt herself gently being lifted into a sitting position. 'Speak to me, Rowan. Please tell me you're not hurt?'

She blinked and shook her head, trying to clear the blurred image that swam before her.

'Jack? But you're not here,' she murmured.

'That bang on the head's made you delirious,' he said, smoothing back her tumble of curls. 'I am very much here.'

'Oh, you are,' she gasped, as his face slowly came into focus.

'Yes, and it's just as well, if you must go clambering about in the bushes. Honestly, Rowan, when I looked out of the window and saw those rhododendrons shaking like billy-o, I wondered what on earth was going on.'

'I was just collecting flowers for my dye. Camilla said I could,' she assured him quickly.

'Blow the flowers, and Camilla for that matter. You could have been hurt, Rowan,' he said, staring at her so tenderly she had to look away quickly.

'But I'm not,' she said, struggling to her feet. 'And I needed the flowers for a special dye.'

'What about that special flower?' he asked, pointing towards the bush where her bonnet was dangling. Grinning, he reached up and retrieved it. 'I'm afraid the ribbon's snapped,' he said, handing the bonnet back to her.

'Nothing that can't be mended,' she reassured him.

'What about us, Rowan? Can we be mended, do you think?'

She stared at him, remembering Camilla's words.

'It was my pride . . .' they both began, then burst into peals of laughter.

'Well, we seem to think the same, so that must be a starting point,' Jack said. 'What do you think, Rowan, could we start again?' Putting his hand in his pocket, he brought out her red ribbon. 'I've carried this everywhere since it caught on my button.'

Smiling, she held out her arm and gently he tied it around her wrist. Immediately, she was filled with a sense of rightness. And as the ribbon gave a gentle tug, she knew they'd come full circle.

Acknowledgements

Grateful thanks to Teresa Chris for believing in me, Clare Bowron for her insightful input and BWC for their invaluable feedback.

He just wanted a decent book to read ...

Not too much to ask, is it? It was in 1935 when Allen Lane, Managing Director of Bodley Head Publishers, stood on a platform at Exeter railway station looking for something good to read on his journey back to London. His choice was limited to popular magazines and poor-quality paperbacks – the same choice faced every day by the vast majority of readers, few of whom could afford hardbacks. Lane's disappointment and subsequent anger at the range of books generally available led him to found a company – and change the world.

'We believed in the existence in this country of a vast reading public for intelligent books at a low price, and staked everything on it'
Sir Allen Lane, 1902–1970, founder of Penguin Books

The quality paperback had arrived – and not just in bookshops. Lane was adamant that his Penguins should appear in chain stores and tobacconists, and should cost no more than a packet of cigarettes.

Reading habits (and cigarette prices) have changed since 1935, but Penguin still believes in publishing the best books for everybody to enjoy. We still believe that good design costs no more than bad design, and we still believe that quality books published passionately and responsibly make the world a better place.

So wherever you see the little bird – whether it's on a piece of prize-winning literary fiction or a celebrity autobiography, political tour de force or historical masterpiece, a serial-killer thriller, reference book, world classic or a piece of pure escapism – you can bet that it represents the very best that the genre has to offer.

Whatever you like to read – trust Penguin.